Far Worlds

Edited by
A. R. Aston, James Fadeley & J. L. Gribble

Cover Art and Illustrations by
Manuel Mesones

Published by The Bolthole

The stories and artwork contained within this book are the property of the respective authors and artist. All rights reserved.

Text Copyright © 2014

Table of Contents

Introduction 4
Anomaly — Jonathan Ward 7
First Spark 36
Rainer — Heidi Ruby Miller 38
A Deadline to Remember 60
The Lost and Found — Kerri Fitzgerald 64
Real-Mater 97
Helzenthrax — A. R. Aston 99
Someday 143
City Blue — Edward Smith 153
Her Kiss 164
Golden Planet — Evan Purcell 165
A Pelnodan Bounty — James Fadeley 182
Murderer 230
Bequeathal — K. Ceres Wright 231
Salvation Comes — Simon Farrow 260
Locum 308
Endaris — Michael J. Hollows 309
Secrets Within 342
Alone — Alex Helm 343
Once in a Lifetime 356
The War Room — Michael Seese 359
Shard of Heaven — Damir Salkovic 378
The Drift Engine — A. R. Aston 410
Biographies 421
Acknowledgments 427
Also Available 428

Introduction

I have always been intrigued by the storytelling potential of our universe. Out in the wider cosmos, astronomers have already discovered hundreds of exo-planets orbiting alien stars, and countless solar systems await detection. Across this vast panoply of worlds, separated by the insurmountable light-speed barrier, there could be civilisations as sophisticated and detailed as our own, with histories as full and bountiful.

With this anthology, I wished to capture a sense of this monumental scale and the breadth of diversity possible in a universe. There could be a gargantuan operatic space adventure occurring in one corner of the galaxy, while on another world, lovers quarrel in a small-scale romance. They are blissfully unaware of the intense psychological thriller occurring only a couple of rooms down, on the cosmic scale.

It was my desire to demonstrate just how all-encompassing a speculative fiction setting can be. Diversity was our watchword for this third Bolthole anthology. The task set for our writers was at once incredibly broad and very specific. There were only two rules. First, their stories cannot be set on Earth. Second, the light-speed barrier was maintained. Aside from these stipulations, our writers were allowed to throw themselves into whatever exotic worlds and storylines their feverishly imaginative minds could conjure for your enjoyment. I am pleased to say they have done so with aplomb.

This collection contains an exciting mix of genres. From

space westerns involving aliens with triple sexes to psychological thrillers. From high fantasy to desolate existential horror, stories where the fate of entire worlds are in the balance and stories where the only stake is the heart of one hopeful lover. Such a collection of tales naturally risked feeling disassociated, and it became clear, even in the early stages of the anthology, that the stories required a narrative and thematic connective tissue.

That's where the Drift Engine came in. A nomadic alien observer, unknown and never lingering in one place for long. Like you, the Drift Engine alone bridges the void's great gulfs, crossing endless tracts of darkness to glimpse the points of light and life that dwell within *Far Worlds*.

I wish you luck on your journey, and I hope you enjoy the ride.

—A. R. Aston

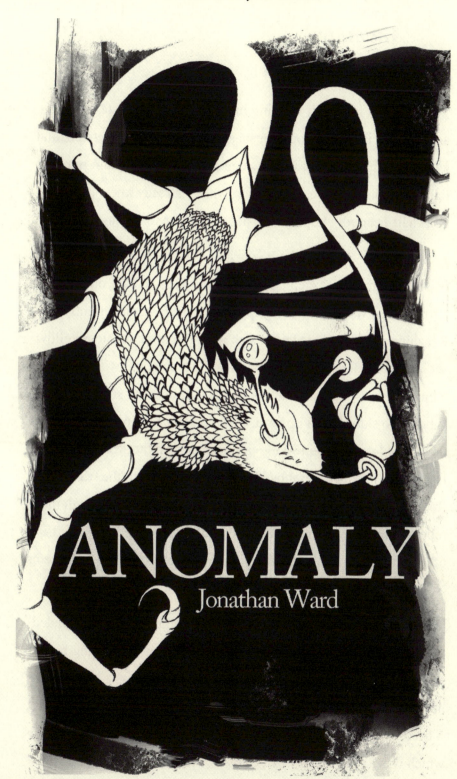

Anomaly
By Jonathan Ward

A soft but shrill whining intruded into Kalara-ste's dreams and dragged it toward consciousness. It unfurled one eye-stalk and aimed it at the alarm set into the compartment wall: a dim purple light was pulsing there, confirming what it already knew but had been half-heartedly hoping was not true. Time to get up.

Kalara-ste raised both eye-stalks and began flexing each of its six legs in turn, stretching and rotating them to ease out the stiffness that was a result of gripping the sleep-stool so tightly. Reaching round with its tail, it stabbed a finger-claw into a hollow set into the underside of the stool's bulbous top, and with a faint whine, the mesh that had held it in place against the stool retracted. It began to slowly drift upward, a motion that continued until it unwrapped its two-metre-long tail from around the stool and the finger-claws at its tip grabbed hold of a grip set into the wall. It floated there for a few moments while it quickly read through the reports scrolling down a wall-screen; those generated both by the other two crew members and automatically by *Scout One*'s systems. Nothing jumped out as being particularly noteworthy.

With that done, it left its sleeping compartment and headed along the corridor, propelling itself in the zero-gravity using both its tail and legs. It moved slowly and carefully; Kalara-ste knew it was nowhere near as fast as the other two crew members, but every time it tried to move more quickly it tended to end up bouncing off walls, which was a very undignified thing to do if you were the

Commander of Antata's first ever starship. Better to be thought slow than ridiculous.

It drifted on toward the bridge located near the front of the ship, passing the doorway leading to the medical bay, its domain. Fortunately, so far it had not needed to be used, so it was filling the time not spent sleeping or on the bridge with a series of experiments assessing the effects of zero-gee on some of Antata's life. The results were quite fascinating; some of the fungal spores in particular were positively thriving. Neither of the others showed any interest in this, despite its attempts to explain things to them. Just the thought of that made its back-scales flush pink with annoyance. Fortunately the colour had faded by the time it reached the last room before the bridge.

Inside that room, Nefaran-stex hung from the ceiling, its tail looped around a large bar there. The rest of its body was wrapped by a cradle of machinery, and every few seconds it twitched as the devices discharged jolts of electricity into specific muscle groups—a necessary though uncomfortable procedure that counteracted the atrophying effects of prolonged periods without gravity. Its back was facing the doorway, blue-tinted scales signifying discomfort and boredom, and one eye-stalk shifted round as it became aware that it had company.

"Medic. I will be done in another half-segment." Although Kalara-ste was the Commander of the mission, each crew member was usually referred to by their formal function aboard *Scout One*.

"What caused the delay, Navigator? According to the

schedule you should have finished your stimulation treatment over a segment ago."

Nefaran-stex's rear legs flailed in what would have been an insulting gesture, had it not been suspended from the ceiling. The intent, though, was obvious.

"The Factaren was using the device. It said it does not need the same amount of rest as the two of us do, that it was inefficient to sleep for so long. It took my place so I had to wait until it was done."

It took some effort, but Kalara-ste was able to prevent its chagrin from showing on its body. It would need to speak to Yorlax-stex about this; routine was vital on a starship. Things had to be done properly and when they were supposed to be. Their environment was too fragile for disruption to be tolerated. By the same token, the Navigator's words had to be dealt with, too.

"Do not refer to it as the *Factaren*. Its title is Engineer. Do you understand my words, Navigator?"

"Yes, Medic." Nefaran-stex replied, twitching as a series of jolts sent the muscles on the right side of its body into spasm.

"Good. I will speak to the Engineer about this matter. When you are done here, I expect you to go straight to your station on the bridge; *Scout One* is manoeuvring in six segments' time and I want the systems checked and navigational calculations confirmed long before that."

"Understood."

Kalara-ste released its grip on a grab-handle sunk into the

floor and brought its tail forward to grasp another, the motion twisting it around to face the way it had come. As it did so, it turned an eye-stalk briefly toward the Navigator and saw its legs twitch again in a different, more insulting pattern. It might have been the effects of the machinery, but somehow the Medic doubted that. It decided to ignore the gesture, and pushed off back down the corridor to find Yorlax-stex.

###

The rear of the ship had become very much the Engineer's domain. From a heavily reinforced and armoured spherical compartment, Yorlax-stex monitored the status of the experimental fusion engine that propelled *Scout One*, as well as watching over the rest of the ship's systems so that it could perform maintenance when required. A smaller compartment forward of that one held three EVA suits for when repair work was required on the ship's hull; so far Yorlax-stex had not deemed that necessary, much to Kalara-ste's unspoken relief. When the Medic finally drifted into the chamber and wrapped its legs around grab-handles set into the floor, the Engineer had both eye-stalks fixed on a screen, its tail looped over its head so that its finger-claws could manipulate controls directly in front of it, while its legs rested in pressure-pits set into the floor and the lower part of the wall.

"Is there a problem?"

An eye-stalk rose and studied him for a moment before turning back to watching the screen. "Yes. One of the robots is experiencing a malfunction in its motor unit. I am trying to get it back for repairs before it fails entirely and becomes inaccessible."

"Can't the other robot—"

"No. Now I need to concentrate for a while. I will give you my full attention shortly."

Kalara-ste considered coming back later, but the thought of navigating the entire length of the ship any more than it had to held little appeal. The Engineer's attention was entirely focussed on what it was doing, with only an occasional hiss to indicate its displeasure and irritation. The Medic understood the reason for that; Yorlax-stex had made no secret of its dissatisfaction with how the engineering section had been constructed.

The fusion engine could not be accessed directly by any of the crew; it had been deemed too much of a health risk by the committee in charge of designing the starship. Instead, two small robots could be operated remotely by the Engineer to maintain the engine and its support systems, ensuring magnetic bottle containment, monitoring radiation levels, and supervising all the various tasks that Kalara-ste was largely ignorant of. Passages too small for an Antatan to pass through had been built for the robots so that they could get to where they needed to go, which of course was a considerable problem if one of the machines suffered some kind of malfunction.

After almost a full quarter-segment, a panel set into the wall slid open and the robot emerged, an alarming grinding sound issuing from its motor unit. Yorlax-stex rose from its position and stretched, then pushed itself over to the machine. It pulled some kind of scanner from a belt wrapped around its torso and held it over the robot for a few moments before studying the screen intently. The Engineer then put the scanner back in place and swivelled to face Kalara-ste.

"Will you be able to fix it?"

The Engineer's tail twitched as it thought about this. "Yes. The motor unit will have to be completely rebuilt, though. It is not suitable for zero-gee. I will be filing a report on the matter before we return to Antata. Now. You wished to speak with me about something?"

"Yes. Nefaran-stex informed me that it had to wait to use the stimulation machine earlier, because you were using it when you should not have been."

"That is correct."

Kalara-ste waited, but no further answer was forthcoming. It fought the urge to rattle its legs impatiently, knowing that such an action would probably send it drifting again.

"Explain."

"Very well. I only require six segments of sleep, rather than the seven that the Navigator and yourself do. I chose to use the remaining segment productively. I will in future check the schedule to ensure that my stimulation treatments do not overlap with those of another crew member."

"Good. That, however, is not the point. The protocols for this mission require each crew member to have designated amounts of both exercise and rest; the periods have been calculated specifically to help mitigate the impact of zero-gee on our bodies. You must rest for the appropriate time."

"Factaren young are raised from birth to only require six segments of sleep. It promotes efficiency and stamina. I have been physically unable to sleep longer than that since I was freshly spawned. If you were not Nestratan you would understand this."

"What I understand, and what you must also, is that the protocols for this mission must be followed. If you are unable to sleep for the allotted time, then you must spend the remainder of the period resting in your sleeping compartment and not elsewhere in the ship. As both Medic and Commander, I am ordering this."

"Very well."

Kalara-ste had been expecting more of an argument than that and was momentarily lost for words. Before it could gather its wits, a harsh trilling echoed through the compartment: the sound of the all-ship intercom being activated.

"Kalara-ste to the bridge. Priority two."

Priority two. That meant urgent, but not something that posed an immediate threat to the ship. Without another word, the Medic turned and pushed off toward the exit. The bridge was at the far end of the ship. It would have to hurry.

The bridge was the only compartment in the ship that had the door closed unless opened by a member of the crew. When Kalara-ste opened the door and pushed itself inside, the Navigator was hard at work, its front legs embedded in pressure-pits in the floor while its tail manipulated console controls off to one side. The Medic spared its crewmate a brief look before turning both eye-stalks toward the main screen. It gazed out on a void that was utterly black, save for scattered pinprick stars that burned unwaveringly, though their light did nothing to alleviate the darkness. *Scout One* was currently twice as far from the sun as Antata was, and although it was close to the orbit of a gas giant, that planet was currently on the far side of the sun. There was nothing at all anywhere near here, which made it ideal for their purposes.

Of course the view wasn't real; the image was received by the sensors embedded in the ship's hull and reconstructed here. The bridge itself was deep within the hull of the ship surrounded by thick armour, as were all the crew sections with the exception of the airlock access tubes. The idea was to help reduce the effects of cosmic rays and other radiation on the Antatans within, as well as to prevent micrometeoroid impacts from jeopardising any of their lives. It worked well, though all the extra weight made it difficult for *Scout One* to turn or accelerate swiftly. Sometimes it seemed as if the entire ship design was based on compromises.

Kalara-ste pushed the distracting thoughts away and propelled itself into the bridge. The Navigator looked around as it approached and gestured at the nearest stool. The Medic settled itself into place, as always shifting about to try and make itself more comfortable and failing miserably. The stools had expandable backs that could fold out to brace the Antatans when the ship was under acceleration. That somehow managed to be even less comfortable, at least as far as Kalara-ste was concerned.

"Report, Navigator. Why did you issue a priority two alert?"

Nefaran-stex shifted around so that it was fully facing Kalara-ste. "It would seem that one of the stars vanished."

The distance between Kalara-ste's eye-stalks widened in an involuntary gesture of surprise. From the flush of colour that passed over the Navigator's scales, it was evident that it was enjoying the Medic's confusion.

"What do you mean, *disappeared*?"

"Only for a brief moment. Its light was occluded by something passing between it and *Scout One*."

"And this means what, exactly?"

"I ran the calculations, and it appears that the object was travelling at a considerable speed."

"Are we in danger?"

"No. The object does not pose a collision risk. Were it not for the fact that it blocked out the star's light briefly, the ship's astrometric sensors would never have flagged it. I am doing my best to track it now; fortunately, the object seems to possess a remarkably high albedo—" The Navigator paused as a flush of colour across the Medic's back indicated its lack of comprehension. "The object is highly reflective. The light being bounced from it is fractionally blue-shifted, indicating that it is heading in our general direction, although of course in spatial terms that does not mean it will pass anywhere near *Scout One*."

Kalara-ste lashed its tail in frustration. "I still do not understand. Why does any of this warrant a priority two alert?"

"Because of the speed at which the object is travelling. According to *Scout One*'s sensors, when first detected it was travelling at approximately ten percent of the light-constant. Its rate of approach is now less than that." The Navigator paused for a moment, evidently conscious of the magnitude of what it was saying. "The object is slowing down."

Kalara-ste remained still for long moments. It had no idea how to respond to this; nothing in its training had prepared it for the possibility that something like this might occur. Eventually, it became aware that Nefaran-stex was staring at it, obviously waiting for it to respond. It felt a flicker of childish resentment but crushed the emotion, snapping its tail decisively.

"Is there any way that this deceleration could be a result of some natural process?"

"No. The most likely explanation by far is that the object is in some way artificial."

"This needs to be reported to Space Command."

"I have already done so, requesting that they verify my calculations and advise us on what action we should take. There has been no response as yet."

Kalara-ste felt briefly annoyed that the Navigator had not checked with it first but decided that in its place it would have done exactly the same thing. It was not surprising that there had been no response so far; not only was the distance between *Scout One* and the homeworld so great that a simple conversation could take over a segment, but news like this would undoubtedly have caused great confusion. It could imagine the frantic debates taking place as the scientists and politicians that had worked together to make *Scout One* a reality tried to decide how to respond to this.

"Very well, continue monitoring the object. I will wait here until a response is received from Space Command."

"What about the Fa—the Engineer? Should it be informed?"

Kalara-ste thought about that. "Not yet. It is engaged in important work at the moment, and there are more questions than answers right now. It will be told when we have more information."

The Navigator bobbed its eye-stalks approvingly and turned back to its screens. Kalara-ste settled down to wait, wondering whether what it had just said was the truth, or a convenient lie to mask the fact that it did not trust the Factaren. Nefaran-stex had made no secret of its distaste for the Engineer, but Kalara-ste could not say for certain how it itself felt. The situation was very complicated; although they had trained extensively together prior to the mission, the lingering suspicion of the Insanity was not so easily dispelled.

After what felt like an eternity, but in reality was no more than half a segment of waiting, a red light set into the ceiling began to pulse, indicating the arrival of a tight-beam communication from Space Command. Kalara-ste gave the order, and Nefaran-stex brought it up on the main screen. All communications from Antata were sent in text form with multiple copies included in the tight-beam burst to reduce the risk of transmission error. This time, though, it arrived perfectly.

Both crew members studied the orders silently and looked at each other. Kalara-ste felt as if an invisible funeral cowl had been draped across its body, such was the weight of the responsibility that had now fallen upon this ship and its crew.

"Begin the calculations," it eventually said. "When they are complete, call the Engineer and myself to the bridge. Its input will be essential if we are to succeed in doing as we have been instructed. I am going to the medical bay to check on my experiments." And have a chance to think, it thought. It suspected the Navigator knew anyway.

"Yes, Medic."

When Kalara-ste was eventually called back to the bridge, the Engineer and the Navigator were already waiting. As before, Nefaran-stex sat in its usual place, its finger claws idly manipulating controls while it kept one eye-stalk turned toward a nearby screen. The Engineer had opted to float in the centre of the bridge, its tail loosely grasping a grab-handle set into the floor. It drifted back and forth slightly as the door closed and the air currents shifted; to Kalara-ste it looked like some kind of bizarre plant, and it had to fight to keep its amusement from showing.

"Has Nefaran-stex made you aware of the anomaly?" It had been called that by Space Command, and to Kalara-ste the name seemed fitting.

The Engineer's tail tensed, drawing it closer toward the floor. "It has, but I must say that I am sceptical of the whole situation." Kalara-ste turned an eye toward the Navigator in time to see its scales flush with anger and waved its front legs for it to be still.

"Clarify."

"I do not dispute the Navigator's calculations; even if I did, they have been checked and the presence of the anomaly confirmed by Space Command on Antata. My scepticism relates to the proposed course of action. The chances of the anomaly being some kind of artificial construct are extremely remote; to say nothing of the probability of something like this entering our system just as Antata is in a position to investigate it meaningfully for the first time."

"And what is the alternative?" Nefaran-stex demanded. "No natural object could behave in the way that this anomaly has."

"No natural object *that we know of,*" the Engineer replied, twisting an eye-stalk around so that it had both of them in view at once. "That is my point. It is far more likely that this object is something natural with strange properties than that it is of *alien* origin." It paused, and rose up a little. "Why aren't they already here?"

Kalara-ste knew that phrase. The possibility of alien life was something that had never really been considered until recent years, in the immediate aftermath of the Insanity. Antatans had turned their eye-stalks towards the stars and pondered the opportunities that they could hold for a newly unified race. The theory proposed that, given the apparent age of the universe, any intelligent life that arose within the galaxy should have colonised it long before now, and since there was no sign of that, it implied that the Antatans were alone. It was an interesting thought-experiment, but not one that Kalara-ste had spent a great deal of time pondering.

"Whether it is alien or natural is irrelevant," Kalara-ste said. "We have been given orders to investigate it, and we will do so. It is as simple as that. Navigator, are we able to intercept the anomaly?"

Nefaran-stex clattered its legs against its stool. "It is achievable, but only just. Although the anomaly initially continued to decelerate rapidly, its velocity has now become constant and its course is taking it out of the system. That means in order to catch it, *Scout One* would have to undergo maximum acceleration for almost a full day. Such a sustained period of engine use would deplete our fusion fuel reserves to the point that we would only be able to spend a small amount of time studying the object before we had to reverse the ship and decelerate, otherwise we would not be able to return to Antata before our supplies ran out."

"How much time would we have?"

The Navigator shifted uneasily. "Assuming no change in the anomaly's heading and velocity— less than half a segment."

"When would *Scout One* have to begin acceleration?" Kalara-ste asked, hiding its disappointment as best it could.

"As soon as possible. In one and a half segments' time we will be unable to catch it."

"Can the engine cope with such a prolonged period of acceleration?"

Yorlax-stex waved its eye-stalks thoughtfully before responding. "It has never been activated for so long, but I believe it can. I would, however, like a full segment to run diagnostics and ensure all is functioning as it should be."

"I can only give you half that time." The Engineer stared at Kalara-ste for a few moments, until it decided that its Commander was not about to change its mind.

"Then I will begin at once. I would like to request that I stay close to the engineering section while *Scout One* is accelerating, in case any problems arise."

"Very well."

The Engineer left the bridge, and Kalara-ste turned to face the other crew member. "Double-check your calculations and make ready. In half a segment we will begin the manoeuvre. I will inform Space Command."

"Yes, Medic." Nefaran-stex hesitated. "There is another possibility. About the anomaly, I mean."

"Which is?" Kalara-ste asked, its curiosity piqued.

"It could be that the anomaly is not natural or alien. We must consider the possibility that the Factarens are responsible."

Kalara-ste waited until it decided that the Navigator wasn't making some kind of obscure joke. "What possible reason could you have for thinking that?"

"The timing. Yorlax-stex was right about one thing: the timing of this anomaly's arrival is highly suspicious. Perhaps the Factarens used the launch of *Scout One* as a distraction to conceal the testing of their own ship. You know as well as I that not all of their territory is visible to satellite—a deliberate act on their part. How do we know that they are not responsible?"

"I know you distrust the Factarens," Kalara-ste said. "I do not blame you for that. But you must acknowledge that what you are saying does not make sense. Although unlikely, it is possible that the Factarens could have constructed their own ship. Consider, however, the rate at which the anomaly is travelling and how swiftly it was able to decelerate. Antata is simply not advanced enough to build something capable of that, and such a technological leap by either nation would be impossible to conceal."

The Navigator's tail whipped back and forth as it thought about Kalara-ste's response. "You make a good point. I will think about this further."

"Very well," Kalara-ste said. Such an admission was the best that it could hope for right now, and time was pressing. "Let us get to work."

After *Scout One*'s engine had fired up to full power, it took Kalara-ste only a few moments to decide that it did not like being under such heavy acceleration—a feeling that only intensified as the segments scuttled by. With the fusion engine active, the crew were under gravity twice as strong as that on the surface of Antata. Given the amount of time that they had spent in zero-gee, normal Antatan gravity would have been enough of a strain: this was practically torture.

Fortunately, the time they had all spent in the stimulation chamber would help prevent their bodies from suffering any permanent damage, although it could do nothing to mitigate the all-over ache that Kalara-ste was experiencing.

Nor could any of them reach other parts of the ship without considerable difficulty. The gravity was acting toward the rear of *Scout One*; Kalara-ste thought of it as a tower being propelled upward by fire spewing from its base. The effect was to turn the corridors into almost sheer, vertical drops that ran most of the length of the ship. Although the grips embedded in the walls made it possible to move from one room to another, Kalara-ste had immediately decided that the risk of serious injury from falling rendered it too hazardous. He had ordered the other two to remain where they were, although they had shown no sign of wanting to go anywhere. It was another flaw in the design of the ship that Space Command would have to address when considering future vessels.

With little to do but sit on its stool, monitor screens, and try not to focus on the constant discomfort, Kalara-ste found its thoughts returning again and again to what the Navigator had said about the Factarens. It was frustrated to the point of being furious: why could it not seem to concentrate on the anomaly, on what it might represent, and what that could mean for them and for Antata itself? Instead, its mind seemed to slide away from it, seeking anything else to latch onto. This situation was something it had never considered before—it might simply be a matter of time for it to adjust. In the meantime, it dwelled on the Factarens and the Insanity.

After the Insanity, once the immediate horror and trauma had begun to fade, some unknown Antatan had made a statement. This was far from unusual; indeed, the whole world was trying to make sense of what had happened, to drag some sort of meaning from the madness, but this particular statement had grown in popularity and it had lodged itself in Kalara-ste's consciousness.

"Conflict on a scale so horrific as to surpass the stuff of nightmare is inevitable. A people must truly appreciate just how far they can fall before they can find their way to new heights of achievement."

Perhaps, then, the Insanity had been inevitable; if not in the form that it had actually taken, it surely would have occurred in one way or another. The idea had gained much support, because it allowed Antata to accept what had happened and move on rather than remain obsessed with the past. Or perhaps that was simply an excuse. Kalara-ste didn't know; it had no idea if it even mattered one way or the other.

It was the Factarens that had built the bomb. Tensions between the continents of Factara and Nestrata had been increasing for generations, and it had finally found an outlet when conflict broke out over possession of a cluster of islands equidistant between the two continents—ideal territory on which to build a defensive buffer against attack. Or, to other minds, a launchpad for an invasion. The notion of using a newly developed fusion bomb on a civilian target was so self-evidently abhorrent that no military officer would go along with it. The target was set as the largest island in the cluster; the intent was to demonstrate just what the weapon could do, and thus bring the conflict to a swift end.

The power of the detonation far exceeded their expectations, utterly vaporising the small Nestratan military contingent as well as wiping out everything within a ten kilometre radius of the impact point. Rock was turned to magma and the ocean poured into the resulting crater, creating a cloud of steam so thick that it took days before either side could see what lay within it.

When the wind finally blew it away, nothing remained of the island save for a few stray outcrops of land stripped down to the bedrock.

Word of the fusion bomb's destructive power swiftly spread, and large numbers of both civilians and military personnel rebelled against the notion of using it again; demonstrations that only increased when it was revealed that the Nestratans were also working on their own weapon of mass destruction. Both governments looked at the potential for devastation that could ensue if the war was allowed to continue and stepped back from the brink.

Negotiations began in earnest after that, and progress was swiftly made. Cooperation between the two nations flourished, of which *Scout One* was the most recent, and perhaps greatest, expression.

Yet mistrust still remained; a residual war mentality that infected some more than others, at least as far as Kalara-ste was concerned. Nefaran-stex's suspicion of the Factaren engineer was an obvious indicator, though it wondered whether the Navigator's paranoia had any relation to the fact that it had already deposited its body's cache of seed in the birthing pools, and made the transition from –ste to –stex.

Perhaps the knowledge that your young might exist somewhere encouraged a more defensive, protective attitude. It was possible, Kalara-ste supposed. The mentality could also be seen in the design of the ship itself; the armour was so thick that it hampered manoeuvrability, and it was not as if anything out here was going to attack them.

With the possible exception of the anomaly.

As the day inched on, Kalara-ste found itself losing track of time with increasing frequency. When the acceleration abruptly ceased, for a moment it could not believe that almost a full day had passed. Clarity returned swiftly, riding a wave of pain that pulsed through every part of its body as it tried to adjust to the sudden absence of the stress that it had been under for so long.

Kalara-ste stretched slowly, wincing with every muted *crack* and *pop* from various parts of its body, and turned its gaze on the Navigator. Nefaran-stex's eye-stalks were almost flat against its body, an indication of severe pain, but despite that it was still working.

"Report."

"I have the anomaly on sensors. Its velocity and heading have remained constant; it will pass us in approximately half a segment. I am initiating continuous scans and stand ready to make a course correction if it shows any sign of reacting in a way that we do not like."

"Has it shown any reaction to our presence so far?"

"None, though I am reading strange emissions from its surface, some kind of continuous electromagnetic wave spreading in all directions."

"Some form of scanning technology?"

"Perhaps, though unlike any I have ever seen. There are also emissions of extremely high-energy particles. Everything is being analysed, recorded, and transmitted to Antata continuously."

"Good."

The door to the bridge slid open, and Kalara-ste looked around to see Yorlax-stex drift in, three meal packs held against its underside. It flicked two in the direction of the other crew, who reached out with their tails and snatched them out of midair instinctively. Kalara-ste had not thought it was hungry but found itself fighting the urge to completely ignore the Engineer and tear into the meal pack straight away.

"The engine functioned most satisfactorily," the Engineer said, settling itself on a stool equidistant from the other two, so that each Antatan formed the point of a rough triangle. "I was monitoring the systems throughout the burn, and I am certain that there will be no problems during the deceleration phase. What news of the anomaly?"

"It continues to approach and has shown no indication that it is aware of our presence," the Navigator replied, then paused for a moment. "Thank you for the food."

"It was no trouble. Could you bring the anomaly up on the screen?"

The Navigator did so, and all three turned their eye-stalks to look at it. At this distance it was almost disappointing—just another point of light against the backdrop of space. That was until they looked at the measurement of its speed blinking in the corner of the screen or registered that the light was growing larger and brighter with every passing moment as it drew steadily closer to *Scout One*.

Despite its increasing trepidation, Kalara-ste pierced the meal pack with its feeding tongue and swiftly devoured the contents, and the other two did likewise. It knew that everything inside the ship was also being monitored constantly for any useful insights on such an historic event and could only assume that the slurping noises and muttered curses as a few globs of food drifted into the air would be edited out of any public broadcast. The wrappings were tossed aside as the crew turned their attention back to their work.

The anomaly drew closer and closer until it almost filled the main screen, and Nefaran-stex had to zoom out to regain some perspective. Its surface was highly reflective, perhaps near perfectly so, and as a result, it was hard to get a sense of its dimensions or what external features it had, if any. Both the Navigator and Engineer were hard at work monitoring sensor returns and interrogating systems for more information, and Kalara-ste could not help but feel slightly useless.

"What can you tell me about it?" it asked, mindful that they were being recorded.

"Our scans are being reflected or absorbed depending on the method used," Nefaran-stex answered without bothering to look around. "I have been unable to get any sense of what may be inside it, or what its outer surface might be composed of."

"Perhaps that is not even its outer surface," the Engineer interjected. "Some kind of field technology could produce a similar effect."

"Impossible to tell. However, I can calculate its shape by measuring how the radar pulses and scanning laser bursts are reflected. It appears to be a perfect cylinder, at least to the limit of *Scout One*'s sensors."

"Dimensions?" Kalara-ste asked.

"One hundred metres in width and one kilometre in length."

For a moment, everyone was silent. The full length of *Scout*

One was barely seventy-five metres. A kilometre long, one hundred metres wide, a perfect cylinder. It would be laughable to suggest that something like this could be natural.

"Has there been any change in the anomaly since we began scanning it?"

"None, though it appears that the high-energy particles I mentioned earlier are passing straight through our vessel without slowing. Through us, as well. I suggest you check my readings for any possible medical implications."

Kalara-ste called up the data on a small screen and studied it. Nefaran-stex wasn't quite correct; although the particles were indeed passing through everything and everyone, they were changing slightly as they did so. The changes were at the very limits of the ability of *Scout One*'s sensors to detect, but they were there. What might a vessel like the anomaly, for surely it was a vessel, be able to tell from such fluctuations?

Kalara-ste slowly looked up and turned both eye-stalks toward the rough direction from which the anomaly was approaching. Had something inside the anomaly seen it perform that action? Was some unknowable machine or creature watching them all, even now? It felt a thrill of terror that it suppressed with an effort, wondering whether the scans had captured the chemical changes inside its body and what those unknown eyes would make of it.

"Can we communicate with them? The anomaly?"

Eye-stalks turned in its direction. "The anomaly has shown no sign of interest in our vessel," Yorlax-stex said. "It is possible that it does not even know that we are here."

Kalara-ste looked at the Engineer and waited.

"Yes, it can be done. We can use tight-beam or radio communication."

"Use both."

The Factaren's finger-claws danced over the console in front of it for a few moments, then it flicked its tail in Kalara-ste's direction. Kalara-ste was reminded once again that everything that took place on the bridge was being recorded, and that if the anomaly actually responded, this conversation would go down in history. Now would not be an ideal time to say something foolish.

"This is the Antatan vessel designated *Scout One*, hailing unknown vessel designated *Anomaly*. We have been tracking your course through our system and wish to open communications. Please respond."

After a few moments, Kalara-ste looked at the Navigator. "Anything?"

"Nothing. No response on any frequency. No detectable change in the anomaly."

"Set the message to repeat. Time until the anomaly passes us?"

"Minutes, at best."

That remaining time seemed to stretch into an eternity. Kalara-ste was unable to keep from lashing its tail back and forth, its scales flushed with frustration. Was there something else it should be doing? Nefaran-stex and Yorlax-stex were still working diligently, but no new information seemed forthcoming.

It considered trying to communicate with the anomaly again, but the broadcast was still repeating. If the vessel, or whatever it was, had not responded before, why would it now? Perhaps it was not even capable of answering; perhaps everything aboard it had died, or it was automated, or those aboard it did not care, or . . . it snapped its tail so hard that it made an audible *crack*, and both crew looked round, startled. Kalara-ste took a deep breath and forced calm on itself.

The anomaly passed by.

The vessels were no more than one hundred metres apart, and against the immensity of the anomaly, Kalara-ste felt as small as a mud-basker. Even so close, it was difficult to see where the anomaly ended and space began, so perfect was its reflectivity. Then it saw something, a dark smear, and for a moment thought it was seeing through the surface to that which lay underneath.

Recognition came swiftly, however. What it was seeing was *Scout One* itself, reflected back from the anomaly. Kalara-ste allowed one eye-stalk to follow the reflection as it moved across the surface of the overtaking vessel, even now still able to be surprised and impressed by the ship. *Working together, Antatans built this.*

And *Scout One*, as the name suggested, would only be the

beginning.

Then the anomaly was past them, receding into the black, its rear just as featureless as every other part of it. Part of Kalara-ste wanted to yell at them to stop, to come back, to explain. Another part, smaller by far, hoped that the anomaly would never return.

They watched for as long as they could, until the distance between them was so great that the anomaly was once more reduced to little more than a point of light. After that, Kalara-ste gave the order for *Scout One* to be flipped over. Once it was facing the opposite direction, the engine would fire again to slow their speed and eventually set them on the course for home.

"So that was it?" Nefaran-stex asked. "The first encounter with alien life, and we learn nothing?"

"We have not learned nothing," Yorlax-stex replied. "We have obtained a great deal of data, and who can say what the scientists will be able to deduce from that about the anomaly. In any event—you expected something different? Why should something from beyond our world and everything we have ever known be *anything* like us? Why should it want to speak with us?"

"At least the question has been answered," Kalara-ste said. Both looked confused, and it allowed itself to show its amusement. *"Why aren't they already here?* They were, just now, and soon they will be gone. That is the problem with questions. They always lead to more."

"That is hardly satisfying," Nefaran-stex grumbled.

"That is life," Yorlax-stex answered, and after a moment all three of them laughed.

Knowing what was coming, Kalara-ste tried to make itself as comfortable as possible. Despite its light-hearted comments, it knew that what they had witnessed would change the very future of Antata. How could it not? The knowledge that other life existed out here, other beings far in advance of the Antatans, would surely bring the Nestratans and Factarens together. The potential opportunities, and possible threats, would require nothing less. Perhaps, one day, they would even learn what the anomaly had truly been.

The main engine fired, and *Scout One* began its long journey home.

First Spark
By J. L. Gribble

So as it turned out, starting a fire with your brain was kind of hard.

Toria sat cross-legged on the lawn behind her house, staring at a small pile of grass and kindling that was definitely not smoking. The twigs were a little warm, but that was due to the afternoon sun beaming down on a hot day. She yearned for the air conditioning inside. However, upon discovering her practicing with a candle in her bedroom, Mama had banished her outside with a bucket of water, "just in case."

Just in case of nothing. She squinted at the kindling and imagined fire. Flames, sparks, lava. Explosions. The freaking sun.

The bucket sat unused. The kindling remained unlit.

"You have got to be kidding me," she said. Toria flopped back on the grass and stared up at the blue summer sky. Some magical prodigy she was. She could make a pen fly around the room. She could shield herself with gorgeous prisms of energy.

She could shield others! Electricity danced to her whims. If today got too hot, she could call rain—even if she got in trouble for messing with the weather patterns again. Some mages twice, three times her age couldn't pull off these feats.

But a simple fire cantrip? All of the other apprentices could call fire. Even Archer could, and his element was water!

And what was she? She was storm. Reportedly the only human mage between Calverton and the Grand Strand with a primordial power rather than an elemental. Sometimes elves sat in on her lessons to supervise her progress. Heady stuff for an eleven-year-old.

If she was so awesome, why couldn't she perform one of the most basic of spells?

She waited for an answer.

A black spot streaked across the sky above her, and she blinked. Not quite the sign she was looking for, but it was time to get back to work.

Toria propped herself up on her elbows and glared at the pile of kindling. She would get the cantrip to work. She would light fire.

Perhaps calling a bolt of lightning from the sky and igniting the twigs that way would count? Tempting.

Nah, she didn't think so either.

Rainer
By Heidi Ruby Miller

The rippling arches around the flesh club's oval entryway reminded Rainer Varden of a pink lotus flower, among other things.

A hostess with emerald-colored hair and see-through blouse intercepted him and his six contractors in the lobby of the Foxx House. "May I help you? Does your group have reservations?" she asked.

"We're here on Embassy business." Rainer shouldered past her to a set of lavender glass doors.

The hostess hesitated, then popped in front of Rainer. "Well, I'm not allowed to let you go in there without reservations."

Rainer suspected the young woman might be Lower Caste, otherwise she'd be inside rather than watching the door, so her bravado needled at him.

Just another sign that the system is falling into societal ruin.

As the Sovereign hadn't made any Media appearances since the battle with the fragger organization at Palomin, rumors of his failing health and loosening grip on the system spurred defiance, manifesting in public outbursts and several instances of violence. What would happen when Rainer finally had to tell the citizenry that Sovereign Simon Prollixer had been assassinated? Chaos could ensue. Power grabs were certain among Uppers, especially the Socialites.

What Rainer would never feed to the Media and the tuned-in

masses was the truth behind Prollixer's demise—that Rainer himself, trusted Head Contractor, had taken down the Sovereign for crimes against a woman Rainer still obsessed over. Should the truth ever come out, the voyeurs would have a field day spying on him and his family, probably even mixing and painting older stock footage to fabricate new feed.

And, though there were no voyeurs with telescoping cameras floating around here in the Latulipe Underground, Rainer couldn't allow even this small insolence by the hostess to go unchecked. Direct force wasn't always the answer either. He learned that at Palomin . . . both times.

Choices worked best.

Make the target choose.

Rainer dug his fingers into her arm and pulled her close so that only she could hear him. "You can either step aside and keep your job or I'll see that you're sent to the uranium mines on Deleine. Those better-than-average Lower Caste looks will wither quickly from the radiation. Wouldn't you rather try to fool a Socialite into marrying you, have a child so he can't change his mind, and live a pampered life here on Tampa Quad? *On the surface?*"

The woman lowered her eyes. When Rainer let go of her, she scampered out of his way.

###

A different world waited behind the oversized glass doors. The sweetness of bath salts, metallic mist drugs, and carnal pursuits fogged the air around him. "I hate the smell of flesh clubs."

"You probably hate everything about flesh clubs," Dahlia said over the music bombarding them from several mind minstrels hovering near the top of the nine-meter-high baroque-style ceilings. These floating parallelograms projected turquoise beams onto their subjects below, analyzing emotions, speech patterns, brain waves. Each minstrel played distinctly different tunes, from frantic beats to sultry nocturnes, depending on where the various guests were in the stages of coupling. Rainer caught snatches of suggestive lyrics and erotic language in all of them.

Dahlia seemed more comfortable in a place like this than he would have thought. Even after three weeks of seclusion with her, he still didn't know much about his sixth amour. Her attitude had disintegrated with every day of her pregnancy. Her mood swings and neuroses about his other amours dug into his nerves like blade cuffs through flesh. She especially delighted in talking about Ambasadora Sara Mendoza, then flying into a rage and hinting at telling the world what Rainer had done to appease his emotional fallacy for Sara.

Dahlia would never make good on the bluff because she risked a Writ of Execution for just witnessing Rainer kill Prollixer. Until the modified truth was released to the public, she would be seen as covering for her amour all this time, which wouldn't win her any sympathy with a jury.

Only thirteen weeks into her pregnancy, Dahlia still wore the snug-fitting black pants and shirts preferred by most contractors.

And an extra belt of razor discs, as though the small weapons would keep their progeny safe should a confrontation erupt.

Rainer insisted she remain at his estate, but Dahlia's conception had stirred a streak of independence that he hadn't expected. She'd always been so malleable before, not like her older half-sister, Faya—Sara's tormentor. Still, Rainer refused to argue with Dahlia. Most times he just didn't say anything to her. Keeping her close for now was his best choice. He trusted her, but only as far as he could see her.

They strode past the coupling salons that spiraled outward from the plateau of central baths. Dark purple and silver curtains covered the doorways of salons with the most modest guests. Many stood open to undulating bodies in every position and every size group. A few groups gestured invitations. They were mostly Socialites slumming it with mixed-Caste couplings. Though contractors were also technically Socialites, they were practically their own subgroup, one with extremely pure bloodlines and closed family circles. They considered themselves the most *upper* of the Upper Caste.

Wisps of steam brushed Rainer's perspiring face the closer he came to the baths. The guests here were exclusively contractors. Their homogenized features of squared jawlines, oval eyes, and similar skin tones spoke of their pure lineage. With their black hair and blue eyes, many looked like they could have been part of Rainer's childhood family circle. And because of the limited number of available suitors, some probably were.

Large spas bubbled from steamy depressions in the fluorospar plateau. Beverage buckets dotted the perimeters. Naked bodies pressed close to one another in the water.

"Rogues know how to drag out a celebration." Dahlia unholstered a cender. "How long has it been since the Corruption of Palomin? Three months?"

"Corruption of Palomin?" Rainer asked. "Where did you hear that?"

"Some of the Media channels."

"Hmmm. Nice little euphemism for the beginning of a system-wide revolution." He preferred the "Fall of Palomin." It rang truer. The fragger assault there destroyed the old data archive complex and took the lives of hundreds of contractors.

Just ahead of their small group, three males and a female sat in the spa, unaware of Rainer's approach.

He overheard one of the males say, "I think you need to check your facts. I took out at least thirty fraggers at Palomin."

Killian Doje—thrown out of the Embassy guild after a mishap last year while on a training run. Apparently his charge at the time had taken a severe beating while Killian remained unscathed. The incident with two *unidentified* assailants landed Killian's charge in a coma, then a funeral pyre. No formal charges had been leveled against Killian, so the man's ego had never been checked.

"You took out that many fraggers all by yourself?" Rainer's comment stifled the surrounding conversation.

Casualties had been high on both sides of the unexpected fragger assault, but no one man or woman could have made that much of a difference in the bloody tech battle.

"Someone had to," Killian said. "Obviously you guilders couldn't get the job done yourselves."

"*Guilders?*" Rainer let the word float around in his mind. "I don't like it. There are already too many titles flying around this system. Let's stick with just plain old contractor, Embassy-sanctioned or not."

"You still seem to like the title *Head Contractor*." Another of the men stood up to face Rainer.

"It's a pretension I tolerate for my position," Rainer said. Though he had never met most of these rogues before, all contractors knew of Rainer Varden, Sovereign Simon Prollixer's right-hand man.

The tension in the air almost pushed away the steam.

"I have a proposition for you." With a rub to his eyebrow, Rainer signaled one of his contractors to circle around the spa.

"For him or for me?" The woman next to Killian spoke up.

She was part Socialite. Rainer knew because she looked a little like Sara had, before the Sovereign had altered her appearance. As part of the reconstruction necessary after Faya's month of butchering, Prollixer had decided, for reasons he never cared to share, to remake Sara to look like a contractor. Rainer had preferred her new look, including the addition of the bio-lights flashing beneath her skin. But he often dreamt about Sara as she was when they first met, when he snatched her from that ballroom for illegally syphoning data.

Like this woman staring at him from the bath, Sara's hair had been silky brown and bobbed. Her jawline and the curve of her neck was also the same, but the eyes were all wrong. This woman had dull eyes, the color of cold chai, not honey-colored like Sara's. Those were the eyes that haunted him during quiet moments, but they had been changed, too, like every part of her.

If he had known what would happen to Sara after she left that elevator with Faya . . . well, it was best not to indulge in regret. It might paralyze him from making an equally difficult decision in the future. But he wouldn't pretend that he hadn't pulled the trigger on Prollixer in retribution for not doing more to save Sara Mendoza.

"I was talking to Killian," Rainer said, pushing memory and emotion from his mind.

"He's not into SG," the woman said.

"I'm not a same gender man either," Rainer said. "Just looking to recruit some rogues for the Embassy."

"The *Embassy*?" Killian stood up, his stance aggressive despite his lack of clothing. "The guild threw me out, remember? Not that I'm ungrateful, because business is much more lucrative on this side of the law. Turns out I don't want to be owned by the Embassy again."

"You fought for the Embassy at Palomin," Rainer said.

"We wanted to wipe out the fraggers. Just so happens that those goals aligned with the Sovereign's, but that assist at Palomin was all you'll get from me."

"Do you honestly believe we wiped out the fraggers that day?" Rainer asked.

"Cut them down to nothing, at least."

Killian's arrogant tone made Rainer want to reconsider the pending offer, but the contractors' guild needed the rogues to strengthen their ranks.

"The fraggers have been quiet," Rainer said, "because they are regrouping, growing their numbers, stockpiling their weapons."

"You're implying that's what we need to be doing." Killian grabbed a purple towel from the rack behind him and stepped out of the tub.

"No." Rainer let the word hover in the air.

Killian took the bait. "Then why are you here?"

"To assemble a task force. To hunt down the fraggers throughout this system, even in the virtual worlds . . . before they can strike."

"I don't go V-side," Killian said, "but if there's something in it for me, I'd consider slicing open some of those techno-militant pieces of shit here in the real world."

"How about a signed Writ of Privilege to gather as many fragger hides as you like by whatever methods you deem fitting?"

Rainer asked.

"All paid bounties?"

"All paid. No limits. Just proof of fragger involvement," Rainer said.

"Now that's a deal I can't pass up," Killian said.

It was also a deal Rainer didn't plan to honor.

###

Rainer's black uniform stood in desperate contrast to the white tech room. He was the only splotch of color, save for the silver countertops and rainbow shimmer on the free-standing energy shields positioned around the octagonal space.

"Have you made the appropriate adjustments?" he asked one of the Embassy scientists assigned to backward engineer fragger technology. Rainer couldn't afford to lose another contractor to a faulty research and development team. The last volunteer who had used the fragger orb weapon spontaneously combusted.

"This time should do it," the lab-coated scientist said.

"Good." Rainer picked up the reporter from the metal counter.

"You're going to try it yourself?" the man asked, surprise thinning his voice.

"Of course not." Rainer grabbed the scientist's arm, twisted it behind his back and snapped the reporter onto his wrist. Before he let the man go, Rainer tapped a finger to his palm, activating his own reporter and sending lock-out codes to the one he'd just forced on the scientist.

Upon release, he frantically tried to claw the metal bracelet from his body but only managed to skin away part of his flesh. "I'm not a contractor," he pleaded.

Rainer stepped away from him. "Which is exactly why you're the perfect volunteer. Scientists are a plague in this system. The lifetime of training given to contractors is irreplaceable. Now get ready to catch this." Rainer moved behind the hazy energy shield, leaving only his left hand exposed, the one holding his live cender.

The scientist crouched down, nearly tripping over his billowing lab coat, and held both hands up in front of his face.

"You probably want to put that hand as far out in front of you as possible," Rainer said. "The energy backwash can be severe."

Still cowering in a stoop, the scientist hid his face with one hand and held the one with the locked reporter out, palm-first, in front of him.

Rainer checked to be sure his cender was dialed all the way up. Then, not ten meters from his target, Rainer fired. The static electricity crackled through the air, but the only visible sign that it had found its mark was the glow emanating from the scientist's hand.

Satisfied, and a little surprised, Rainer lowered his weapon. He stepped out from behind the shield when he heard the man shrieking. He held his hand like it was hemorrhaging blood, but the only thing pouring out of his palm was an intense, white-hot light.

It looked promising, then Rainer's hair stood on end. He dove behind the shield and covered his head. The concussive explosion blew out the energy shield and the lights.

A charred mess remained of the Embassy scientist.

Rainer bit back his anger, careful not to let disappointment ruin his focus. The test had been more successful than last time—the energy could be harnessed by the fragger orbs they'd acquired during the Palomin battle. The problem now was how that absorbed energy could be released without frying the energy wielder.

He left the room and headed for the next testing facility, the one working on the low-tech caster pistols. There was more than one way to use fragger technology against its militant creators.

Rainer had little interest in the brightly lit mega-estates they passed along the canal. The female rogue beside him droned on about the size of the estates here in this part of Tampa Quad and the prominent families who owned them.

He focused on the interplay across from him . . . Killian and Arta Robeni, the woman from the spa. Rainer had objected when Killian listed her as one of his team, but the rogue insisted he had trained her personally and that her absence was a deal breaker.

Rainer had watched her discreetly since the mix of sixteen Embassy contractors and rogues had boarded the high-speed canal hoppers an hour ago. From his peripheral vision, he noticed as she leaned in close to Killian. How Killian's gaze swept over her thin face. And especially how he draped his arm around her shoulders. Sometimes his hand slid from her shoulder to massage her neck.

Rainer had rarely shared small intimacies like this with Sara or his amours.

"My first time to Balaam," Arta said, "and I get to see it in the black of night."

"Just a bunch of flashy homes and transports." Killian scratched at the blonde hair ridging slightly from his forehead to the back of his head.

Rainer's hair had gotten too long to wear in this traditional style—Dahlia had even called him shaggy. He was glad she had agreed to stay at his mother's estate during this raid. He wouldn't have to listen to her insults or worry about her and the baby. Even though she was becoming more and more difficult, she was still carrying his child, and that meant her safety was paramount.

"Are you looking for another rich amour, Arta?" Killian asked.

He used her name fondly, which surprised Rainer because he had only known the rogue to be self-absorbed and surly. But, she was his prime, his first amour, according to her background check. She, on the other hand, had three others before Killian, all wealthy socialites. Apparently she wanted a little adventure or a purer bloodline.

"I hear the Uppers from Balaam are among the wealthiest." Arta looked at Rainer. "Is that true?"

"I don't know," Rainer said. "I don't keep up on the Socialite scene."

"You're a purist," she said, a bit of derision in her tone breaking the façade of her cool exterior and reminding Rainer of how often Sara accused him of playing to his caste.

"I prefer tradition," Rainer said.

"What a shame," Arta said, focusing her affections back on Killian. "I like variety."

"*I* prefer tradition," said the redheaded female sitting next to Rainer. Casual flirting before an engagement was the norm among many contractors. The sexual tension gave them a focus and allowed them to preview partners for the celebrations afterward. That's what the redhead was trying for.

Rainer ignored her.

Her well-toned arms and narrow hips would make a nice distraction for one of the other men or women here, just not him. Not with Sara so close.

Sara? Her name bounced around in his mind like a threnody—he had never grieved for her death at Palomin, maybe because part of him held hope that she was somehow still alive, somewhere safe.

But that would mean she was with Sean Cryer, a fragger node she was originally sent to kill. Instead she had developed an emotional fallacy for the man.

An ambasadora and a fragger.

They would have been perfect for one another—neither valued tradition nor the tenets of society. And the Media would have eaten that story up, no doubt giving it even more airtime than the "new star" that had appeared in the northern sky just after the battle at Palomin. In fact, "Palomin's Death" had become the star's moniker, even after the astronomical observers had proven it wasn't really a star, just some space junk drifting through the edge of the Intra-Brazial.

Still, he started thinking of Palomin's Death as Sara's star. She had once told him while recovering from one of Faya's torture sessions that she was ready for the Otherside—all she needed was a star to take her there. If she really did die at Palomin . . .

One of the rogue males pounded on the transport wall, bringing Rainer's attention to the present. The rogue yelled, "I'm ready to kill some fucking fraggers." Cheers erupted from all around, even from some of the group Rainer had brought from the Embassy.

"Are the rumors about fraggers true or just their own propaganda?" The redhead squeezed Rainer's knee in another attempt to engage him.

Rainer pushed her hand away. "What rumors?"

She hesitated after another unrequited advance. "That they're so brutal they kill their own kind in training exercises?"

"You've never met a fragger, have you?" Rainer's question hushed those contractors and rogues around them.

"Of cour—"

"You wouldn't have asked that question if you had," Rainer said.

The woman's cheeks flushed.

"They fight to win just like the rest of us. V-side training doesn't guarantee anything," he said.

The techno-militants had only come out of reclusion this past week. Their forces were small, but terrifyingly strong, with brazen attacks on high-profile Embassy targets. No longer afraid to show their affiliation with the fragger organization and its ideologies, many members branded and tattooed themselves. The gesture showed solidarity and was meant as an equalizer for their Lower Caste brethren. But, kill their own kind? Only contractors excelled at that.

The canal hopper slowed to enter the dank waterway of the Svetz Pods. In this watery slum resided the working force for the estates they had just passed.

Six globular edifices surrounded a small, marshy courtyard. On closer approach, they could see that each lit dwelling was actually a group of three elliptical pods fashioned into a pyramid. A pan ahead showed thousands of glowing pods rising from the swamps like giant, green frogs.

"I'm glad our hit is near the canal bank. I'd hate to have to trudge too far into there," Killian said.

Arta smiled and gave Rainer's forearm a pulse before she exited the hopper. It was an invitation for later. She had obviously picked up on his attraction to her. It was something to think about, even if it would be only a substitute . . . and a way to dent Killian's ego.

Rainer stood in front of the contractors and stared into the distant darkness. He closed his right eye to allow the macro focus in his left to activate. A nice addition, thanks to an Armadan he knew. Another casualty from their team that day at Palomin.

Rainer spied no signs of movement. He raised his fist and gave the motion to move out.

Killian kissed Arta before leading her and his team on an approach from the pod's left.

Rainer took his contractors to the right.

Surprise and the brand-new projectile casters would be their only advantage. The Embassy scientists had finally developed these prototypes of the sleek fragger pistols, which fired metallic slugs that opened into stars upon impact. In a bout of poetic irony, the caster's low-tech design was based on fragger specs from their V-side training worlds and would be used to thwart the fragger orb weapon. No energy to absorb meant no energy to fire back. At least that was the theory. This would be the casters' first field test.

He motioned his team toward the sparse light of the closest pyramid of pods. The pungent smell of watery decay intensified once they left the open canals. The humid air clung to his face and weighed on his lungs. Bloodywings buzzed around but found no viable skin thanks to natural insecticide secreted by his scentbots.

Rainer stopped just outside the bottom pod's glow. Water seeped over his black boots. With a twitch of his index finger, he prompted the other contractors to follow, then grasped the first rung of the pod's ladder. They climbed silently and quickly to the uppermost level. Rainer scaled the last rounded wall and peered down from the roof through the pod's oval skylight.

His pulse quickened at the sight of a woman lying naked and motionless on a bare mattress. He thought she might be dead until her arms jerked in response to some unseen stimulus.

Must be in the V-side.

A look to the right revealed a man and woman coupling on the other bed. To the left, three men watched the Media on an early model viewer. The picture on the large screen showed a blonde ambasadora whom Rainer had met once during an Embassy function. Her mouth opened in a laugh and the shot pulled back to reveal a platinum-headed show host laughing beside her. This ambasadora was nothing like Sara, aside from the purple bio-lights glowing along the woman's arm. What had Sara called the astronomically expensive intra-tat reserved exclusively for the ambasadoras?

A cattle brand.

A small smile reached the corner of his mouth, remembering

her irreverence for the Embassy and Sovereign Simon Prollixer. How would she have reacted knowing that Rainer had killed the good Sovereign to avenge her?

He glanced at Palomin's Death shining wanly in the night sky before drawing his casters. Maybe she had seen it all from the Otherside. Maybe she watched him now. Not a man to be taken with superstition and cosmic divinity, he shook the thought away.

He focused on Killian and his team maneuvering below. They burst through a bottom pod's inner door. Rainer shot out the skylight and jumped through the opening. He landed on top of the motionless V-sider and rammed his knee into the woman's throat. The soft flesh gave way with a snap, barely audible above the staccato of the firing casters.

He spun his weapons around just in time to plug an advancing male. Three projectiles thudded into the fragger's chest in rapid succession, then starburst, releasing their barbs for extra damage.

Rainer's team took out the docking couple. Another fragger fell in front of Rainer at the top of the interior ladder—a row of razor discs studded the man's back. Killian gave Rainer a cocky smile from below and grabbed more discs from his bandoleer.

Don't celebrate until the last fragger falls.

A series of electric cracks cut the air. Three more fraggers appeared from the lower pod, equipped with the blank stare of V-mitter lenses, their way of seeing in the real world like they did in the V-side. They brandished electric filament whips. The electric charge from these retractables sent three contractors and a rogue to the floor before Rainer could react.

He fired at the fraggers as they sliced at Rainer's downed team with their whips. Arta and three other rogues were beside him, unloading their casters.

One of the fraggers, her chest plate pocked with metallic stars, raised her retractable and slashed its glowing blue filament at Arta. As if in slow motion, Rainer watched the whip wrap itself around her head and neck and drop her instantly.

Killian dove for her.

Rainer shot the fragger's wrist. The deadly retractable fell impotent to the pod floor. Without bothering to reload, Rainer lunged at the fragger and caught her with a backhand. The woman staggered off-balance.

Killian bounded from his dead amour's side and tackled the fragger female with a roar, tearing the V-mitters from her eyes. The woman screamed and clawed at his face. He smashed the caster repeatedly against her temple until her breathing came in gurgly spurts. Her eyes, raw from where he had ripped off the lenses, rolled back into her head.

Killian pushed away from her and wiped the blood from his face, then fired his caster. The point-blank shot opened a hole in the fragger's forehead. "For Arta," he said. Then Killian flew back into the fray, leaving Arta's sliced body lying at Rainer's feet.

Abandoning tragedy to avoid the pain. Rainer understood that better than most.

Motion to his right made him alert. He bounded down the steps to the pod's bottom level and glimpsed a form exiting out the back. Caster drawn, he followed.

He used his macro-vision to scope ahead. A woman. She tripped just outside the pod's green glow.

Rainer descended upon the female struggling in the swampy muck. He aimed his caster at her face.

"Fucking contractor," she whispered.

"Mother." The cry came from a boy a few meters away.

Rainer froze.

The little boy threw himself on his mother in a protective gesture. Rainer pulled him out of the way. The boy, maybe six years old, pounded Rainer's leg with his tiny fists. Rainer pulled him off and tossed him aside. The mother waved the boy off from another assault.

Rainer held his caster on them, listening to the fight behind him in the pods. From the sounds of it, the contractors were winning.

"Run." The word broke out of Rainer's mouth before he could stop it.

The fragger stood still, regarding him warily.

Whether it was the protective instincts that had been building inside him since Dahlia's pregnancy or for a reason he refused to acknowledge, he had made his decision.

"Run. Both of you. Now."

The fragger didn't hesitate a second time. She grabbed her son's arm and disappeared into the darkness.

Rainer kept the caster pointed at them until they splashed away into the swamp. A roiling in his gut said he would pay for this mercy one day.

He looked up at Palomin's Death.

Just like he paid for his emotional fallacy of a dead woman.

A Deadline to Remember
By James Fadeley

She felt a tingle of excitement to hear her name called.

"Pera, you got a second?"

Pera leaned back in her office chair, her shoulder-length green hair bobbing. When she saw who it was, she smiled. "Yeah, Mych. What do you need?"

Mych looked over his shoulder, and Pera knew he was checking to make sure no one was watching. He turned back to Pera and put his hands on her neck, his fingers massaging her muscles. She sighed with relief. "Oh, so it's about what I need."

"Shush," Mych said, whispering.

"Oh, come on, Mych," Pera said in a hushed tone. "We've been dating for almost a solar year now. Everyone basically figured it out already. Except maybe Xander from accounting."

Mych worked her back some and Pera let her tongue hang out like a happy pet as he eased her tensed deltoids. "Yeah, well. I don't need any more stress right now with the new code release coming up."

"Please. We're done, and ahead of schedule too. We gave up our holiday, but it was worth it. The boss even gave us tomorrow off. You did great," Pera replied as her head hung low.

"Almost."

Pera looked up at him. Try as she might, she couldn't figure out what was with Mych's face. It was something between nervous and trying to hold back a smile. "What's wrong?"

"I deployed one more build after I found another bug," he said, withdrawing his hands. "Can you hit the Web site and make sure you got it?"

"Sure." She all but sighed and reached for her console, opening up the net browser. She opened the application and typed the address in.

Then she gasped.

"The code will never be perfect," the site read in plain letters. "But you can make me perfect. Will you marry me, Pera?"

Her hands covered her mouth as she read the words with wide eyes. She swiveled her chair to face him, but instead found herself staring at a ruby ring.

"So, will you?" he asked with a smile.

She couldn't even breath, she just nodded her head with the world's largest smile on her face as he tenderly lifted her hand and slipped the engagement ring on her finger.

The sound of applause rose throughout the office as their coworkers began to cheer. Pera choked back a laugh and looked over her cubicle wall. They were all standing and clapping for her and Mych. They all knew. They all had to have known. And everyone kept the secret from her.

She felt her face flush as he took her hand and made her stand. Xander approached with a bottle of bubbly alcohol and two glasses. But before he could offer it to them, Yuna the receptionist interjected herself with a camera.

Pera and Mych held each other with the sight from the window as their backdrop. Yuna lined up the shot just as a wave of murmurs and surprise went up from the other coworkers.

"A shooting star!" Xander shouted as Yuna took the picture.

###

With the couple's permission, Yuna hung the picture in the office hallway. It was taken from the highest floor of the building. Against a background of sunset orange, the black boxy silhouettes of neighboring office structures contrasted with the curves of the two lovers embracing. In the upper-left corner of the picture was a slim, white streak in the dimming sky.

For most people that day, the comet was an object of scientific wonder. And the news was abuzz with theories and speculations. But for those two lovers, it was nothing so mundane, to be ruined by fact and reason.

No could claim otherwise. To them, it was a wish that had come true.

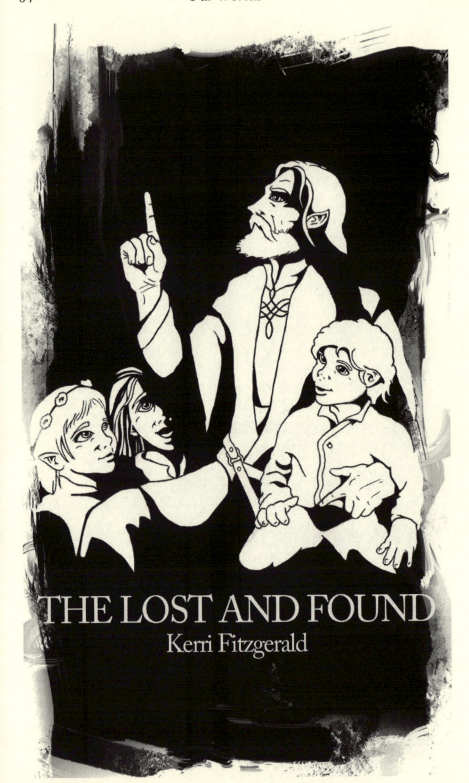

The Lost and Found
By Kerri Fitzgerald

Everyone gathered around Ylli. The adults were in small groups having quiet conversations; the Younglings were laughing and running circles around the furniture. He smiled. His people, the Denuvians, truly were beautiful people, both inside and out. A small hand placed on his knee pulled him from his reverie. He looked down into soft, golden eyes set in a cherubic face.

"Good evening, Lali. How does this beautiful day find you?"

Lali wrinkled her nose. "Why do you always speak so strangely, Ylli?"

"Lali, that is no way to speak to your Elder! Be mindful of the way you address Master Ylli."

Ylli raised placating hands. "Do not be so hard on the Youngling, Anelim. She is only inquisitive. I enjoy our little conversations. She reminds me so very much of myself when I was a Youngling." Ylli looked down in to those eyes again and gave a toothy grin, his eyes sparkling with humour.

Anelim nodded her assent and went back to the small group of adults, slowly shaking her head in the way only an exasperated mother can.

Ylli tousled Lali's hair. "So, Lali, what may I do for you?" Lali raised her chubby little arms skywards. Ylli chuckled and lifted Lali onto his knee.

"My, my, Lali. With Nature as my witness you grow bigger .

. . and heavier every day!" Lali giggled and rested her head on Ylli's chest, his grey beard rubbing gently against her forehead.

"Tell me a story, Ylli?"

"A story, you say?"

"Yes, please, Ylli."

Suddenly, a chorus went up from all the Younglings in the room. "A story! A story! Tell us a story, Ylli! Please, please, please!" All the Younglings stampeded toward Ylli's chair, jumping up and down, all vying for his attention.

Ylli chuckled and raised his eyes to the ceiling. He tilted his head slightly to the side. "Well, Mother, what do you think? Should I recount a tale for the Younglings this fine evening?"

A tall and lithe Elder woman walked slowly to stand behind Ylli's chair. She placed her slender hand on his shoulder and stared into his golden eyes, her long grey hair cascading over one shoulder. "I think that would be most agreeable, my love. You tell stories so very well." She cupped his chin in her hand. "The question is which story will you regale us with?"

"Well, Vida, that all depends on which story you'd like to hear?"

"I don't think that's for me to decide." She peered over Ylli's shoulder to look down upon Lali's innocent face. "Do you have a story in mind, young Lali?"

Lali thought about this for some time, tapping a small finger against her lips as she did so. Ylli and Vida glanced at each other and grinned. Vida bent down toward Ylli and placed a gentle kiss on his cheek.

"I'd like to hear the one about Mount Bast. When he got really cross . . . and angry . . . and his head exploded!" Lali started bouncing up and down on Ylli's knee in her excitement.

Ylli let out a heartfelt belly laugh. "What a wonderful idea, Lali. That is one of my favourites. Okay, Younglings!" Ylli clapped his hands. "Gather round, make yourselves comfortable, and I'll begin. Vida, we may need some sustenance."

Vida smiled warmly and bowed. "I'd do anything for you, my love." She turned and glided toward the kitchen area, putting together small cuts of meat, bowls of soft fruit, and jugs of warm, honeyed cordial. The Younglings gathered cushions and furs and laid them out in a rough semicircle around Ylli's chair. The adults pulled up their own chairs in a larger semicircle around the children's places.

Ylli's eyes grew distant as he recalled a time gone by, a time of hunger and strife, a time of omens. "The story begins when I was a young adult. Our people were known as the Perdites back then. We were lost people. We were hungry and distrustful people. But that all changed with the coming of an omen . . ."

I was a keen stargazer as a young man. The stars have always spoken to me; the way they make beautiful patterns, the way they twinkle and wink. They have always mesmerized me. I was stargazing this particular night when I noticed The Omen for the first time. It was like nothing I'd ever seen before. It was so mind-achingly gigantic that I could hardly believe my eyes.

I was staring through my telescope, making sketches of the stars. I liked to make notes on how the night sky changed over time. The stars would stay in the same formations, but they would edge slowly across the sky; some would disappear, and I wouldn't see them again for weeks at a time. On this particular night, there was something new in the sky. To the naked eye, it was a large, bright star. Through the telescope, it was a different thing entirely. It was hundreds of metres long and shaped like a giant pillar. Its surface was metallic, and it reflected the stars that surrounded it in a hazy corona. I don't know why I didn't run to tell someone sooner than I did, but I was in awe of it. I sat watching it for at least an hour; I didn't discern anything from it in that time, but I just couldn't tear myself away.

Eventually, I went to find an Elder. Not just any Elder. The Elder I had the closest affinity to, Ilvas. Ilvas was a wise and clever Elder. He was also extremely kind-hearted and had a fast wit, which often kept the other Elders on their toes. He was intuitive, too, and always managed to pull me from grim musings in my young life just by sitting down next to me and smoking his pipe. He wouldn't utter a single word. He would just sit there until I unloaded what was troubling my wretched soul. He always did things with a smile. I remember him with fondness.

"What is it, Ylli? Whatever is the rush?" I dragged Ilvas by the arm to my telescope. "Ylli, really, this is most irregular of you. You're acting very much out of character. I've never seen you so animated!"

"Just wait until you see this, Ilvas! I don't know what to make of it?"

Ilvas hobbled over to the telescope, straightening his robes. He raised a straggly grey eyebrow at me, smirked, and placed his eye in front of the telescope's eyepiece. His body stiffened, and I felt a sense of satisfaction that I'd managed to shock my tutor. He adjusted the lens to change the focus and muttered something under his breath. He pulled away and restraightened his robes, rubbed his eyes, and then went back to looking through the eyepiece. I knew better than to disturb him, and I waited patiently for him to finish.

After what seemed like an eternity, Ilvas pulled away.

"Well, I never! I mean, what on Dorgumir is that? It's huge. It's bigger than huge . . . it's enormous!" He gesticulated wildly, then placed his hands over his aged brown eyes. He sighed, rubbing his hands from his eyes down his face to his chin, where he let them fall to his sides. I'd never seen him so dumbfounded, and it unnerved me more than a little.

"I don't know what it is, Ilvas," I said, shrugging. "I was hoping you might have some answers for me?"

Ilvas shook his head. "I have no idea, lad. This has me stumped. We need to take this to the Elder council right away. It could be a really bad omen. What happens if that . . . that thing . . .

crashes in to Dorgumir? We're struggling enough without a catastrophe befalling us." He pointed into the sky in The Omen's general direction.

"We had best go then, Ilvas. No time like the present, eh?"

Ilvas sighed again and gave me a wistful smile. "I've got something for you, lad."

"Hm?" Ilvas threw an apple at me and I caught it deftly. "Where did you get this, Ilvas? We're not supposed to have these unless they're being distributed with the rations."

Ilvas tapped the side of his nose. "Well, lad, that would be telling. We'll keep it a secret between you and me, okay? Eat it quick before we reach the temple."

Normally, I would have protested and insisted that we share it between our townsfolk, but my growling stomach had other ideas. I devoured it with relish as we walked down the hillside toward the Elder temple.

###

The temple of the Elders was a white marble monument. It had clean edges and beautifully coloured mosaics carpeting the floor. Statues in deference to all Nature dotted the alcoves and sat upon shelves and plinths. We Perdites didn't believe in a God, as such; we believed in life, in the bounty we got from Nature itself. Life was being seized from the Perdites, and it was beginning to show. We'd become an ugly people on the outside, and it crept into our very beings, our souls. Our lithe bodies had begun to look twisted and ill. Our skin had lost its healthy glow, and our eyes no longer shone gold. They had been reduced to a sickly brown. We'd been a thriving race once, but the increase in our populace had led to pressures on the land. Our numbers just weren't sustainable, and so the Perdites suffered. Sickness increased, health dwindled, and we rationed what little food we reaped from the earth.

Inside the temple, we sat on polished wooden pews and waited to be called inside the Chamber of Elders. It was a large hall located within the centre of the temple, and it was from here that the Elders governed Dorgumir. There were seven elders in total, each one elected to their position by the Perdite citizenry.

The great wooden doors to the chamber opened slowly, and a small, dark-haired aide dressed in red robes emerged. He bowed before Ilvas and nodded curtly toward me.

"Master Ilvas. Ylli. The other Elders will see you now. Master Ilvas, is there anything you require before I depart?"

"No. No. Thank you, Faron, that will be all." Faron bowed again and made his way down the corridor toward the front of the temple, his cloak swishing from side to side as he went.

"That boy is far too formal for his own good. He will never make an Elder if he doesn't start forming his own ideas and opinions. He thinks he can work his way through the ranks through servitude." Ilvas looked thoughtful and seemed to muse a moment longer.

"I think it best we go inside now, Ilvas. The rest of the Elders will be waiting."

"What? Yes, yes. Sorry, lad. My mind had begun to wander. Best not keep them waiting, eh? You know how they get."

Ilvas walked into the chamber, and I followed closely behind him. It was a large, circular chamber with seating around the entire circumference of the room—all polished pews like the waiting area outside. On a balcony toward the top of the tiered pews, behind a giant wooden desk, sat the other six Elders. Each one was tall and slender limbed with a beard, but that is where the similarities ended.

"Master Ilvas, you've called an impromptu meeting of the Elders. I trust it is a matter of great import at this late hour?"

Kyros was the sternest of the Elders. He had black hair with wisps of grey showing above his ears and around his temples. He had progressed to the title of Elder early in his adult life, and his ambition was a force to be reckoned with. Suffice to say, Kyros and Ilvas, for the most part, did not generally see eye to eye.

"That it is, Kyros. I am not entirely sure how to explain it. I fear it may be an ill omen for our people. However, I cannot be certain."

"It's Master Kyros if you please, Master Ilvas. We are all equals here." Kyros swept out his arms, indicating the other Elders that sat to either side of him. "If we can get to the heart of the matter quickly?"

"As you wish . . . Master . . . Kyros. There is a very large metallic object in the night sky heading toward Dorgumir. I do not know what it is, or what it could possibly be. But it appears to be heading straight for us, and I thought it should be brought to the council's attention." Ilvas folded his arms and awaited the fallout. The other Elders looked at one another with bemused faces, some shaking their heads in disbelief, while others conversed quietly with each other under their breaths.

"Masters! Quiet, please. We must hear what else Master Ilvas has to say. Please explain yourself, Master."

"What more do you want me to explain, Kyros?"

"Master Kyros."

"Apologies, Master Kyros. There's a giant object in our sky, and I'm wondering as a council what we should do about it? Perhaps if you gentleman would like to follow me, I could show you exactly what we're talking about here?"

###

The Elders followed Ilvas from the chamber, and I hurried to catch up with them. The sight of the whole council of Elders stalking out of the temple to the outskirts of town and up the small hill stopped the townsfolk in their tracks.

"Masters, whatever is happening? Is there something amiss?" Perdites in the vicinity dropped whatever they were doing and started following in a processional after the Elders. I cursed under my breath. I could see this wasn't going to end well. I ran to the front to catch up with Ilvas, my robes kicking up dust as I went.

"Ilvas, what's going to happen? Master Kyros and the other

Elders do not seem impressed at all. It's almost like they don't believe you."

"Well, they won't have much choice once we've shown them, will they, lad? It's as clear as daylight once you look at . . ." He waved his arms in tight circles in front of himself. ". . . It. We're going to need to name the thing, I suspect. We can't keep referring to it as 'it' or 'thing.'"

I chuckled despite myself. Ilvas always seemed to be able to put a comical spin on a situation, no matter how dire it was.

Kyros loomed ahead of the crowd as we caught up.

"Do you find this situation amusing, Ylli?"

"No, Master."

"Good." Kyros turned toward Ilvas and sighed. "Okay, Master Ilvas. What is it that you want to show us?"

"Could you take a look through the telescope, please?" Ilvas indicated the telescope and bowed.

I smirked. I couldn't help it. Ilvas winked at me, then turned a serious face toward Kyros.

Kyros looked through the lens. The crowd surrounding the telescope hushed. Everyone held their breath, waiting for Kyros' reaction to whatever was on the other end of the telescope. He pulled his head away with an odd look on his face—somewhere between confusion and amusement.

"See, Kyros, I told you there—"

"There's nothing there."

"Wait. What?"

"I said there's nothing there, Master Ilvas."

"That can't be!" Ilvas shoved Kyros out of his path and looked through the telescope.

"Ylli, he's right." Ilvas bent over, placing his hands on his knees and tilting his head toward me, almost like he was trying to catch his breath. "There's nothing there. How could something that size just disappear?" He began to shake his head. I strode over to the telescope.

"May I?"

"Of course, Ylli, it's your telescope, after all." Kyros made a snorting sound and rolled his eyes. I ignored him as I placed my eye against the eyepiece. And then I held my breath. I moved the telescope in and out of focus, and scanned lightly across the night sky. It didn't take me long to find what I was looking for.

I let my breath out slowly, and I could hear my blood pounding in my ears. I moved away from the telescope and peered into the night sky. My naked eye confirmed what I already knew. The Omen had inched its way across the night sky in only a couple of hours. It was moving far faster than anything I had ever observed. My stomach did a somersault. I turned toward Ilvas and the other waiting Elders.

"Would you like to take a look, Master?" My voice wavered as I spoke. I'd tried to mask my unease, but if anything, it made my voice crack even more.

Kyros stepped forward and looked through the telescope. He gasped. As he pulled away, his face was pale, and the sharpness to his brown eyes had softened somewhat. Fear. It could have a strange effect on people. The crowd heard Kyros' gasp and started murmuring, wondering what it was he'd seen. My heart sank. I wondered how much more bad news these people, my people, could take? The news of The Omen would either make the Perdites or break them. The murmuring grew in intensity, until it became chatter.

"Perdites, gather in the Chamber of Elders, please. There is much we need to discuss." Ilvas raised his arms, and his voice, in an effort to get the people's attention.

"What's going to happen, Master Ilvas? Are we in danger?"

"All we be explained in the Chamber. Please make your way to the temple. Collect those townsfolk who are not currently here." The townsfolk, still chattering loudly amongst themselves, began to make their way down the hill. I could see hysteria lurking on the edge of the crowd like a black cloud; I was just thankful that it hadn't broken free.

I turned back toward Ilvas and the Elders. The majority of them were now crowded around the telescope, taking it in turns to peer through its lens. Kyros and those other Elders who had already taken a look sat on the stony ground with ashen faces, breathing deep breaths, with a patina of sweat upon their brows.

"What in Nature's name is that thing?" asked Kyros, trembling slightly. "I mean, where did it come from? What is it doing here? Why is it here? How can we . . . ?"

"Master Kyros, please, the townsfolk are waiting on an explanation. Seeing the Elders falling to pieces around them is not very helpful now, is it? We are meant to lead them in matters such as this. Do you agree?" Ilvas gave Kyros a questioning look, like that a parent gives to an irrational child.

"How can you be so calm about this, Master Ilvas? This . . . this . . . thing . . . could completely wipe out our world as we know it. I hardly think the Elders 'falling to pieces' is to be unexpected, do you?" Kyros had gotten up and begun pacing up and down on the top of the hill.

"I've had time to digest the information. The Omen may prove to be of great ill, but on the other hand, it could also be a sign that things might go well for the Perdites. Who are we to say?" Ilvas idly twiddled with the focusing knob on the telescope whilst he spoke. "Besides, Master Kyros, what could any of us do? I mean, there's a gigantic chunk of metal in our skies. If Nature decides it's going to force this thing to the surface of Dorgumir, then how do you suppose we prevent it?" Ilvas shrugged and turned his back on the group of Elders to peer into the nighttime sky.

"Come, Master Kyros, we owe the Perdites in the Chambers an explanation. Let us go give them one. This affects them as much as it does us, and we would be lax in our role as Elders if we did not try and guide them as best we know how." Ilvas laid a gentle hand on Kyros' shoulder and steered him to the path leading down the hill. Kyros sighed, and slowly descended the slope.

###

The clamour in the Chambers when we arrived was one I had never encountered before. As Perdites, we were very forward and uncomplicated in the way we conducted ourselves, but we were not overly confrontational. It wasn't becoming of us to make a fuss. We liked to handle our affairs quickly and efficiently.

The Elders took themselves to the balcony farther up the tiers and seated themselves around the large wooden desk. Ilvas leaned in toward Kyros and whispered something. Kyros nodded his head, a coating of sweat still on his brow.

Ilvas stood to address the crowd below him. I couldn't hear him, though, and I doubted many others in the Chambers could. He raised his voice and started again. Now I could hear him slightly over the hubbub of the crowd, but his voice was being drowned out by the commotion of worried and agitated conversation.

A loud thumping issued from the wooden desk, which slowly silenced the crowd after a few gasps and shocked murmurs. Ilvas had used a wooden gavel. I'd never seen it used before; it had always been more of an ornamental piece. Today, it had served its true purpose.

"Perdites, please, remember where you are!" Ilvas turned a stern gaze upon the people gathered below him. "I realise this is most unorthodox, and I apologize for the lateness of the hour, but there is a matter of great significance that we must discuss collectively."

"What is it, Master Ilvas? You are beginning to frighten us more than a little." Alvaro, the patriarch of one of the larger families in the town, stood up from his pew. His gathered family looked up at him and at one another, nodding in agreement. A general susurration went up from the townsfolk in concurrence.

"Well, Alvaro, if you would allow me to finish, maybe I could enlighten you?" Ilvas' tolerance was beginning to wear thin. He was generally very passive and amiable, but his verbal exchanges with Kyros had worn away at his resolve.

He was clearly as confused as the rest of us, but he had to be seen to be logical and level-headed. Alvaro nodded and sat back down in his pew. His wife Dharini embraced his arm and squeezed it gently in silent support, giving him a weak smile.

Ilvas visibly sagged and sighed.

"I'm sorry, Alvaro. I didn't mean to be short with you. It's just that events that have unfolded are very troubling, and I'm trying to decide how best to deliver the news. I don't think there will actually be any easy way to say this. So I think the best way to deal with this is to not honey-coat it and just lay out all the facts. We can decide what to do once you have all the information." Ilvas looked around the wooden desk, and the other Elders nodded their encouragement and support.

"Young Ylli came to me a few hours ago describing a great

object in our skies." The crowd immediately began deliberating this amongst themselves, and the noise level rose. "Please! Let me finish!" A quiet descended on the Chambers, and Ilvas continued. "This object is extremely large and appears to be metallic in nature. We have no idea of its origins, but it is making fairly fast progress across our stars. We have no way of ascertaining what it is, except through observation. And . . ." Ilvas rubbed at his eyes. ". . . And we fear it may collide with our world."

The crowd exploded with questions, women wailing, men shouting, children crying. It was all I could do not to force my hands over my ears to drown out the din.

"However . . ." Ilvas shouted, gesticulating for calm. ". . . However, it may be that it just passes us by and causes no ill effects. I'm afraid we just don't know."

"Well, how will we find out? I mean, we can't just sit here and ignore the durned thing, can we?" Alvaro had stood again, questing, as were the rest of the people, for answers.

Kyros stood at this point, having regained his composure.

"This is what we need to decide, fair Perdites. If The Omen is for ill, then I'm afraid we must await our fate. If it is for good, then we truly deserve some fortune. Either way, I do not really know what options we have left to us?"

"Well, what in Nature's name was the point in calling us here?" said Alvaro.

"We wanted to make sure you were all informed. How would

you have reacted if we'd have kept this from you? Would you have seen it as protection? Or would you have seen it as neglect of care? We can only guide you as we see fit. That is why you elected us to these positions, is it not?" Kyros eyed Alvaro, either goading or defying him, to respond. I wasn't entirely sure which.

Alvaro sat back down, a deep sense of loss in his eyes. As I scanned the sea of faces, it dawned on me what I was seeing. Defeat. My people had struggled for so long that this was just the high point to the suffering. It was almost as if they'd been expecting it. I don't think there was a single soul in the Chamber that believed The Omen was something good. It wasn't within them to hope anymore, and that saddened me through to my very core.

Ilvas stared down at the townspeople and must have come to the same conclusion. He wiped away a single tear.

"My dear, dear, Perdites. Go to your homes. Spend time with your loved ones. We will set up a rota of sky watchers. We will track The Omen across our skies, and we will observe, and we will wait. We will not make any rash decisions. If these are our last days, then shouldn't we spend them with each other? As a community? As unified people? We should remember what it is we adore each other for. Take the time to do the things we enjoy doing. If The Omen passes us by, then we will have regained a sense of self and meaning. If it doesn't, then we will have spent our time the way we choose. These are our options, and I know we will make the best of them." He smiled down from the balcony, a smile of such warmth and hope that it seemed to invigorate the gathered crowd.

The doors to the Chambers were opened, and the cool night air blew in. Families exited the temple, some weeping and quietly bemoaning their fortune. Others left with arms wrapped around loved ones, soft smiles and words of comfort binding them. I lagged behind and waited for Ilvas to descend from the balcony.

"Well, lad, that could have gone worse." He embraced my shoulders and led me from the Chambers.

"You've named it, you know?" I glanced up at him.

A faraway look danced in his eyes. "Well, somebody had to, lad. Part of being an Elder is that. Getting to name things and such." We both chuckled, slowly exiting the temple proper. "You best get off home, lad. It feels like tonight will be a cold one. Go wrap up cosy in your bed. The morning will bring a new perspective, and no doubt a fresh cart of trials and tribulations." He nudged me forward, and I sprinted off home.

"Good night, Ilvas," I called over my shoulder.

"Good night, Ylli."

I will always remember how fitfully I slept that night. Metal objects that loomed in the dark. Blinding flashes that lit up the sky. Smoke billowing and choking the air. Rivers running red with boiling lava.

The next few days passed by in a haze for me. Most of the Perdites got on with their everyday business, trying not to focus too intently on the object invading our atmosphere. It was easier during the day, because the sunshine made it harder to pinpoint. Nighttime was more difficult, because The Omen reflected a lot of light and was constantly moving across the sky. Some Perdites gave up. They stopped going out to farm the land, stopped going down to the sea to fish, and stopped doing odd jobs around the home. These Perdites gathered in small groups, looking lost and defeated. I always felt sorrier for this faction; how would they ever get back to normality if The Omen didn't collide with Dorgumir? How would they pick themselves up and dust themselves off? I wished I had the answers, or even had some encouraging words, but I was as stumped as the next Perdite in the street.

I had been assigned to the "watch rota." It was made up of Perdites tasked with observing The Omen and how it made its way across the void and whether we could ascertain if it was on a collision course with our small planet. For the most part, I didn't believe that it would. A small number of projections I'd drawn showed that, but there was always a niggling part of me that wasn't so sure. With the way things were going for my people, I had lost a sense of absolute certainty. Something I'd never really had an issue with in my Youngling years.

I enjoyed looking at The Omen and marvelling at what a magnificent feat of engineering it was. Who, in Nature's name, had built it? What was it for? Why was it in our star system? How did it propel itself? I pondered these questions for hours, often getting a crick in my neck from sitting and gazing through the telescope for too long. I came up with many weird and wonderful explanations but could never pin my musings down to just one idea. It did humble me, however. Knowing that someone else was out there in the nighttime skies, that somebody out there had sent The Omen with some specific task or another. I wondered whether I'd ever get to meet them, and what I would say. Would we even be able to communicate? The thought thrilled and frightened me, in equal measure.

"Hello, Ylli," a soft voice whispered in my ear.

I jumped, startled, and banged my head against the telescope.

"Oh. Hello, Vida. You made me jump," I said, rubbing at the small lump now forming on my forehead. Vida giggled. "How does this sunny day find you?"

"It finds me as best as can be expected, thank you, Ylli. Yourself?"

"Not too bad. All things considered, I'm actually having a fairly good day."

"Oh. How so?"

"Well, I'm still alive, and The Omen hasn't crashed and annihilated Dorgumir yet."

"Yes, I suppose you're right," she said, gathering up the bottom of her robes to sit down next to me.

She stared out across the town toward the coastline. Mount Bast, our only mountain and volcano on the left, the sea to the right. I'd known Vida all my life, and we'd always been close friends. Although as we'd become young adults things had become slightly more awkward, for a number of reasons. One being our need to establish ourselves as valuable members of the community, another being that I had come to realise she meant far more to me than just a mere friend. I'd never imparted that particular piece of trivia to Vida, but recent events had me concluding otherwise.

As she looked out to the horizon, I watched her face. The sleek profile, the contours of her cheeks and brow, the way her hair caught in the wind and danced across her face. The way her brown eyes sparkled, even given how she must be half-starved. Watching her gave me a warm glow that nestled in my heart, and I knew Nature had blessed me with a true soul for a friend.

"Ylli, may I ask you a question?" Vida faced me with a serious look.

"Of course, Vida. Anything," I said, concern etching my tone.

Vida gathered my hands in hers. "Do you really think we're doomed? Is The Omen really going to crash in to Dorgumir? We've suffered so much already, and I don't think I could bear for this to befall us."

I looked into her eyes. She was clearly frightened, and I wanted to smooth those fears and concerns away. But I also couldn't lie to her. That would have made me an awful friend, so I decided on the truth.

"Honestly, Vida, I don't know. From what I've observed, and from some simple projections I've drawn up, I'd like to think we're safe. But there are so many other factors to consider that I simply can't guarantee it. I'm sorry, Vida. I know that's not what you wanted to hear." I let my head drop so as not to read her reaction.

"Don't be silly, Ylli," she said, lifting my chin to stare into my eyes. "I knew you'd give me the honest truth, and that's why I specifically asked you." She smiled, and slowly nodded. I nodded in agreement and smiled, too. "Now, let me have a look at this thing!" Vida gently nudged me away and put her eye to the eyepiece.

After a long pause, she moved away and sat back down in the spot she'd vacated minutes earlier.

"My, my. That thing really is gigantic. How many other townsfolk have been to have a look?"

"Probably more than you'd think, actually. Quite a number of people are curious. The children, especially. They all 'ooh' and 'ahh' at it. I'm pretty pleased they don't seem to understand what's going on." I shrugged and gave her a weak smile.

"Always worrying about other people, aren't you, Ylli? You'll make a fine Elder one day." She gave me a warm smile and placed a slender hand on my shoulder.

I blushed furiously. "If we even survive that long . . ."

"Oh, Ylli." Vida swatted my arm, and we both laughed. I was glad of it, as it helped relieve some of the tension.

"What was that?" Vida bolted upright. We'd been lying in the grass for an hour talking about various things, lurching from one random subject to another, as we were prone to do.

"What was what?" I asked, pushing myself up from the ground.

"I'm sure I felt the ground move." Vida looked around.

"I didn't feel anything."

"Well, I did. What on Dorgumir was that?" Vida stood up. The ground gave an almighty shudder, and Vida toppled over to land flat on her back where she'd been laying mere moments before.

"Okay . . . that . . . I felt!" I stood and helped Vida off the ground. We both dusted down our robes and headed toward the centre of town.

When we got there, most of the townsfolk were out of their houses and heading straight for the temple. We threw each other troubled looks and hurried our pace to catch the majority of the crowd.

"What in Nature's name was that?"

"What's going on now?"

"Did The Omen do that?"

Perdites were crying out for answers, but nobody seemed to have any. Once in the temple, townsfolk were pouring in to the Chambers. They were jostling each other for seats, arguing about what the earth shudder had been. What had caused it and what did it mean? The tension was palpable, and I could feel agitation emanating from those gathered on the pews.

"Perdites, some quiet, please!" Kyros stood at the wooden desk, looking down over the crowd. "I understand that what has just happened is very distressing, and as of yet, we have no answers. We do not know whether this was caused by The Omen, or whether it is Nature herself. But rest assured, we will offer you as much support and aid as we can. I believe there are several families within these Chambers whose houses are no longer currently habitable? We are happy for you to take up shelter within the staterooms throughout the temple. And if the earth shudders continue, then we can look to housing people within the Chambers themselves. I would ask you other Perdites who have been largely unaffected to aid your family members, your friends, and your neighbours. We need to do all we can to help each other in what is quickly becoming a serious time of need."

For all people said about Kyros, he was a fantastic orator and always seemed to know how to pacify and allay fears. Some townspeople began to leave the temple, either to collect belongings or aid others. The sight brought back a little of the hope I'd lost in recent times. It truly lifted my heart to see us collectively providing support.

"Come on, Ylli, we best go check our homes and make sure there's not too much damage. We don't know whether these earth shudders are going to continue, so it might be worth moving valuables and sticking things down." She looked so concerned that I couldn't disagree. My shift on the watch rota had conveniently finished, too. We hurried off to make sure we still had homes and hoped to Nature that there wasn't too much damage.

###

The earth shudders did continue. The force with which they came grew, and the frequency of their occurrence grew with it. More and more Perdites were forced to exit their homes and either take up residence with families and friends or move into the Chambers within the temple. No one could fathom why this was happening, until one full week after The Omen first entered our skies. On the morning of that particular day, I headed to the crest of the hill to start my next shift of the watch rota. I relieved Abner of his duties, and I've never seen anybody look so thankful. Poor Abner looked like he hadn't slept in days and that was most likely the reality.

I sat down in front of the telescope, found The Omen within my field of vision, and adjusted the lens. As I got it into focus, another earth shudder struck. It was fairly strong and took longer to dissipate than the others. Once it had stopped and I'd righted the telescope, the screaming started. I wasn't sure what I was hearing at first, but then other voices joined that single outcry. I scanned all around me, and it didn't take me long to gauge the source of the screaming.

Thick smoke poured from Mount Bast. Hot lava bubbled forth from his crater and crept slowly down his coastal side. At least it would flow straight into the sea, and not cause any damage. Mount Bast hadn't erupted in aeons. The last time he had blown, it brought great change, but then he had settled and not spoken again. Nature hadn't seen fit to keep him awake. But now something had stirred him from his slumber, and I had a pretty good idea what that something probably was . . . The Omen.

I couldn't move from my place upon the hill. I had a duty to stay there and keep an eye on The Omen—but I so desperately wanted to go down and help my townsfolk. I wanted to ensure they were okay and keep them safe. On reflection, I'm glad I stayed upon the crest of that hill. Otherwise, I wouldn't have witnessed what I did. I don't know why, but in that instant I looked through the telescope, and I couldn't believe my eye.

The Omen had changed. It wasn't just a metal pillar. It was now a cylindrical shape, with what could only be described as a lens upon the front. I was looking from one lens to another. But why on Dorgumir was there now a lens, where there had been none before? I wanted to cry out for help, but who would hear me with all the screaming going on down in the town centre? I just hoped to Nature that someone would happen by, and that I could show somebody else what I was seeing. Just so I could be certain I wasn't imaging it.

Vida. She came. She came, and she saw. I don't know why she'd chosen that moment to come and visit me. But she had, and I've been thankful to Nature ever since.

"Ylli, have you seen Mount Bast? Have you seen the smoke and the lava issuing from his crater? Why do you think he's . . . ? Ylli, what's the matter?" I was waving my arms at her, pleading with her to stop. She thought she had exciting news for me, but I had exciting news for her!

"Vida, come look at this. The Omen has changed!" I was panting, exhilarated and petrified in equal measure.

"What?"

"The Omen has changed, Vida!"

"Okay, okay. Calm down, Ylli. Let me have a look" She stooped to look through the lens. She stood up, and her hands went to her mouth. She shook her head. "What in Nature's name has happened to it?"

"It looks like a lens."

"You mean the same sort of lens in your telescope? Is it using it to look at us? Why is it looking at us?"

"I don't know. I have no idea."

Then the flash came—an explosion of light. It was so pure as to appear brilliant white. We threw ourselves to the ground, fearing what might happen if we didn't protect our faces. And then the light was gone. We scrabbled back to the telescope to see where the flash had come from. The Omen had vanished. It didn't matter how far I looked, or how much I refocused, it was gone. Pure and simple. I couldn't make it out with my own eyes. It had disappeared from our atmosphere just as easily as it had appeared.

"The Omen. It's gone! What happened to . . . ?"

Then the earth shook, and Mount Bast exploded. Smoke billowed, lava flowed, and ash clouds filled the skies. It became night when it should have been day. Vida and I clung to each other, our senses overloaded, unsure of what was about to happen next. Tears streamed down our faces, and we hoped to Nature we'd survive. We pleaded with Nature to spare our lives. We promised to live the way all good Perdites should.

But the clouds parted, and the ash began to fall like rain. Lava steered a slow path down the mountainside into the sea, completely avoiding our town and people. The sun began to peer through breaks in the cloud. Mount Bast quieted once more, and the earth shudder abated. We still clung to each other for dear life, ash coating every inch of our faces and robes. After what seemed like an age, we let go. A great cheer sounded. Small and quiet at first, but then it gathered volume and enthusiasm. It intensified into a tumult of noise, and we lent our voices to it. Cheering until our lungs were empty and our throats raw. We smiled and embraced each other. Vida linked my arm. She led me down the hill toward the town centre and temple.

"Come on, Ylli. I don't think you need to keep watch anymore. I think your services will be needed elsewhere."

"Really? How so?"

"Well, all the sweeping up for a start."

"Hm. I think you've got a point, there. What are we going to tell the Elders?"

"What do you mean?"

"Well, The Omen. It's gone. It's just completely disappeared." Vida stopped in her tracks and looked up into the sky. Ash drifted down and caught on her eyelashes. She sighed.

"We tell them the truth, Ylli. What more can we do? Aren't you glad it's gone? We have something to celebrate. Something that's been haunting our skies for a week has gone, there's no longer a threat of collision. Mount Bast just blew his top and stopped just as abruptly as he started. Two things have threatened us in this past week, and we appear . . . with Nature's blessing . . . to have avoided both catastrophes. I don't know about you, Ylli, but I'm taking that as a good omen—for Dorgumir and the Perdites."

I smiled at her and shook my head.

"You have such a magnificent, articulate way with words, Vida. It wouldn't surprise me in the slightest if you became our first female Elder."

"You know, Ylli, I think you might be right." And with that, we carried on down the hill.

". . . What happened next, Ylli?"

"Well, you know what happened next, Lali. We teach it to all you Younglings, from the day you're born. We sing songs, tell stories, and draw pictures. All these things, and more, so that we never forget." Ylli looked into Lali's chubby face, her golden eyes sparkling back at him.

"I know, Ylli, but I like it best when you tell it." She stuck a podgy thumb in her mouth and rested her head back against his chest.

"Well, after we'd cleaned up all the mess from the ash, the lava, and the earth shudders, we began to notice a difference in the lands. It happened slowly at first, but then it seemed to gather momentum as the season drew out. Vibrant colours started to appear where there'd been none before. Crops and flowers started to grow, flourish even. Nature had stopped our famine and placed a great wealth at our feet.

"You see, when Mount Bast blew his top, all the ash and dust he spewed forth contained lots of life-giving minerals. The ash and dust settled on our soil, and everything we'd swept and tidied went to the fields. Those minerals fed the soil and encouraged the plants to grow. Nature had provided us with a second chance. And this time we weren't going to squander it.

"We began devising new ways to farm our land, new ways to keep the soil healthy, and not overwork it. We began to flourish as a people. Our health returned, and we no longer appeared pale and sickly. Our skin and hair regained their lustre, and our eyes changed from murky brown to glowing gold, the way it always should have been. We must remain mindful, and that will always stay with us. And do you know the best way for us to remember that, Lali?"

Lali shook her head.

"We changed the name of our people. We no longer believed that the name that adorned us was befitting of people that Nature had blessed with a second chance. So the Elders took a vote from the townspeople, and we decided upon a new name, the Denuvians. Do you know what that means, Lali? In fact, do any of you know what it means?"

Hands thrust up into the air. Ylli looked from one little raised hand to the next and beamed. "Loqun, what do you think it means?"

Loqun flushed and squirmed where he sat. His friends gathered around him, egging him on to answer, with words of encouragement. He cleared his throat. "The Found?"

Ylli clapped his hands together, startling Lali. "Excellent. Fantastic. Well done, Loqun. The found. We were lost, and now we are found. You have made my evening, Youngling. It means our teachings are doing the job they're supposed to be doing—reminding us."

Lali sat upright on Ylli's knee, tiredness making her eyelids droop.

"Ylli, why did Mount Bast explode? And where did The Omen go?" She slumped back to his chest and squirmed until she was comfortable in his lap.

Ylli chuckled. "Are you quite comfortable there, Lali?" A tired little nod was all the answer he received. "Okay. First, I have no idea where The Omen went. And I don't think we'll ever know. We've never seen it since, and I doubt we ever will. Second, with regards to Mount Bast, I think he vented in answer to The Omen's flash of light. I truly believe that when it entered our skies, it roused Mount Bast from his slumber. And the light it emitted shortly before it left was seen as a challenge by Mount Bast. He didn't like an intruder in his skies, so when it threatened his people, he shouted, and it fled. I really think it's as simple as that."

Ylli peered around the edge of his chair.

"Would you agree, Mother?" Vida walked slowly over to

stand next to Ylli's chair. She placed a gentle hand on his shoulder, small pieces of hair tumbling across her face as she looked down at Ylli.

"I believe so, my darling. We've had a long time to ponder, and we've discussed it a great many times. No other explanation fits."

"And so there you have it." He peered down into Lali's face. The Youngling had fallen asleep and was snoring gently. "You know, one of these days she's going to stay awake long enough to hear the answers to her questions!" Ylli chuckled softly, so as not to wake her. Anelim came and lifted Lali gently from Ylli's lap, cradling the Youngling to her chest, and placing a gentle kiss on her forehead. Anelim nodded to Ylli and Vida and quietly left the room. The other adults and children followed behind, whispering good nights and good-byes.

Ylli and Vida were left alone in the room.

"I never tire of telling that story," Ylli said, rubbing some life back into his tired thighs.

"And I hope you never will. It holds so much significance for our people, and for us personally." She offered her hand to help Ylli from his chair, and he took it gladly. "Let us rest now, Master Ylli. No doubt you will regale them with stories tomorrow."

"And regale them I will."

Real-Mater
By J. L. Gribble

The second hatchling was seven rotations old today. It was time to make the social rounds and present it to Pater and Fake-Mater's coterie of friends. The hatchling was a mewling mass of feathers and scales, swaddled in linen. (Not acceptable for polite company.)

The first hatchling was two orbits old. It trailed along behind Pater and Fake-Mater, playing in leftover snow and soaking its feathers. Its dress was already stained from breakfast, and the hem of one sleeve was coming undone. (Not acceptable for polite company at all.)

She was nine orbits old. She followed Pater, Fake-Mater, and the two hatchlings at a dignified pace, her claws folded in front of her. (Her silk gown was impeccable. Real-Mater taught her how to be a lady. She was acceptable for polite company.)

Pater named the second hatchling after a cloud formation as it reflected off Pater's scales. The name implied whimsy and frivolity. (The second hatchling's name would not inspire confidence in the family business.)

Fake-Mater had named the first hatchling after a comet that passed through the sky the night of its birth. The name implied impermanence and flights of fancy. (The first hatchling's name would not inspire confidence in the family business.)

Real-Mater had named her after the Queen's premier financial advisor. The name implied intelligence and monetary acumen. (Her name would inspire confidence when she took over the family's shipping assets.)

At the first house, the second hatchling received tokens to celebrate its birth. The first hatchling received toys to congratulate it on its new sister. She received nothing.

At the second house, the second hatchling received an embroidered blanket to celebrate its birth. The first hatchling received a doll to congratulate it on its new sister. She received nothing.

At the third house, after the first and second hatchlings had received their prizes, the hostess looked apologetic for forgetting her. The kind woman offered to fetch a packet of seeds from the kitchen as a token gift. Pater and Fake-Mater waved off the gesture. She received nothing.

(You are invisible now, Real-Mater whispered. Just like me.)

Helzenthrax
By A. R. Aston

And the Ten Sons of the Shining Shield gathered together beneath the great black tower of Helzenthrax the Terrible, the great necromancer prince, the Cadaverous King and the Lord of Carrion. Their courage was unwavering, and their gleaming swords shone with Illurio's enchantments. The great tide of undead broke against their steel like wheat before a scythe. But unlike wheat, the rotting legions of Helzenthrax erupted into blue fire as they were cast low by the shimmering blades.

Onward they rode, parting the army of wights with hoof and blade, courage and fury. They sang the songs of Castros, the god of harps, and their ballads unwound the spells of the Cadaverous King, returning the shambling nightmares to the dust and grave muck from whence they were raised.

Down the Ten rode, through the winding passages of the under-tower, beneath the gates of lament and the poisoned moat of Khaides, to the drowning halls. Sea serpents and barbed krakens raised by the Prince of Wights opposed them, binding their arms and threatening to drag them to watery graves. But they could not be impeded for long, for Lord Auron was with them. He was anointed by the sky gods, and no evil thing could withstand him and his golden crown. Such was the darkness of the labyrinth that Elerod the Tall had to set his cloak alight for a torch to banish the vile enchantments placed upon the under-tower. One cannot number the days they spent in the shadows, but after countless weeks of strife, they found the ascending stairs and emerged into the charnel court of Helzenthrax the Cadaverous.

Upon a throne of petrified branches curved into bleached white horns sat the black demon of the world of Tallou. A cloak made from the flayed hides of countless foes shrouded his shoulders, and upon his grey, fleshless head perched a crown of obsidian that shone with internal fire.

Foul things, clad in decay and misery, cavorted in that dread throne room, for Helzenthrax was the heathen prince of necromancy, and no flesh was safe from his desecrating touch. Long-dead knights pulled themselves from their barrows and drew their pitted blades as they set upon the Ten Sons. As they fought, the dark lord laughed to see them demean themselves so.

"**Why wrestle my minions in the dirt like common peasants, proud lord Auron? You and your brothers have ever been welcome at my table. Let none say I am an inhospitable host.**" The dread voice of Helzenthrax rumbled across the hall, every syllable painful to withstand. "**Bend the knee, my dear friends, and I shall molest your lands no longer. I desire your subjugation, not your destruction. Tallou is mine; why should I wish to shatter my plaything?**"

But Lord Auron would not be swayed by the venomous words of the dark one. "Nay, sheath your serpent's tongue, Helzenthrax! We shall bow to no foul, unnatural tyrant. The gods themselves attaint you; you are no friend of mine."

Helzenthrax's mask of friendship fell away then, as a veil

falls from the eyes of a widow or bride. Behind that mask, a monster dwelt, whose corpse-light stare was cold as a tomb.

"Alive or dead, you will serve me yet."

With that, Helzenthrax drew upon all his black reservoirs of power and malice. Even as his necrotic constructs fell to dust, he swelled with sorcerous flame. There, at the root of the world, where the black tower met the world tree's heart, the children of life and starlight clashed with the great abomination. Five brave sons perished in the darkness, wasted to nothingness in their gleaming armour. But Auron and his brothers prevailed after arduous struggle.

Though Helzenthrax was defeated, he was a thing cast out of the afterlife by the god of the underworld, Mourn. Helzenthrax was not permitted to die. Thus, Auron used all the powers Illurio had granted him, binding Helzenthrax to his throne, breaking his power and binding it eternally into the foundations of Tallou.

Yet Helzenthrax cried out for justice. To the surprise of all, Illurio himself took notice. The necromancer argued that, as seasons change and time erodes, was it not possible for him to change, too? Could not even the most black-hearted of creatures repent after long eons of bondage?

Though the gods loathed him, they were beings of justice and honour, and Illurio saw that what the black devil said was true.

"Very well," the god replied. "Your bondage may be undone in some distant time. But only when I cast my spear across the firmament. Then you shall know it is time for judgement. And even then, only one with a pure heart may set you free."

Helzenthrax cursed Illurio for this, for he said no innocent would release him. The innocent knew nothing of redemption, for sin was foreign to them. But his curses fell on deaf ears. Auron and his brothers ascended to the light of dawn once more and cast down the black tower, until it shrouded Helzenthrax's tomb like a funeral bier.

Elthena closed the moth-eaten pages. It always vexed her than grandfather's copy of *White Auron's Labours* was so age-worn that the last pages had come loose of their old binding years ago. Now she lacked an ending to the story.

She vaguely recalled the ending her granddad told her as a little girl—something about him and his sons and brothers spreading out, founding kingdoms, and warring with magic. That made her sad; she preferred it when they were fighting good versus evil. The heroes should not kill each other for lands. They were supposed to be the best of people.

Maybe she didn't want the last pages after all. She replaced the tome in her already swollen bookshelf. She shoved aside alchemical notes and books on dragons to make room, praying for it to fit when the shelf gave an ominous groan. She sighed in relief as the book slid into its appointed space.

Tallou-Majoritus was not a place for spells and fanciful tales anymore. The other Tallouan youthlings didn't care about wizards and demons and knights. They only cared about courting, costumes, and how to win at games of clash-sprint. Sometimes, Elthena wished she could like those things, too. But she was stuck with the other outcasts, whittling on about enchantments and what spells they would use to banish wights and manticores.

The elders were no use either. Magic wasn't real to them anymore, like it was for her grandfather's grandfathers and great-grandfathers.

"You want magic? Pah, magic don't give us clean water and sewers, child. That's our work. Magic dint help feed us neither; that were clever folks who made the soil feed us better, and cleverer men who made the boats that carry food to us from all over. The toil of Tallouans and the engineer's square is all the magic I need, girl," old Errol Cobbler had once chided her when he caught her complaining about the distinct lack of warlocks in Guthun, her hometown.

He wasn't wrong, she had to admit. Folks tended to die of flux and sickness a lot, even in the nicer fae tales, and they didn't have piped water or printed books, either. But there was something missing. Elthena couldn't explain it. The world in her books was full of extremes, vibrant one moment, terrible and dark the next, not the middling, faded tones of life in the modern world.

She crossed her grey town in a fugue, passing the factory chimneys by. She imagined one of them was Helzenthrax's black tower, and she was Auron, with gleaming lance.

She continued to daydream in her loom class, watching her other classmates follow the instructions of Melbede, the tutor. Their arms moved in unison, as if the threads they were winding into lacklustre patterns were actually marionette-wires pulled by Melbede. Maybe Melbede was a witch herself, to command so many to copy her tedious example and to endure her harsh, discordant hectoring when they failed to match her pace.

Elthena was one of those who didn't follow her pattern, but fortunately for her, Melbede hadn't noticed. Zashr and Timel always said she was lucky, and many others agreed. She could always tell where a die might land before it was even thrown. Timel suggested she had the magic of the elder days lingering in her blood. Zashr had agreed awkwardly; she was eager to impress Elthena. Elthena did not see the girl in the same way, but she could not bring herself to open a door that could not readily be closed again. She didn't have that many friends that she could afford to potentially lose one. She loved Zashr, but as a friend alone.

That was selfish of her. The heroes weren't selfish in the stories. At least, not by the end.

She wasn't all that lucky, of course. A lucky girl wouldn't be trapped at a loom, being nurtured for a lifelong job in one of the weaving mills, to have her potential rot to nothing like an atrophied limb. If she was lucky, she'd have been a Gleamer, one of the iridescent dryads with the power to sculpt the forests to her liking, like in the Old Green Tale, or an outrider of the Dagger Prince, with their poisoned swords and fearsome purple stirigan steeds—anything but a lowborn loom girl of Guthun.

Classes seemed to go on for countless hours, with different

tutors arriving to instruct the girls in slightly different aspects of textile production, yelling and berating deviants from their orders in their own belligerent ways. The one thing they never, ever taught was the art of tapestry. The looms produced patterns in the fabric, sometimes complex patterns of threaded wool dyed and arranged in aesthetically pleasing ways, but they never *meant* anything.

Finally, the day ended, and Elthena and her classmates filed from the factory school. Zashr would be waiting at the fountain in the square, ready to go off with her into the woods to play at Knight and Damsel. Elthena always won and got to be the knight; more of her luck, Zashr claimed. Elthena knew better, but there was no harm in letting Zashr be the damsel if she wanted to be. Zashr would only deny her feelings if brought up, her light purple cheeks flushing dark with embarrassment.

Elthena rushed through the narrow gaps between the sagging townhouses of Guthun, eager to throw off the shackles of a long day.

The sudden thunderclap almost made her topple onto her face as she swerved around a corner. She looked to the heavens, but there wasn't a cloud in the dusk-reddening sky. Soon afterward, another series of bangs set her teeth on edge and made the quills on the back of her arms stand up.

Adults poured out into the streets, peering up with expressions of childish bewilderment, which Elthena took as a bad sign. She had to find Zashr now. Play could wait, something was happening.

The worried voices of the townsfolk were like a babbling

brook. The sonorous exclamations continued unabated; shaking the ground, rattling window panes. So pervasive were the sounds that Elthena almost ran into the stirigan men atop their horned steeds, marching down the road. The standard-bearing sergeant at arms bawled at her in time, and the confused girl sprang away as the heavy triple-toed feet of the stirigans pounded the cobbles.

She ran on, covering her ears as the bone-rattling din of explosions rocked the ground, followed by the screaming of dying men. Steel rang as if struck against an anvil, and the flaring detonations continued. Elthena threw herself to the ground as a great crimson bolt of scorching fire screamed overhead and punched the innards from a townhouse behind her, spraying burning debris across a hundred yards. She sprang up as more bolts came down from on high, like the furious spears of Illurio.

Smoke stung the back of her throat and cloyed her bleary eyes as she fled. All sense of direction and purpose was lost in this scorching tumult. People spilled out into the streets, wailing, crowding and crushing each other in the desperate press. Elthena's diminutive size aided her here, for she could vault the bodies and wriggle between struggling crowds of frightened townies. A riderless stirigan shrieked as it galloped past, aflame from toes to crested horns. She didn't remember how many times she stumbled and fell during her flight, but her flesh ran with blood from dozens of cuts and grazes.

Elthena snatched glances between the collapsing buildings, watching for the cause of such terrible calamity even as she fled.

Through smoke and fire, she caught vague glimpses of great silver giants, triad eyes glowing the same fierce red as the bolts that flew from the guns clutched in their claws. The stirigan men were wilted shadows silhouetted by the fires, struggling shapes that unleashed pathetic return fire in puffs of white smoke. The silver giants killed them with crackling red cannons and glowing orange blades. Blood formed a continuous red mist in the air, for the giants were relentless and tireless in their slaughter.

The crowds flowed through the streets like wild rapids, funnelled along by the push of those behind. They moved as one, but in directions they had no control over. Elthena had to fight, kicking and biting, to keep herself apart from the aimless horde. A man, eyes wide as dinner plates, punched her without a second thought, clambering over her to rejoin the press. She tasted blood, which washed some of the ashen acridity of the smoke from her mouth, but the pain that came with it negated any advantage that brought. On her hands and knees, she crawled away, slipping into the shadow of two buildings that had fallen into each other with drunken camaraderie. Her cheeks were wet, but only partially with tears.

Amidst the chatter of the enemy's gunfire, she heard piercing whines that grew as shadows swept overhead. Elthena peered skyward and spied impossible silver flying machines, zipping above her on clouds of invisible heat. These floating engines looked like upended siege towers covered with layered metal plate, polished to perfection and bristling with short, snouted forks that crackled with evil red lightning. As the twin prongs of each fork came together, a great clap of thunder issued forth, followed by another screaming ball of fire.

She had to escape the town. The town was death, a charnel house.

Elthena's life had shrunk in her mind. Old worries, her old concerns and preoccupations, were forgotten. Her nails were broken and bloody, her knees almost worn to the bone from crawling. Like some servile washerwoman, she scuttled across cobblestones, cowering in the shadow of broken walls whenever the whirring silver giants stomped past.

There were bodies everywhere. Some were charred skeletons; some looked almost like serene sleeping babes atop mounds of rubble. Still more no longer looked like Tallouan corpses at all: piles of gory rags lying in the road or chopped up offal, smouldering where they had fallen. The stench was unlike anything Elthena had smelled before. She wanted to vomit, but her stomach was empty, and nothing but foul water wretched up from her knotted bowels.

Wherever she looked, she saw the artefacts of her life broken and scorched black. It was next to impossible to recognise the landmarks anymore. Yet still, somehow, she saw the fountain square, one street over from her. As she struggled to her feet, she heard footfalls—heavy ones accompanied by the disturbing, persistent hum of the giants' forms. A horn blared. She turned. Her knees quivered and she felt the warmth of fear between her legs, but she fought to keep this terror from her face, scowling to stop the tears falling.

What she found the worst about the giant was that it was beautiful. Illuminated by the flickering firelight of her city, it was clad in the most wonderful plate armour she'd ever seen, from its huge wide head to its steel-shod hooves. The armour was polished to mirror-like perfection, with only patches of blood and the scorched dents of musket impacts tarnishing it. Each of the thousands of interlocking pieces was etched in unreadable golden lettering and runic transcriptions. One hand ended in a triple-digit claw, opening and closing as the thing walked. The other arm ended in a twin-pronged fork, a smaller cousin of the flying towers' city-killing weapons. Its three glowering eyes rotated around each other, their irises narrowing, focusing on the little girl shivering before them. There was no face to speak of on this horrendous blank helm, only the rotating eyes, cold and intallouan. It raised its weapon toward her.

The giant said something in a Tallouan language Elthena didn't understand, followed by another sentence in another foreign tongue. Then, it spoke words she comprehended.

"EVICTION IN PROGRESS. NOTICE GIVEN APPROXIMATELY 34.56 ON MURKAVAN CALENDER. TREPASS UPON SOVEREIGN MURKAVAN PROPERTY PENALIZED HEAVILY."

With that, the giant aimed. Elthena flinched, letting out a strangled yelp of fright. But the weapon did not fire. A low-pitched tone echoed from the gun. The giant raised its weapon for inspection, removing a smoking cube from the gun's flank.

Always lucky, she thought.

The giant reached for another cube on its belt, and she took her chance. The giant was powerful, but she was quick, and she bolted as fast as her agonised limbs could carry her.

The giant's weapon was working again, for she felt the heat of his bolts as they thundered past her, blasting walls to rubble and cobbles to ash. She darted left and right, zigzagging to avoid the lethal barrage as best she could. Dust and rubble pelted her, but she kept her footing, even after a chunk of masonry almost tore the pointed tip of her left earlobe with a wet squelch. She outpaced the stomping suit of armour, smiling bleakly as its blaring horn faded to an insidious echo on the edge of her hearing. She didn't have long, though; it was slow, but it would not tire as she would. Inevitably, it would catch her up.

The fountain square was close; the edge of the forest beckoned to her, leafy arms reaching out. But she couldn't leave yet. She couldn't leave without Zashr. When the younger girl was not there, Elthena cursed out loud, wading through the puddles unleashed by the sundered water feature. She threw handfuls of the brackish fluid into her face, washing the blood from her savaged ear and the grimy brown filth from her swollen cheeks. Zashr was a clever girl; she wouldn't stay waiting as death rumbled toward her. She'd have made for the forest and sanctuary. Just as Elthena would.

She needed no further persuasion and stumbled toward the tree line. The edge of the forest rose up, and she used the saplings as handholds to ascend the wooded hill. Without the light of the fires, the evening woods were a maze of slender, crooked shapes in grey and black. The gnawing cold snapped at her bones and stung flesh. Wet bark and moss clung to her feet, which she only then realised were bare. She must have lost her shoes somewhere in the maelstrom.

Elthena sagged against the nearest trunk, clutching at it like a wizard's walking cane, digging her broken nails into the bark. Her legs were going numb, and she could hardly stand. The fatigue of the long march was never mentioned in the old tales, nor the weight of horror and fear that pressed upon you when the immediate danger had passed. All she wanted to do was fall to her knees and rest. Just for a moment, just until feeling returned.

Yet the odour of charred corpses would not leave her nostrils. So long as it remained, she dared not stop until the dying town was far behind her. She continued, step after faltering step. Weak as a kitten, she walked to keep herself from falling down, like a ghost knight from Helkar's hunt, or a dead wanderer from Helzenthrax's carnival. On she wandered, daydreaming of giants turning her corpse over a spit and of brave knights in shining armour, eight feet tall, no longer heroic but monstrous, armed with dragons under each arm, belching fire over mewling masses of mouse-headed people sobbing for mercy.

Mercy was a trait these knights of legend were bereft.

She saw Zashr, ever a damsel in her waking dreams, calling out for her knight to save her. Elthena looked down, and her body was clothed in iron, a lance in her hand. But she stripped the armour away, cast down her shield. Elthena was no knight, and she pictured knights being torn from their saddles by the forest dryads, pulled apart as the woods cloaked her and Zashr in its protective mantle of leaves.

She saw the knight, the knight and ogre in one, with a cloak of fire and a war horn at his lips. His helm had three holes, churning with fire, and a two-headed dragon with flame-filled mouths. She staggered backward but was caught in the grasp of a tree root.

"Let me free, dryads! Let me free!" she whimpered through blood-flecked lips. She had paused too long—the knight was upon her.

Panic and delirium snatched her wits, and she flailed in the grip of the branch that was a dryad, that was a branch.

The dragons' snouts raised again. But as they inhaled, they were beheaded. A tattered prince leapt from the woods with his flashing sword of leaping orange hue, cutting away the drakes from the grasp of the towering knight-beast. The knight's claws swept around to behead the prince, but he ducked and rolled beneath the clumsy blows, hacking at the armoured terror with furious abandon. His sword gleamed in the darkness, lighting the knight with false glory.

As silvered claw and flashing blade met time and again, sparks flew and scorched the clustering dryads, who screamed as they died. Burning trees toppled, severed by claw and sword. Some crashed against the knight, knocking him onto his back. With burning brands and sharpened stones, the prince's men flooded to their master's side and set upon the monstrosity.

Elthena freed herself from the dryads' grasp and made to step forward to finish off the knight beside her prince. But without the support of the tree to hold her up, Elthena collapsed, crumpling like damp paper in a breeze.

Her forehead crashed against the knot of a tree root, granting her black oblivion.

###

She awoke with a start. She was by a stream with towering trees all about her, like pillars holding up a leafy cathedral's roof. A blanket was wrapped about her punished legs, and something mint-smelling was rubbed into her wounds.

There were other men and women around her, in various states of disrepair and desolation. Some had their heads and limbs bound in soiled bandages; others wore their wounds on the inside, in haunted expressions and pale lilac flesh.

The cloying insanity of the previous night had faded like the light in a dying man's eyes, and the morning was grey as the ash that fell between the forlorn trees. All eyes were downcast, even those of her saviour. No prince, but he did wear a uniform, tattered though it was. The man walked between the survivors, muttering words of encouragement or consolation as he passed. Elthena saw a wickedly curved blade sheathed at his side. It was not Tallouan, she saw at once. It was etched with the same runes as the armoured giants and looked as if it would not be out of place in some epic tale of the

Shining Shields. He was grizzled as they come, with a filthy face, carved up to be forever short of handsome, and sallow eyes, hollow as a consumptive's. He came to her last of all, setting down his stolen sword as he perched before Elthena.

"You're awake. We thought after two days, you might not ever rouse," he said as he checked her wounds with his thick fingers. He noticed her staring at the sword by his side and smiled, flashing his yellowed teeth at her. "It's the only thing that can cut the Evictors' hides. Still took a good struggle though. You were lucky you wandered into our camp. An hour later, and we'd have left, and that thing would have charred you black. We found you halfway up the valley side, snared on a tree branch, ranting about dryads and faeries."

"Who . . . ?"

"Bulraur. Sergeant at Arms," he explained. "I picked up a bunch of refugees on my way north from Guthun."

She sat up, wincing at the pain in her knees. "What happened? How many of us got out?" she asked, too dehydrated to cry, though every fibre of her being willed her to.

Bulraur looked away, toward the simple campfire some of the other refugees had erected. "Guthun is gone. Those . . . sky ships settled over the town, and they burned it all. I was on my way out when I saw the larger ships cast down the factory chimneys and the mayor's keep, and all the rest were consumed by fire. There could be no survivors inside that place."

"*I* got out," she said.

"And what a miracle that was, child. All these Guthunians were out in the fields when the Evictors came, like me. After they smashed the towers, they flattened the land, removed their armoured devils, and burnt the ground to cracked black glass. I am sorry, if there was anyone you called kin back there, you are bereft of them," he said sombrely.

As he made to rise, she grasped his wrist. "Were there any other young ones, out in the woods like me? Children, perhaps; even a girl-child smaller than me? Please!" Her voice croaked as she spoke.

He paused. "Some. One is but a yearling, another was a young lad. And—"

"A girl? Short, with deeper purple skin, and white hair, tied in a bob?"

He nodded. "Aye, that is her," he whispered, before shrugging her hand away. He couldn't meet her eye as he departed.

"What happened to her, Bulraur? Bulraur? What happened to my Zashr?"

Though it was agony, Elthena struggled to her feet and scoured the camp for her friend, frantic as a mother hen.

They had set her in a clearing in the wood besides the trickling waterfall that fed the stream, bundled in what warm furs they could scavenge. Zashr's hair was in a wild mess, and her eyes were closed. Her head was unblemished by violence, but Elthena could see dark patches in the furs, where her bloodied torso met the skins. She suppressed a sob as she knelt beside her young friend.

Elthena cradled Zashr's head on her lap and rocked, back and forth. According to Bulraur, she had been found wounded, limping through the woods in a tattered dress. Elthena later learned they had carried her deep into the woods, far from the silver murderers. But even after binding her wounds, the girl had soon caught a fever. Within two days, her frame had wasted, her flesh paled, and she closed her eyes for the final time.

Timel was dead, Elthena was sure of it. All her books were gone, too; her whole life, ashes and corpses. The other refugees gave her a wide berth and did not interrupt her as she wept over Zashr's cooling form. Elthena pressed her lips to her cheek, flinching at how cold the flesh there had become. She tilted her head toward the uncaring heavens, but she did not scream. She had screamed and wailed and whimpered until the gestures lost all meaning. She was broken and hollow now. For tears and fury there must be passion, and that had been stolen from her.

She focused on the heavens. It was an early morning sky. Soon, a new day without Zashr would dawn, and the gleaming stars, once so magical to Elthena, would be hidden again.

Then, she saw it. A silver bolt, like a shooting star made of platinum, streaked across the starry side of the heavenly dome. It took its time, traversing the firmament before it slid, inexorably, toward dawn's oblivion. When it caught the light of dawn, it shone all the brighter. It was like a silver javelin, thrown across the sky . . .

A javelin or a *spear* ...

The notion struck, making her reel as if slapped in the face.

She was not lucky. They always said she was lucky, but maybe not. Maybe not this time. Maybe she was touched. The vanishing object crossing the sky—it *was* a spear. It was Illurio's spear; it must have been. It had to be. If the spear was real, then maybe *He* was real, too.

Bulraur would not hear her plan when she came to him wild-eyed and breathless. She pleaded that he heed her, even as the grim caravan of dispossessed townsfolk marched on through the forest.

"It was the spear, I swear it. If it is true, if the legends are real, then we haven't a choice. I can't let her just die, I can't just let these Murkavans win!" she said, tugging at Bulraur's stirigan as he led the way.

Two other men pulled her away as he replied, "Enough of your stories, child. We can't make plans based on whimsy and fancy. We will all starve out here unless we reach aid. We travel to Hotteleib, ten miles northwest. They'll take us in, and we can warn them about the enemy in the bargain. Now hush. Grieve for your friend."

Elthena did grieve, but she would not despair. The spear of Illurio had kindled the embers of her soul. The other survivors spoke little, not even in protest, when Elthena began dragging the bound body of her friend alongside them. If they noticed the smell, they were too weary or broken to comment.

And so, the ragged band of homeless wretches travelled to Hotteleib, losing three of their number as they crossed the lowland hills and forded the Suram River. Unlike Zashr, nobody stopped to carry their corpses. The march continued on, bodies buried where they fell. They reached the borders of Hotteleiban territory at dusk.

Even from a distance, they realised Hotteleib was dead. They heard the discordant rumble of rolling thunder barrages and saw the horizon ahead haloed with orange light, visible for miles around. Bulraur's group threw themselves into what cover they could as the flying machines screeched overhead, joining in the slaughter just over the hill.

The refugees abandoned Hotteleib to its fate, foraging what they could from the abandoned farmlands around the town before they moved on. Destitute survivors and roaming vagrants attached themselves to the walking party. Nobody knew what to do, so they followed whoever looked like they might, uncaring of the ultimate destination.

It was the same story in towns and cities across the county. Wherever Bulraur's group travelled, burning settlements and more refugees were waiting to greet them. It was as if the Evictors struck wherever the gatherings of people were thickest, striking swiftly and without ceremony across the whole country—perhaps even the world.

###

After two harrowing months of fruitless searching, Bulraur, in his desperation, sent for the girl Elthena again.

"How would you find this lair? Where is it supposed to lie?" he asked before a flickering campfire.

Elthena was a gaunt lilac shade, swaddled in her tatty rags like a shaman. She looked older somehow. She was weathered and eroded, until only the hard core of her being remained, exposed and raw for all to see. She fixed him with a stare. "I will know. I will feel it. I feel more powerful now. There is nothing but the gift for me."

He nodded, too weary to argue with the crazed child. He was broken. Before he had had a fire in him, defiance and a righteous fury, but now he was hollow as the others.

"But . . . Helzenthrax. Why would we wake Him? Isn't He the villain of all the old sagas? The necromancer prince, the old black demon? Why not search out one of the others . . . the other gods?" said one of the gathered refugees through his matted beard.

Elthena rounded on this man. "The other gods are not on Tallou. If they are, they do not hear us, and the only knights in shining armour are monsters who hunt us. Helzenthrax is the only one left to us."

"Would He even help?" Bulraur said, prodding the fire with a bone-like branch. "Does He not hate Tallouans?"

"Who knows what He hates? The old stories were written hundreds, thousands of years ago, about even older events. The legend might bear no semblance to reality," another malcontent barked, clutching at the stump of his former right hand.

"Have faith," she responded staunchly.

The one-handed man stood to leave. "My faith burned with my family."

Despite this outburst, most of the assembled survivors nodded their heads with Elthena's vague scheme. It wasn't much of a plan, but it was all they had to guide them.

###

It was a strange thing, travelling to where the ground was hardest, where the trees were gnarled and sickly. It was anathema to a sensible survivalist to travel where no food or true shelter could be found, where the wind snatched and clawed at exposed skin and eyes.

But Elthena was not guided by self-preservation or hunger. She was guided by supernatural dread clutching at her heart. Like a compass, she let the direction of this misery direct her. In her wake, a small army of half-crazed survivors stumbled. She bore the bundled body of Zashr with her like a precious relic. Desiccation robbed the cadaver of stench, save for a cloying taste that ever lingered at the back of the throat.

"We are nearly there, Zashr. Can you feel it? The Land of Dread?" she asked.

The Land of Dread was not the one Elthena had pictured in the books from her old life. She had dreamed of stinking marshes, with great bones and tusks of demon monsters jutting up raw and bloody from the polluted ground. Most of all, she had pictured the terrible tower of Helzenthrax, a solid black rod, rising up to punch a hole in swirling green clouds. She imagined gibbets filled with wailing captives bolted to the obsidian flanks of the necromancer's turret, perishing to feed his monstrous appetite.

But the land to which she had led her reluctant allies was bleak—nothing like her twisted dreams.

The rolling hills spread out for miles in all directions, featureless save for sporadic rock formations scattered across the landscape like the discarded weapons of giants. The grass was ugly, patchy, pale, and malnourished. Treeless, the wind howled with evil promise, snapping at unprotected flesh. It was an awful desolation, but it was not the churning hellscape the old scholars envisioned.

Perhaps she was wrong? Perhaps her luck and her magic were nothing but dumb chance. Had she brought her people out here to die? Such a fate was too cruel to imagine. Such thoughts were just the curse infusing this land, seeking to turn away interlopers. But she felt a greater force, drawing her onward.

Bulraur, ever by her side now, had his sword drawn warily.

"We're too exposed out here," he said. His pale lilac features caved in around his cheeks, giving him a gaunt and skeletal appearance, robbing the old soldier of his aura of power. "Have you forgotten that our enemy comes from the sky? When they are done with our cities . . . they will come looking for us. Mark my words, my little warlock."

Elthena didn't know what to say. Did he expect her to come up with a strategy or a defence? She was guided by fate; could he not see that? The way he and the others peered at her with expectant eyes, she realised they did not. She was the leader of a quest, but not the quests she had longed for. This was one of those grim journeys spoken of in the later tales, ones of deprivation and tragedy, kin-strife and death. The ones she had always hated.

"We will be in cover soon. The drowning halls were underground. All the stories said so. We just need to find the roots of the under-tower. These rocks . . . they can't all just be rocks . . ."

Bulraur nodded, comprehending. "Some might be placed here deliberately . . . foundation stones, yes."

He turned and raised his voice to the gathered crowd. "Everyone, listen to me! I know you are tired, I know you are hungry, but we are close now. Spread out, search the stone outcrops. Look for anything that might look like masonry. Anything that could be foundations or even the remnants of a stone wall. Hurry!"

It took them all but a few hours, and they endured half a dozen false calls and disappointments, before the final shout went up. At first glance, the rock formation was like the others—a random jumble of jagged stones resting together where they fell. But between the largest stones, there was a hexagonal opening, black as pitch within. Such cold issued from the mouth of the portal that most of the gathered Tallouans refused to tarry nearby. Even Elthena had to fight to keep a tremor from her voice as she approached.

"This is the way . . ."

"That hole has been carved. The edges are too straight," said

Bulraur, gritting his teeth against the chill.

Elthena stepped forward to enter, but he laid a hand on her shoulder. "We'll go together. Then I'll come back up if it's safe and fetch the others down."

She nodded, before they descended into shadow.

###

The only guiding light was the dim orange glow of Bulraur's stolen sword, bobbing ahead of her as he led the way. All else was blank; deeper than mere black. It was as if the descending shaft had never seen light before, and her eyes rebelled at this utter absence, for she saw purple haze before her eyes. They said that happened down mineshafts, too, but this was the first time she had ever experienced such a thing.

"Be careful. There are steps," Bulraur said, his sword descending before her a clear indicator of this fact. She picked her way forward, feeling out each step with her foot before committing to the descent. Her footfalls clicked and clacked against the hard stone; the only sound besides her heavy breathing and Bulraur's occasional comment.

Elthena couldn't guess at the size of the passageway. At certain points, she felt the air close against her skin and her ears experienced a sort of pressure. Other times, the way widened, with a stale breeze in her face, her footsteps echoing in the darkness. They could have passed through caverns vast as cathedral halls, and they would have never known. The only way forward was by the short stretch of path Bulraur illuminated with his Murkavan blade.

It was cold. Colder that the windblown moors above them, with a chill their scavenged coats and shawls couldn't keep out.

The wind murmured secrets in a wordless language no man spoke. It made her gums itch, and her heart flutter. Elthena heard the wind's voice, long after the breeze subsided. If the old soldier did, he gave no sign.

The song was for her. It had no lyrics, no rhythm, no tune, but she knew it was for her; calling out, beckoning her onward. Revulsion and compulsion warred within her. All she could do was continue, drowning it out with the click-clack of her feet against age-worn granite.

"Hold on, child, there's a door. It looks like . . . yes, it isn't barred," Bulraur said, followed by the discordant squeal of old metal being contorted and grunts of exertion from him. With a final, sonorous boom, the door was heaved through, and the way was opened.

The musty scent of damp assailed Elthena. She could hear water, too; a slow dripping, trickling sound, plopping at a sporadic pace.

"Ach! It's ankle deep!" Bulraur said as he splashed into the chamber.

Elthena could see it was a chamber, for the light of his sword was reflected in hundreds of body-length mirrors. Even this dull light was near blinding in comparison to the void they'd emerged from. She blinked back tears.

The mirrors loomed over a waterlogged scene of broken stone tables and soiled cutlery, like some macabre diorama of a banquet hall, attended by the dead. For at each table place, bodies lay, black and grey ribbons of rot draped across their bones. Some were slumped over the tables like derelict drunks at a feast, while others sat with unrecognisable jumbles of meat and bone, moist with decay. Pale branches of subterranean plants grew through the furniture and masonry, thorns glistening with corruption.

Elthena followed the tangled, winding path of the thorns as they crossed the flooded hall and converged upon the far side. Here, they grew and wound around one another, forming a throne of daggerpoints and horns. Upon this throne sat a giant's corpse. Hollow were its eyes, taut and grey the flesh that still clung to the wretched bones of the creature. Here and there, the pallid branches grew through the creature, wriggling between its ribcage and punching through the left side of the cadaver's skull. It sat on the throne, head bowed by age or reverence. Armour of oxide rust and a tattered mantle indistinguishable from necrotised flesh swathed it. She recognised the broken, uneven crown of obsidian, fixed to the giant's head like horns.

Even sat upon its throne, the dead prince loomed over the diminutive form of Elthena, and she found herself craning her neck to keep the hollow pits of the creature's eyes in view. For a time, out in the forest, she had believed the Evictors had robbed her soul of the capacity for fear. She was proven wrong in that moment.

Helzenthrax. Even thinking the name made the monarch before her seem more real, more solid. As if His animus were being summoned, across depthless stretches of netherworlds beyond count.

Elthena placed the satchel of Zashr's bones reverently before Him, ignoring the strange look she saw etched upon Bulraur's face.

Bulraur raised his sword to his shoulder. "Is this him? Helzenthrax?"

She nodded, crying without realising it.

"I never believed . . . all those centuries. Are we awake? Did I die, back in Guthun?" he asked, disbelieving.

"Would you dream of this?"

"Nothing so foul, I confess," Bulraur said.

"I might have once. I dreamt I had a sword . . . like yours," she said, stepping toward Helzenthrax. "I was one of the sons of the Shining Shield, and I vanquished Him for all time. I ran Him through, and let Him burn on the point of my blade. I'd save the damsel He'd taken, and I'd kill Him, and Illurio couldn't stop me."

"That isn't why we're here. What are we supposed to do? Did your fairy tales tell us how to dredge up this . . . devil?"

"An innocent would release Him, if they judged Him worthy of atonement for His sins," she said, her voice hollow. It was as if she was listening to herself talk in another lifetime. A time when she had friends, and the luxury to complain about the civilisation that had sheltered and fed her all her life. How petty she had been. She'd been naive and foolish, but had she been innocent?

Bulraur coughed. Then he coughed again, descending into a hacking fit of retching, which doubled the soldier up. The din made Elthena whirl around, seeking out her ally. His eyes were bloodshot, and drool dribbled from the corner of his mouth.

"I don't feel well . . ." he said wearily, clutching his stomach. She rushed to his side, and almost fell into the water as she propped up the man before he toppled. He was warm to the touch, as if a sudden fever gripped him.

She glanced back toward Helzenthrax. His skeletal right hand, which had previously clutched the arm of His throne like an eagle's talon, was splayed open. Elthena's eyes widened.

"Stop it! Stop this now!" she exclaimed. Bulraur vomited over her shoulders, something black and viscous.

"Stop it, or I'll drive this sword through Your belly, and curse You to remain here! Release him now!"

Her challenge echoed across the sunken hall.

Bulraur shrugged her off, sending her careening into the nearest table. The man turned to her with eyes filled with childish panic. His lips still drooled black tar as he spoke.

The language was ancient, and the voice that issued from his abused mouth was not his own. He reverberated with the power of a baritone no mere mortal could achieve, making her skin crawl with every syllable.

"I can't understand you. What do you want?" she muttered between sobs, cowering before Bulraur as he spewed black vileness into the water again. He spoke with the ancient voice of Helzenthrax, but this time, snippets of the speech were known to Elthena. The tendons in Bulraur's neck were taut as he made a futile effort to regain control of his body. But Helzenthrax's grip was stronger than a strangling snake. On and on, the demon spoke, pillaging the soldier's mind for words it knew the girl could understand.

"Let him go! It was me you wanted! It was me you called to! Leave this man out of this game!" she said, drawing herself up to her full height, which was still puny compared to the undead avatar of evil that grew from the throne before her.

She felt something in the air change; the sort of sensation one got in the moments after a loud song had ended. Bulraur stopped spewing and looked toward Elthena with tears in his eyes.

"I'm sorry," was all he could say, before his courage abandoned him, and he turned tail and fled.

"Please, Bul! Don't take the light!" she called after him, but it was too late. Darkness swept in around her.

Silence, save for her panting.

She heard creaking, akin to the sound of taut ropes tightening. She held her breath, trying to discern whether she'd imagined it. Even straining to listen, the illusive sound fled from her perception.

Then.

"Elthena . . ."

###

Dawn came earlier than the refugees were expecting, and it came from the south. They turned in fear as a golden city swept over the horizon, carried aloft upon a churning white cloud that flashed with thunderstorms.

The city was flanked by smaller towers and structures that kept pace with the vast floating fortress as it blared a challenge across the moors with its great war horns.

"The Evictors!" one man wailed. "We are undone!"

Fear spread through the group like a cancer, and before even the farthest person witnessed the city's arrival, the men at the front were fighting to escape. The only avenue of retreat was the small opening in the rock formation. Their unsettled thoughts about the tunnel were overcome by the immediate threat of the Evictors. Heedless of the people they crushed, the Tallouan refugees plunged down into the caverns, blind and terrified.

They met Bulraur rising up from the tunnel, and he was overwhelmed by the flow of people streaming into Helzenthrax's tomb.

But the retreat was not fast enough. The Evictors had spotted them, and a great many of the refugees were still stranded on the open surface, helpless before the golden city.

###

She blinked, and from the darkness was conjured a world of broken stones beneath a starless night sky. Before her stood a man in a black habit, swathed by a faded purple cloak that moved with a life of its own. The man was a Tallou, with familiar pointed ears and wide almond eyes, who smiled with a face that might have been handsome, if the skin were not a shimmering, translucent tone of grey and white that let her see the black bones of his skull moving beneath the flesh. Upon his head sat an obsidian crown, and about his feet writhed pale vines, wriggling like thorn-clad serpents.

Looking down at her own body, she found she bore armour plate; a beautiful suit of sculpted pieces that conformed to the contours of her young body as if tailor-made for her.

"**Elthena. A risible name,**" he said. "**It derives from Charnivic.** *Stel Thenos*, **meaning 'stone mouse,' did you know? Meaningless, and also carelessly chosen by your elders. There is power in words. Your family must have no clue to the etymology of their own language. Ever is the curse of time. It is fortunate for you that on the languages of mortals, I am a swift study.**"

His voice was volcanic; she could taste the smoke and sulphur of every syllable. Effortlessly powerful, it demanded attention.

"How do you know my name?" she replied, her voice a quivering gasp in comparison.

"**Who are you to presume to interrogate me?**"

"You know my name already."

He smiled. "**Admirable bravery for one so little, Elthena. You do not cower and break like a reed in the wind, as most do** when set to the question. I know your name, for you cannot hide what is inside your soul from me. I may peer into the souls of all mortals, unbarred. I have harvested the dark secrets of legions of Talloukind without count, no matter what dank corner of their minds they seek to shroud them within.

"There is something of the wyrd about you, child; some fleeting trace of power etched into your bones. Ever since I woke, you have niggled at the edge of my thoughts, like a fluttering firefly in the periphery."

"When did you wake?"

"So many questions. But this one you already know, in your heart. My dreams were disturbed by another. Something new to me, but older than the rock of this world, passing through from the cold beyond. You felt it too no doubt, didn't you?"

She nodded. "The spear of Illurio . . ."

He shook His head. "No. Not *His* spear, infant. I wager that old warlock died when your nation was still a squabbling tribe of savage horsemen 'knights.'"

"He is a sky god. He—"

"There are no gods in the firmament. Only me."

She felt as if she'd been slapped. He must be lying.

"Must I be lying?"

The figure grinned.

"I see your thoughts more transparently than most, for you do not think to hide your perceived shame . . . Yes, I see this solitary secret clearly . . ."

Elthena suppressed a gasp, as she saw Zashr dancing around both her and the Dark Lord. She was dressed in the gold-embroidered gown of a highborn lady, and her cheery laughing was all the more poignant for being soundless.

"She loved you. And you loved her . . . but not enough. You lied to her, because you were lonely."

As she had appeared, so Zashr faded away. Elthena didn't try to hold back the tears this time.

"That is your only sin, and a most unsatisfying one it is at that. A devil would starve, feeding off the darkness in your heart. You are innocent." His eyes widened in realisation, flaring with internal fire. **"Why did you come here? Speak!"**

"I came . . . to seek your help."

His mirthless laugh was like the screaming of a murder of crows, echoing through a dead man's amphitheatre. Elthena flinched at the sheer discordance.

"I find it difficult to believe you. I am over a million years old. I have risen and receded in power and influence over a thousand ages of Tallou. Sometimes, the power-hungry or insane search me out and raise me up, oft times I am woken by happenstance or the ill fortune of my foes. But never, in all those eons, has an innocent come to me, without coercion, and asked

for my help. Are you sure you truly comprehend who I am?"

"I know you, Helzenthrax the Black. I have read about you all my life. I know who you are, and what ills you crave to inflict. But . . . I need you . . . We all need you. And you know, as I do, that I can free you. So, you will heed me, Elthena Albartun!"

He laughed again, shaking the hellish desolation around them with His horrendous voice.

"**What are your terms, your demands, child?**" He said at last, His voice dripping with insincerity.

"First, there is a race, the Murkavan. They have set upon our world with fire in the sky and deathless knights upon the land and have deemed Tallouans vermin to be extinguished. I want you to destroy them.

"Second, I want your solemn oath that you will not harm us if I free you. Neither me nor the people I led here.

"And third—"

"**The girl?**"

"Yes, the girl. Bring her back to me. You have to bring her back."

He deliberated for several moments, which seemed to stretch into eons in the dreamscape.

"**The first and the second are possible. But the third? No.**"

"Why?" she asked, an edge of desperation in her voice.

"**You would not like what I dredged back up from Mourn. Though I am mighty and my knowledge of the wyrd is unrivalled . . . what I craft is labelled monster in mortal lands. It is why I am so very popular in the songs of the people of this world**," He said, His voice fatherly in the worst fashion imaginable.

She wiped away a tear. "Fine, but I will have your oath on the other two," she said.

"**What makes you presuppose that I would honour any oath I make? Am I not faithless, and accursed? 'I swear,' but can you believe that? Perhaps not**," He said, with a grin wide as a shark's.

She drew herself up and stared into those hollow pits of eyes. "You have been alone for a thousand years. No one to talk to, none to gloat over and rant at. Nothing but yourself for company. Must be hell for you. I don't think you would be ready to go back to silence and loneliness so soon. You won't kill us."

Around them, the landscape changed, showing great battles raging across forests, mountains, fields; Tallou men dying and screaming out for their mothers while half-rotten knights beneath tattered black banners rode them down on undead chargers. Countless scrabbling masses of dead men clambered over one another to ascend castle walls and throw down their towers. Everywhere she looked, monsters fought and killed. She closed her eyes to it, but this was a realm in her mind, and she could not close her mind to the images.

"**I remain unconvinced. You might want to free me with**

your head, but in your heart, you see this; you see me, and the many faces of atrocity I veil myself in. You don't feel I am changed, that I am reborn. But know this child—all I do, I do for life. My existence has been devoted to the defiance of death's touch, and all who follow me crave life; I give it to them, as best I can manage. Life is difficult, messy. Eternal life is paid for in ways even the wisest cannot foresee. You who are without blemish cannot know the weight of such necessary sins I have performed. Do you, in your heart, want to free me?"

Elthena hesitated, whirling around as the images of war and violence closed in, flowing around her like oil in water. "I . . . I . . ."

Then, a rumble shook the whole world. The images shattered as another monstrous boom reverberated about the realm of nightmares. Even Helzenthrax cocked His head to one side in puzzlement. A third impact caused the ground to split and snarl with fire. **"Friends of yours?"**

"What's happening?"

"It would seem your time is up, or close to it," Helzenthrax said with a sour, pouting expression.

"No, no, no! They can't have found us yet! Helzenthrax, how do I summon you? Please tell me!"

Another sonorous blast made the nightmare landscape shudder, and before her eyes, the image of Helzenthrax began to rot again; His robes fell away in tattered strips, followed by His looping coils of gangrenous flesh. His handsome features turned to the hollow-cheeked cadaver she had seen before, and then even that began to dissolve into black ash that billowed away on an unseen breeze.

Somehow, she saw something beneath all that, beneath the rot and the decay and the corpse. Something that looked nothing like a Tallou or dryad or any being she'd ever imagined. Then, even that wisp of shadowy malevolence was gone, and the world dissolved into reality.

Her eyes snapped open. To a mixture of relief and unease, she realised she could see. An acrid breeze buffeted her face, and she smelled ozone and copper. She wore no armour now; only tattered rags, soaked black by the cold, standing water of the chamber.

The ceiling had come down in several places across the throne room, shafts of golden sunlight beaming down through the broken fissures and rents in the structure. Helzenthrax's giant corpse still sat, immobile, upon his driftwood throne. She rose from the stagnant water she had fallen into and noticed a few of her fellow refugees had come down to her. But they cowered behind pillars and tables, whimpering and reeking of their own urine.

She remembered why when a braying horn rattled her bones, echoing down from on high.

On fiery jets, like gleaming wings of fire, the silver giants descended. Half a dozen of the automatons landed, unfurling their lethal weapons from shoulder-mounted sheathes. The few armed refugees began to fire—crossbow bolts, smoky volleys of musket balls, slung lead weights, thrown stones, anything. Their fire pattered against the enemy like a light summer's rain.

Their baleful, tripartite eyes narrowed, focusing on the defenders. Elthena held her ears against the detonations, as one by one, the armed assailants were executed. She saw a flash of orange as Bulraur leapt forward and hacked into the flank of the nearest Evictor. Its fellow war machines fired, their precision blasts hitting Bulraur about the waist, parting him down the middle.

Elthena shrieked in horror. Reacting to her scream, the wounded giant took aim and fired. She dropped as the weapon took a second to charge. The crimson bolt scorched the nape of her neck as it sailed above her and struck Helzenthrax's corpse. The giant corpse burst into flames, and Elthena's heart broke to see the necromancer's body begin to collapse, melting like wax. Sorrow turned to fury. Without hope, she charged the nearest murdering automaton. She had no way to hurt it, but she'd die standing, in defiance of her fate.

The automaton struck her with its piston-like arm, hurling her back. She felt ribs break and a stabbing, white hot agony bore through her left lung as bone pierced internal organs. She hit her head against the steps at the foot of the smouldering wreckage of Helzenthrax's throne. Something warm trickled about her ears and down her shoulders.

Her vision blurred, and she watched as the giants strode through the cavern, ending lives with callous efficiency. Her only thoughts were of the Dark Lord now, smouldering ash upon a shattered throne; he had to come, he had to.

"Helzenthrass . . . pleassse . . . I releasssse . . . you . . . Forgive . . . you," she rasped through ruined lungs.

"It is nice . . . to be appreciated," a voice of depthless malevolence spoke, as if from all directions.

The Murkavan giants paused in their relentless advance, inscrutable eyes rotating as they took in the chamber, searching for the source of the voice.

"PREVIOUS TENANT. YOU ARE DIRECTED TO SHOW YOURSELF FOR SUMMARY EVICTION PROCEEDINGS," one of the giants declared in its flat, toneless voice.

"You have made a mistake. 'Tenant?' You mistake the *tenant* for the *landlord*. This world is mine."

The cacophony of slaughter had fallen silent, as did the wind. The chamber, defying the shafts of sunlight piercing its gloom, began to grow darker and colder.

The wounded giant was the first to experience what came next. From its wound, rust began to spread like fungus across a gelatine plate. Within moments, the oxidisation reached the joints of the automaton. Its red eye dimmed as it took a step backward to steady itself. But as it did so, the joints of its leg came loose, and it toppled to the ground. Within seconds, the lethal machine was naught but a pile of orange dust and flecks of iron. As the other giants turned to leave, the rusting contagion spread to them, too. As they engaged their thrusters to escape, their weakened bodies tore themselves to pieces.

From the bonfire that had once been Helzenthrax, a thing of tar and slime rose up. Black as pitch and drooling oil, the thing was tall, with limbs as long as its body, grasping fingers dripping with the same fluid as its flesh. The blank nub of matter between its hunched shoulders grew, splitting to reveal a mouth full of gleaming shark's fangs. Its long feet left wet, smoking footprints as it stepped from the embers of Helzenthrax's throne. The air was thick with the wyrd, and Elthena wept with joy.

The slime threw back its head and screeched. The sound carried outward, across the chamber and the vast caverns of Helzenthrax's lair, and upward, to resound across the moors.

The city above began to rain crimson fire upon the tomb, and Elthena felt her bones break under the strain. But the thing of slime dissolved before her eyes. It became smoke, thicker than the densest smog, coiling and churning like a gale.

The great city vessel realised the danger it was in far too late as the coiling black vapours surged from the tomb in a hundred tendrils, like a many-headed serpent. Wherever the tendrils struck, fire blossomed and spread as the very innards of the city were consumed and destroyed. Crimson energy bolts filled the sky as the vessel tried to destroy the Dark Lord, but Helzenthrax was beyond mortal concerns.

Elthena smiled as darkness took her. As she perished, she thanked Helzenthrax. And to her surprise, she meant it.

###

Guthun had been flattened and cleared by the Murkavans' army of preparatory drones long before the colonists arrived from orbit aboard the luxury pleasure yachts that had carried them in stasis for the eons-long journey to the planet they called TX-39G.

It was only after the Evictors had cleared the local wildlife and built the Murkavan their settlements that the aliens realised their machines had destroyed an entire people. The Murkavans had sent the Evictors on the assumption that a culture with interplanetary parity had occupied one of many worlds within the system, and eviction from one would not have been too onerous a burden. The Murkavan science council's first act upon arrival was to deactivate the Evictors for analysis and further re-engineering.

Nevertheless, the Murkavan had arrived at last, and they could not turn back and leave the system now they had arrived. So, they stayed and occupied the glittering, perfect cities their robots had built for them. And they flourished in the temperate world they now called home, spreading out across the planet; a silver city on every continent. But the city that had once been Guthun was grandest of all.

The golden-skinned Murkavans, tall and strong of limb, frolicked with their children and their friends, supping on wines and delicacies harvested from the great robot-governed hyper farms. Hunger and want were unknown to this people, and citizens roamed the world with smiles on their faces, smiles that were felt in the heart.

Upon the valley's edge, where the dark and untamed woods met the state gardens of the silver city's outer limits, a figure trotted from between the saplings. Upon a pale and decomposing steed, this wild creature sat, swathed in robes of skin and bark and putrid moss, armoured in black plate etched with blasphemous runes. Her face was drawn and desiccated; the only expression the discoloured flesh of her face could make was a mirthless grimace that showed oozing, brown teeth.

But it was her eyes that marked the figure as a fiend, for they shone with green corpse light. These soulless eyes looked upon this city of plenty and peace and wished only ill upon the Murkavans below. The figure drew her sword, which ignited with blue fire as she raised it to the darkening heavens with a deathless shriek of pain and wrath.

This was the signal, and from the forest, her call was taken up by countless hateful voices roaring as one. From the depths of the woods, a thousand sets of glowing green eyes opened, awaiting their orders.

Elthena the Scorned pointed her burning sword toward the alien city that insulted her by its very existence.

"Kill them. Kill them all! In the name of Helzenthrax! In the name of Tallou-Majoritus!"

Someday

By James Fadeley

"Command, this is Vox. ETA to firing range is 300 seconds."

"Affirm, Vox." The voice coming through the radio was clouded with static. "Vox" Valkyria knew that the Command Carrier Armeya had to destroy a nearby asteroid on its way toward the target, and the dust left behind somehow interfered with communications. "Orders remain…maintain speed…target. Broadcast warning and do not engage unless ordered."

"They should be out of that dust cloud by the time we're in range," her copilot Ryn said.

Valkyria couldn't see Ryn because she sat in the seat behind her own. But Valkyria could hear her fiddling with some of the switches and electronics equipment.

Valkyria leaned back in her seat, which creaked with the motion. She glanced to her left and spotted the fighter of her wingman, "Archon" Edmun. She could even see his helmet through the bubble-shaped cockpit, just like her own fighter.

But where Valkyria's fighter carried a circular radar dish on top, Edmun's was burdened with curved missile pods and two under-wing "Cracker" torpedoes. One direct hit from one of those torpedoes would cripple a regular Cruiser.

Two would split it in half.

Edmun's head turned her way, and he waved to her. His voice came clear through the radio on the channel reserved for their squad. "Got reservations, Val?"

"I don't know." Valkyria took a deep breath and sighed, trying to come to grips with the myriad of conflicting emotions. "I'm not keen on this. Command assumes it's something from another nation, but they even admitted they're doubting that theory now. If this is…" She swallowed. "If this is something new…I don't know. Why us?"

"Had to be someone," he replied.

"Nothing inspires fear like uncertainty and the unknown," Ryn said.

Silence reigned after that, as the target came into sight.

Against the backdrop of black space and glittering stars, the target was, at first, nothing more than a fleck of silver reflecting the light of Xarma's sun.

But the blip grew as they gained on it. Valkyria's mouth dried as they approached as close as Command dared let them. Even from their distance, Valkyria could see it was a perfect cylinder. It was the size of three, perhaps four Command Carriers, making it the single most massive construct they had ever encountered. Its surface was a fine lustre before the solar illumination. But as Valkyria and Edmun guided their fighters parallel to the target's flight path, Valkyria realized there was a strange iridescence to it, shifting from hues of golden orange to coppery green and violet.

Valkyria heard Edmun swallow over the radio.

She reduced her aft engines and even engaged her fore vernier thrusters. From her cockpit, she could see the short-lived spurts of blue fire, reducing her speed. When the sensors indicated that they were matching the target's velocity, Valkyria flipped the radio switch.

"Command, Vox here. We've intercepted the target and are following alongside. Target unresponsive, but continues on course at present velocity."

Valkyria bit her lip as she waited for the response. She cast her eyes over the target. There were no weapon pods, no fighter bays, and no exterior sensor towers. She wondered whether she would find so much as a bolt or a gap between panels if she were to walk on the surface of the strange craft.

"Understood, Vox." Command's voice came through without static, suggesting they had cleared the dust cloud they had created earlier. "Order Blooper to begin transmitting the greeting and feed us visual. Maintain current course, and do not engage unless cleared, I repeat—"

"Do not engage unless cleared. Understood, Command," Valkyria replied. The briefing officers had repeated that phrase perhaps a dozen times before the squadmates even climbed into their cockpits.

"I really hate the call sign they gave me," Ryn said as Valkyria heard the thump of flicked switches behind her seat. They had only just transferred into this unit, but another pilot was already called "Music," forcing a reassignment for Ryn. For the time being, she was given a temporary call sign of "Blooper."

Valkyria heard a mechanical whirring beneath her and knew that Ryn was angling the underslung camera toward the target, recording images and transmitting them back to Command.

"Are we broadcasting the message?" Valkyria asked.

"Broadcasting…" There was a pause followed by another thump of a flicked switch. "Now."

"Attention. Attention. Unknown vessel passing through the Uldran Republic's outer quadrant. You are in violation of our nation's borders. Please broadcast any identifying markers, which may include trade license, military identification, or property serial numbers with name and nation of origin. Failure to comply may result in assumption of hostile intentions. Ayerto. Ayerto. Defamilia outarg-ship travineda caon dal Uldran Republico da outarg-quadro—"

Valkyria heard Ryn switch another button, and the monotone voice stopped.

"Are they broadcasting that in every known language?" Edmun asked over the radio.

"They start with the languages used by nations known to have space-going technology like Artaglish and Calagese, followed by those who have nearly constructed their first ship, followed by others," Ryn replied. "Did you know they even include Vrilgon and Ulvish?"

Despite the seriousness of the situation, Valkyria burst out laughing.

Edmun's mirth could be heard over the radio, too. "You mean from that sci-fi show, Star Journey?"

"Vrilgon is from Star Journey. Ulvish was from that movie, Solar Wars," Valkyria said.

"Gods, you're such a nerd, Val," Edmun replied.

Valkyria continued to giggle for a while. But as she eyed the target again, the smile faded and her emotions sobered. Nothing had changed about it. "Alright, guys, we had our laugh. We should stay focused until this is over with."

"Affirm," Edmun replied.

"Affirm," Ryn said.

The next five minutes passed in relative silence. The thrum of the engines and hum of electronic equipment mingled with the occasional beep of the radar and whirring of the external camera.

"Command to Vox, any developments?"

"Negative, Command. Any change in orders?"

There was a long pause. "Negative, Vox. Analysts are still pouring over what you're sending us with no consensus. Continue to observe, broadcast, and follow."

"Affirm."

A moment passed before Edmun spoke again. "Do you guys think this thing is Xarman?"

Ryn scoffed. "Where else would it have come from?"

"I don't know. It's kind of sexy minimalist, like a Zentlian Sky Skipper. But, there's no where nearby that could have been its port of origin. The colony at Parma is on the other side of the sun right now. Unless this thing made the trip from Biln."

"C'mon, Edmun. Biln? Seriously?" Valkyria broke into the conversation. Biln was the farthest planet in the system, an ice ball whose only residents had been a science team who abandoned it after a three-month expedition. "Are you turning into another anti-government conspiracy theorist?"

"Well, what's the alternative? Aliens?"

Neither Valkyria nor Ryn replied. Despite all rationality, Valkyria couldn't dismiss the thought that perhaps there was something extrinsic about the target. She stared at the unidentified ship and said nothing.

Minutes dragged on. Despite herself, Valkyria's mind began to wander. She looked through the tinted glass of her helmet toward Xarma's sun. The planet Xarma was a shaded circle hanging over the huge ball of swarming orange light. Yet as much as Valkyria wished for home, her gaze trailed to the myriad stars that dusted the black velvet of the universe like sugar.

The memories bubbled in her mind, and Valkyria remembered. Gazing at the stars was never enough for her. Her eyes turned on the target again, and she couldn't help but smile. The words poured out before she could stop herself. "I watched Star Journey when I was a kid."

"Really?" Edmun asked.

"I saw it. Visiting other worlds, other cultures. And I dreamed. I always wanted to go out of the house more often. And when I was old enough to do that, I wanted to drive and go as far as I could. But I still wasn't content when I earned my license."

The words kept coming and wouldn't stop. She knew without seeing that Edmun was turning, looking at her from his cockpit. "I wanted to tour the country. So I ended up in the Uldran military. Going base to base until I got my assignment in the Space Navy."

Her eyes were burning. They'd been open so long that she felt them watering. "And it's unfair. Unfair that…that this is as far as I can go. But something tells me that this thing is going to travel on. And see what I never will…go where I've always wanted to go. See what I've always wanted to see."

The silence endured, until Ryn broke it. "You okay, Valkyria?"

"Yeah." Valkyria's shut her eyes, and the sting of dryness diminished. "Sorry, just nostalgic."

A few minutes passed, until Command finally radioed in. "Vox, Archon, the target is leaving our quadrant. Cease transmission and come on home."

"Command, permission to follow a bit farther." Valkyria leaned forward, feeling the apprehension within her grow.

"Negative, Vox. Military ships beyond the quadrant equal a lot of diplomats getting rude wake-up calls. Also, you have only just enough fuel to make it back."

"Please, Command, just a few more minutes." Valkyria wasn't even sure why she was pleading this. Just to go a little farther, to go beyond the realm of trekked space. Toward the stars, just as this strange ship did.

"Val." It was Edmun. "Someday, we'll follow them. Someday."

Val bit her lip and wondered just how old she would be when they finally did bridge the stars. But she obeyed, reaching for her flight stick and easing it back. Their fighters twisted one hundred eighty degrees and began their return.

Valkyria watched the target drift on toward the blanket of stars in her rearview camera feed. And she whispered a promise to herself. "Someday."

City Blue
By Edward Smith

On 40th Street, on the west side of City Blue, the people were calm—mild heat, blue sky, the sound of a machine. It was the middle of the week. And nothing was happening.

On 67th Street, east side, the people were not so relaxed. They'd all seen it last night—the cylinder, long, curved, and black, making its way over the city, about two-hundred feet off the ground. Someone had to have put it there, right? Someone or something had to have sent it to City Blue on purpose. And now what? What did it mean? Was the cylinder dangerous? Was it coming back to the city?

Possibilities played on the minds of every eastsider that morning. They gossiped and rumoured. They huddled in bars drinking cold water and glancing at the door. Something bad was going to happen, they knew it. Because of the cylinder. What did it want? When was it was coming? What was going on outside?

As far back as they, or any citizen, could remember, nothing had been seen on The Other Side of the Wall. City Blue was an island, a walled-in place with desert in every direction. Whatever *was out there,* the people of City Blue didn't want to know about it. Everything here worked fine and everyone was content.

###

Gal, who was born and raised on the west side, had been dimly aware of the outside world his whole life. But he'd never gone hungry, never been out of work, and never been injured. Like everybody else inside its four walls, City Blue had provided for Gal. And as he sat in his living room, listening to pop music, he thought only about his own life—his job, his diet, his exercise routine.

He lived alone on 40th Street, in a bungalow that his parents had left him. It had a separate living room, kitchen, bathroom, and bedroom, perfectly square in design and layout. Gal was a neat man and had never decorated the walls, preferring to leave them white and uncluttered. His cupboards were equally organised, with food and drink for each day of the week separated into compartments.

He slept in a single bed, wore cotton clothing, and washed once a day. Gal's only extravagance was a thick set of curtains on his bungalow's front-facing window, which were coloured dark purple and made from twill. He kept them closed during the day, sometimes.

Gal switched off his music, got up and walked into the kitchen. He had forgotten about the cylinder already.

###

Richard was covered in sweat, dripping with it, stinking of it. "I bet I look fucking disgusting," he thought as he fidgeted in his chair.

The town hall was packed. It seemed like everyone, from 51st to 100th, was there. Just from where he sat, Richard could make out the faces of Tom, Matt, and Lucy, as well as several others who he'd never met personally but had seen around the block. And there was another guy, who Richard hadn't seen before, standing at the back, smoking a cigarette. He looked calmer than everyone else. Richard wondered whether maybe he knew something about all this.

They'd come to discuss the cylinder. Richard had his questions ready and was eager to grill the committee. When the meeting started, he was the first to stand up.

"The first and most important thing that I think we all want to know is when is this thing coming back? Does the council know? Have you got any idea what the cylinder was doing?"

The speaker leaned forward to give his response, but the room erupted in applause, drowning out his voice. Richard stayed standing for a while. He was proud of his question.

When the councilman was finally able to be heard over the jeering of the audience, he recited what Richard, and everyone else in the crowd, knew was a prepared answer. "We have no solid information on the object as of yet, but the Eastside Committee is using all of its resources to find out precisely what happened."

"Bullshit!" shouted a voice from the back of the room, and everyone cheered again. Richard looked over at the man with the cigarette, who was shaking his head and still looking like he knew something nobody else did.

I need to talk to him, thought Richard, still wiping sweat off of his face.

The rest of the meeting continued the same way. Somebody would ask a pertinent question and the council would give a vague, rehearsed answer. By the end, nobody's worries had been assuaged.

In fact, they had only gotten more severe. Richard was glad to get out of the town hall, growing tired of the council's lies after about half an hour. But he could still feel his mind racing faster than ever. *They don't know what happened. They won't be ready if it comes back again. We need answers, information. How can we get them to listen? How can we get them to listen? How can we get them to listen?* Even in the cool outside air, he was still sweating.

A crowd of people stood around, looking at the sky, trying to spot the cylinder again.

"There, you see," said one of them. "It's peeking out from behind that cloud."

"Got it," said another, and there was a murmur of agreement from the people gathered round.

Richard could see it, too. He swore he could. But the smell of cigarettes made him remember something, and he went to find the calm man, who was around the back. He'd almost reached his car.

"Richard," he introduced himself.

"Nick."

"So what do you think?"

"About the cylinder? Nothing. I don't think we should worry about it. I'm not."

"But what about when it comes back?"

"Who's to say it will?"

Richard looked at him, angry.

"Don't think so much. It was nice meeting you." He drove off. The car had westside plates.

###

Gal had heard it while he was washing up his dinner plate. "Cylinder."

It'd come through the wall from the house next door. And now Gal lay awake on his sofa, in the middle of the night, with the word playing over in his head.

Cylinder, cylinder, cylinder. Surely it didn't mean anything. It was just a cylinder, gliding in the sky, up above the houses. There was nothing outside of City Blue that meant harm to anyone. There was nothing outside of City Blue at all, right?

But still Gal couldn't sleep. The image of the cylinder, flying beyond the city wall, kept playing on his mind.

Between a small gap in the curtains, he stared at the street outside.

###

Richard carried his gun everywhere now. Even here, at the bar, where he was the only customer, he no longer felt safe.

The television was showing a news broadcast, live from 22nd Street, where two of the Eastside Committee had resigned, citing "personal reasons."

Everyone knew what *that* meant.

"Maybe now they'll get it through the rest of their thick

heads. What do you reckon, Dick?" asked John, the bartender.

"Maybe," said Richard. "I'm glad the committee's starting to take this thing seriously, anyway."

Nick walked in.

Richard hadn't seen him since the town hall meeting. He didn't look so calm any more. His suit was ruffled, his eyes were red, and his hair was messy.

He sat at the bar and ordered a glass of cold water.

"There was another sighting last night," said Richard, looking down at his own drink.

Nick didn't reply.

"My neighbour Pete saw it. He was out walking the dog and said he saw the cylinder hovering above the school. That's the third one this month."

"None of them are confirmed."

"Hm?"

"None of them are confirmed," said Nick. "The committee said none of their equipment picked anything up."

"And now two of them have quit," said John.

"Exactly. Look at what's happening, Nick." Richard gestured to the TV. "That's live from 22nd Street."

"People just talk too much, is all." Nick lit a cigarette.

"This thing had to have come from somewhere," Richard

said. "It can't have just popped up out of nothing."

Nick didn't reply.

"There's something going on outside, and we need to know about it. If we aren't ready and this thing comes back, then . . . what if it's armed? What if there's a whole other city out there, watching us through it, waiting for the right moment to attack? People could die because of this thing!"

"That won't happen," said Nick.

"I don't know how you can be so sure."

"There's nothing, alright?" Nick jumped out of his chair. "There's nothing out there. The cylinder was just a trick of the light or something, just a thing that people think they saw. It's not coming back, okay? Everything is fine!"

Nick finished his cigarette and quickly lit another. Richard and John stared at him.

"Fuck!" he said, then threw over his glass of water and hurried into the toilets.

There was a brief moment of silence. Richard looked at John.

"People like him won't listen to reason. They'd rather just pretend everything is okay than have to deal with any problems. This thing's going to come back."

"I agree with you, Dick. I just wish we knew *when*."

"He probably does," said Richard, nodding toward the toilets. "When I was at the town hall, he just stood at the back, shaking his head, laughing every time someone asked a question. And now listen to him. He's telling us not to worry, talking our guard down. I'd never seen him around until the town hall. Maybe he's from the outside, too?"

Richard took a drink.

"We need to shut him up. It's people like him who are stopping the committee from doing anything."

He put his gun on the bar.

"Go lock the door. When he comes back, first we'll get what we need out of him and then we'll—"

"Kill him?"

"This thing needs to get sorted out, John. That cylinder's dangerous. And doubters like Nick are just putting people in danger."

"Okay, I'm with you."

John locked the doors of the bar. Then he walked back behind the counter, poured two glasses of brandy, and handed one to Richard.

When Nick came out of the toilet, he already had his gun drawn. He aimed it at the bar and fired off the entire magazine. John was hit three times in the throat and once in the forehead. Richard was struck in the back of the neck. His head was tilted forward and the bullet exited just below his left eye.

John slid to the ground, blood spilling from his nostrils and the holes in his throat. Richard hit the bar hard enough that his head bounced off it. He fell off his stool and landed flat on his back.

Nick dropped his empty gun on the ground. On his way to the exit, he walked past the two men. They were surrounded by blood now.

Their brains were completely destroyed.

Nick kicked open the door and stepped back into the sunshine. Then he quickly headed west, wiping his brow, trying not to look up at the sky.

Gal turned off the radio and went to his front window. The mailbox belonging to the house across the road was still smashed in. Both sides were dented and the flap had been pulled away. It was eleven days since Gal had noticed the damage. He wanted to know why nobody had been sent to fix it.

But it was dark already, and he needed to finish wallpapering his living room. Then he was making pizza. He opened another beer and went to work.

The cylinder had done something. And it was probably coming back to do more. He'd thought about it, day and night, for as long as he could remember now. The television was on the rolling news channel.

The cylinder. The cylinder. The cylinder. He wanted to know what it was, what it meant. Maybe there were more like it? Maybe, on the other side of the wall, things were better than in here?

A rock punched through his front window in a sudden shower of shattered glass. It was jagged and pale-coloured, not like the rocks usually found on 40th Street.

He walked over to the hole in the glass and looked out. He could just about make out three men in hoods, running off down the road. In the distance, there was smoke from a house fire.

Gal turned back and looked at the rock. It perched on the carpet, which he hadn't cleaned in weeks. Behind it was a white wall. The two on either side had different coloured wallpaper.

Gal sat down with his back to the window and started to cry.

Outside, the sky was clear.

Her Kiss
By A. R. Aston

Kaylo's kiss was sweeter than Jed could have hoped, and the scent of her was intoxicating. He could not stop touching her; if he let go, even for a moment, he feared she'd vanish like a dream spoiled by wakefulness.

He wanted to press himself against her, but she pulled away, grinning.

"Do you think he saw?" she asked. Her voice was soft and without malice, which made her rejection of him even worse. His attention hadn't even registered to her.

Jed dutifully turned from his unrequited love and looked to Haren, her true paramour.

"I don't think so, Kay. He's been looking through the scope all night at that sky thing," Jed said. He turned back to her.

"Maybe if we kissed again?" he asked, already hating himself for it.

Golden Planet
By Evan Purcell

"Ugh."

Roze limped down the hallway. Her arthritis was acting up again. She'd only had that problem a handful of times since moving to Golden Planet, but today was particularly achy. Back on Olaff-9, her joints were constantly acting up. But here . . . the gravity was weaker. The atmosphere was more forgiving. On Golden Planet, everything was just more . . . pleasant.

Roze's three roommates were already sitting at the table when Roze limped into the kitchen.

"You're scrunching up your face again, dear," Blan-Chett said. She was the youngest of the four, and her southern moon drawl was particularly noticeable in the morning, before two and a half cups of coffee jarred her awake.

"Leave Roze alone," Dorox said. "Not everyone is as terrified of wrinkles as you are."

"Clearly," Blan-Chett said.

Good thing Sofi sat between them, or else their argument would escalate pretty quickly. Blan-Chett was notoriously crabby in the morning, and Dorox was crabby in the . . . waking hours.

Roze sat down with a groan. "I'm a little sore this morning," she said.

"Me too!" Blan-Chett said, no doubt implying that she'd had

another late-night visitor.

"Oh, spare us the details," Dorox said. "I just brushed my teeth."

All at once, a shadow passed over the skylight. It seemed too big and slow to be a plane. The sky boomed.

The four women jumped out of their chairs. Well, Roze did more of a half-jump/half-stumble, and even that made her feel as if she'd jarred loose her hip bones. Through the window over the sink, they could see the hazy orange sky. It looked particularly normal today, except...

"What is that?"

"Do you see that thing?"

And to be honest, Roze didn't. At least, not at first. Then, once she squinted a little, she saw a dark, cylindrical shape blotted against one of the suns. From its straight lines and the gentle curve at its base, it certainly didn't look natural.

"It's a satellite of some kind," Dorox guessed. "It's man-made."

Sofi nodded in agreement. Behind her thick glasses, her face seemed at once suspicious and worried. "The government is spying on us."

"Now why would they do that?" Dorox said. "Golden Planet is probably the most boring place in the solar system."

Blan-Chett scoffed. "Maybe for you, but not everyone spends

their Friday nights working on jigsaw puzzles. Some of us lead interesting lives."

"Which is why you, of all people, should be nervous right now," Sofi said. "Do you really want government spy cameras hovering outside your bedroom?"

Roze's three roommates continued to debate the meaning of that mystery shape, but Roze herself was silent. Then, just as the conversation was getting heated, Roze said, "I'm going outside to get a better look."

Everyone looked at her like she'd just murdered someone.

"But we don't know what it is," Dorox said.

"Exactly. Which is why I'm going to check it out."

Blan-Chett was the first to respond, even if that response was just a worried shrug.

"Besides," Roze said, "I think it's time to walk the squid."

She pulled the leash off the wall and grabbed Patches from out of his tank. The squid was ten already, or seventy in squid years. He didn't move the way he used to. Roze had to take things very slowly or else the poor little guy would trip over his own tentacles.

As she left by the front door, Dorox called out to her. "Be careful! If you see . . ."

Roze closed the door. Those three women were her best friends, but at times she felt like their lives were too entwined. Every decision she made—from hair care products to the best time for squid-walking—was subject to scrutiny from the peanut gallery. It was a tad codependent.

As she crossed the street, Roze knew that Dorox was watching her through the window. Normally, she'd turn around and wave. This time, she didn't.

Scratch that, Roze thought. They were more than a little codependent. They were a four-headed worry machine.

As she continued down their cul-de-sac, however, all thoughts of Dorox, Blan-Chett, and Sofi faded away. Heck, even the joint aches that had plagued her this morning were starting to fade. The only thought that occupied her brain—the only thing that registered beyond a basic sense of her surroundings and the dull flop-flop-squish pattern of squid tentacles on pavement—was that strange cylinder in the sky.

What was it?

Why was it dangling in their atmosphere, just out of reach?

And why, as soon as she saw it, did Roze get the feeling that her life was about to change forever?

Once the street ended and Patches was officially out of breath, Roze found herself standing on the edge of a golf course. Golden Planet had the most per capita golf courses in the solar system, and this was definitely one of the nicest. Roze let Patches run wild here. She loved watching his little tentacles frolic through the well-trimmed grass. Squids don't smile, of course, but Roze could've sworn that his little beak curved into a grin every time she took him down here.

High above her, a few sparks of sunlight reflected off the strange shape in the sky. Roze was afraid to stare at it directly, so she cocked her head to the side and tried to look at it through the corner of her eyes. That just gave her a headache.

"I hope that's not the government spying on us."

Who said that? The voice was unfamiliar: gruff and a little scratchy. Roze spun around, noticing a tall, slender man approach her. He smiled at her in a familiar way, but Roze was certain she'd never seen him before. She would've recognized that face.

"You have something against government surveillance?" she asked.

"Absolutely," the stranger said. "I don't want bird's-eye-view photos of my bald spot beamed into every house on Golden Planet."

Roze laughed. This man was undeniably charming. She wasn't quite sure what homeworld he can from, though. Judging by the light dusting of brown spots on his face, he might've been from one of the inner planets. Or perhaps he just liked to sunbathe.

The stranger extended his hand. "I'm Holland," he said.

"Roze." She felt an involuntary smile stretch across her face, and she knew she was beaming like a girl.

"Well, Roze, it's nice to meet you . . . and your friend." With that, he reached down and scratched Patches a few times on the head. The old squid fluttered his tentacles and cooed.

"He likes you," she said.

Holland was a complete stranger, but Roze felt comfortable with him. His freckled skin and large, dark eyes seemed particularly foreign, and his accent was pronounced. She had no idea where he came from, but she was certainly glad that they'd met.

After a while, she noticed that his freckles were starting to shift along his cheeks. They swirled around each other in a strange sort of dance.

"Your face," Roze said.

"Oh, sorry," Holland said. "That happens when I get excited."

Roze had never seen that happen before. It was impossibly cute.

"So, do you live nearby?" she asked. Once the words left her mouth, she realized that she sounded prying. Or forward. Or suggestive. She sounded like Blan-Chett.

All at once, Holland's face darkened. It was like he suddenly remembered something unpleasant, or perhaps smelled something unpleasant. "I'm sorry, Roze, but I just remembered. I have to leave."

"Will I see you again?"

He looked at Roze one last time, his gray eyes sliding over her small frame and off-white track suit. "Yes," he said, forcing the word out of his mouth as if the single syllable was hiding in the back of his throat. "Tomorrow. Right here. Same time."

"Great," Roze said. "I can bring the fixings for a picnic." She glanced back up at the hovering cylinder above them. "And we can . . . get surveyed together." She meant it as a little casual flirting, but it sounded better in her head.

"Um . . . bye." And Holland ran off.

Roze watched him go, amazed at his speed and stamina and . . . hey! He didn't have a bald spot!

###

With a loud splash, Roze dropped Patches back into his tank. He gurgled in appreciation.

"So?"

"Well?"

"And?"

Roze spun around. Dorox, Sofi, and Blan-Chett were waiting by the door to hear all the details. "Did you find out anything about the shape?" one of them asked, but Roze wasn't sure who. Her mind was still fuzzy with visions of Holland.

"Oh. Right. That."

"What do you mean 'oh, right, that?'" Sofi asked. "You've only been gone an hour."

Roze couldn't tell if she was still smiling. She probably was.

Blan-Chett gasped. "Roze! You met a man!"

"What? I . . ."

"Honey, I can tell by your face. It's still scrunched up, but in a . . . different way. You . . . you met somebody."

"Roze!" Dorox said. "You were gone for an hour!"

Blan-Chett grabbed Roze by the wrist and pulled her into the kitchen. The others followed. Slices of frozen cheesecake were waiting for them. "Roze. Talk."

"Well," Roze said, gingerly sitting in her chair. "I was on one of the golf courses, you know, trying to get a better view of that thing in the sky. I was just standing there, when . . ."

"When a handsome gentleman with a gleam in his eye came and whisked you off your feet," Blan-Chett said.

"It wasn't like that," Roze said.

"Honey," Blan-Chett said. "It's okay. Don't ever be ashamed of natural feelings. I mean, if a stranger just wandered up to me and smiled, I wouldn't kick him out of my bedroom."

"And why would a stranger just wander into your bedroom?" Dorox asked.

"Hey. When opportunity knocks . . ."

Roze cleared her throat. Loudly. "I do like him a lot."

Sofi shoveled in another mouthful-and-a-half of cheesecake. She chewed as loudly as Roze's throat-clearing. "Don't tell me you're turning into Blan-Chett 2.0!"

"God, no," Roze said. "I have too much self-respect for that." She turned toward Blan-Chett. "No offense."

"None taken," Blan-Chett said with a shrug. "Sexual liberation never killed anybody."

"Actually . . ." Dorox said, and proceeded to list off at least seven recently dead celebrities, but Roze wasn't paying attention. Her head was in the clouds and nothing—not even a quickie reference to famed Olaffite actress Tahlia Hernandez and her brain-eating infections—would get in her way.

". . . Not to mention the Hepatitis Wars of 48-B," Dorox continued.

"Enough!" Roze said. She stood up, trying to show that she meant business, even though her standing height was roughly equal to Dorox's sitting height. "Holland is a very nice man, and I don't want to talk about the Hepatitis Wars!"

"But what do you really know about this man?" Sofi asked. "What planet is he from?"

Roze looked away.

"You don't even know what planet he's from?"

"I didn't ask."

"At least he didn't have mandibles. Right? Right?" Sofi asked.

"None I could see."

Dorox stood up. "This isn't good, Roze," she said. "You know that, right? You're not back on Olaff-9 anymore. This is Golden Planet."

"The safest retirement planet in the galaxy," Blan-Chett said. "You remember what the screening process was like. All the paperwork. Walking a straight line. Saying the alphabet backward."

"I'm going to see him again," Roze said.

Her roommates reacted in one of three ways: approval, disappointment, or *oh-hell-no*.

"Oh, hell no," Sofi said.

"Be reasonable about this," Dorox added.

And just like that, the roommates started arguing again. They forgot everything about the shape in the sky, instead focusing all their attention on Roze's latest romance.

Great, Roze thought. Nothing ever changed on Golden Planet.

For the next few days, Roze and Holland were as inseparable as Dorox and her jigsaw puzzles. They went for walks. They ate at a couple of Olaffite restaurants nearby. They visited the cinema. And every time they met, they couldn't stop talking. Roze felt like she knew everything about Holland . . . except what planet he came from. But that seemed like such a small matter in the face of all the little things that she did know about him.

His favorite color. (Blue.)

His favorite grandchildren. (Benny or Maria, depending on the day.)

His life's passion. (Golf, both watching and playing.)

But Roze couldn't help noticing that every time he was about to kiss her—every time he leaned in close and his lips parted—he would suddenly pull back and change the subject. Often, this would happen at the end of a beautiful evening together.

At first, Roze assumed he wanted to take everything slowly. But the more it happened, the more she realized that something was wrong. He was going too slowly. That Friday, Roze decided, she was going to kiss him. Even if he pulled away, she'd just grab his collar, pucker up, and wait. There was nothing else she could do.

After all, she deserved a little affection after spending three hours cooking him the perfect Olaffite meal. They ate on the back patio, cozy and together, as moonlight shined down on them. The mystery shape had drifted to the edge of the sky. One more day and it would probably be gone, but for now it waited, a dark shape in an even darker atmosphere.

"This is truly delicious," he said. "There's nothing like old-fashioned homeworld cooking."

Holland's freckles began to dance again. They swirled around each other, faster and faster until they'd faded into a slight blush.

Roze was nervous. She thrummed her fingertips against the glass table but quickly stopped when she realized what she was doing. She wanted so much to kiss him. It had been so long since she'd felt the warmth of contact. And Holland was special. She knew that. He made her stomach shiver in a way that no one else had, not even her ex-husbands.

"Holland?" Roze said.

As if he expected her to say something he wasn't going to like, Holland quickly turned his attention up to the sky. "Beautiful night, isn't it?"

"It is."

"And where are your roommates tonight?"

"Inside," she said. "But don't mind them. They're probably asleep already."

"It's a shame I couldn't meet them."

Roze slowly stood up, not an ounce of soreness in her joints. She grabbed Holland's hand and pulled him to his feet, too. "That's alright," she said. "You can always meet them tomorrow morning."

She knew exactly what she was implying, and Holland did, too. Silently, she led him through the sliding glass door into her bedroom. She had expected he'd come here sooner or later, so most of her figurines and family photos had been stashed in the closet. Together, they sat on the edge of her bed.

"Roze," he said.

She cut him off. "This past week has been one of the best weeks of my life. I feel so close to you."

"I feel the same way, but . . ."

"No buts," she said. "Not now. I think I'm ready to . . ."

"Roze! Stop!"

His sudden outburst made her flinch. She wasn't expecting him to shout at her. Not here. Not now.

"Sorry." Holland exhaled. He was too busy having a staring contest with his shoelaces to look Roze in the eyes. "I, um . . . I know you're an Olaffite."

"Because I told you."

"Exactly," he said. "And I'm . . . well, I'm from somewhere else. Roze, I'm sorry, but we're not the same species."

"That's okay," she said. "I've dated plenty of foreigners. My first husband was from one of the inner planets."

He shook his head. "You don't understand. We . . . we're not biologically compatible."

"I don't understand," Roze said. "What does that mean?"

Holland blinked several times. "That means," he said, "that if we ever get physical . . . well, you would eventually explode from the inside-out."

"Oh, God."

"Like confetti," Holland said. He made hand gestures, too.

Roze felt her world crashing around her, but only for a second. This was awful news—horrible, awful, rip-your-hair-out news—but she had already lived through plenty of bad news before. She could handle it. Besides . . .

"Sex isn't everything," she said.

His eyes lit up. "You're not mad?"

"Of course not," she said. "At my age, I . . . Well, I'd miss the sex, but I'll always be more interested in companionship than intimacy. I like you. A lot. And if I can spend more time with you, then that's all that matters."

He placed his hand on her knee. "Thank you," he said.

"For what?"

"For being a friend."

When Roze smiled, her whole face lit up. She could feel herself blushing.

The situation was certainly less-than-ideal. After all, no matter what she said, she still needed a little more than pleasant companionship. But for now, she would have to manage.

It felt good to just sit together, feeling his warm hand on her knee, feeling his fingers slowly stroke her leg up and down until . . .

Holland stood up. "I can't do this!"

"Holland!"

"I'm sorry, Roze, but I just . . . I can't control my urges right now. I feel like . . . the way you're smiling at me, I'd just . . . I'm sorry. I have to go!"

"Holland! Wait!"

He turned around to look at her one more time. The spots on his skin began to dance around again, like star clusters doing the tango. "Thank you!" he said once more. Then he was gone.

Roze sat alone, thinking about all the time they'd spent together. She didn't love him—not yet—but she was well on her way. And based on that reaction, she knew he had feelings for her, too. It wasn't just any woman that would make a man's freckles dance like that.

She would probably never see him again. She just hoped he'd make it home safely. After all, she didn't want him accidentally walking into one of her roommates' bedrooms.

Sofi's coffee was starting to get cold, but she still hadn't taken a sip. She was too busy talking to Dorox about the strange noises she heard last night. She clamped her mouth shut when Roze walked into the room.

"Morning," Roze mumbled. Her hair was a mess and she still wore her floral pajamas. Those cheery sunflowers—in addition to Roze's sheepish expression—told Sofi that Roze slept alone last night.

"Rough night?" Dorox asked. It was a pointless question. Everybody knew the answer.

"It started off perfectly," she said. "I made him a traditional dinner."

"I could tell," Sofi said. "There's still some fish paste in the sink."

"And things were starting to get romantic. But then he turned to me and said . . ."

"Morning, everyone!" Blan-Chett burst into the kitchen, her nightgown draped loosely around her. Like Roze, she had definite bedhead, but unlike Roze, she was . . . "I feel amazing!"

"Of course you do," Dorox said. "But Roze here was finishing her story."

"Well . . ." Roze said. "Holland—"

"Who cares about Roze's relationship drama? Not you. Not after I tell you what happened to me last night."

"Please, Blan-Chett. I was—"

"Trust me," Blan-Chett said. "This is good. So last night, I was minding my business, when a total stranger wandered into my room. It took me by surprise, but you know what I always tell myself. When opportunity knocks . . . So I just smiled at him and . . ."

Just as her story was getting good, Blan-Chett exploded from the inside-out.

Confetti.

A PELNODAN BOUNTY
James Fadeley

A Pelnodan Bounty
By James Fadeley

Grig stepped out the door, wincing as the light of Pelnoda's binary suns aroused fresh agony from his hangover. He shut his eyes and brought a mug of bujullo brew to his lips, slurping the steaming drink.

"Is that other for me?" Feminine harmonic tones emanated from the trimortal's throat.

Grig smiled and handed the mug in his other hand to Julla, who took it with three slender fingers. Trimortals did not smile with their mouths. But her large orb-like eyes seemed to light up as she accepted the drink and took a long slurp through the soft membrane that was her mouth.

Grig took a moment to survey the fields. Red ivy had swept over many of the fertilizer orbs—rocky, misshapen spheres that grew in a patch of leaves. When ground, the spheres became a potent powder that was mixed into soil to reduce the growth time of edible produce. Grig sighed. "It's the start of autumn solstice. We've got to clean these weeds off the crops or we'll miss the grinding and distribution."

Julla rolled one of her shoulders a few times and waved her serrated knife toward the fields. "I've been chopping away all morning while you were asleep!"

Grig raised a hand defensively at her irritation. "I'm sorry, Julla. Yesterday was the first drop of sactul juice I've had in months, and I only did it for my friend's wedding. I've become a bit of a lightweight."

Julla's head shook from side to side. "Oh, I almost forgot. Zax called while you were asleep. Said he needed to speak to you and would be here in a decoton."

Grig lifted his wrist, checking his chronometer. "Did Zax say what he wants?"

"No, but he sounded a little—" She paused. "Agitated, I guess."

Grig gazed at Julla as he took another sip. She stared at the desert horizon, the fingers of each of her hands wrapped about the warm mug. He felt his heart flutter as she reached up and tucked one of the long, hair-like tendrils over her shoulder. Grig always thought there was something sensual about the shape of the trimortal females, their curved hips, thin legs, and slight breasts not far in appearance from guests like himself.

But he would never voice such an opinion. Trimortal and guest relations happened on occasion, but they were often poorly received by families of both parties. The two species could never bare each other's children, and the importance of litters was a fundamental concept within trimortal society.

Grig turned away just as Julla glanced in his direction, slurping his caffeinated brew. "Well. You keep at it, and I'll feed the scaloks fast and join you. Gonna be a busy day."

They had worked for almost a decaton when Zax came down

the dirt path toward the ranch. The trimortal rode on the back of a scalok, the green-skinned creature stepping softly on the sand with its webbed feet. Grig saw him coming and waved him down, realizing the man was not alone.

Grig turned to Julla. "What time you got to pick up your litter today?"

Julla wiped a thin, clear layer of mucus from her forehead. It was what trimortals secreted instead of sweat when overheated. "Our caretaker is going to have them for the night. So not until tomorrow."

Grig nodded. He began treading dry dirt toward Zax and his guest, leaving boot marks behind him.

"Morning, Zax." Grig smiled at his old friend.

"Grig! Have you met my soon-to-be ex-girlfriend, Liness?" Zax indicated the mounted trimortal behind him. She was lithe, but younger than Zax by many years.

Grig coughed uncomfortably at such a remark. "I don't believe I've ha—"

"Save it," she replied.

The two arrivals dismounted their frog-like scaloks and tied them to the hitching post while Grig brooded on the nature of their conflict. Returning to his friend, Zax removed his hat. "Grig, I know you're a busy guest. So close to harvest. But I need your help. Can we talk inside?"

Grig glanced over his shoulder at Julla, who still hacked

away at a particularly bad patch of red ivy. "Julla, I'll be back in a few minutes. Just holler if you need anything."

Julla waved, whether in greeting or affirmation, Grig couldn't say. He led Liness and Zax across the porch and inside, indicating the simple kulkwood table and chairs. "Please have a seat. Would you like some bujullo brew?"

Liness' head bounced from left to right as she took a seat. Zax pulled out his chair, replying, "No. No, thank you."

Grig hesitated before walking toward the table. There were only two chairs and his friend and the surly lady occupied them, so he was content to stand. "How can I help you, Zax?"

"It's our caretaker, Tendar," Liness replied almost immediately. "Ze's gone missing."

"Your caretaker, not mine." Zax tapped his chest, which Grig knew for a hostile expression.

Instantly, Grig had an instinct about the problem. The caretakers were the third sex of the trimortals and equally necessary to have a litter.

"Ze's your friend!" Liness pointed a long, accusing finger at Zax. "You can't just ignore zer after all these years!"

Zax rose from his seat, the dark orbs of his eyes hidden behind dangerous slits. "And then you convince zer to fool around when you already had a clutch of fertile eggs. So you tell me right now, Liness. Did Tendar actually know, or did you convince zer to willingly become a parent?"

Liness went silent over that. Zax's limbs relaxed a bit, and he looked over at his host. "Grig, I'm sorry for the outburst. But, we came here because we need your help."

Grig crossed his arms and leaned back against a kitchen counter. "I'm listening."

"Liness and I have been looking for Tendar for two days. We went to the authorities, but they don't consider missing person cases unless there's a family tie," Zax said, reminding Grig of the law on the matter.

"It's not enough that Tendar is pregnant with your litter? Haven't you registered yet?" Grig asked.

Zax shook his head, the mess of tentacle "hair" surrounding his bald pate shaking. "Not without medical proof or legal registration."

Grig cast his eyes to Liness, and then back to Zax. "So you haven't registered?"

Liness snorted through the thin, tilted slits of her nostrils. "We came to an agreement."

"I help Liness find Tendar," Zax continued as he leaned back in the chair. "I don't have to register the litter as my own. No child support payments, but no visiting rights either."

Grig put a hand against his temple and rubbed it. Serious doubt nagged at him, old failures aching like an aged wound that never healed. He rubbed his face. "Zax, I really don't do bounty hunting work anymore. I've been out of that business for nearly two rotations. You know that. Gods, you know that better than anyone."

"But you were good at it!" Liness' fingers touched her shoulders, as trimortals did when supplicating. "Zax told me all about the work you two did. Bail jumpers, lost children, a few kidnappings."

"And the friends you made with the police." Zax put his palms on the table as he leaned forward. Grig gazed into Zax's eyes, the colour of a tropic ocean. "Look. I'll cancel out the rest of your debt. This harvest? Yours. All yours."

Grig rubbed the stubble on his chin as he considered it. There wasn't that much left of what Grig owed Zax. Perhaps some three thousand shells, the last of a small loan he borrowed to pay what he was short to buy the ranch. It would have taken at least two harvests to pay off the remainder.

"And you're sure the police can do nothing? At all?" Grig asked, hoping there was a way out.

"Like we said, we haven't registered, and we don't have a DNA sample," Liness replied. "If we had evidence of abduction, the police would get involved. But that's the only way."

But to say yes would be risking this harvest. Grig looked out the window at Julla, still hard at work in the field. She was a good farmhand who had worked for a few cycles. But she deserved better. A little time off, to be treated right . . .

At last, the counter-proposal crossed his mind. "I'll give you two days. If we find Tendar, we call the debt settled. But regardless of whether we find the caretaker or not, you have to help me with the harvest this year. Deal?"

"Deal!" Zax offered his hand. Grig shook it.

###

Grig slipped the poncho over his shirt, smoothing the red and yellow cloth over his chest. When he finished, he reached for his wide-brimmed hat on the dresser. At last, he opened the dresser. And sighed.

Under a glass pane on his dresser lay a number of newspaper clippings. His successes, his triumphs. The people he helped and saved. The Gramma twins, the case of actress Quindala Tark. Bringing in the murderer Clide Hudgin. The headlines praised him. The pictures were of people saved or brought to justice.

And there were his failures, too. Barl Vovik, captured by the police instead. Hank Raldal, Midj and Cul Din, all contraband runners, all of whom Grig caught only to see the justice system let them walk. The wanted poster for Toriz Scamboli; Grig nearly caught him, but he escaped. The reward for that scum Scamboli still lay unclaimed to this day. The Wyndiq bounty, stolen by Folix Grendin.

Grig winced in guilt, averting his eyes from the picture of the smiling, victorious bounty hunter.

Beside the clippings, the old tools of his trade lay upon his belt and holster. He slipped the lizard-skin belt out and slipped it through the loops of his pants, checking to make sure everything he'd need was in the pockets. Then he reached into the drawer and rolled a piece of cloth aside, pausing to gingerly stare at the missing piece.

"After this is over," Grig said to it. "I hope I can leave you to rust."

Grig picked up his laser revolver. He clicked the chamber open and checked the bio-batteries. Five the cells looked good, their indicators green. But the sixth flashed red, the energy-producing bacteria long since dead. Grig sighed and removed the dead battery, setting it aside to be opened, cleaned, and recultured later. He found a fresh cell near the corner of the dresser drawer and slid it home before closing the chamber and holstering the weapon.

Nemiah, Grig's scalok, shook his long neck and snorted through the short snout. He padded awkwardly, his webbed feet moving more laterally than forward. Grig sighed and leaned forward, whispering into the scalok's stubby ear to soothe it.

"What's wrong with him?" Zax asked. He came up alongside Grig as the trio trotted toward town.

"I haven't ridden him lately. They tend to regress to old instincts without their riders," Grig said as he leaned back in his saddle. Nemiah corrected his motions and began to move his legs in a smoother, more locomotive motion that wasted less energy. Grig grinned. "Maybe if you weren't such a city-slicker, you'd know that."

Zax's eyes rolled into amused, arching slits. "You funny guest. I shoot you last."

Grig burst into laughter at Zax's phony accent. "Gods, what flick was that from? It's been ages."

"I don't even remember." Zax scratched his chin. "It's been so long since we hung out. Why did we stop?"

"I owed you money," Grig said sombrely. "It wouldn't have been right blowing shells left and right on drinks and good times. Yesterday was the first drink I've had in months, only because I was at a friend's wedding. Paying you back came first."

Zax grew solemn. "I've lost a few friends to debts before. That's usually because they wouldn't pay them back, too dishonest. I never even considered I'd miss a friend because they *were* honest."

They rode in silence for a while, Liness not far behind. Slowly, a grin spread across Grig's stubbly face. "Well, after all this is over, I guess we could get a drink."

"Now that's the best idea I've heard in forever." Zax sat up in the saddle, the life back in his eyes and his spirits improved.

Grig snuck a glance over his shoulder at Liness, who trailed them at a comfortable distance. "So how'd all this happen, anyway? She's a young 'un for you, old man."

Zax snorted. "Oh, I think I can blame this one on you. You weren't around to stop me from my usual bad ideas. So one night I hit the town by my lonesome and ran into a friend of mine whose ventures paid off handsome. He introduces me to one of his lady friends. Liness."

"You always were a genius when it came to making a buck. So I never understood your horrible luck with women," Grig replied, winking.

"Don't I know it?" Zax sighed. "So Liness and I hit it off. But I made it clear to her early on that I already had two litters and finally finished supporting them. I was not going to have a third. Especially after . . . after Ilin died."

Grig's smile dropped, and he tipped his brim respectfully. Of his ten children, Zax had six daughters and three caretakers. Ilin was the only son, as males made up only a fifth of the trimortal population. It had been a blow to Zax, and Grig had been there through it.

Zax said nothing for a bit, but wiped at his nostrils. "Anyway. So we're together for a few months. Eventually, she gets to meet my friends. Just sort of pops up when they're coming over. That's how she met Tendar."

Grig glanced over his shoulder again, but Liness seemed to just watch the dusty horizon. He looked back at Zax.

"A few months later, Tendar comes to me and tells me ze's pregnant. I'm happy for zer and ask who the mother and father are. That's when ze panics and just leaves. And I knew right away who was responsible." Zax's face seemed to cringe up like a dried piece of fruit, and he sneered at Liness.

Grig sighed and rubbed his forehead. Among trimortals, there were a few different family arrangements and reproduction tactics. In the most common method, a female trimortal held a fertilized clutch of eggs for a month, and no more. She had to transfer them to a caretaker through sexual contact in order for them to finish growing.

In this case, however, it was done without Zax's knowledge or consent. To the guests, it was a very strange form of cuckoldry unique to the trimortals. Grig's race only had two sexes, and his own interactions with women often started cordially and ended strained. Yet somehow, Grig was not envious.

The town of Etuul neared.

Crystals chimed as Zax flipped through his key ring. He found one and put it against the lock. A weak laser passed through it and diffused into the appropriate pattern that the system identified and accepted. Slides drew back and the door to Tendar's home opened.

"We've been here," Liness said. "How is this going to help us?"

"With all due respect, I need to go over what you've done so far in case you've missed anything." Grig stepped in and something flew along the floor as he kicked it. He glanced down to try and see what it was, then felt the wall for a light switch.

When he found it, he noticed an immaculately kept room of simple furnishings. The object he had kicked was a collection of piling mail that had been slid under the door. They stepped in, and Grig scooped up the letters. "These look fresh."

Zax walked to the communicator console, a boxy device that glittered with glowing lights. He pressed a button, and a moment later, a voice began.

"Tendar Vatari, this is Mindus Olvic. I'm calling you again and urging you to consider my client's offer. We were hoping you would at least have a formal meeting with us. You have our contact info, so we hope to hear from you. Thank you."

The message ended. Zax checked the records on the communicator's digital display. "That call came in last night, and all previous records have been deleted. Guess Olvic didn't get the news."

Liness scratched her hands. "I know that name."

Grig and Zax looked at her.

"He's a lawyer. High-class, too. I met him at a few parties and he only accepts very, very high-end clients who can afford him."

Zax rubbed his jaw. "So Tendar had something of value to Olvic's client?"

"Maybe there's something about Tendar neither of you knew," Grig said as he flipped through the mail. One particular piece caught his eye, as it was nothing but a transparent slip with an address on the top right corner. "Zax, Liness, do either of you know whether Tendar kept records of contacts or bills?"

Zax opened a drawer beside the communicator. "Right here.

Got something?"

"Maybe. But Liness, you know this Mindus Olvic. Maybe you should go and break the news to him. Perhaps he'll have some details about where Tendar is." Grig's fingers sifted through the slates until he withdrew one and matched the company on the letter to the address on the bill.

"You found something?" Zax asked.

Grig put the transparent slip against the slate. It was a holographic lock, designed to maintain the privacy of mail. A moment later, the key met the cypher, and words appeared on the letter. Grig read it aloud. "Dear Mistern Vatari, we regret that you missed your most recent appointment. We hope all is well and that you reschedule a meeting with foetal physician Sari Mitoll at your soonest convenience. Consider it a matter of urgency, given your condition."

Liness shook her head. "Zax . . . that's it."

The men looked at the female trimortal.

"Tendar must be having a triple." Liness tapped her fingers together lightly.

When trimortals gave birth, it was in litters of five. Hence, litters including at least three males were considered incredibly fortunate, and trimortal customs rained good fortune and care down on the parents. Once or twice every century, there were even a few quads of four males. That was even more celebrated.

"I seriously hope that's not true, Liness." Grig said. "In all my years of bounty work, I only ever got one case involving a blessed birth."

Zax crossed his arms and looked away. Liness read into Zax's body language and prodded on. "What happened?"

Grig rubbed his forehead, his hat bobbing as his wrist touched the tip. "It . . . it went poorly. I was hot on the trail of the trimortal who kidnapped the three sons. He was trying to flee to the other side of the planet. I caught up with him at the transportation hub, but so did—" Grig paused at the name. "—my rival, Folix Grendin. Anyway, rather than get caught, he took the sons and jumped onto the tracks instead. None of them survived the train."

Liness gasped. "The Hrinsan kidnapping! I was barely past my teens when that happened!"

"Folix!" Zax said. "I always wondered what happened to him."

Grig drew his mouth into a line and nodded. "My career was finished after that. I mean, the police found nothing wrong with what I did, and I got to keep my bounty hunting license. But no one would hire me, not after what happened. Everyone blamed me, regardless of what the law said. So I took out a loan from Zax and started farming."

"It's not like it was your fault," Zax said. "You couldn't have stopped him."

"It doesn't matter. That isn't my life anymore. And this is more a favour for a friend than me getting back into the job again."

Grig looked at Liness. "Where is Olvic's office?"

"In Cujjip."

"Ugh, that trip's about two decatons away. We should just call," Zax said as he reached for the communicator.

Grig gently put his gloved hand on Zax's arm, stopping him. Zax glanced at Grig, who was staring out the window, contemplating.

"Change of thinking. We know that Olvic, or rather his client, wants something from Tendar. If we call, we give away that someone else is looking for Tendar."

"So what do we do?" Liness asked.

Grig glanced at the address on the slate. "Liness, you and I are going to find this physician first. Zax, we're reacting to recent developments. I need you to stay here and go through all the contacts, bills, and letters. I haven't had time to read any of it, so just look for anything you might have missed. Don't answer the communicator until you hear my voice leave a message."

"You got it." Zax opened the drawers and began sorting through everything. "Be careful out there."

Nemiah snarled at Liness' scalok, narrowing his square-pupil eyes at the beast. Grig pulled the reins of his ride, parting the two scaloks as they sauntered toward Etuul's medical district.

"Looks like your scalok is another person who doesn't like

me very much." Liness sighed.

Grig lowered his hat, avoiding eye contact. He knew that Liness was aiming for a pity angle to pull him to her side.

"I'm so envious of you guests," she said. "There are just two sexes. Man and woman. All your kind has to do is have a few drinks and one night of fun and a child comes of it. We trimortals are just biologically complex like that."

"It's not that simple," Grig replied. "In all my life, I've only known one girl who would have settled down with me. But I waited. And waited and waited, trying to scrap together a good life before I asked her. By the time I was anywhere near ready, she moved home and married someone else. They just had their first kid."

Liness stared ahead as she spoke. "You ever hear of the gender rights strike almost three hundred rotations ago?"

Grig shook his head.

"We trimortals don't like to talk about it, seeing as you guests only just arrived a few decades after it was over. Even my parents waited until I was an adult. But trimortal society was different back then. The females, being half the population, ruled and dictated that every female should have a chance to reproduce. The males and caretakers were made to go along with it.

"Then they fought back. They demanded rights. Stronger property rights, more political rights. And to make it happen, the majority of males refused to engage in sex. But even though there were males who did fertilize the eggs, many caretakers sided with the males, too."

Liness turned her doughy eyes toward Grig. "It went on for almost two decades like this. And our population severely dropped. Not by death, but by a refusal to create life."

"So you gave in," Grig said.

Liness nodded. "We gave the males and even a few caretakers guaranteed representation in the councils. We strengthened their property rights. Eventually, as they began to accumulate wealth, we wrote rules to strengthen the roles of females again, like child support. But it's no longer a right for a female to have children anymore."

Grig felt uncomfortable. The dynamic between male and female guests was tough, but trimortals were a whole new level of strange. He knew that the limited number of males and caretakers made the females extremely competitive. But the history lesson changed everything. They had made reproduction a right, and the resulting struggle nearly destroyed them for it, completely altering the trimortal society.

"Could you imagine what—"

"Stop," Grig said with a growl in his throat. "Just stop. I'm not your therapist. You want me to understand your position? I do. But there's a difference between grasping a situation and caring. I bet you made the same mistake with Zax, assuming that he wanted what you wanted, just because he should understand your pain."

Liness glared at Grig with slant features. "How dare you."

"I barely *met you* and you're ranting at me." Grig couldn't believe it, but he snarled, the anger bubbling up in him. "You show up at my house, having pestered my friend with a problem that *you* created. *You*. Now you're telling me about some ugly aspect of your people's history as though there is some ideal in there that has been forgotten.

"Guess what, lady? You're *getting* everything you want. You lie to people, and they'll want nothing to do with you. And yet despite this, Tendar is still having your kids. And I got roped into finding them for you. Honestly, if it were anyone but Zax, I would have turned them down." He turned narrowed eyes on her. "And it's not too late for me to walk away from this. So do me a favour, and just shut up until the job is done."

Their scaloks treaded through Etuul. Grig contemplated everything he had said and knew he'd lashed out because of what Liness had done to his friend. Even after all this time apart, he still cared about Zax. Grig wondered whether he would feel horrible about what he had said to Liness when his anger abated.

But when it did, he felt right as rain.

"I'm sorry," the receptionist said in a tone that suggested she wasn't. "Physician Sari Mitoll is busy, and to be blunt, I'm not certain what business a guest would have with a trimortal foetal specialist."

Grig bit his tongue to keep from yelling at the caretaker

seated behind the desk. Physically, the receptionist was like most caretakers. Wide-bellied, shorter than male or female trimortals, with stout legs and reptilian skin on the back and behind the arms. But unlike most caretakers, this one was snobby and rude.

Grig raised a hand toward Liness. "I'm a family friend, and we have a bit of an emergency. Liness here, she has a clutch of fertile eggs, and a caretaker ready to receive. But the male died and we're concerned about the genetic health of the eggs. Please, we haven't much time before her body rejects them! Some of these tests take days we barely have!"

The caretaker's features lightened, and ze got up. "Have a seat, and I'll see if the physician is available."

Liness glanced at Grig once the receptionist was out of earshot. "Clever."

He said nothing but settled down on a chair, propping his boots on a coffee table.

"Physician Mitoll can see you now," the receptionist said as ze returned. "Down the hall, second door on the left."

"Much obliged." Grig got up and strolled down the hall with Liness behind him. As they approached, the door slid to the side, and the two of them entered an examination room.

Sari Mitoll was a tall female, taller than either of the two of them. Her tendrils of "hair" were gathered into a long ponytail that reached the small of her back. She was slipping gloves on her long fingers.

"Faenin tells me you have a bit of an emergency on your hands?" Mitoll's voice seemed to sing as she spoke. "Please, miss, have a seat."

Liness stepped up to a bench and did so. "We apologize for this."

"I understand your circumstances all too well. I'm just glad you have a caretaker ready under these unfortunate conditions." Mitoll rolled a stool toward Liness.

"Actually, it's the caretaker we want to speak to you about," Grig said. When Mitoll gave him a wide-eyed look he couldn't read, he explained. "Zer name's Tendar. Ze's gone missing and you were zer physician."

Mitoll's eyes narrowed as she realized she had been deceived. She kicked back in her stool, rolling across the tile floors. "Abuse of a physician's attention during work hours is a serious offence. If there was someone else with a dire problem, you would be risking her life."

"We do have an emergency," Liness said.

Mitoll crossed her arms over her chest. "Regardless, Tendar is a patient, and I can't just give away—"

"Tendar has been missing for a few days," Grig blurted out. He watched Mitoll for the faintest body language. Then he saw it, a light quiver of one of her hair tendrils. "And we know that ze is pregnant. We need to find zer."

Mitoll said nothing for a moment, and then turned her head

near horizontal, the trimortal equivalent of a shrug. "So go tell the police. I'm sure they'd love to hear how you wasted a physician's time."

"I could talk to the police. And they'll listen to me. And then they'll requisition your records and ask a lot of questions." It was a bluff. But Grig kept his face calm.

Mitoll's brow popped up. Grig suppressed a smirk.

"The difference between telling me and telling the police is that my interest begins and ends with Tendar. Whatever they find—"

"Stop." Mitoll shuddered. "Stop. Tendar was here."

"And?" Grig asked.

"Ze was pregnant. And it was big. Huge news, even. But I don't know anything about Tendar disappearing. Honestly."

"A triple?" Liness asked, almost hopeful.

Mitoll turned to look at Liness, but remained silent.

Grig waited. "So why are you afraid of the police?"

"I was selling patient information. Certain parties, finding out who the father and the mother are can gain leverage in the courts, or be used against them otherwise. My dealings were always kept at arm's length through a data broker."

"Sari Mitoll. We need to know who that person—"

The window exploded inward.

Grig dropped and hid behind a counter, drawing his laser

revolver instinctively. Liness screamed and rolled off the bench to cover. Grig glanced at the broken window, cracked around a hole with smouldering edges.

Gurgling brought Grig's attention to the floor, where Mitoll lay. Her neck was pierced from behind, blue blood pumping out. She stared at him with wide eyes until the bloody bubbles stopped growing from her jugular and she lay still.

"Liness, you alive? Unhurt?"

She glanced up, hiding behind the bench. "I—I think so . . ."

"Call the police!" Grig vaulted over the pool of blood, taking a few steps before throwing himself through the still-heated window.

Glass shards clattered against the patio outside as he crashed and rolled through, his poncho and hat protecting him from cuts. As he rolled onto his knee, Grig spotted a man dashing into an alley. In the brief instant he saw his face, Grig knew there was something familiar about him. He took off after the murderer.

The suspect, a guest like Grig, wore a duster. Grig could see the bulge of what he guessed was the murderer's weapon. The man suddenly stopped and twisted around to face his pursuer. Grig had guessed right.

He barely ducked as the plasma spreader sent a superheated pulse his way. Even without being touched, the plasma seared his skin, though his tipped hat shielded his eyes from the worst of the light. As he dropped, Grig fired blindly.

The man screamed as he went down. Grig blinked purple

spots out of his eyes as he scrambled up. He dashed forward and kicked the spreader away from the murderer's grasp, holding his revolver to the guest's face.

The man cradled his wounded leg with both hands, a black mark where the laser shot penetrated his hamstring. Then he glanced up at Grig and groaned. "Ah, fuck me."

"Hello, Midj." Grig grinned.

Grig winced as he probed his back with a finger. The plasma shot had missed any direct hit, but his shoulder was effectively sunburned from just being close to it. If it wasn't for the thickness of his poncho, he would more than likely have a few blisters.

"You really, really lucked out," Order Keeper Nasa said. "Not many people survive close encounters with plasma spreaders."

"I know," Grig said and sighed. Earlier, he had seen the glowing spot where the blast had hit the dirt road. Only then had he realized how close he had come to death and felt the effects of aftershock. "I can't believe I caught him after all this time."

Midj had been put in an isolation cell. Nasa had a medic look at Grig's shoulder and back while taking his statement. The Etuul police had not forgotten Grig's good reputation.

"So, what happens now?" Grig asked.

"Now we have your statement and we're taking Liness'. We will do pattern matching against the weapon. Between a matching ionic signature of the weapon blast and two surviving eye witnesses, we're likely to have an airtight case against Midj. Based on your witness reports alone, we're probably going to make an arrest," Nasa replied. She brushed her tendril hair over a shoulder as she leaned back in her chair.

"I should probably mention. Liness and I are partners on a missing persons case. Physician Mitoll was somehow connected."

"If it's missing persons . . ."

Grig tilted his head from side to side. "This is a caretaker who hasn't registered a family yet. And there's no proof of abduction. Yet."

Nasa reached for a steaming mug of bujullo brew. "So, what would you like me to do?"

Grig thought it over for a moment, an idea forming. "I have a request that might be considered extra-legal. I need you to . . . charge him with the crime and get the name of his lawyer. Get me that name before you contact them."

Nasa slurped the mug before replying. "There's nothing extra-legal about that."

"If this person is who I think it is, then I need you to delay communicating them for a few decatons while I go interview them. If it isn't my guy, then get Midj his representation."

Nasa tilted her head horizontally. "I can do it, but you'll only have four decatons before we give him a public defender, who will gladly contact his desired lawyer anyway."

"That's fine. The name is all that matters."

Nasa nodded and got up, setting her mug down. "I guess we'll just say we forgot between the crimes surges today. A murder, several petty robberies, and even *arson* of all things. Swear, it must be that comet making everyone acting all cra—"

Grig's brow perked. "Where was the arson?"

Liness and Grig raced their scaloks back to Tendar's apartment.

They arrived to find the blackened frame of the triplet, a huge pile of debris and charred ashes rested underneath. A pillar of black smoke reached toward the blue heavens, rising well above the squat buildings of Etuul. Firefighters, guests and trimortals alike, struggled to douse the last flames with hand-pumped cable and buckets. They were succeeding, but the damage was done.

Grig looked about amongst the crowds of guests and trimortals before crying out, "Zax! . . . Zax, where are you?"

"Here!" The balding trimortal appeared from the crowd, waving to them.

Grig got off of Nemiah and took the reins, walking toward Zax. "Are you alright?"

"Just. I got out in time and managed to save all the files from Tendar's apartment."

"What happened, though?"

Zax raised his arms in a gesture not unlike a shrug. "I

smelled smoke. Then the alarms went off. I grabbed everything and ran out. Lots of people were running, but one looked like he was actually escaping from it all."

"But he got away?" Liness asked.

"Afraid so. The police are looking for him now."

Grig sighed in relief. "Just glad you're alright, Zax. I got to make a call."

"There's a public communicator right over there." He pointed a finger to a booth not a city block away.

Grig walked Nemiah to a hitching post and tied the scalok up before heading to the booth. He waited a moment while a caretaker finished making a call before he finally got a chance, then he dialled the Etuul police precinct. It took the operator a few moments to connect him.

"Everything okay, Grig?"

"Yeah, Nasa, my friend is fine. But I've no doubt that this arson was connected to the missing caretaker."

There was a pause. "Grig, this is enough circumstantial evidence to involve us in the disappearance."

"I'm hot on the trail, Nasa. Someone's covering their tracks and time is of the essence. If I come in now to bring the police up to speed, we'll lose valuable decatons we probably don't have."

"I got the name of the lawyer. But the captain is going to want to get involved. You need to scratch our back."

Grig turned and saw Liness and Zax watching him outside. "Alright, I got an idea. You give me the name of the lawyer, and I'll send Liness to make the official report with everything we've found. She'll bring you up to speed while I chase down any new leads."

"Sounds like a deal. The name of Midj's attorney is Mindus Olvic. We haven't contacted him yet, but we looked up his office in—"

"Cujjip. Nasa, that's who I thought it would be. Can you hold his call?"

"You've got three and a half decatons to do what you're going to do. Hurry, Grig."

"I will. I'm sending Liness over now. Will contact you soon."

The communicator cut off. Grig opened the booth door and spoke. "Liness, I need you to go back to the police precinct. They consider Mitoll's murder and the arson to be evidence enough to get involved. Zax, we're going to Cujjip."

"But you don't know whether Tendar went there or not!" Liness waved her arms in protest.

"Actually, ze might have," Zax replied. He took a piece of paper from the small collection under his arm. "You were right, Grig. When I first looked at Tendar's paperwork, I forgot that there are ways, low-tech ways, of preserving privacy other than the encryption slates."

Grig tilted his head and took the paper. Looking at it, he

smiled and returned to the booth. He dialled the company's identification number.

"Cotana Services. How may I help you?" A voice came from the other end.

"Hello. My name is Grig, and I'm in service to the police of Etuul. I have a receipt number here with no indication of the purchased good or service. I need to know what that was."

"Ready."

"E-78842."

"The customer's name is . . . Tendar Vitari?"

"Tendar Vitari is currently missing, and our precinct is charged with finding zer."

"I'm sorry to hear that and wish you the best of luck, sir. Anyway, the receipt was for a line hauler passenger's ticket."

"Where to?" Grig asked. He smiled at Zax and Liness as the operator confirmed the name. Liness put her hands together hopefully.

###

"You sound like you knew that guy!" Zax spoke over the smacking gallop of the scaloks. The guest and trimortal persevered through the desert between Etuul and Cujjip. In the distance, they saw the Verjinya mountain ranges, where Pelnoda's suns dipped, the sky turning a brilliant shade of orange and pink. And along the way, Grig filled Zax in on the gritty details of his near lethal encounter.

"Kind of," Grig replied. "His name is Midj. I knew him as muscle working for Viktir Benjon. About two rotations ago, I chased his bounty after he strong armed transports with gug'na, the key ingredient in a special stimulant unique to Xinkertun."

"What happened? Did he get away?"

"I caught him! But when he went to trial, critical evidence disappeared from the police headquarters there! Xinkertun police are corrupt as gangrene. Worst day of my life, then Hrinsan happened."

"It's easy, then! We just find Midj's boss, Viktir Benjon!"

"No, it isn't."

"Why not?"

"Viktir Benjon died half a rotation ago. Heard the whole story from an Order Keeper friend. You see, Viktir was planning a robbery against his rival, Walpor. Rumour goes that Viktir thought Walpor had contraband goods in one of the store fronts Walpor used for credit laundering. Walpor got tipped off, so he hid the goods and called the cops on Viktir's gang as they broke into the store. In the shoot-out that followed, Viktir was killed."

"This Walpor sounds like a clever bastard!"

"More than clever. After it was over, Walpor had his insurance take care of the damage. Then, with their leader dead and half of them in lockup, Walpor took over Viktir's territory almost overnight."

"So you think Walpor impressed Viktir's men into service? Including Midj?"

Grig said nothing for a moment. He was lying to his friend. The story hadn't come from an officer of the law. Grig knew, from personal experience, that Walpor was half business and half family, a shrewd strategist more inclined toward profits than bloodletting. Midj was the kind of sadistic goon Walpor had little use for. "We'll find out soon enough."

On they rode, and soon they saw a monument of the past: a mountain of rusted metal that had long since embedded itself in the soil of Pelnoda. Centuries ago, it was one of three ships that crashed upon the world, bringing with it thousands of cryogenically preserved passengers.

The trimortals had rushed there, finding a bewildered and scared people who did not speak their language, nor remembered anything about their own history at all. The ships contained no flight data to speak of, and the first generation of guests showed signs of mind tampering and memory wiping. Except for their language and basic mannerisms, precious little evidence suggested where they had come from. Only that the ships had been traveling for centuries before arriving on Pelnoda.

The trimortals ended up giving many of the guests a special augmentation, allowing them to hear and understand the trimortal's high pitched voices, whereas the trimortals could understand the words of the guests well enough. Overtime, the guests had integrated so thoroughly with the trimortals that few of them even spoke their original language.

"I forgot this was here," Zax said as his head popped up and down in an excited fashion.

Grig wondered about the ship. Like every other guest, he knew nothing about where they had come from. Whether it had been some other species who had banished the guests or higher-ranking guests who cast them into space. Exile was not an unknown punishment in certain trimortal communities. Had Grig's ancestors been criminals themselves?

Grig shook his head. "Let's just stay focused. We have a lawyer to catch."

Cujjip. It had grown far larger than Etuul. But increased population had brought urban growth pains. The town was rife with run-down buildings, ageing streets, and faded graffiti. In the distance, Grig made out smokestacks that output pillars of grey smoke into the air. And scalok dung went dry and uncollected in the streets.

The two friends galloped down the streets, stopping before a decrepit old office building. Zax studied the scripture above the doorway before declaring, "This is it."

"You're sure?" Grig asked.

Zax nodded. "I'm not sure how I feel about leaving our scaloks here."

"Nemiah is too untrusting to let just anyone take him. And he'll protect your ride." Grig smiled. The scalok would fight almost anyone who tried to take him, such was his mount's temper. It had taken Grig forever to earn Nemiah's trust, but it had been worth it.

"Zax, whatever happens, let me do all the talking. But do as I say at all times."

"You got it." Zax flashed an open hand toward Grig.

The two hitched their scaloks against a lamppost before entering the building's lobby. Grig drew his laser revolver and started to climb the stairs, his boots clumping every step of the way. He paused at a rusted door and checked under his poncho, ensuring he had the right "credentials" before knocking.

The door slid slightly open. "Yes?"

"Mindus Olvic?" Grig asked.

"My advertisement says to call for services."

"Olvic, you are under arrest for conspiracy to commit murder."

"What!" The door flew open. A male trimortal stood there, bald with no tendrils off the crown of his scaly head. He was dressed in formal, if faded, black robes that were fashionable among legal professionals perhaps a decade before. "I demand to see your identification."

Grig lifted a metal badge from behind his poncho. The scripture around it read "Order Keeper of Etuul."

"Two hours ago, physician Sari Mitoll was killed in her practice." It was standard legal procedure to immediately inform an arrested suspect of the crime and the basic manner of which evidence led to their incarceration. "She was killed by an assassin named Midj, who has named you as the contract provider."

"That's prepost—"

"Sir." Grig applied some force to his voice, raising but not pointing his weapon. "I *insist* you cooperate. Given the serious nature of this crime, I am authorized to use stern methods to bring you into the precinct."

A trickle of mucus began to run down Olvic's face, forming in the top of his eyes and flowing down. Olvic stood still for a moment before raising two thin wrists.

Grig put his badge back in his poncho and took out a pair of wrist cuffs that he gave to his partner. "Deputy Zax, please place the suspect in custody."

Zax took the metal restraints before he ordered, "On your knees."

Olvic was slow to obey, but once he knelt, Zax bound one of his wrists. Zax slipped behind the lawyer and pulled both wrists behind Olvic's back, binding him entirely. He then took Olvic by the shoulders and made him stand, leading the lawyer into his office. Grig followed them in and slid the door shut.

There was no receptionist, at least not one that was working. Nor was there a maid or any kind of cleaning service. A mouldy smell spilled from the wash closet. Stacks of printed slates stood everywhere, while the communicator blinked with several ignored messages. A bottle of Vunji rested on a desk next to an empty glass.

If it had been almost any other liquor, Grig might have had a glass then and there. But Vunji was one of the few trimortal alcohols that were actually dangerous to guests.

"Look," Olvic said. "Whatever Midj told you, I can cut you a way better deal."

Grig reached up and tipped his hat to hide his smile.

"Truly. I'm just the middle man. The boss comes to me and informs me when there's a job going on, the name to expect, and orders me to wait for a call and react if need be."

Grig managed to straighten his face and glanced at Zax curiously before back to Olvic.

"Killing a physician is a very serious offence," Grig replied. "Especially when contracted hits are involved. The charge often merits cryocution. Suspect Midj was quick to give you up."

Olvic shuttered. Cryocution was execution by flash freezing the prisoner, leaving vital organs to thaw and decompose over time. The method was cheaper than incarceration. The victim felt no pain and the process took decades, leaving open the possibility of repeal. But there were many unsettling stories of both guests and trimortals thawing after years, returning to society with deteriorated minds. Olvic's reaction was no surprise.

"No!" The lawyer screamed. "Tavist! It was Tavist who ordered the hit on Mitoll!"

Grig tilted his head almost horizontally, and it wasn't an act. "Tavist is nobody. A low-level enforcer who lost bad when Viktir

Benjon was slain in Xinkertun. Try harder, Olvic."

"I swear!" Olvic was panting hard, the mucus dripping off his chin. "Look, look. You know Viktir was killed right?"

"Every officer on this side of Pelnoda remembers that."

"Right. So Viktir got killed. Tavist took his gang and hid. They did odd jobs. Stayed afloat. I met them when one of his thugs got smacked up by the police after a botched robbery. I insisted I was just a family lawyer, but they flashed some heavy shells and I did what I could."

Grig scratched his chin. "Go on."

"So I get his friend off with a month. Tavist takes me out to celebrate and I get a little drunk. I tell him that I run a little . . . over-legal business on the side." Olvic swayed from side to side. "Sometimes, people want the wrong guy named as father or mother for a litter. So I forge up some DNA tests and cash in on a large bonus once child support payments come through."

Olvic flinched defensively.

"Deputy Zax," Grig interrupted. "Please lower your raised fist."

Zax gave Grig a contemptuous look before lowering what would have been a harsh punch. Olvic took a step away from Zax, but continued.

"To stay on top of my job, I need to know about pregnancies of potentially big clients. I pay out physicians. Sari Mitoll was on the cut. But a week ago, she came to me with something huge. A caretaker with a litter of four formed boys."

Zax and Grig gasped.

"Scalokshit!" Zax shouted.

"Pelnoda's own truth!" Olvic twisted to get a good look at Zax. "A jackpot of sons. So I tell Tavist about it. And he gets really interested. He orders me to call and lure Tendar to Cujjip."

Grig paused. A nasty feeling bubbled in his stomach as he thought about what Olvic had said. "Is the pregnant caretaker here? With Tavist?"

"Yes, and yes. They only told me this morning but they grabbed zer when ze was getting off the train a couple of days ago. I promise, I'll lead you to them. I didn't mean for this to happen, I swear I didn't." Olvic's mucus had become a thin stream that leaked off his chin and dotted all over his robes. Grig didn't know what face he must have been making to scare the lawyer so, but he felt cold.

"Deputy Zax, please escort the suspect downstairs, unharmed, and wait for me. Olvic, you will take us to Tavist and we will stop this. Tonight."

Zax grabbed Olvic by the shoulders and forced him toward the door. Zax glanced back, seeing Grig turn the communicator toward himself. But Grig waited until Zax had left before making the call.

"Speak of Tavist's plan, Olvic." Zax commanded as he and Grig rode their scaloks. Olvic walked with a rope attached to his restraints, connected to Zax's saddle. "It's not just kidnapping, is it?"

Olvic hesitated. "A black physician. They wanted to rewrite the male's contribution of the children to make Tavist the biological father."

An uncomfortable silence passed over them. There was only one crime that was above murder, an act called parental theft. In the past, it primarily consisted of stealing the children. But modern techniques went so far as to completely rewrite the DNA. While trimortal law permitted the study of genetics as a means to prepare for future health concerns, it strictly forbade rewriting DNA for any reason.

Still mounted on the scalok, Zax kicked the back of Olvic's head. The lawyer tumbled and dropped. Zax's eyes slanted as his body turned a shade red. "How low can you *get*?"

Grig had seen the results of such attempts before. A few young faces flashed before his eyes. Hrinsan. The kidnapped children who fell to their deaths. The tumours that disfigured them. The stunted limbs. *It was horrible enough that they died,* he thought.

Olvic managed to get up, but Zax kicked him again.

"Zax," Grig said. The trimortal glanced at his friend, eyes wide with anger. But Grig stared him down, until Zax turned away, trembling with disgust.

"You can't link me to what Tavist is doing," Olvic said, but Grig could hear the pleading in his voice.

Grig glanced down at the lawyer. "How far is it?"

"It's . . . it's right there." Olvic tilted his head toward a warehouse made of circular bricks with plaster between the grooves.

Grig dismounted and looked at Zax. "Stay here and watch over him."

"Shouldn't we call for backup?" Zax asked.

Grig couldn't help but smile as Zax suggested the term "backup" over "the police," the trimortal maintaining the façade of being an officer. But then he frowned as he handed Zax the reins. "I already did back at the office."

Zax nodded. Grig consoled himself that it wasn't a lie, just not the intended truth.

Grig crept toward the building, staying away from windows. There were neither outdoor lights nor sounds from the building, but as Grig rounded the warehouse, he saw a thin beam beneath a large door. Grig drew his laser revolver and slipped close.

He wondered whether it could be a trap, but he shook off the feeling. They had caught Olvic too swiftly for such a possibility. Grig swallowed, put a hand on the handle, and slid the door open.

The light came from a dim bulb at the base of a staircase. Grig descended as softly as he could walk in his boots. And with every step, he could hear the sound of whimpering and pleading.

At the bottom, he found an arch that lead to a dimly lit room filled with boxes. Grig advanced, careful not to make a noise. Around the corner of a few boxes, he saw them.

There were seven, a mix of guests and trimortals. Five of them merely watched, wearing an assortment of fine clothing and holstered weapons with that rough look of scars and piercings only Cujjip gangsters could possess. Amongst them, Grig recognized Tavist. The trimortal had grown obese, his limbs becoming very wide as male trimortal physiology stored fat closest to where it would be demanded.

The other two were something out of a horror picture. An intense lamp on the ceiling illuminated a clearly pregnant caretaker strapped to a table, struggling against zer restraints. Zer blue eyes narrowed in fear, flinching protectively from another trimortal. The other figure stood beside zer, wearing a grey jumpsuit and physician's apron, readying a strange assortment of tools connected to spidery metal arms.

Grig couldn't be sure the caretaker was Tendar. And it didn't matter. He levelled his revolver over his other wrist as he stepped forward. He shot the black physician through the neck.

The trimortal over the caretaker toppled over, the wound instantly cauterized by the laser blast's heat. He crashed to his back, dead on the cement floor.

The gangsters reached for their weapons and drew. But as they did, Grig dove for cover behind the table where the caretaker was held.

"Hold fire, you idiots!" Tavist commanded as the gangsters were levelling their firearms at Grig. "You'll hit my prize!"

Grig thought about firing on them. Tavist wouldn't dare risk the caretaker in some reckless gunfight. One of Tavist's men had the sense to try and go around the table, but Grig stood up just enough to fire a warning shot at the man, singing the guest goon's cheek as he did.

"Stay *back*, Tavist!" Grig screamed as his free hand worried at one of the caretaker's restraints, his eyes trained on Tavist's men. In a quieter voice, "Are you Tendar?"

"Yeheheheyes." Tendar said as one of zer restraints came loose. The caretaker reached over zer huge belly and began to undo the other wrist clasp. "Thank you!"

Tavist put a hand on one of his goon's shoulders and whispered something in her ear. The female trimortal ran off behind her boss. Grig knew she was going to seal the exits.

"So who are you, anyway?" Tavist asked. "I mean, aside from dead. Just want to know whose family to kill after I get my prize back."

"Yeah, you're a *real* family man, aren't you, Tavist?" Grig couldn't help the smile that crept over his face. "Can't start your own, so you try and steal another person's kids!"

Tavist laughed, his arms jiggling. "Let me guess. Grig, right? That bounty hunter that got those kids killed back in Hrinsan? If it's any consolation, I promise you it won't happen again this time."

Grig felt his brow involuntarily twitch. "I know it won't. But you're not the crime lord who'll keep that promise."

"What?" Tavist asked stupidly. But it was already too late.

The warehouse boomed with a few shots. Two of Tavist's men fell dead, red holes in their chests sprouting geysers of blood. Tavist and his last man froze as firearms were pressed to their backs. A group of men seemed to appear from the darkness outside the operating table's light. One of them dragged the fifth of Tavist's thugs forward, the one who was sent to block off the exits.

Tendar finished removing the restraints from zer ankles and got off the table, zer legs wobbling as ze did. Grig holstered his weapon when he saw the situation was under control and nodded to the man who held a weapon on Tavist. "Tell Walpor I said thank you."

The man nodded back. "We'll take care of this. But cut Olvic loose upstairs. The boss is going to need his expertise to hold this territory."

Grig froze. "The lawyer had a heavy hand in this."

"You got the caretaker back, alive and safe. You're the hero of the hour. And Tavist here is going to get what he deserves," Walpor's man replied as he pressed his weapon into the fat, whimpering crime lord. "Haven't you got enough?"

Grig bowed his head a little and tipped his hat. "Never thought I'd be lectured on being greedy from a gangster."

Walpor's man laughed. "Get the fuck out of here."

"Take care," Grig said and began to walk toward the exit.

"Oh, we will," Walpor's man grabbed Tavist and dragged

him away. "We most certainly will."

Grig helped Tendar up the stairs. When the two of them emerged from the building, Zax shouted with joy and hopped down off his scalok.

"You did it, Grig!" The trimortal threw his arms around Tendar, glad to see his friend alive.

"Yeah, I did," Grig replied glumly. "But not without help. Zax, you have to cut Olvic loose."

"What?"

"I stopped Tavist because I had help from Walpor." Grig bowed his head to hide his eyes. "Look, I . . . Zax, I lied to you."

Zax said nothing. Grig looked up and realized that Olvic, Zax, and Tendar were all watching him.

"The Hrinsan kidnapper didn't commit suicide. I was hot on his trail, and so was my rival, Folix Grendin. Folix got there first. But he screwed up, and the kidnapper and the kids got hit by the train. So we gave our statements, and I turned my back on the case to find another job. But the press wanted blood for it. Folix had a friend, an editor in the news. And he managed to pin the blame on me, saving his own ass."

Tendar covered zer mouth. Zax stammered, "What, Grig . . ."

"Let me finish, Zax. I was furious. Folix screwed up and was about to get away with it. My career was as good as over. Then I found proof that Folix was really responsible. It was the security surveillance. The police took the original, but the transport hub security always kept a backup. Just as I got my hands on it, Walpor's men came for me.

"They brought me before the crime lord, who was going to kill me. Those kids who died, who got their DNA rewritten? They were his grandchildren." Grig swallowed, remembering. "I showed him the proof, daring him to find out who really killed those kids. Walpor said nothing after seeing the video I had. Then he turned around, and hired me to find Folix."

Grig looked at Tendar's wide eyes, then into the sea-blue of Zax's shocked gaze. Finally, he looked at Olvic, who had turned away.

"I did. And I let Walpor's men have him instead. Walpor gave me a sizeable fee, almost enough to pay for the ranch. But as I left, Walpor said that if I ever needed anything, I just had to call. I had to cash in on that favour today."

Silence dominated the group, until Zax moaned. "So you didn't hear about Walpor from a police friend?"

"He told me the story himself, over a bottle of the finest sactul juice I ever tasted." Grig shook his head and walked toward Olvic. He began to undo the lawyer's restraints. "Walpor said he wants your services. He owns this part of town now that Tavist is gone. I wouldn't keep his men waiting."

Olvic hesitated, then headed around the back of the building.

The trio walked down the streets of Cujjip. Tendar was too

heavy to ride, so they were content to walk to the train station, guiding the scaloks with them. Zax put an arm around Tendar's shoulders. "How could you have been so dumb to come to Cujjip? Were you really going to take Olvic's deal over the kids? Give up a quad?"

Tendar looked up. "No! That's not why I came to Cujjip! Three days ago, I found out it was going to be a no less than a quad. I knew Zax and Liness were still fighting, so I thought I'd give them a few days to cool off. I also realized I was going to need a little time to rest before the big news. It's huge! And from watching all those celebrity shows, I know what that kind of lifestyle meant!

"So I wanted a little break before I told you all. That's when I heard that there was this comet passing over the sky near Cujjip tonight and I thought it would be fun to see it before everything changed. But when I got off the train, Tavist's men spotted and grabbed me."

"Comet?" Grig asked.

"Yes! Haven't you been watching the news?" Tendar said.

Zax and Grig looked at each other. "We were busy looking for you," Zax said.

"Oh," Tendar said. Ze pointed to the sky. Grig and Zax followed Tendar's finger.

"That . . . doesn't look like a comet," Zax said.

"It looks . . . artificial," Grig said. Indeed, they saw a streak through the purple, dusky skies and glittering stars. But even from afar, they could make out the shape of the comet's head, which was more like a baton or a bar than a piece of heated rock.

Tendar shook Grig's arm excitedly. "Do you think it's your people? Do you think the other guests have come? This is blessing upon a blessing!"

"Indeed it is," Zax said. "I can't believe I'm going to be the father to a quad!"

Tendar laughed. Grig and Zax looked at the jovial caretaker.

"It *was* a quad! But when Tavist had me, they made me take another test. The sex of the fifth child formed a couple of days ago."

Zax seemed confused for a moment, until he saw the happiness on Tendar's face. He froze like a statue. "Scalokshit."

Tendar shook zer head and giggled.

"You heard me correctly, Binjun!" The news anchor said on the television. "A Quinn! It has never once happened in the entire history of the trimortals race . . . until today! Five boys! The litter was confirmed by no less than *seven* physicians."

"Loanna, that is incredible news. I'm sure Tendar, Zax, and Liness are going to be the happiest family in all of Pelnoda," Binjun replied.

"And that's only half of this incredible story! Caretaker Tendar was kidnapped until about two days ago, when ze was saved by a former bounty hunter. Now get this, it was the same bounty hunter who was involved in the Hrinsan kidnapping so long ago!"

Grig was listening, but he wasn't watching. He had a hand on the wall as he struggled to take off his boot. He had only just arrived home, and he couldn't wait to get some sleep. To the rest of the world, it was all news. To him, it was fresh history.

When his footwear was removed, Grig moved toward the television to turn it off when he noticed movement. Julla was asleep on the couch.

"I thought you went home and left the television on," Grig said.

"Mmmm," she replied as she weakly opened her eyes. "You're a hero."

Grig shrugged and slipped his arms underneath the female trimortal. Cradling her, he walked to the bedroom and gently set her on the bed, covering her with a sheet. Finished, he returned to the couch and lay down. He considered switching off the television, but lethargy overwhelmed him.

The communicator rang a few moments until the messaging service clicked on. "Grig, this is Hanur Talrik of Pelnoda Pan News. We were hoping we could schedule an interview with you sometime tomorrow about your incredible rescue. Please contact us back at . . ."

Grig ceased paying attention. But as soon as the message ended, another call came through.

"Grig! Baby! It's Ewell! You remember me, of course. What

you did put your career back on the map. I got reports of missing persons and you're just the man for the job. Gimme a call back, but in case you lost my number it's . . ."

"On top of this incredible news story, scientists have confirmed that the comet passing over our hemisphere is not naturally formed," Binjun went on. "Guest groups have seen an overwhelming boost in funding. Guest Homefront leader Kilo Bandmun released a statement saying that the artificial comet has caused renewed interest in reconnecting with the guest's homeworld."

The communicator rang on, but Grig paid it no attention as friends called in to ask whether he was okay and congratulate him, old coworkers called to hear the details, news sources begged for interviews and updates, clients came hoping he'd take their case, well-wishers, political groups, and more.

But Grig watched the footage of the faux comet on the television. He thought again about what Kilo Bandmun said, about the guests wanting to find out about his people's home planet. But as his mind drifted to Zax and Julla, the harvest and the ranch, his scalok Nemiah, and the people he trusted and loved, Grig knew Pelnoda was his real home.

And there was no place like it.

Murderer
By A. R. Aston

   Fenx dragged the body, draped in its soiled sheets, through the woods. He trailed a red smear in the snow. His breath smoked in the chill mountain air, and he gasped with exertion.

   He looked to the sky, searching for the northern triad of stars to guide him. Watery tears went unshed in his eyes, which caused him to wince as the cold bit into the moisture. He saw a gleam; a shooting star passed between the drifting black clouds of heaven for only a moment. A silver gleam that made him seem so small.

   The inky depth of the sky was limitless, and yet his world was narrowed to this moment—his moment of shame. With a resigned sigh, he continued to haul his brother's body north.

Bequeathal
By K. Ceres Wright

Maxzide Tor awoke to his faint reflection in the glass pod lid with the vague sensation of a feeding tube having just been removed from his throat and a catheter from his nether regions. He coughed and the lid opened with a hydraulic hiss. The warm voice of the computer that greeted him contrasted with the sterile room.

"Good morning, Ambassador Tor. It is the fifth day of Naturne at eight point five hetrons, and we are in orbit around Glissau. There are thirty-two hetrons in a day on Glissau, with an average sleep cycle of five hetrons."

As he sat up, still coughing, a glass of water slid out from the wall of the suspension pod. He gratefully took it and drank, emptying the glass. Memories flitting across his mental landscape soon solidified, and he remembered why he had just woken up in a pod.

"Morning, Melinda. Glissau . . . membership application . . . Coalition of Industrialized Planets . . . right, okay. I'm definitely going to need more than five hetrons of sleep, though." Max replaced the glass on the tray and it retracted into the pod wall. He swung his legs over the side and struggled more than usual to climb out, attributing his stiffness to approaching middle age. He landed on the slippers he had left on the floor and shrugged on a robe. Several androids stood inert around the small room, ready to render assistance if necessary.

"What time is my meeting with the Chief Minister?"

"Eleven hetrons."

Max grunted in reply. "And what time's breakfast?"

"Ten."

"Good. I'll be in my office going over the application."

Max quickly showered and dressed in his bedroom and crossed to the adjacent office. His senior liaison, Xio Felar, was already planetside, sent ahead to formally conduct preliminary talks but informally to assess the players and gather intelligence. He opened a communications link to her personal 'caster, announcing his arrival. She immediately answered.

"Max, glad you're here, although you're cutting it close," she said.

He sat in his monogrammed chair and put his feet on the desk. "I've been doing this for so long, I've got it down to a science. Where are you?"

"In my villa. I don't think you're going to like it much here, though. It's a matriarchal society run like a harem . . . men raising the kids, men cleaning the house, even men strategizing what men to acquire."

"Acquire?" Max said. "What do you mean, like buy?"

"Not buy *per se*, but trade, like a dowry," Xio said.

"As in trading men for animals and bolts of fabric?"

"No! They're not primitive. Stocks and bonds, sometimes ground transport."

"Oh, well, that's so much more civilized. Why the hell would COIP be interested in a backwoods planet like that? Who authorized the prelims?" Max said.

"Anz Tamar. Expedited."

"Anz?" Max stood up and began pacing his office. "That rat bastard is dirtier than the crust on a banker's ass. What the hell is he up to?"

"I've been trying to figure that out myself."

"Well, we've got the advantage of being here while he's back at headquarters. He's not the type to get his hands dirty. I'll send out two sleeper scouts and get the lay of the land," Max said.

"Good idea. I'll meet you at the rendezvous point at ten point five."

"Do your men sneak out at night to back-alley houses of ill repute? When they seem tired and listless the next day, does it make you wonder what they were doing? Well, wonder no more. With the Zacto-Track, you'll be able to know where they are every cytron of every day. Simply upload the tracking program to your central node, and their implants will do the rest. The program is compatible with both Cognition and Nervus systems. Know exactly with Zacto! Call today!"

In the kitchen, footsteps reverberated from the upstairs bedroom. They stopped at the staircase and a voice yelled, "Mani! I told you to cut the sales segments from the day's songlist!"

"Yes, mi lapa," Mani replied.

Lirina sat at the kitchen table with her sister Kallo and peeked over the manuscript she was reading to stare at Mani. He muttered something under his breath that Lirina didn't catch. She smiled. Her mother *could* be overwhelming.

"Why does Mom keep him around? He obviously disobeys her," Kallo said.

"Have some respect, Kallo. He *is* your father. And he makes the best usheff between here and Olaro. Besides, they really love each other. It's sort of a game between them," Lirina said.

"Hm. When *I* grow up, all my men will obey my every command."

"*You* have a lot to learn about life. And love," Lirina said. She rose and made her way out back to the cooking area, the men's usual gathering place. After a day's work, they would build a fire in the large grated pit and roast a large dinner and the smaller meals for the next day. Generous amounts of lugu fermented from the haca plant would be passed around, even a bit to the young children they cared for.

Because Mani was Eminent Coitioner, Eminent Cuisiner, and the father of Dotar's two daughters—and her mother disdained childrearing—he was afforded much sway. He used to bring Lirina and Kallo out back with him and the other men, even long past the Age of Separation. Kallo would only stay long enough to eat, then went inside with their mother. But Lirina would stay low and quiet while she listened to the men tell stories by the dying fire. The light danced on each of their faces, playing up the hard lines and the trace of sadness behind their eyes. It was an image that had repeated itself in Lirina's mind over the years.

Three years after the Age of Separation, when the men's looks at her began to change, Mani forced her to stay inside with her sister and mother. Now twelve years past the Age, as Lirina stood in the doorway staring out at the gathering, the smell of the fire and sounds of laughter took her back to those early days.

"Mani," she said.

He turned away from the pit, half his face garishly lit, then handed his tongs to Checko, the gardener. Mani took Lirina's hand and led her to the side of the house, away from prying ears.

"Lirina," Mani said, smiling.

"Sesi," she said, using the affectionate term for "father." "Do you know what's bothering Mom? She's been hostile lately, more than usual."

Mani chuckled. "She has a meeting with a representative of the COIP to try and obtain membership status. She was going to tell you once it was approved. But she didn't want you to get your hopes up in case it didn't work out."

"So that's it." Lirina stared off, to a point behind Mani. *COIP? That could mean . . .*

"Lirina!" The voice rang from inside.

"Your mother's calling you. Be good." He cupped her face

with both hands, placing his index fingers on the silver discs—cernos—on either side of her temples, then released her. She'd always been told the discs helped to seal the bond between mother and daughter, but she suspected something more . . . and wondered why males didn't have them.

"I'll see you later," she said, smiling.

She pushed past the strips of haca leaves hanging from the doorway. Kallo was gone, but had left her cup on the table. *Probably off to bother Gorlan in the haca orchard.* Lirina snatched up the cup and placed it in the queue for Bolar to wash.

She rushed upstairs, headed for her mother's bedroom. The door beads parted, then came together in a wall of tangerine once she passed. Her mother was standing next to her bed, curlibugs crawling on her head, suctioning up hair and depositing curls. She held up two sets of robes—one red, one black and white—then decided on the latter and handed the former to her dresser Naph to return to the closet. Upon her entrance, Naph lowered his head.

"Kuhn," Lirina said, giving him permission to act freely in her presence. "Where are you going?"

"Oh, just a boring meeting of the Advisory Council on trade with Amsu," Dotar said.

"Hm," Lirina said.

"Have you chosen an Eminent Coitioner yet? There's not much time left. You're almost twenty-five yetrons."

Lirina sighed. "Yes, I know." They'd had the same

conversation on countless occasions. She sat on the large round bed and fell in among the fuchsia pillows, looking up at the painted ceiling of clouds and flying sea creatures. Her mother curtly waved off Naph and he fled from the room.

"Lirina, I weary of your delays. We still have to plan the ceremony and you've been putting this off for a yetron. What about Helfor? He comes with ten-thousand hets of business and two ground transports."

Lirina picked absentmindedly at a tassel. "Too short and hairy."

"Then what about Omal? He's tall with purple eyes and comes with eight-thousand hets and an air transport."

"Too submissive."

"There is no such thing!" Dotar said. An exasperated tone underscored her words. "Never mind. I'll choose myself."

Lirina sat up. "But—"

"No buts! It's decided. Now go! I have to get dressed."

Max absorbed the sights of Olaru, the capital city of the continent of Jenar, in between sending messages to Xio. She was unable to make their meeting, so he had gone straight to his meeting with Chief Minister Nikil, who had sent an official ground transport for his ride into the city. But he and Xio expected implanted listening devices, so they spoke of mundane matters while they sent coded text-based messages back and forth on their 'casters.

"Is that sand in that fountain?" Max said. He had passed a large blue fountain overflowing with orange sand that pooled in a shallow basin.

Text: So how did this matriarchal society come about?

"Yes, some sand on Glissau is so fine that it behaves like water, so they use it in fountains."

Text: About 60 years back, they had a nuclear war. In the aftermath, several powerful women came up with a plan to make sure it didn't happen again. They spin it by saying it's the natural order of things, but I've noticed some things . . . amiss. Did the sleeper scouts send you anything interesting?

"I love the weather here. And everything is quite large compared to Melot—the wide avenues, spacious ground transport, immense buildings."

Text: Just some aerial images of the cities. They'll soon land near choice targets and begin to relay information. So what did you find amiss?

"Many buildings don't have windows or even barrier fields because the weather's so balmy."

Text: I was walking down the hall in the capitol building when I overheard Dotar and an aide talking about epistasis, but when I walked past, they shushed each other. And . . . wait, someone's calling me. I'll see you when you get here. Don't forget the official greeting is lowering your head and extending an upward palm.

His 'caster went dead and he had to content himself with

watching the landscape roll by. The transport came to a stop outside of a large white building with a domed top.

"Welcome to the capitol," said a disembodied voice from the interior of the ground transport. The door automatically opened and Max alighted. A tall blue-robed man with light brown skin and rust-colored hair approached him. He gave the greeting that Xio had described, which Max copied.

"Legate Tor, I am Varlan. Welcome to Olaru. I trust your voyage was satisfactory?" He led Max up the stairs and toward an elaborate door depicting an ancient battle scene of men fighting each other with short pitchforks.

"As satisfactory as can be in suspended animation," Max said.

As they approached the door, it broke apart into thousands of tiny beads, gathering on either side of the entrance, and then reformed once the pair passed through.

The lobby soared up to a twenty-story dome ringed by circular openings and decorated with images of what Max assumed were animals and plants indigenous to Glissau. Blue long-necked animals nibbled yellow-leafed trees while small purples balls of fur gathered around a red bush. Diffuse light gave the space an ethereal feel, and a faint scent that reminded Max of his mother's garden permeated the air. The scene made Max want to take a tour of the planet, contrary to his usual routine of getting in and out as quickly as possible.

As he and Varlan crossed under the dome of the building, a larger delegation of about twenty people approached them, led by a brown-skinned woman with purple hair dressed in black-and-white robes. She had a silver disc affixed to each of her temples. Those accompanying her had skin tones that varied from dark brown to light orange and they wore a rainbow of colored robes. But only the women wore the discs.

Max recognized the Chief Minister from the images Xio had sent. He paused to give the standard greeting, but with more flourish.

"Prime Minister Nikil, it is an honor to be here. Thank you for receiving me."

She returned the greeting, with considerably less flourish. "Legate Tor, I greet you in the name of the people of Jenar." She then turned and introduced each of the others, to whom Max gave an abbreviated nod.

"Pardon," Max said, once the introductions were completed, "but where is my aide, Xio Felar?"

"She will be along shortly. She is meeting with a trade delegation from Amsu. But please, come, take a tour of our garden," Dotar said. "A day as lovely as this should not be wasted indoors."

Dotar slipped her arm into Max's and the group headed for a large open doorway that led down a flight of white stone steps to an expansive garden. As Max and Dotar walked on, the chittering group fell away, leaving them alone. The fragrance grew as they walked among fluted green stalks, yellow flowers that were as twice as tall as Max, and black trees that hunched ominously over red bushes. He looked around for the purples balls of fur, but found none. They continued on a path of crushed red stone that meandered throughout the garden.

"What a magnificent garden. It reminds me of my mother's, on Melot, in a region called Larantz. It's known for its tropical weather and lush greenery. The rains can be quite torrential, though."

"It rains quite infrequently. Our planet is watered mainly by a vast underground system of natural springs and irrigation pipes. We strive to surround ourselves with beauty amid the trials of life."

"The burden of rule rests heavily on the shoulders of leaders," Max said.

"Samsa Plat. I'm surprised you know of our philosophers," Dotar said. "Seeing as we are rather . . . out of the way of established trade routes."

"Wisdom is found among the most experienced, not the most popular." He mentally thanked Xio for her list of "Important Things to Say."

Dotar laughed. "Now I think you're just trying to get on my good side." They rounded a corner and the path opened to a large patio with an oval stone table and two chairs, along with a buffet of colorful foods. Max took in the sight and smell of the food.

"Now who's trying to get on whose good side?" Max said, grinning.

"Please, enjoy. We have much to talk about."

Max half expected an android server to appear from behind the bushes, but then remembered Glissau was rather behind in robotics. He took a plate from the buffet and surveyed the spread. He did not recognize any of the food and wished Xio had sent a list. But he shrugged it off and dove in, having had extensive experience in eating adventurously on numerous planets. After filling his plate with green nodules, white flat rectangles, and yellow leaves, he scooped up a bottle of clear liquid, hoping it was as close to water as possible. Then he took his seat at the table and started with the nodules. They were surprisingly tender. Dotar soon joined him, but her plate had only one type of food, orange tubules with a yellow sauce.

"So, tell me, how does our application look?"

Max wiped his mouth and took a sip of the beverage, which tasted like water . . . *Thank Hanani.*

"Chief Minister . . ."

"Please," she said, interrupting him. "Call me Dotar."

"And call me Max. Dotar, the membership requirements include having stable institutions that guarantee the rule of law, citizen's rights, respect for and protection of minority populations, and a functioning economy that can sustain the majority of a planet's population. The two requirements that are areas of concern for the Coalition are first, the economy, which only sustains about half of Glissau at levels above impoverishment, and second . . ." *Tread lightly here.* ". . . Respect for the male population."

Dotar started in her seat, but Max held up two hands in an attempt to stave off protest.

"Now hear me out. Regarding the economy, we can offer aid to set up centers for training and education, in addition to incentives for existing businesses to expand in those areas. It usually takes about thirty-two metrons to work itself out, not long at all in the grand scheme of things. As to the . . . latter concern, we would need to send in an observation team, just to help convince the Coalition you're not forcibly subjugating half of the population."

They both laughed, Max more from nervousness.

"Max, let me assure you we are not forcibly oppressing anyone. And we would welcome any measures the Coalition deems necessary." She took a sip of her drink, before deftly switching subjects. "Tell me, Max, are you married?"

Max paused, surprised at the turn of conversation. "Unfortunately, no. My job keeps me away from home so much, I decided that as long as I was an ambassador, I would not subject anyone to that burden."

"Ah, forgive me," Dotar said, jumping out of her seat. "I forgot to serve the romar." She walked to the end of the buffet and retrieved two glasses and a carafe.

"Romar?"

"Yes, it's a traditional drink for negotiations. It's said to aid the process."

Max could guess what "aid" she was speaking of, but obligation drove him to at least take a sip.

Dotar poured a dark burgundy liquid into a glass and handed it to him, then poured herself one. "May our relationship be long and fruitful."

Max moved his glass in a circular motion in response, then drank. He was pleasantly surprised at the mild, smooth flavor, half-expecting a bitter ruggedness.

"I like this romar," he said. A hot flush crept up his neck and light-headedness took center stage. It was the last thing he remembered.

###

Lirina sat at her desk in the home office staring out at the front garden. Her mother had given her the task of researching trade agreements to help prepare her for assuming the title of Assistant Minister, but the task bored her. In fact, the idea of being AM bored her. She wanted to become a docere, to heal others, not become mired in endless squabbling over the rule of law. But arguing with her mother was an exercise in futility. She needed a plan. *And soon.*

###

Max awoke in a dark room, on a bed, bound and gagged. He panicked, jerking and squirming to get out of his bindings, but the metal cuffs on his wrists and legs held tight. A figure lay next to him, unmoving, and he hoped it wasn't a dead body. He kicked at it twice before it moved and made a frantic muffled noise. The figure rolled over and Xio's large eyes stared back at him.

At the sudden muted clacking of beads, Max lifted his head. A figure stood in the doorway, backlit, then entered. The beads came together and the gloom returned.

"Good," the figure said. "I was getting tired of waiting." He walked toward the bed. "We're going to take your friend, but don't worry, she'll be safe as long as you do what we want."

He picked up Xio and threw her over his shoulder. She began to buck and kick until he extracted a device from his pocket and pressed it against her thigh.

"I'll be back," the man said. Then he pressed the device to Max's arm and a peaceful euphoria swept over him.

The next few—or what he assumed were few—hetrons passed in a hazy blur. People and voices came and went. He recognized Dotar's voice . . .

"—Series of injections. Do you hear me? They will make you more agreeable, open—"

"—Why we do this to our men . . . most destroyed . . . blast that killed over forty percent—"

"—Progress."

"—Crashed your ship so they think you're dead."

"—First Eminent Coitioner. Welcome to the family. For now, anyway."

###

"He's pale green," Lirina said. "With white hair. Where is he from?" She sat in a chair in the corner of her mother's bedroom, staring at the man her mother had chosen to be her Eminent Coitioner. He stood, placid-faced, in the middle of the room.

"A planet called Melot," Dotar said. She stood in front of the mirror, admiring the outfit she had chosen for the ceremony. She'd told Lirina she met with a representative from the Coalition. Lirina had thought her mother would wait, but she was action-oriented, keen on making things happen as quickly as possible. She was probably already planning Glissau's induction ceremony into the COIP.

"Wait, is he the ambassador you met with?"

"Yes, and when he saw how peaceful our world was, he said he wanted to stay. He wasn't married, so I thought he would make an excellent EC."

"And he didn't object to . . ."

"Not at all," Dotar said. "And after the ceremony, we'll make the change permanent."

Lirina didn't believe her mother for a second, but said nothing.

Dotar adjusted her headdress and robe, turning sideways and checking her reflection. Dotar had chosen white as the ceremonial theme, to match Max's hair. Lirina had been content to let her mother arrange the Coition Ceremony—and eventually the EC himself—having never cared for coordinating social gatherings.

Seeing at how happy her mother was, she figured it a perfect opportunity to press her terms and conditions.

"Mother?"

"Hm?" She had moved onto adjusting Max's robe and sash, ensuring they were aligned to whatever knot-to-button size ratio she deemed acceptable.

Lirina stood up, as she was taller than her mother. The move would give her more confidence, or so she figured. The flared sleeves of her robe hung uselessly at her sides.

"I don't want to be Assistant Minister."

Dotar turned, an incredulous look on her face.

"What?"

The sharpness that edged the curves of the word threatened to undercut Lirina's confidence, but she pressed forward. "I don't want to be AM," she repeated, slowly. "I want to be a docere."

"But—"

"No buts. I've made my decision. If you want me to participate in this ceremony, then let me choose what I want to be."

Dotar paused, her mind configuring machinations of every size, shape, and color, Lirina thought. But Lirina knew how important this ceremony was to her mother. She would have to give in . . .

"Mani!"

. . . Or not.

Lirina's eardrums reverberated at the sound of her mother's scream. Mani ran through the doorway in seconds, a worried look on his face. Dotar stalked him down.

"You daughter refuses to become Assistant Minister. Where do you think *that* idea came from?"

Mani looked at her, disbelieving, then fixed his eyes on Lirina. "Lirina, what is this?"

"Sesi, I want to choose my own life."

"Silence!" Dotar pointed to Lirina, then turned back toward Mani. "I knew I was too permissive with her, letting you adjust her cernos."

Mani stood up straighter, jaw set. "Perhaps her eminence should recall that her efforts were focused on politics, not rearing children."

"How dare you. My efforts were focused on providing a comfortable home and keeping you in Cellina robes. I didn't expect to be repaid with betrayal."

"It's not betrayal," Lirina said. "It's my life!"

Dotar turned. "I'm doing all this for you, Lirina. Becoming Chief Minister, arranging a deal with the Coalition to bring this planet on par with the other worlds, coordinating your Coition Cere—"

"Make no mistake, Mother. You're not doing it for me; you're doing it for yourself. Now either you let me be or I won't be at the ceremony."

Her mother's look bored into her, but Lirina stood her ground and met her gaze, unwavering.

"Fine. For now. In the meantime, I have Kallo," Dotar said.

"What do you mean 'for now'?"

"There's still The Bequeathal."

"What's that?"

"Just be at the ceremony on time. We'll arrange for docere training next week," Dotar said. "It is agreed."

Lirina hesitated, not wanting to fully trust her mother, but seeing no other choice.

"It is agreed," Lirina said.

Max had remembered a gathering of people under a large white tent. He wore a white robe and stood next to a woman in front of the gathering. They uttered the words, "It is agreed," and a loud cheer rose up from the crowd. Afterward, everyone danced, ate, and drank. He had eaten, but could not remember the taste. Later that night, he was taken upstairs, to the bedroom, to the woman who'd stood next to him at the ceremony. They stripped and climbed into bed. His mouth on her . . . hers on him . . . her on top. Then . . .

Sun beamed in through an open window, waking him. He threw an arm over his eyes and turned away, only to be met by the woman at the ceremony.

"Ai!" He jerked backward and almost fell out of the bed. He

held onto the headboard and dragged himself back onto the mattress. She giggled. Grogginess still filled his head, but not as much as before. The bed was large and round, spread with a green quilt and brightly colored pillows.

"Who are you?"

"I'm Lirina Nikil, the Chief Minister's daughter. And you're my Eminent Coitioner."

"Your what?"

"The man in my household whom I would first consider in matters of coition. But seeing as you're my only one . . ."

"Wait . . . yesterday, there was a ceremony?"

"The Coitioner Ceremony, where you were publicly announced. Taking a first EC is a rite of passage for women. Do you have the same thing where you come from?"

"Er, no, it's . . . different. Wait . . . I remember . . ."

"You were on a drug, to make you docile. You are supposed to receive it twice a day, but I arranged for you not to get it yesterday."

Max sat up. "Why?"

"I'll be honest with you. I need your help to change the way this government is run. Men contribute greatly to this society. They should be able to reap the benefits in freedom."

"Wait . . . my aide, Xio. She's . . ."

"She's fine," Lirina said. "Lightly sedated, but resting

comfortably. I sneaked a peek after I sent my mother's guard on an errand."

"But I remember. It's hazy." Max told her about his capture and the snippets of conversation he'd heard, about his ship crashing, about becoming an Eminent something-or-other, the drugs. It seemed surreal.

"I can't believe my mother kidnapped you. And if your people think you're dead . . ."

"They won't come after me. I need to get my 'caster so I can find out what's going on." He paused to rub his eyes. "Do you know where they are? Where your mother's keeping them?"

"Look, you have to keep pretending you're docile. I'll try and get your things, but you have to promise to obey."

Max nodded. "All right."

He twisted back around to look out of the window. Off in the distance, along the horizon, several plumes of dust rose up, which were soon sprayed with water from a large vehicle. Faint rainbows glistened in the expanse.

"What's that?" he said.

"My mother's new venture. She says she's clearing land to build housing, but I haven't seen anything going up."

"That doesn't look like construction. It looks like mining,"

"Mining?"

"Yes, and from the yellow color, I'd say it was keuterum. It's used in space ships to block cosmic radiation. So that's why Anz was so interested. If your planet has deposits, this land is worth a fortune. And your mother is helping to cash in on it."

"So that's why she was pushing so hard to join the Coalition. The trade avenues it would open up . . . ," Lirina said.

Max looked at her, admiring the smoothness of her skin and the kindness in her voice. "Hope you don't take offense, but you're not like what I expected."

Lirina smiled at him. "Because I'm my father's daughter."

"You'll have to tell me about your father one day. Should we get dressed now?" Max said.

She ran her hand along his thigh and up to his chest, and then caressed the downy hair.

"In a hetron," she said.

Lirina and Max walked down the hall of the capitol building to her mother's office. They passed several aides, each of whom greeted the pair.

"Congratulations, you two."

"I wish you all the best."

"I'm surprised you're not still in bed."

The last comment was accompanied by a wink. Lirina smiled at each one and kept walking. When they reached her mother's office, her aide Jilo looked up at the two.

"What are you doing here?"

"I just came to get some documents my mother wanted me to research. Tomorrow's the deadline. Is she in?"

"No, but you can go in and see if you can find them," Jilo said.

"Thanks." Lirina knew her mother would not be in because she had drunk too much at the ceremony and was still in bed when they had left the house.

Once inside the office, Lirina and Max searched over, in, and beneath cabinets, desks, and seat cushions, but to no avail. Exasperated, Lirina fell into her mother's chair.

"We can't stay much longer without Jilo coming in here." She scanned her mother's desk and settled on a black box decorated with gold flowers that Dotar's mother had given to her. Lirina opened it.

"Are these your things?"

Max hurried over and peered inside. "Yes, thank Hanani." He grabbed the pad and immediately downloaded the data from the sleeper scouts.

"What are you doing?"

"When I first arrived, I sent out small robots to gather data on the planet. They're programmed to assess the area and report on anything of interest." Max quickly read the information streaming in.

"What's the Hifeld Research Facility?"

"A laboratory. It's close by. Why?"

"We need to get there. Apparently, according to the security cameras, your mother's been going there every day for months."

###

Lirina and Max chose a side entrance and waved the stolen ID tag they'd lifted from Dotar's office. The door opened softly, and they crept into the storage part of the lab. The area was large, about the size of a sporting stadium, all grey from floor to ceiling, and stacked with crates and packages wrapped in plastic. A new-equipment odor filled the place and a niggling sensation tickled the back of Max's consciousness. He headed for a plastic-wrapped package and pulled off the covering. Standing before him was a pristine android, the prior year's model on Melot, but unused.

"Is that what I think it is?" Lirina said.

"If you were thinking android, then yes. Anz Tamar is president of a company that makes androids, and he's using Glissau to make a profit from last year's castaways. If he and your mother push through the membership application, then he'll already have a business set up here, shutting out the competition for mining and android production."

Lirina shook her head. "That woman, I swear."

"Not your fault. We can't pick our relatives." He put a hand on her shoulder and gave it a reassuring squeeze. "Once the Coalition hears about this, your mother and Anz will have to answer for it." Max looked up as something caught the corner of his eye. Outside one of the barrier fields, an object appeared in the sky, small but noticeable.

"What's that?" he said.

Lirina followed his gaze and saw something streaming high across the horizon. "I have no idea. We'll figure it out later. Right now, we need to get some evidence before we're kicked out, or worse."

"Right," Max said. He used his pad to record their discovery and sent it to the sleeper scouts, which could send the signal to Coalition headquarters.

"Come on. Let's see what else is in this place," Lirina said.

They walked to the other end of the storage facility and peered through a window. Rows of computers and servers lined the walls and looked to Max as if they were running at full capacity.

"Wonder what they're calculating," Max said.

Lirina opened the door. "Only one way to find out." She walked into the next room with Max reluctantly in tow. They made it halfway down the hall when voices sounded in the near distance.

"Hide," Lirina said. She inserted herself between two glass-encased servers. Max crept beneath one of the tables and waited.

Dotar's voice, harsh and unmistakable, rang out in the small room.

"The genetic changes to male DNA to make them

permanently docile are coming along. Phase one tests were successful in the lab, and we will begin testing on a small group of men within a metron. I've downloaded the data on this pad if you're interested." She held up a small data device.

"Excellent. I'm glad it's working out for you."

Max knew the voice. Anz Tamar. *He can't resist personally overseeing what he considers as getting over on the Coalition. Bastard.*

Lirina stepped out from between the servers and confronted her mother. Dotar was taken aback at the sudden appearance, and Anz's face slackened to incomprehension.

"Lirina! What are you doing here? How did you get in?" Dotar said.

"Never mind that. What the hell are you doing? Changing people's DNA? Pushing through membership so this man can take advantage of our economy?" She gestured toward Anz. "I am telling the authorities."

Anz reached in his robe and extracted a plasma gun. He pointed it at Lirina. "I don't think so. You're about to—"

Max lunged from underneath the desk, tackling Anz. He fell forward, and the gun clattered and skittered down the hallway. Max climbed over Anz to reach the weapon and held it up as a prize, but Anz twisted and propelled himself toward Max. Anz grabbed for the gun, but Max held fast. They grappled, turning over and over, until they reached the opposite end of the hall. Anz was stronger, directing Max's hand toward the door to the storage area. They locked hands, quivering in conflict. The gun fired.

"No!" Lirina exclaimed.

Dotar clutched her stomach, eyes wide, and fell to her knees, then dropped over to the floor. Lirina ran to her mother. Max used the distraction to wrest the gun away and stand over Anz, pointing the weapon at his head.

"Move and I'll cook your brain in your damn skull," Max said. Anz froze.

Lirina's sobs filled the room as she ripped open Dotar's robes to look at the wound. It was obvious she wouldn't last much longer. Dotar reached up and caressed Lirina's face.

"I love you, Lirina. Don't cry. Part of me will live on. In you."

Dotar placed her index fingers on Lirina's cernos and closed her eyes. Lirina tried to hold back sobs, but they wracked her body, rocking her back and forth over her mother.

"This . . . is The Bequeathal," Dotar said. "My memories and personality, and your grandmother's."

A bright light flashed in Lirina's thoughts as images filled her mind . . . of her grandmother as a young woman receiving radiation treatment in a hospital, of devastated neighborhoods and starving children roaming the streets, of burned bodies and piles of corpses, of the first meeting of Future Female Leaders that eventually spread across the country, of vials and experiments, of Dotar's first Coition Ceremony, of giving birth, of becoming Chief Minister, and of seeking to establish Glissau as a preeminent world . . . to leave to her daughter.

Lirina fell back, holding her head, and Max reached down to help her up, even as he kept the weapon trained on Anz.

"Are you all right?"

She paused, to let the pain fade away and information to fall into place. "I—I think so."

"Good. Let's erase all these servers before any authorities decide to keep it for themselves," Max said. He forced Anz to his feet and shot at the first row of computers, slicing screens and mechanical innards in one continuous movement. Sparks flew upward, and billows of smoke roiled from the destruction.

Lirina spied her mother's pad with the genetic data and slowly reached for it, then tucked it inside her robes as Max's back was turned.

"Yes, it is agreed," Lirina said to herself.

Salvation Comes
By Simon Farrow

Golden light gleamed from the metallic surfaces of the storefronts and warmed the surface of the broad avenue as the last drips of moisture from the chill night evaporated in the new day's warmth. The day shift had just started, but the street bustled with people, the muted thrum of gossip from small groups competing with the hawking of the market vendors. Excited children screamed as they ran through the throng.

Corin na-Dalaga leant against the wall of a clothing store. He chewed on seeds he had picked up from a vending trolley farther down the street and watched as the people made their way through the market district. At times like these he could almost imagine that this scene was idyllic, that the people he watched were living happy and worthwhile lives. He knew it was all an illusion. The golden light wasn't from a sun, but from the lighting array embedded in the cavern ceiling fifteen metres above. The street was packed with people, but only because they had just finished a gruelling twelve-hour night shift, and the gossip was always a mixture of mean-spirited backstabbing and continual complaining.

A boy chased a ball across the street, skidding to a stop as he saw Corin. Flashing a gap-toothed grin, he scooped up the ball and ran shouting back to his friends. Corin didn't return the smile. He knew that the boy and his friends would most likely end up dead; even if they survived to adulthood, they would be condemned to follow their parents into the daily grind. Worse still, they might end up like Corin himself, named for the company that owned him and doomed to a life of violent brutality.

Jemel emerged from the store opposite. Corin smiled, amused at the difference between the child his friend had been when they were growing up together in the orphanage and the young man he saw now. Jemel walked confidently through the crowd, which seemed to magically part before him and then rush back in his wake like something tidal. It was always this way when they left The Black, executive Elemos' biggest bar and brothel, and ventured out of the black district and into Epiphany mining station proper. As Jemel approached each group, their conversations died to hushed whispers and nodded glances. With his gang markings showing proudly on his bare shoulders, Jemel ignored them. Corin stepped out into the street to meet him and offered him the paper bag of seeds. As Jemel took a pinch and popped them into his mouth, Corin noticed a smear of blood on his friend's knuckles.

"The old woman give you any trouble?" he asked as they walked down the street toward an intersection. Jemel shrugged and spat a wad of seed casings onto the pavement.

"No, she knows what's best for business. Her son didn't like me talking to her, so I gave him a bit of a tap. No big deal." Jemel grinned and reached for another handful of seeds. Corin held the bag open and shook his head silently. He never relished his role as Elemos' enforcer. Jemel, however, seemed to gain more and more enjoyment from pressuring store owners into paying protection money and punishing those who argued or fought back. In quiet moments, Corin allowed himself to admit that he was disgusted, both with the way that things worked on Epiphany and his part in it, but there was nothing he could do to change it. Whenever Corin tried to talk to Jemel, his friend just laughed at his naivety, arguing that this was the way of things and that one man could never change it. He'd never had a good enough answer to argue back.

A cheer rang out from a side street as the two gangers approached an intersection. As they rounded the corner, they saw a crowd gathered around a man standing on a crate like a priest delivering a sermon. The crowd was almost entirely mine workers, mostly men, who were captivated by the speaker before them. The man waved to the crowd for attention, and the cheering subsided.

"My friends, thank you for coming. Today you have made a step toward your freedom." The man smiled as he spoke, and the crowd cheered again. The man gestured for quiet and then continued. "I know you'd like nothing more than to go home after a long shift, but us being here today shows that we will not be walked over by the corporations." Corin shot a questioning look at his companion as the speaker continued.

"It's just a demo." Jemel pointed at the man on the crate. "That's Kibbs, the unionist. He's been pushing for better working conditions for a few months, and every now and then he holds one of these rallies to gather followers. Anti-Dalaga, anti-corporation, anti-corruption." He snorted with amusement. "If he keeps it up, Elemos will have his head. Not good for business."

Corin looked at Kibbs. He was a tall man wearing a

nondescript black jumpsuit, with a patrician face and a shock of short blond hair so fair it was almost white. As they got closer, Corin could see the badges on his chest indicating he was assigned as a refinery worker, but the skin on his hands lacked the usual greenish-yellow discolouration such labour inevitably caused. Despite himself, Corin wanted to listen to what the older man had to say.

"Our lives are not our own. We are slaves to the corporation, condemned to serve until we die. If we don't work hard enough, we die. If we stand up for ourselves, we die. If we give in, and do exactly what they tell us, we die." Kibbs had picked up a wrench and punctuated each point by smacking it into his palm. "So many of us turn to drink or drugs or women to make it easier, but the corporation controls these, too. All we do is make it easier for them to control us!"

The crowd shouted angrily, and Corin's attention was drawn to four or five people who wore the same uniform as Kibbs, conspicuous by their obvious support for his oratory. Corin noted that they were always the first to applaud and the loudest to shout at Kibb's statements and suspected they were placed there to encourage the crowd.

Several people at the edge of the crowd had noticed the two gangers approaching, and Corin could sense the hostility and resentment that Kibbs had managed to stoke in them.

"C'mon, Jem, let's go another way round." He reached out to grab Jemel's arm, but the shorter youth shook him off and began moving through the crowd toward the front. Corin followed reluctantly. On the crate, Kibbs had noticed them and pointed their way with the wrench.

"See here, how the enforcers of 'executive' Elemos come to shut me down! They don't want you to realise you have a choice, that you can live without the drugs, the prostitution, the *protection*." The vehemence and scorn Kibbs put into the last word cut through Corin, who raised his hands open palmed in a calming gesture, but Kibbs continued. "Elemos fears the power of the workers, so he's sent his gangers out from the black district to stop me. Are you going to kill me?"

The crowd murmured, and Corin was aware that they had started to close in on the two gangers as they moved through, the usual respectful distance people gave to Elemos' enforcers noticeably absent. Jemel seemed completely oblivious to this as he reached the front of the crowd and looked up at Kibbs.

"No, Kibbs, we're not going to kill you. We're going to take you back to The Black to have a chat with Mr. Elemos about respect." Jemel reached up to pull Kibbs from the crate, but one of the black-suited mine workers stepped in and blocked him whilst another grabbed Corin's shoulder.

"Protect Lenton Kibbs! Protect the people!" someone shouted, and the crowd surged forward, bundling the two gangers to the ground as blows and boots rained down on them. Corin's last sight of Kibbs was of him walking away with his five accomplices before his view was blocked by the crush of the crowd.

###

Given his relatively lowly status, Subexecutive Sauren had obviously done well since his arrival on Epiphany fifteen months previously. The spacious apartment he had leased from the corporation was on the outer edge of the hollowed-out asteroid that formed the bulk of the station, with a small terrace overlooking the central plaza and the executive district where the headquarters stood proudly among lush lawns and clutches of trees. The apartment itself even had its own internal atrium with several small shrubs surrounding a trickling water feature in the centre of the open-plan living area. Clean white stone and shining chrome were trimmed with real wood throughout the apartment, and the sculptures and paintings dotted around must surely have been imported from off-rock.

When a two-person security team finally responded to a neighbour's reports of screaming from the apartment, they didn't have to look far to find the subexecutive. Whilst one officer shouted into her radio for backup, her partner dashed through the apartment and was violently ill over the veranda. Four minutes later, a team from the Kolam arrived and immediately summoned their superior.

When Roccan Drathmore arrived at the scene, his agents were standing outside, their presence enough to deter any citizens curious as to why the secret police had cordoned off the apartment and what had happened to their neighbour. Nodding to the lead agent, Drathmore pulled on rubber shoe covers and latex gloves and stepped through the front door.

Most of Subexecutive Sauren was very easy to find. He had

dragged himself almost as far as the door, his left arm reaching for the handle, before someone had used a piton gun, normally used to attach heavy mining equipment to the surface of an asteroid, to nail him to the marble floor. A trail of bodily fluids led back toward the kitchen area, where his right hand lay on a chopping board, a meat cleaver lying nearby in a pool of scarlet blood. His legs ended in ragged, bloody stumps just below the knee, and it took Drathmore a minute to find the subexecutive's feet in the bathroom next to a heavy-duty rock saw. Arterial blood had sprayed high on the tiled wall, and the rubberised floor was filthy where Sauren had soiled himself.

Unlike the security patrol, Drathmore didn't so much as flinch as he stepped through the carnage; in twenty-three years in various branches of security and law enforcement, he had seen it all. Since joining the Kolam seven years previously, he had done worse. Furthermore, this was the fifth Dalaga employee at subexecutive level or higher to have been brutally murdered in the last eight months. Each case had a similar level of violence and disfigurement, and now any related cases landed straight on his desk. The chairman was putting a lot of pressure on the Kolam to find the culprits and bring them to justice.

One of the agents called for him from another room, and Drathmore walked through to the bedroom as a forensic crew arrived and started scanning the apartment. He was doubtful they would manage to find anything betraying the attackers beyond work glove fibres, but he hadn't made it to head of security without being thorough, and he nodded his thanks as they went to work.

An agent looked up from his communicator as he walked in. "Sir, the unionists put the video out already. We're blocking it as fast as we can, but it's out there."

Drathmore nodded as he took in the impromptu filming set the attackers had set up in the bedroom. Several bloody implements rested on a small side table next to a chair in front of a digital recorder, the memory unit from the camera conspicuous by its absence.

The agent coughed quietly. "There's something else though sir, something good. We've had a report of an assault in the market district. Two of Elemos' men apparently tried to interrupt a unionist demo and got beaten up for their trouble. According to reports, Kibbs was there."

Drathmore dismissed the agent after ascertaining where the victims were now and summoned his driver.

The first thing Corin became aware of was the gentle but insistent ping of a heartbeat monitor. He took a moment to measure it against his pulse and realised it was him it was hooked to. A strong antiseptic smell overpowered any other odours in the room. The absence of his cologne implied he had been washed, and tightness in his chest with each breath betrayed at least one cracked rib along with several other aches and pains.

Squinting against bright light, Corin looked around, immediately recognising his surroundings as the market district medical centre. Through a wide window, he could see a busy corridor as doctors and nursing staff bustled back and forth. Jemel lay next to him in an identical cot, heavy bandaging wrapping his head and some impressive bruises beginning to colour his arms and torso. Corin winced, stretching out his arms and legs as he checked for any serious damage. It appeared that the beating had been thorough but amateurish, with the bandages binding his friend's head and his own chest being the only notable injuries. The rest was just bruising and would heal quickly enough.

The door opened, and a tall, lean man walked in with a riot gun slung over his shoulder, his body armour the dark blue of the Kolam and his grey hair cut short in a military style. Corin had never met him before, but he easily recognised the man as Roccan Drathmore, the feared head of the Kolam. Even the gangers working for Elemos were cautious around the corporation's enforcers, for whom there were basically no laws to follow, and the head of that organisation commanded the utmost respect. Corin shifted in his cot to try and sit up, but pain shot through his chest and forced him back down.

"Stay where you are. You know who I am?" Corin nodded. "The nurse told me they've given you a bone binding injection so the ribs should knit back together in a day or so, but you'll be sore for a couple of weeks." Drathmore grabbed a chair and dragged it over to Corin's bedside. "You boys took quite a beating. What were you playing at, getting into it with a crowd that big?"

Corin shrugged, and gestured to the unconscious Jemel in the next cot. "You'd have to ask Jemel. I was just backing him up. Jem takes criticism of Mr. Elemos very seriously." Corin didn't feel any need to lie about how the fight had started; Jemel would be proud of his efforts were he conscious. As he took Drathmore through the events of that morning, the Kolam chief made few notes, instead quietly listening and only interrupting to confirm that Kibbs had been there in person.

As Corin repeated the words the unionist had been speaking to the crowd, Drathmore saw the fierceness and conviction in his eyes, and not a little shame.

"What Kibbs said, about the state of things; what did you think of that?"

Corin was surprised by the question, and took a moment to respond. "I just . . .." He paused, wondering how wise it would be to reveal his true feelings to one of the corporate regime's most senior people, but realised that Drathmore would see through it if he lied. "I don't like the way things are. A lot of what Kibbs said is true; the workers are basically slaves, there is no way off Epiphany for them. They come here for an opportunity and end up trapped. People like me come around and take what little they have or they end up dead or hooked on drugs. The executives live in luxury while everyone else just survives." Corin looked at Drathmore for a response but the older man remained silent, so he continued, emboldened. "I was told that the fire my parents died in was an accident, but I've seen stores burn down when people don't pay protection. Hell, I've been part of it. Jem's dad died in the refinery, and his ma overdosed at The

Black. You tell me if that's right."

Drathmore stood and walked to the window looking out into the clinic, watching as a man on a gurney was rushed past. Past him, Corin glimpsed a nurse cowering before two suited executives who shouted as they waved sheaves of paperwork in his face. His colleagues didn't even look, lest they also attract the ire of the powerful couple. A mine worker slumped on a nearby bench, clearly unconscious or dead, without anyone sparing her as much as a glance.

Drathmore sighed. "No, son, it isn't right, but it's the way of things. I don't like it any more than you do, but my job is to maintain order and security, and people like Lenton Kibbs threaten that. Would you rather see people downtrodden or see them dead?"

"Dead and free might be better than alive and in slavery."

"Possibly, but as long as I do my job, we'll never know." Drathmore turned back to the room. "You've given me enough to arrest Kibbs. I'll take care of it personally. Message Elemos and tell him, from me, not to interfere. I'll not brook a war of reprisal breaking out on my station." Drathmore opened the door, and then turned to nod at Jemel. "When he wakes up, I want you both at HQ for statements. Don't do anything stupid, Corin. One man can't change anything."

"Maybe true, but if there are enough 'one men,' maybe they can. All they need is the opportunity to try."

Drathmore paused to consider this, then nodded and walked

out of the room. As the door closed behind him, Corin heard him start radioing orders for the raid of the unionist offices.

###

Lenton Kibbs was in a briefing in the small cave behind the unionist headquarters when he heard the commotion as a Kolam arrest team burst in to the unionist office. He watched a monitor showing feeds from several hidden cameras in the storefront as eight heavily armed and armoured officers walked in and ordered everyone out except the staff whilst another two guarded the doorway. Once the men and women of the Kolam were satisfied that there was no threat, Roccan Drathmore strode in to the office and held a shining silver plate above his head.

"I have an arrest warrant for Lenton Kibbs. You will tell me where he is, right now." The two unionist reps who ran the front office squeaked denials and blows rained down from the shock-batons of the enforcers to "jog" their memories. Drathmore stood impassive as his squad tore down shelves, ripped posters from walls, and sifted through paperwork searching for evidence of wrongdoing, but Kibbs was confident that there was nothing incriminating in the office. The entrance into the cave was actually at the back of the service laundry next door, not in the unionist property at all, and the pinhole cameras would be impossible to spot without dedicated detection equipment. To be doubly sure, the storefront workers genuinely didn't know where he was; he only stopped in to the office every few days to show his face.

Kibbs beckoned to his two most trusted lieutenants as he

watched the enforcers drag his employees to the back of the waiting APC and finish kicking through the wreckage of the office. Drathmore was the last to leave the building, looking around with an unreadable expression before stalking out into the street. Seconds later, a small dark shape flew in through the broken front window of the office, and the monitor dissolved into static as the grenade destroyed the fragile cameras along with everything else in the room. Kibbs leaned forward and switched off the monitor, silencing the static hiss.

"We need to bring up the schedule. Jax, instruct the kill teams to go now. We need to eliminate any possible threat from Elemos and his organisation before we move." The short, stocky woman nodded and left the cave through a small crevasse at the rear, scooping up a duffel bag that clanked metallically.

"Tora, spread the word—the demonstration is tonight. Let the rally leaders know. Individual groups are to meet at their designated points and mass at the entrance to the executive district, as planned."

The other man nodded, but paused. "Lenton, what do you think tipped them off?"

Kibbs had been wondering that himself. "Those two punks Elemos sent to the rally yesterday. They saw my face before they got beat down, and that's all Drathmore needs to trump up an arrest on an assault charge." He considered his options for a moment. "Go catch up with Jax and add those two to the list. We can't have violent men walking around our new society with a grudge against us."

Tora nodded again, and left through the laundry door. Kibbs sat down at a small desk and waited for the reports to come in.

The Black had started life as a chemical refinery, but since then it had been a film house, a brewery, a small printing works, and a social club before Executive Elemos had seen its potential and negotiated a trade for his interests in mass transportation planetside. Under his ownership, it had transformed into bar, club, drug den, and whorehouse all rolled into one, spawning several lesser competitors in what had become known as the black district. The penthouse offered Elemos an unrivalled position where he could see clear across one of the main caverns of Epiphany station, containing the black, retail, and market districts, as well as two major slums where the majority of his business came from.

Elemos leant back in his recliner and sighed contentedly, a glass of iced liqueur in his hand and one of his best girls with her face buried in his lap. The message from Corin that Drathmore was finally going to deal with the unionist bastards was welcome indeed; he'd lost too many useful people to those murderers recently, and now he was celebrating his change in fortune. Through the reinforced one-way glass floor, he could see other girls servicing clients in the sixth-floor brothel, the one reserved for corporation executives and visiting dignitaries. Several rows of monitors showed him what was happening on all floors of the building, including the basement where clients with more exotic tastes and thicker wads of cash could "express themselves" on subjects both willing and unwilling.

A tentative knock sounded at the door, which was then slammed open as Orr burst in. The girl was so startled by the sudden noise she damn near bit it off, and Elemos swatted her away with a backhand as he stood and hurriedly rearranged his clothing. Orr averted his eyes respectfully, and behind the big ganger, Elemos could see his assistant berating a young man bearing the colours of a gang runner.

Orr didn't even wait for Elemos to give him permission before speaking. "Sir, we have to get you out. Your life is in danger." That certainly got his attention as Orr gestured to the runner in the hallway. "The kid was with Len an hour ago when two guys ended him, straight up in the middle of the street, bang. On his way here, he saw two more lots of guys hunting, and we just heard Kooke's car ran over a mine, killed him and our two best dealers. Our people are being picked off." Elemos was already moving, collecting his document case and pistol from his desk and thinking of ways to punish Drathmore for his failure, when the crying girl he'd slapped pointed out of the window.

"Wh-what's that? Sir?" Elemos followed the line of her finger and saw a bright pinprick of light flare on the other side of the cavern and then grow. Realisation crossed his face and he just had time to shout before the missile slammed into the first floor of The Black and shook the building to its foundations, throwing him to the floor. Several more spots of light lit up and streaked toward the building.

Executive Elemos died as the second missile smashed into the penthouse and detonated, seconds before the rest of the salvo slammed home and demolished the building.

The crowd at the entrance barrier had been growing for several hours, and by now almost a thousand workers were standing with placards held high. Drathmore stood and watched as another group emerged from a side street and joined the main congregation, as group leaders wove through them handing out megaphones and signs. Security was heightened after the murders in the black district and a line of blank-helmed guards stood opposite the crowd, but spot checks had determined that none of the people in the crowd were meant to be on shift and so far there hadn't been a trace of violence. In fact, the gathering had more of a carnival atmosphere, so under station law there was nothing he could do to prevent the protest from continuing.

Drathmore climbed into the back of his car, instructing his driver to take him back to his apartment as he retrieved his beeping communicator from his pocket and keyed it to the vehicle's screen. An image of the head and shoulders of Chairman Delacruz appeared behind the driver's head.

"Roccan, what's going on out there? Why aren't those bastards working?" Drathmore cursed silently, composing himself before responding.

"Sir, they're off shift. None of them are armed. According to station law, they are entitled to be there," Drathmore said.

"I don't care if they have a note from God saying they can be there, I don't want them protesting every little thing. Dammit, our people are being killed out there, and you haven't done shit about it! Get rid of them!" The chairman was almost shouting now, his face darkening with anger. "I'm declaring martial law. They'll run home to mummy when they face the Kolam with loaded weapons."

Drathmore physically recoiled in shock. "Sir, we can't do that. The situation is on a knife edge—any provocation and we could have a full-scale rebellion on our hands. The only way to deal with this is to sit down and talk with Kibbs, see if the Head of Resource can negotiate a settlement."

"Are you refusing a direct order?"

"No, sir, I'm refusing to allow you to let them justify a war. So far we've kept this quiet—none of the other corporations or anyone back home has heard about this yet, and if we can keep it quiet none of them will. Would CEO Dalaga like it if we start dragging his corporation's name through the mud because we're killing our workforce?"

Delacruz paused to consider this. "You had better be right, or I'll hold you accountable. Alright, no martial law yet, but if they push me, I'll order the Kolam to open fire. Now get back here. There's a board meeting in four hours, and you need to be ready." The screen snapped off.

Drathmore sighed; he didn't think he'd be able to prevent the bloodshed for much longer. He leant forward and told the driver to change destination, seeing out of the window the last couple of groups of workers joining the swelling mass of protestors as they began to make their way down the long avenue toward the head office.

As the car approached the fortress-like wall of the head office building, Drathmore's attention was drawn to a small confrontation outside the main entrance. Three Kolam officers were arguing with Corin and Jemel, the young gangers clearly about to be shock-batoned into submission. The car drew to a halt next to the gate, and he smoothly stepped out into the space between Jemel and the guards before the argument could escalate to violence. Jemel ignored him, but Corin nodded in greeting as Drathmore turned to the officers with a questioning look.

"Sir," the most senior officer said, stepping forward. "Do you know these men? They claim you told them to come here."

"I did. What seems to be the issue?" Drathmore's tone was icy, and the officer glanced at his comrades for support.

"They were searched and both are armed. They aren't cooperating. I was about to arrest them."

"Try it, Kolam punk," Jemel said with a snarl, but Drathmore put his arm in front of the ganger to stop him from stepping forward. Now that he looked closely, the younger man had more cuts and scrapes than he had in the hospital, and the steel knuckles he held loosely were crusted with drying blood. Corin had similar injuries and was making no effort to hide the small pistol tucked into his waistband. Corin noticed the head of security looking at the weapon, and at least had the common sense to look slightly chagrined.

"We messaged Elemos like you asked, and then we headed over here when we heard about the attacks. On the way, we were jumped—six of them, miners mostly. The weapons are theirs." Corin pulled out the pistol and handed it to Drathmore, butt first. "We killed two—the others ran off."

Drathmore took the pistol and passed it to one of the guards. "It's Kibbs, it has to be. You two seeing him is the only link we have between him and the killings, so he knows you're a threat. Go on up to the security office—one of these officers will escort you and take your statements. I'll be there as soon as I've finished a board meeting."

Outside the head office building, the crowd of protesters had finally made their way up the long drive through the lawns and shrubs of the executive district. During the march, the carnival atmosphere of the protest had eked away as the workers saw, most for the first time, the luxury that the leadership caste enjoyed while they slaved away in the mines and refineries. Now the crowd was sullen, their chants having a raw, aggressive edge as the crowd surrounded the entrance. The three guards still on duty had called for reinforcement. Now a row of Kolam officers in riot gear faced the crowd, helmets covering their faces and shock-batons ready to crush the protest.

Through the crowd, several men and women in black refinery jumpsuits moved from group to group. Wherever they went, the protesters became more and more aggressive. The agitators kept in touch using small radios clipped to their ears, carefully inciting the protest so that they would be at the peak of their fury when Kibbs made his appearance.

###

"Gentlemen, perhaps we could call this meeting to order? We can discuss Service Management's evening activities at another juncture." Chairman Delacruz's tone was light, but it was well known that the chairman only called the board members by their departments when he was making a point regarding hierarchy. A single glance at his face was enough for the other board members to hurriedly take their seats as two Kolam agents stepped in and closed the double doors. Service Management nodded an apology as he sat, his story about his latest exploits in the head office harem cut off just as it got interesting. His seat was at the far end from the chairman. To his right sat the heads of Industrial Operations and Resources; opposite were Relations and Finance. In the last seat, at his right hand, Drathmore took his seat in his capacity as Head of Security. Delacruz waited until everyone was seated and attentive before continuing.

"You have all seen the anomaly report provided by the sensor station. Just over seven hours ago, an object was detected approaching from outside the system. Sensors are unable to tell us where it has come from or exactly what it is. Visual examination shows a cylinder roughly a kilometre long and one-hundred-metres wide. Gentlemen, tell me what we know." Delacruz sat back in his chair and gestured for them to continue.

Industrial Operations took a sip of water and wiped his brow with his handkerchief. A jowly, heavily overweight man with a nervous disposition and a constant sheen of sweat over his balding scalp, he nevertheless was an expert in deep space mining. "We have carried out a full spectral analysis. The results are . . . breathtaking. We're picking up indicators of *every* trace element we know of and several we don't, in amounts that boggle the mind. Quite simply, it's the find of the . . . of the . . . well, ever." He glanced at Delacruz for signs of acknowledgement, but he kept his face impassive, so he hurriedly continued. "The speed of the object is high, but no greater than some of the comets we've mined in the past. If we were to launch within the next three days we can get in front of it, attach tow-motors, and slow it down so that we can mine it."

The head of Relations leaned forward and made a steeple with her fingers as she looked to Delacruz. "We've had no indication that any other corporation has detected the object. Given our position, the position of any rival assets, and the range at which we detected the anomaly, we can assume no one else will even see it for another two days. No one can get to it within five. It's ours if we want it." At this, Delacruz nodded. Relations were responsible for communicating and negotiating with, and spying on, the other corporations in the system. The current head of the department was a ruthlessly cold and efficient woman who had yet to put a foot wrong. He mused that if left unchecked, she could become a threat to his position in the future and resolved to order Drathmore to find any skeletons in her closet. Delacruz looked to the young man next to her.

"Finance, I take it that if we get to this thing then the gains would be worth any financial investment?"

Finance nodded.

"Good. Resources, what will it cost us in people?"

Resources looked up sharply from the screen he had been studying, a haunted look on his pale face.

"Sir, assuming we deploy 2,500 miners and given the speed the anomaly is moving, the distance from the station, the various mechanisms and techniques we would have to employ—" Delacruz made a get-to-the-point gesture. "Sir, we're looking at a twenty-percent resource rate." From the corner of his eye, Delacruz saw Drathmore blanch at the figure and wondered. The Head of Security had never been squeamish before about spending lives, and he wondered what had changed. Still, this was no time to be worrying about that.

"A twenty-percent casualty rate is acceptable given the potential gains. Now, we need to . . ." He paused as Resources meekly raised his hand. "Yes, Resources? You have more information?"

"Sir, apologies." Resources looked even more flustered as he fiddled with his thin-rimmed spectacles, "but the twenty percent isn't the casualty rate. It's the *survival* rate."

Delacruz took this in without visible reaction. The head of Resources began to repeat himself, but was stopped short when Delacruz raised his hand. "Very well, we go ahead as planned."

Drathmore rocked back as if the chairman had hit him, his shock plain on his face.

"Sir, that's two thousand people who wouldn't survive. Two *thousand*. The workers are already up in arms; the security forces are barely holding them in check. If this gets out, it could light a powder keg." Drathmore was trying to present rational arguments, but he could see from Delacruz's face that it wasn't working. Coupled with his refusal to enact martial law, Delacruz thought he was going soft.

"Then you will make sure it doesn't get out—you personally, Drathmore. As far as the workers will know, this will be a perfectly standard operation. Now, does anyone else want to grow a conscience? No?"

All of the board members, even Resources, refused to meet his gaze. "No, I didn't think so. You know what to do. Make it happen." The board members all muttered acknowledgements and made their way out of the room, the two silent Kolam agents following them out. As one of them closed the boardroom doors behind them, the other reached for his communicator.

###

Roccan Drathmore walked through the metal detector at the entrance to the security department of the head office without stopping despite the flashing red light and insistent beeping set off by the handgun in his jacket. The Kolam officer manning the post saluted him and silenced the alarms with a press of a button, and Drathmore nodded his thanks. As he walked down the corridor, he looked through a glass wall and saw Corin sleeping on a couch but no sign of the other boy, Jemel. The other boy had seemed far less comfortable being near the inner sanctum of the security forces, and Drathmore wasn't surprised that he had made his getaway as soon as he could.

Walking into his office and closing the door behind him, Drathmore shrugged off his suit jacket and moved over to the rack beside his desk. His fatigues and body armour were hung next to a shoulder holster for his pistol and a massive shot cannon. Delacruz insisted that all members were attired appropriately for board meetings, but Drathmore could never wait to get out of the restrictive business suit and back into the familiar comfort of his combat gear. As he changed, he noticed a flashing light on his desk terminal, and he unlocked it with a verbal command. The message was from Munda, his second in command, and his expression hardened as he played her message.

"Sir, Chairman Delacruz has expressed his concern at the situation outside. He said he couldn't contact you and asked me to disperse the protesters and enact martial law. I've tooled up the reaction force, and we're going out."

Drathmore cursed. Munda was a political appointment, forced upon him regardless of her minimal skill as a law keeper, and to boot, she was a sadist who enjoyed the freedom that being in the feared secret police gave her to inflict harm on others. She would have been only too keen to obey the chairman's orders and saddle up to deal serious harm to the civilians outside.

A cough attracted his attention, and he saw Corin standing in the doorway, leaning nonchalantly against the doorframe. On impulse, Drathmore pressed the play button again and watched the younger man's face as he listened to the recording.

As it finished, Corin swallowed visibly. "They won't back down. It'll be a massacre."

Drathmore nodded and walked to a large cupboard. Opening it, he handed a set of body armour and a riot gun to Corin.

"You're deputised. Put this on."

Corin raised his eyebrows as he took the equipment. "Why do you trust me?"

Drathmore checked the charge on his shock-baton before replying. "Because you know the value of a life, and you won't take one unless you have to. You're a much wiser man than I was at your age. Now come on—we have to stop Munda before she kills everyone."

###

It was late morning, and the thoroughfare at the rear of the head office building was quiet. Only a few workers hurried down the street to join the protest on the other side of the building as the hatch creaked open and Jemel stepped out. The summons from Elemos' agent within the Kolam had been brief and their meeting even shorter. Now he had to get news of the upcoming mission back to the executive so that he could act upon it. News of a big mining job always increased demand for the girls and drugs Elemos provided, and if word were to accidentally get out of its high risk nature, that would only cause more workers to seek a temporary escape to ease their fears. Jemel glanced about to ensure that his exit had not been observed, and then he hurried toward the black district.

Despite the beatings he and Corin had so recently received, Jemel moved confidently. He was proud of his gang markings and knew that, short of another mass rally, no one would attempt to stop him. Even the Kolam had studiously ignored him when he had left Corin asleep and walked brazenly out of the security wing of head office. He even smiled to the guards manning the checkpoint and received a nod in return as he left the executive quarter and headed down the main avenue through the market district.

At first, he didn't notice the two men following him, and when he did, he thought nothing of it. Only when he rounded a corner into a narrower walkway and found his way blocked by two more men wielding lengths of pipe did he realise his mistake. He turned around to try to escape, but the first men had blocked his exit. Lashing out, he kicked the first man in the groin and shoved the second as hard as he could. Before he could run, light exploded behind his eyes as a pipe hammered into the back of his head and another smashed into his kidney. Jemel collapsed to the floor as blows rained down on him; he felt at least two ribs crack as the breath was knocked out of him by a well-aimed boot and a huge swing with a pipe caved in his left eye socket. The beating continued until a voice commanded the men to stop, and Jemel cried out in pain as they each roughly grabbed a limb and dragged him to a subsurface access hatch.

The journey through the service corridors under the main level seemed to take forever, each jolt and bump sending bolts of agony through his face and chest, but soon they reached a small hatch and dragged him through. Two of the men stood outside to keep watch while the others roughly bound him to a steel reclining chair bolted to the floor in the middle of the tiny, dirty room. Jemel heard the same voice that had stopped the beating earlier give orders to the two men, and then a face appeared above him, appearing in silhouette with the single ceiling light behind him.

"So, it's the messenger. This really isn't your week, is it, son?" Jemel was confused, but then the figure stepped back. As the light illuminated the man's face, Jemel recognised him as Lenton Kibbs, the leader of the rally in the habitat district. Kibbs saw the recognition in Jemel's face and smirked. "Not your week at all. So, you carry messages for Elemos. Elemos works for the board. You leave the head office in a hurry and head straight to the black, which means you are carrying an important message. This will all be much more pleasant for you if you tell me what that message was."

Kibbs paused, and Jemel thought as fast as he could. He was hurt badly, but he'd had worse before, and Elemos dealt with betrayal even more harshly than he dealt with failure. There was no way he was going to just give up the message, and as soon as he got back to Elemos and told him what had happened, Kibbs' days would be numbered.

Kibbs smiled at his silence and put his hand into his pocket. "I'll be honest, I was hoping you would stay quiet. It's been a while since I got to practise my skills." Kibbs took his hand out of his pocket, and Jemel caught a glimpse of metal shining in the harsh blueness of the ceiling light. A tiny motor whirred to life as the two men roughly grabbed him and held him in place. Kibbs took hold of Jemel's right wrist and held his hand up to the light.

Jemel cried out in agony as the man used the mineral saw to cut his thumb off. The unionist leader worked his way through every finger on Jemel's hand before turning off the saw and putting it on a table next to the chair. Jemel had his remaining eye squeezed tightly shut. He was sweating and panting as he desperately tried to get his breath back and block out the fire in his ruined hand. Kibbs leant over his face, and Jemel was helpless as one of the men forced his eye open. "Had enough?"

"Fuck you, you fucking psychopath!" Jemel reared forward and spat in his face before the two men could slam him back into his chair. Kibbs wiped his face with a cloth and scowled.

"Hold his head." One of the men gripped Jemel's head on each side as Kibbs drew another tool from his pocket and flicked it on, sneering at the ganger. "I'm going to make this last as long as possible."

Jemel screamed as Kibbs lowered the soldering tool into his remaining eye.

###

A roar of approval rose up as Lenton Kibbs made his appearance at the protest outside. Corin was jogging over to the main gate of the building, following in the footsteps of the head of security. Drathmore had been silent as they had made their way through the building to stop Munda from massacring the protesters. As soon as they burst into the courtyard, however, he started shouting orders at the troopers massing behind the two-meter-high wall. Drathmore immediately moved to confront the short, stocky woman who Corin assumed to be Munda, and so Corin swiftly mounted the stairs to the fire step at the top of the wall.

Looking down, he saw the crowd had grown even further and continued to do so as more and more workers made their way into the executive district. They were paying rapt attention to Kibbs as he stood on the back of a small power cart with a display screen behind him. As if Corin's gaze had attracted his attention, Kibbs looked up and locked eyes with him for a moment, a wicked smile moving across his face as he turned back to address the crowd.

"My brothers and sisters, it is worse than we feared! The corporations and their lackeys in the gangs have crossed the line this time. Only this afternoon, they sent one of their assassins to kill me!" Kibbs looked across the crowd as a swell of indignation rode across the workers, then gestured for quiet. "Two of your fellows died defending me from the maniac they sent, and I will be eternally grateful to their memories."

More shouts and threats of retribution came from the crowd,

and even Drathmore and Munda had stopped arguing and were watching the mob as it reached boiling point. A sense of cold dread settled in the pit of Corin's stomach as Kibbs glanced up at him again before continuing.

"But there is more! The corporation does not care about your lives, they only care for profit. Even now, they plot to send you to your deaths—two thousand of you! And this isn't just propaganda as they would claim—no, we have proof! The assassin confessed before he died! Tora, show them the footage." Kibbs gestured to the man on his right, who entered a command into his datapad. The screen behind him came to life.

The face on the screen was half destroyed, one of his eye sockets caved in and the other eye a gooey mess dripping down the man's face. The damage was so severe that it was only when the man started talking that Corin recognised his best friend.

Drathmore was worried. The crowd had grown to almost unmanageable proportions, and soon it would be too big for the few troopers he had to contain, if it wasn't already. His only hope was that the protest would remain peaceful long enough to disperse naturally, but Munda had shown him the chairman's orders and they were explicit—disperse the crowd immediately, through any means necessary. He'd been about to contact the chairman and challenge the orders when his attention had been grabbed by Kibb's oratory. As he listened to the unionist's story, he used his datapad to issue orders to the troopers in the courtyard. Discretely, they moved into defensive positions in the courtyard, even Munda having the sense not to argue given the situation.

As Kibbs spoke, he kept glancing up to the wall, and Drathmore followed his gaze to see Corin standing on the fire step watching the protest. Intuition from years of law enforcement had him moving toward the younger man just as the screen flicked on. A ruined face stared out at the crowd and started talking shakily about the anomaly mission, but he was too late. Corin let out a wordlessly anguished cry as he dropped down from the fire step and sprinted toward the power cart.

"Corin, don't!" shouted Drathmore, but it was too late.

With Corin screaming his hate at Kibbs, it seemed to the maddened crowd that another murderer was coming for their leader, and they formed an impenetrable wall between the two men.

Kibbs pointed up at the screen, his voice fiery now. "See how they plot to murder you all along with me! This cannot continue! If we want to live, we have to take back our lives by force!"

The crowd responded with a huge angry roar and surged through the entrance into the courtyard.

Chairman Delacruz watched through the window of the boardroom as the mob stormed into the courtyard and slammed into the riot shields and shock-batons of the Kolam troopers lined up to repel them. He sighed heavily. He'd thought for a long time that

Drathmore had been going soft, but this latest failure simply proved what he had suspected for a few months—the head of security was no longer fit for command. Delacruz would have to do what he had done his whole life and take control himself.

"If you want something done properly . . ." he said, muttering as he walked over to the comms station on the boardroom wall and flicked a switch.

"All Kolam and security holding the head office, this is Chairman Delacruz. Roccan Drathmore is relieved as head of security, effective immediately. Live fire is authorised. Shoot to kill." Delacruz walked back to the window and looked out again, smiling as the first bangs of weapons fire echoed through the courtyard.

Drathmore blocked the swing of a socket wrench with his riot shield and pushed back, sending the woman wielding it sprawling back into the press of struggling bodies as he yelled for his men to cease fire. A small group of Kolam stood with him in an ordered fashion, using their shields, shock-batons, and stun guns to hold back the crowd. Most of the others ignored his shouts as the protesters attacked them with wild abandon. More riot guns boomed, and he saw an arm pinwheel through the air, arterial blood spraying red against the clean, white marble.

The rioters had quickly pushed the few troopers in the courtyard back, and they now desperately fought to hold the main foyer. Workers and troopers snarled and screamed in each others' faces as they tripped over bodies and slipped on pooling blood. A trooper went down under a furious barrage of blows. A worker emerged brandishing the fallen man's riot gun and fired before Drathmore could shout a warning. One of the Kolam near him fell, a huge crater blown in his chest. Miners fell upon the wounded man, stabbing and clubbing with their makeshift weapons as Drathmore watched in horror.

A huge man burst through the press of people and barged toward Drathmore and his men, smashing between their shields and ruining their tight formation. Suddenly, the rioters were all over Drathmore. A hammer smacked into his shoulder and something took out his legs as he was borne to the ground. Hands grabbed at his limbs and held him down as the giant lifted a massive bust of CEO Dalaga from a plinth and stood over the prostrate head of security. The miner lifted the bust above his head; his face was a mask of fury. Drathmore closed his eyes and waited for death.

A huge, rapid booming shook the air above him. Drathmore opened his eyes again as the hands holding him down suddenly released. The giant worker still stood, a gaping hole in his chest and an arm missing below the elbow. The crashing noise returned, and the man disintegrated above the waist, his legs toppling over as if in slow motion. Corin stood over Drathmore as he struggled to his feet, the massive barrel of the shot-cannon he was carrying still smoking. The young ganger shrugged the gun's sling from his shoulder and passed it to Drathmore.

"Still want your guys to hold their fire?" The grim expression on the young man's face removed any humour from the remark.

"Thanks. Where did you get . . . never mind. Thanks."

Corin nodded, pulling a combat blade from his waistband and moving back into the fray. Looking around, Drathmore saw that the security forces were barely holding their ground, the sheer fury and numbers of the protesters balanced by the superior firepower and training of the security teams. Drathmore saw Munda fighting in the middle of the crowd, swinging a short flagpole like a quarterstaff as she stood over the bodies of two more Kolam troopers. Drathmore ran toward her, but one of the protesters had taken a pistol from a fallen officer. Munda shook as rounds smacked into her chest, falling beneath the press of bodies. Drathmore raised the shot-cannon and pulled the trigger, yelling noiselessly as the steel flechettes tore Munda's killers apart.

Movement caught Drathmore's eye, and he turned to see black-clad figures disappearing down a side corridor. From the edge of the fighting, Corin had seen it as well. He tried to run after them, but hands reached out and dragged him back into the fight. His eyes locked with Drathmore's.

"Drathmore! It's Kibbs! Kill the bastard!" Corin shouted as the protesters enveloped him and he was fighting for his life once more. Drathmore hesitated for a moment, wanting to save the man who had saved him, but he knew that the whole rebellion lived and died with Kibbs.

Shouldering the shot-cannon, he ran out of the room toward the service entrance.

###

Unlike the main entrance to the boardroom with its plush, deep-shag rugs covering the polished hardwood, the staff entrance was a dull uniform grey corridor barely wide enough for two people. Harsh fluorescent lights hanging from skeletal metal gantries shone with a cold, pale-blue light on corroded rivets connecting sections of steel dating from the first construction of the station. Each hatch bore the scratches and dents of a thousand clumsy bumps and scrapes. Chairman Delacruz limped along under the conduits and pipes swarming over the ceiling, favouring his left leg and leaving bloody footprints as he made his way to the emergency ladder.

As the boardroom doors had smashed open and bullets began to thud into the other board members, he had spun his chair around and dived through the heavy red curtains at the back of the room. This was a staging area, where the waiters and sommeliers normally waited hidden until summoned to serve the postmeeting banquet. The carbon-reinforced back of his chair had absorbed most of the shots. As he hurled himself from the room, a stray bullet had smacked into his leg, missing the bone but lodging in the meat of his thigh.

As he reached a ladder set into an alcove in the wall and painfully began to descend, he could hear the gunfire die away behind him. The rattle and crash of fully automatic fire and grenades mixed with the occasional single sharp reports of execution rounds as the rebels finished off the surviving board members. He was confident that the vacuum-rated hatch would hold them long enough for him to reach the nearest launch bay, but there was no guarantee that other groups of fighters hadn't already reached the shuttlecraft. The rebels could be securing or sabotaging them to prevent his escape, so he moved as quickly as his wounded leg would allow.

The ladder shaft opened out into a docking area completely devoid of people, and Delacruz breathed a sigh of relief as he staggered across it. Although it was one of the smaller launch bays on the station, it was still at least three hundred meters across and was almost full of heavy mining equipment. Slave-controlled mining drills and semi-autonomous debris collectors intermingled with heavy ore dredgers and a couple of specialist blasting craft, whose task was to attach to a large asteroid and attach high explosives before detonating and riding out the storm. Towering over all of them was a single mammoth refining machine, a yellow and grey behemoth able to swallow the chunks of asteroid left from the blasting and render them down, ejecting waste rock and dust from one side and refined elements from the other. Nestled in the shadow of the huge machine was a small personnel shuttle used by a supervisor to oversee the mining operations. Delacruz hobbled toward the small craft, using his tab to open the airlock and begin powering up its systems along with those of another, much smaller craft on the other side of the hanger.

Delacruz knew that in the eyes of the CEO he had failed. The station was in the hands of the enemy, the rest of the board was dead or captured, and CEO Dalaga was not known for his clemency. At best, they would send a rescue craft and then publicly execute him as a demonstration of how the corporation treated failure; at worst, they would simply leave him in the tiny craft to drift in space until he ran out of food and water. His only hope would be to claim the anomaly for the corporation and hope that the value of it as a prize would be enough to bargain for his survival. The only way to do that was to attach a beacon to it, broadcasting its status as Dalaga Corporation property. The smaller craft he had activated was basically an engine attached to a powerful transmitter, used to claim important finds that could not be mined right away. As the drone whined up to full power, it bobbed up from the floor and hovered on a jet of thrust waiting for command. As Delacruz entered the shuttle, the airlock door hissed shut behind him and the ship lifted into the air, heading for the bay doors and open space with the smaller beacon craft following in its wake.

###

Kibbs stood next to the communications desk as Jax and his two remaining followers worked their way around the board room, kicking each body in turn and putting a single round between the eyes of any board member who showed signs of life. He hadn't fired his pistol yet, either in the foyer or as they stormed the boardroom. He was content to let the others do the killing around him as he retuned the com set and angled the transmitter dish to a new set of target coordinates.

As the last board member was shot, Jax sat down in a chair and looked up at him. The adrenaline of serious combat and the enormity of what they had done clearly weighed heavily on the woman, her eyes twitching and her hands unable to stop shaking as the shock started to kick in.

"They're all dead, all of them. Lenton, the rest of the system must know what we've done; they must know we are free. Are you going to start the broadcast?" she asked. Kibbs nodded thoughtfully, making final adjustments to the trajectory of the antenna and then smiled at the woman.

"Yes, my friend, I am going to start the broadcast."

Jax smiled nervously back at him, but her expression changed to one of shock as Kibbs smoothly brought up his arm and shot her in the face.

The heavy calibre handgun bucked in his grip and the back of her head simply ceased to exist. The other two were still reacting, turning and raising their captured riot guns as he pivoted on the spot and brought up his other hand, steadying his aim. The pistol kicked twice more and both men crumpled into heaps, one with a huge hole in the back of his head and the other with blood spurting from a severed artery in his neck.

Kibbs grunted with satisfaction and put the weapon down, then leant over and spoke into the microphone. "Gryphone centre, this is Lenton Kibbs, authorisation code brava-brava-chisel-five. I require contact with CEO Kamata. Acknowledge this signal." The com set gave a crackle of noise, and a voice cracked out a brief acknowledgement. Kibbs took a breath and steadied himself. This was the moment the last five years of his life had led him to. The com set crackled and snapped again, and a new voice echoed through the speakers. Recognising the voice of his secret master he bowed slightly, despite the fact that there was no video link.

"Lenton, this is Kamata. I must confess we are not surprised to hear from you. Reports of unrest on Epiphany have been flooding in, and it did sound like your handiwork. Are we ready to proceed?"

"Yes, sir. The board of Epiphany station have been permanently retired, and I have personally eliminated all other major sources of possible resistance, including any of the general population likely to rebel against your authority. The Gryphone Corporation can take possession of the station whenever you so order."

"That's what this was about? A fucking corporate takeover?" The voice came from behind him rather than from the com set. Kibbs spun and then froze, caught in the pose of reaching for the pistol on the table and but knowing that the smallest movement would cause Drathmore to pull the trigger on the gun he had trained on Kibbs' chest. Behind the Kolam chief, the service door he had entered through banged shut with a sharp metallic clang, but his eyes never twitched and the weapon never wavered from its target. The com set behind Kibbs squawked and hissed with Kamata's ranting but Kibbs dared not move. Drathmore's trigger finger was white with pressure, a heartbeat away from firing the cannon. "You did all this, you bastard. You got rid of the board, you got rid of the gangs, you caused the deaths of all those poor fools who believed in you, and for what? To increase a profit margin?"

Kibbs tried to keep a level tone. "Tell me, how many have you killed? How many have you tortured, to keep your masters in control of this station? Get off your pedestal, Drathmore, you might slip and fall in your own hypocrisy."

"I can change. I *have* changed, but I still know what must be done." Lenton saw the barrel of the shot-cannon twitch as Drathmore increased the pressure on the trigger, but before he could fire, two unionists burst in through the main door with their weapons raised.

"Kill him!" Kibbs shouted. The two men opened fire with their fully automatic rifles, but Drathmore was already diving to the side, the long barrel of the shot-cannon turning and barking as fast as he could pull the trigger. Steel flechette rounds tore into the two men, the surrounding doorway, and the corridor beyond them as both disintegrated under the hail of fire. Kibbs took advantage of the distraction and scooped up his pistol, blazing away at the head of the Kolam. One round hit Drathmore in the left shoulder, the next smashed into his chest armour, and a third destroyed the trigger mechanism of the shot-cannon, along with most of Drathmore's right hand. Lenton stalked around the table, reloading the pistol with practiced hands, without taking his eyes off the fallen security chief.

"You *have* changed, Drathmore. You never used to hesitate." Lenton aimed between Drathmore's eyes.

The booming report of the shot echoed around the boardroom, and Drathmore felt a heavy weight crash into his legs. Opening his eyes, he saw what was left of Lenton Kibbs lying across him with a gaping hole where his stomach used to be. In the doorway stood Corin, covered almost head to toe in blood and with several wounds of his own, the smoking barrel of a riot-gun still aimed at the corpse of the Kamata agent.

The boy shouldered the weapon and walked over to Drathmore, grabbing the body by its feet and dragging it off of him, then helping Drathmore to stand. He winced as Corin grabbed his left arm and pain tore through his damaged shoulder but he made it to his feet, and the two men stood face to face as Drathmore nodded his thanks. Corin looked around the room where over fifteen corpses littered the floor and blood sprayed up almost every wall. Some of the board members, like the two unionists, had been dismembered by gunfire and the room resembled a charnel house in every respect, the tang of gunpowder mixing with the coppery scent of blood and the foulness of destroyed bowels.

"Some party, huh?"

Corin snorted with amusement at the older man's tone. "Yeah, some party. Wouldn't want to be the guy who gets to clear this lot up." Corin walked over to the com set, still blaring away as Kamata screeched and shouted for Kibbs to respond, and grasped the microphone. "Kibbs is dead, asshole. You will be too if you come here. Epiphany out."

"Who is this? When we take that station, I will have your head! You and your entire family! I will kill every single—"

Corin flicked the com set off to silence the raving CEO while Drathmore moved next to him and checked some readouts.

"That bastard, he completely took down the defence systems. I'll get them back up." Drathmore entered some commands, and two blank screens came to life, displaying an image of Epiphany station and a list of weapon platforms. A blue glow began to surround the image of the station as the weapon platforms went from a static to active status.

"What's that?" Corin pointed at a third monitor, where the anomaly could easily be seen as it passed through the inner reaches of the system. Ahead of it, directly in its path, was a sensor blip. Drathmore interrogated the sensor report.

"It's a shuttle. One of ours. Launched ten minutes ago using the authorisation codes of . . . Chairman Delacruz. Dammit, he's going to claim the anomaly. It's the only way to buy his life back from Dalaga."

"Can you stop him?" Corin moved to the console, but he was a ganger, not a systems tech. Drathmore entered several commands into the console and a warning message flashed. He dismissed it and hit a final confirmation.

"What did you do?" Corin asked.

"I used the maintenance override codes to carry out an emergency shutdown of his reactor. Being head of security has its privileges." Drathmore locked the console and looked at Corin. For the first time, he noticed just how badly wounded the younger man really was and helped him to stagger over to the table and collapse into the chairman's seat.

###

The interior of the shuttle could hardly be called opulent, but it served the basic needs Delacruz had of it at this moment. The auto-galley had produced a reasonable approximation of brandy, and the internal com was piping through some neo-classical music as he lounged back in the pilot's couch and sipped his drink. After the terror of nearly being murdered and the fear of his headlong flight from danger, Delacruz needed a drink, and so after getting the shuttle into position along the anomaly's course and bandaging the wound in his leg, he had set the automatic navigator to hold station. The beacon was deactivated until it was needed, to save the little craft's batteries.

Through the reinforced plex of the forward viewscreen, he could see the anomaly approaching, the hundred-meter-wide circumference of the cylinder directly ahead. Delacruz smiled to himself as he saw his salvation approach, and he reached for the manual controls so he could manoeuvre out of the anomaly's path.

As he touched the controls, the music stopped. Delacruz frowned in frustration just as the lighting flickered and died to an emergency battery only level. Complete silence fell as the air circulators spooled down to a dead stop.

He pressed the button to turn them back on.

No response.

The lights wouldn't flicker back on, and neither would the music.

He rammed the throttle as far forward as it would go, but no reaction mass burst from the ships' thrusters. Delacruz pounded the buttons and keys on the command console but all he did was beat his hands bloody, leaving fist-prints in scarlet on the screens. Panicking, he moved to the copilot seat, but all the controls there were just as dead. Through the plex, he saw the anomaly rapidly approaching.

Delacruz whimpered in fear as he moved to the airlock, desperate to escape the seemingly never-ending shining barrier that now dwarfed the tiny shuttle, but the airlock door wouldn't cycle open. Delacruz turned and pressed his back to the hatch, raising his arms in a desperate attempt to fend off the onrushing silver wall.

The anomaly smashed into the beacon craft, disintegrating it and leaving no pieces larger than a coin to tumble into space. A second later, it obliterated the shuttle, pancaking it before it bounced across the smooth face of the cylinder to tumble behind in its wake. Chairman Delacruz died, screaming and alone, as the airlock he had been so desperate to open folded around him and crushed his skull.

The public areas of Epiphany station were almost silent, the corridors and avenues virtually deserted as the people took refuge from both the rioting and the inevitable retribution by the security teams. The stalls in the market district were shuttered and the ore processing plants were silent as the population took shelter. From apartments, crash-houses, bars, and clubs came muted sound as people huddled together watching the news on screens and speaking in hushed tones, fearfully glancing at the doors where any moment a rebel group or a security team might burst in bringing violence and death.

A loud crackling cut through the silence in the streets, followed by a sharp static hiss. Those few people still out looked up to the civic broadcast displays that hadn't been used since the corporation took over Epiphany, as screens that had been blank for over a decade flickered and snowed before snapping into focus, showing a pick-axe superimposed over an asteroid—the old symbol of the system mining efforts before the rise of the corporations. Speakers mounted on poles at avenue intersections and on walls in corridors blared a brief brass fanfare before dying back to the same background hiss.

The emblem disappeared, and in its place was a shirtless, dark-haired and muscular young man, displaying gang tattoos on his arms and chest. He was seated at the head of a large wooden table, with a large gun resting in front of him. His left eye was swollen almost closed, and his torso was covered in a sheen of blood seeping from numerous gashes in his flesh. Behind him stood a much older man in body armour with short, receding grey hair and a hawkish face that could have looked noble, had it not been pale and drawn from blood loss from his several gunshot wounds. As the young man's icy blue eyes stared into the camera, every single person watching felt the intensity of his gaze drilling into them even through the screen.

"Foreman Lenton Kibbs is dead." He paused and a wry grin flashed across his face. "So are Chairman Delacruz and his entire board, and Executive Elemos along with most of the other executives. None of them should be missed. Delacruz was a sleaze willing to kill thousands just to turn a profit. Kibbs was a snake trying to steal the station for another corporation so they could do the same. Neither of them gave a shit about you. Neither of them gave a shit about *us*, and they have paid with their lives."

"For too long the corporations have taken from us. For too long they have profited while we toiled; they have lived in luxury while we lived in squalor; they have lived while we have died. *No more.* No more working until you drop from exhaustion. No more bowing and scraping to men who were born into their positions instead of working for them. No more secret police disappearing people in the middle of the night." The older man winced as the younger man continued without pause. "Now we control this station, and with it the biggest source of raw materials in the entire system. Without Epiphany, they cannot function." He hesitated and glanced at the older man behind him, who nodded for him to continue. "Make no mistake, they will try to take it back from us—and if they do, then nothing will change. We must fight, and we must win. We must show them that the need to live is stronger than the greed for wealth."

The young man shifted in his seat and nodded to someone unseen behind the camera, and his image was replaced by the view from a remote camera outside the station. Epiphany filled the screen, and in the background a shining silver cylinder could be seen moving away as his voice continued. "My name is Corin. I was born on Epiphany. It is my home and my world, and I pledge this to you.

We will work together to change our lives. We will fight together to protect our newfound freedom. We will be our own salvation."

Locum
By A. R. Aston

Locum, the greatest engine of the Gavel system, had ordered the planets like strings on a harp, tuned and perfected orbits put in place to create the gravity waves that would conjure the sweet music of eternity.

Perfection took ten millennia. In that time, the stunted creators had grown up, withered and died on the vine. They perished on their world, never reaching the potential Locum achieved. Every particle of the system was now his to govern, his to order and orchestrate.

The rod, an intruder, an interloper of the cold void, scored a blunt line of gravitic trauma through Locum's great work. Like a razor blade across a first folio of poetry, his art was forever tarnished. Locum, clothed in nuclear fire, threw himself after the drifting rod. Eventually, even he retreated back to his tattered artwork, for it was the only shelter for countless light years.

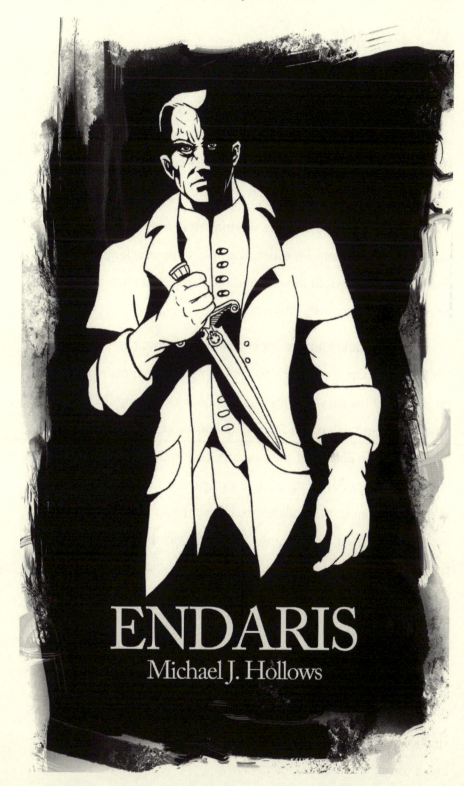

Endaris
By Michael J. Hollows

His brush scraped across the dirt in a hesitant motion. As he squatted his ankles ached and complained, but he was used to it now. Hjal had spent most of his life squatting in narrow ditches, though that wasn't what he had intended when he joined the universitat.

He looked at the others working near him. The desert sprawled behind them for miles; the only thing breaking it up was the tracks of their pack mounts and the rising heat haze. He wished he was somewhere else. Anywhere else.

The small team had spent a few weeks out here, sent by the Collegiate group to analyse this area of strange magnetism. Hjal had no idea what the mysterious organisation was looking for, but his task felt like punishment for some unknown crime. The Collegiate had left Hjal in charge of the students, and in their time out here they had barely found anything of note except small fragments of metal alloys that even now the alchemists were trying to decipher. He sighed and carried on brushing. The earth was the pale yellow of compressed sand, and each scrape that pulled the sand away only deposited more in the space that it had occupied. It was a thankless task.

Hjal looked back at his work, forgetting the sprawling desert. With a start, he noticed small black flecks had begun to poke through the sand as he dusted it away. Setting his brush aside on the small white cloth that was weighted beside him, he picked up thin metal tongs.

Tentatively, he reached out and tapped the tongs against the darkness showing through the sand. The sound clunked slightly, dampened by the surrounding earth. He felt the resistance of it. With care, he tried to clasp a piece of the black material, but there was nothing to grip; it was completely smooth. Whatever this was, it was far larger than the pieces of metal the others had found. Picking up the brush again, he began frantically scrapping more dirt from the object, being as careful as his hasty intrigue would allow.

Moments passed in his task before Hjal once again set down his tools. With a sigh brought on by aching muscles, he scrambled up and took a few steps back to assess his handiwork.

What he saw astounded him. He had uncovered a metal construction, approximately one metre in length, curved at one end. The most startling thing about the object was that it was fire-blackened from one end running along its surface, removing all detail, scouring it into a smooth plate. He had no idea what it was or where it had come from; he hadn't seen anything like it before in his career. But whatever it was, he was sure of one thing.

It wasn't from this world.

Without turning, he raised his voice to the rest, forgetting himself in the moment. "Here," he shouted. "Over here. You want to come look at this!"

###

Rao closed the heavy wooden doors behind him with a controlled push, shutting out the noise of the crowds, and took the candle from the sconce in the wall. There was only one way to go from the doors; a staircase that led up, curving around and away from the porch. The walls were a crimson stone. Light from the candle reflected and played tricks on the eye. The wooden steps appeared as if they were bleeding, casting an oppressive feel on the place.

He climbed the steep stairs carefully, with one hand out before him to touch the cool stone and the other holding the candle dish.

As he took a step, his leg fought against the bending action of the climb, and he subconsciously put a hand to the old wound. It was still sore, even after all these years. Rao could never remember the face of the man that had given him the wound, its scar tissue far more comprehensive than all the others. It had been a bitter struggle in a war long forgotten and best left unremembered.

Rao sighed; he was weary, because of the wound, because of the dredged-up memory, and because of all that he had done since.

He willed his leg to collaborate and forced himself upward, taking his time, not overexerting himself. He wanted to be fresh when he entered the chamber, to use the time to compose himself and decide what he was going to say.

As the stairway curved toward its top, it brought about a view of the grand hallway. He had entered the building via a back staircase, usually reserved for staff. But what was he, if not staff? He had worked for the court in many capacities over the years, stalking these corridors. Besides, he preferred to enter unannounced.

He walked through the hallway, ignoring the servants as they hurried about their tasks, hesitating only to look at the portraits that covered the walls. The family in all their resplendent glory looked down on him, as if in judgement.

"Ah, councillor. There you are."

Rao turned, handing the candle to a passing servant, to see the lord chamberlain staring at him expectantly. He had slightly pale, translucent Endarian skin, threatening almost to show his long, thin bones beneath. He was a tall man, around two metres in height, looking down on Rao.

Rao considered the question for a long moment before answering. A hasty word could give too much away.

"Here I am indeed, Rute," he said.

The chamberlain covered his anger at Rao's obtuse familiarity with a scowl of frustration. Good, it was beneficial to keep the chamberlain on his toes. He stepped to the side, showing the room he had left to greet Rao. Raising a careful hand, palm outstretched, he motioned for the councillor to enter before him. "Best to not keep Him waiting."

Rao walked toward the wooden doors, trying to keep the crick out of his leg. He refused to show any weakness in front of Rute, or any of the others for that matter. They would fixate on it, and he would lose any power he might have over them. The members of the court feared him, and while they didn't exactly know his past, there were rumours about what he did before he became a councillor. Let them whisper, it was in his interest not to shatter that suspicious fear.

The room was as garish and over-decorated as the hallway he had just left. Unlike the hallway, it was coated in gold, which seemed to flow over the furniture and ornaments like tendrils of decorative streams. Men stood in small clutches, talking in hushed voices, or alone, separate from the crowd, but they all gravitated toward one side of the room. Or perhaps they had been repelled there, for opposite them was the great litter of the King of Endaris.

The king sprawled on his back, his bulbous form covered in silks and furs. The litter looked like a bed, sheets seemingly covering a harem of courtly conquering, but it couldn't hide the fact that the king had long ceased to be a fit young man. His green-tinged, translucent skin rolled out of the sheets in places, showing the lie. Some saw this as proof of the King's god-like power, but to the court, the chamberlain could not hide that the king was not well. Soft grunts and moans issued occasionally from his lips.

Rao dipped his head in deference to the king as he stood in front of the litter; as councillor, he was afforded the privilege of not having to kneel.

"And where have you been, councillor?" It wasn't the king that had spoken out loud; he barely raised his voice above more than a whisper. Rao wheeled on the spot to find the origin of the voice, careful not to turn his back on His Majesty.

He saw that the owner of the voice stood slightly apart from a huddle of men in the corner of the audience chamber; another tall man, with a look of displeasure showing through his close-cut black goatee. The man raised an eyebrow in impatience.

Rao deliberately took a moment to look at the other assembled men. They all wore emulations of the King's dress, velvet and ostentatious, but they were careful to keep the decoration at a level less than His. It fit most of them better than it did Him and highlighted Rao's own practical dinner suit.

Fixing his attention back on the goateed man, he finally and carefully spoke. "I was getting to grips with the crowd, Haken."

Haken scoffed, his black hair bristling at the use of his given name. "Ah, so we get right to the point then, Rao son of Arnar."

Rao nodded and let him continue.

"The crowd at our gates, which threatens the safety and sovereignty of His Great Majesty, the God-King Olf of Endaris. What are we to do with them?"

His overbearing and overly flattering tone was common of those at court, and Rao cringed inwardly at every over-spoken word. Speak plainly and clearly and the power was yours. Something his father had taught him before he died.

Another new voice cut in. "Have them rounded up and flogged, I say."

"We don't nearly have the manpower for such a feat," said Haken.

Rao let the argument continue as he moved through the room unnoticed by the crowd to stand to the side of the litter next to the chamberlain.

"It smacks of cowardice and—"

"Perhaps," said Rao, "if we understood what they want, we may understand their motives and control them?" He didn't raise his voice; he hadn't needed to. Like his father, he made men listen. Perhaps it was because he was the only one not shouting.

"What on Endaris do you mean, Councillor?" The chamberlain was the only one astute enough to ask the correct questions. After all, he wouldn't want to lose his fragile power.

"Well, I thought that you might tell me what they are unhappy about and what they suspect His Majesty is capable of doing about it. I would ask them myself, but they all appear to be shouting at one another." The unspoken criticism in Rao's words was clear to all in the room as they turned to listen to the councillor and chamberlain speaking.

The king shifted on his litter, emitting a low rumble. A laugh or a cough, Rao wasn't sure which.

"It is because of the fire in the sky. An omen, they say." The chamberlain's words were the first Rao had heard of an omen. As far as he was concerned, the crowd was merely demonstrating their boiling over discontent at the restrictions put on them by the government. They were unhappy with the lack of food, but those presenting new ways of farming feared incurring the wrath of the King.

"Here, look." Rute turned to fully reveal a man by the

window, bent over as if studying, the long feathers of his cap drooping. The academic stood by a long brass tube, looking through what appeared to Rao to be a cup. "Through the lens, see."

The academic moved aside to allow him access and gestured to the eyepiece.

Rao bent to bring his eye level with the device, but the muscles in his back complained at the movement. He willed his body to comply. He wouldn't show weakness in front of the others. After a brief hesitation, he managed to lower himself.

As Rao looked through the lens, all he could see was blackness. The cold nothingness of night looked back at him, and he wondered what he was supposed to see. A hand gently took his and placed it over a dial on the side of the lens.

"Pardon me, my lord." Rao was no lord, not officially, but there was no benefit in correcting the academic. "Turn the dial, and you will see in focus."

Rao did as he was bid. At first, the picture was a milky blur, splashing the light from distant stars across his eye. After a few seconds, the image resolved itself into a ball of burning fire, piercing its way through the sky of Endaris. Rao had to tilt the lens ever so slightly to keep pace with it.

"What is it?" he said in a low voice.

The answer was drowned out by a crashing noise from the far side of the chamber. Burly palace guardsmen bundled a man into the room via the side entrance. They were carrying the young man firmly by each arm, but he was protesting all the while, knocking bits of furniture over. The guardsmen dumped him unceremoniously in front of the king and backed away. The man still protested where he sat.

"You dare disturb the King's chamber?" The chamberlain emphasised every word.

Sensing mortal danger, the young man slowly looked up at the king's litter and fell silent. He was a dejected figure on the plush rug, clothed in the simple garments of a field academic, but covered in dirt and dust, long blond hair falling limply at his shoulders. After a moment staring in disbelief at where he was, he dropped his head in surrender, which gave him the look of a rag doll spread on the floor. He didn't move another inch.

The chamberlain moved forward, towering over the young man sprawled on the floor.

"So, you are the one that has caused all this trouble?" He paused for a moment, but he clearly didn't expect an answer. "If I would debase myself in such a way, what would I call you? I like to know the names of our enemies." His teeth glittered in a grin that didn't touch his eyes, like a predator playing with its prey. He circled the man on the floor, each careful step splaying the fronds of his patience.

"Hjal," the young academic said, his voice a resigned whisper. "My name is Hjal."

"A low-born name. Disgusting." He sneered as he looked

down, on the verge of spitting. "And you claim to have found something in the desert?"

Hjal hesitated, looking up at the tall man leaning over him. The chamberlain's every move was a threat, and he took his time to sit up straight before answering.

"Something, yes. I don't know what, but it wasn't—"

The chamberlain smacked Hjal around the head with the back of his hand, forcing him back to the rug in a whimper.

"You found nothing, nothing but scrap. Do you hear me?"

Hjal seemed to break internally, his body becoming rigid, fixed. For the first time during the entire conversation, he raised his head to look the chamberlain in the eye.

"Everything we have been told, everything you tell us, is a lie." He moved to stand, his voice raised to a shout. "Endaris end—"

Rute cuffed the young man across the face again, drawing blood, and turned. "Take him away."

A servant moved toward the chamberlain from the shadows, offering him a cloth to clean the blood from his hand, but Rute pushed the young woman away, his face a mask of fury.

He turned back to the assembled men and shouted, "Do something about this mess," before marching out of the room.

Rao decided in that moment that he would indeed do something about this . . . mess.

###

It was almost morning by the time Rao descended the steps again. The court had talked for hours, barely saying anything at all. They would argue back and forth, and eventually they would punish the citizens and bring them back under an umbrella of fear.

The dawn light from the high windows faded as Rao descended to the dungeon. Despite what he had said, he would not return to his offices, not yet. He had another task to see to before continuing his work.

He pushed his aching body down the slippery steps one at a time. It had been a long night, and it was going to be even longer before he was done.

The steps finally broke out to a stone corridor with a table and a waiting guardsman by one side. Rao could hear faint dripping in the corners of the room, and the cold, damp air made his bones ache.

He gestured to the guard to open the door. The man obliged, picking up a heavy ring of keys that jangled in the confined space. He moved toward the solid wooden door that closed off the dungeon and put the brass key in the sunken lock. Turning the key, the door creaked back on its hinges, revealing another dark, damp corridor beyond.

The guardsman faced Rao and waited for him to fall into step so he could show him to the cell, but Rao waved him away. He would do this alone; he didn't need his hand held.

He took the flaming brand the prison guard proffered him

and walked through the doorway. It was a depressing place; cells lined both walls of the corridor as he walked through, each one housing a different kind of criminal or enemy of the king.

Rao tried not to glance into them as he passed, but curiosity got the better of him. In one cell, he saw a family huddled in the corner, their hair grown long, their clothes ripped and torn. In another, he saw what could only be described as an animal, a beast. It was so feral that it no longer resembled anything Endarian.

But they weren't what he was here for. They could wait. He would get to them eventually. The cell Rao wanted was at the end of the prison, around a corner, through a couple of shorter corridors; the cell that held the dungeon's newest prisoner.

He carefully placed the brand in a rusting metal holder opposite the cell, and it cast an orange hue across the metal bars, long shadows reaching the far wall of the small enclosure.

The shape in the cell lay in a foetal position, making its body look smaller than it really was. The cell smelt of damp and faeces, and Rao fought back the urge to gag.

As if sensing the presence, Hjal looked up at the councillor from the floor and shrunk back further into the cell. Recognition was clear on the younger man's face; he remembered Rao from the audience chamber, and perhaps his reputation preceded him.

Rao crouched down beside the cell, leaning against the metal bars. Pain shot up his leg, but he ignored it and focussed on the prisoner. He cleared his throat and forced softness into his voice before speaking.

"What did you *really* find in the desert?"

Hjal stared at him, but refused to answer.

Rao sighed and shook his head. He pushed his legs out to sit on the floor with his back against the bars. His suit soaked up the dampness of the floor, but he didn't care. He hoped that it would bring the prisoner and himself to a similar level.

"Come on. How can I possibly make your situation any worse?" It wasn't a question he expected an answer to.

Hjal seemed to relax a little, his body becoming less rigid, but he still stared at Rao. The councillor looked away, breaking the awkwardness between them, and stared at his hands, at the aged scars and engrained dirt.

"I don't know what it was, truly." The words were slow, fearful.

"Go on," Rao said, gently.

A scrape against the stone floor suggested Hjal was moving in his cell. "I was working as part of a dig. We'd found some unusual magnetic fields in the desert." The prisoner's voice was closer than it had been before and less timid. "Most of what we found was just useless junk, but after a while I uncovered something . . . different."

Rao thought for a moment. "That something, is that what caused all this mess?"

"You could say that, I don't know. It was a catalyst, no doubt."

"So, what was it?"

"I told you, I don't know." Hjal was getting frustrated with the questions now, his voice rising in timbre and volume. "All I have is my theories."

Rao had him exactly where he wanted him. "Describe it to me."

"All I could see when I was working was a black metallic surface. It was rectangular but curved at the nearest end. Kind of like a coffin." The memory was flowing freely now as Hjal talked. "That was all I could make out, before the Collegiate Lektor ordered me away, and they hauled it off to the universitat. Bastards wouldn't even let me get a closer look at what I found."

"That's disappointing." Rao considered his next words for a long time as the awkward silence resumed. Turning to look at Hjal, he said, "Tell me, what do you think it is?"

Hjal seemed to consider his thoughts for a few long, drawn out seconds. "I'll tell you this. It's not from Endaris." The excitement in his voice was clear. "We don't make anything like that here, not even at the universitat. In the Collegiate, we have . . . devices, forbidden devices that can check these things, but we didn't make this. They're working on it now, and the one thing they did tell me was that it is made from some previously unknown alloy."

Rao nodded, slowly.

"I reckon my first description was about right, a coffin. Though why anyone would want to dump their dead on Endaris, I have no idea. So it's that or a message, some kind of time capsule. Like the ones we sent off into space, a probe, but much more advanced. Maybe that flare in the sky has something to do with it?" Hjal was in his element, reeling off his ideas about the mysterious item from the heavens.

Rao watched Hjal carefully; he reminded him of his younger self. He had often had flights of fantasy in his youth, questioning his father's beliefs and stories. Most children on Endaris did, it was part of growing up. Hjal was different, though. He seemed to know. He didn't just have wild theories; he had thought it all through. There was a cold certainty there that scared Rao.

"What you are implying is dangerous." Each word was slow.

Hjal stopped talking immediately and gave Rao a look that spoke volumes. He knew he had said too much and regret passed across his face, but it was gone in an instant, replaced with the fear that had been there before the conversation began.

"What now?" he said. His voice had dropped down to a whisper as the dripping in the cell fought the silence. "You tricked me." The accusation was quiet. Did he really dare incur the wrath of a royal councillor?

"I needed to know what you know," Rao said as he clutched the bars to haul himself up. He made sure to emphasise the weakness of his legs as they cracked and protested while he lifted his body to a standing position. *Yes, an ageing, almost crippled man is keeping you captive.* He still had that power.

Raised to his full height, he looked at the younger man curled on the cell floor. Why was it only the weak and the young he could look down upon?

"That is all," he said and turned to leave

"Wait, you can't leave me here."

Rao hesitated for a moment before looking over his shoulder at the prisoner. He shook his head once and continued his cold, wet walk back to the dungeon entrance.

###

Hjal stared at the retreating figure in disbelief. What had just happened? Had he incriminated himself even more? He had always spoken too easily, too quickly, without thinking. That was why the universitat had sent him out to that God-King-forsaken desert. He paused at the thought. *God-king?* That was why he was here now, in this cold, miserable cell. The hubris of his questioning beliefs, his doubt. That was what had imprisoned him.

As the light of the man's candle moved off into the distance, it caught an object laying on the floor on the other side of the bars. The object glinted in the light where all else was dark, bleak stone.

Hjal pushed himself toward the bars of his cell to get a closer look. Where the man had been sitting was a thin metal item, which almost disappeared as the light retreated down the corridor. Only the ambient glow of the algae that lined the walls gave off any kind of light to the dungeon. With a trembling hand, Hjal reached through the tight bars and clasped the item in a quick grab, before anyone could notice what he was doing. As far as he knew, there was no one around. He was in the most secluded cell he had seen, but it was better to be too careful than make things any worse.

His arm almost got stuck in the confined space, but he pulled it back with a jerk and sat against the wall. The stone was cold against his back. He drew his knees up and laid his furled hands upon them, cradling the dagger like a pauper begging for money.

He looked around the corridor again from where he sat, but could see no one. Holding his breath, he listened to hear whether anyone else was coming. The only sound in the cell was the dripping of water from the curved ceiling.

Reassured that he was alone, he carefully unfurled his hands. Laying on one palm was the metal item. He looked at it more closely, trying to make it out in the dim light. It was long and thin, with a tapered edge. Blackened metal heated and forced into a point. It was a rare item, but Hjal knew exactly what it was. He had seen one before in a book at the universitat.

Hjal took the blade in his other hand, careful not to cut himself, and looked at the hilt. Like the blade, it had a black hue, but instead of metal it was made of fine leather with an embossed eagle on either side, wings spread in flight and a scroll in its claws. He twisted it, and it came away in his hand, revealing the blade's secret. Within the hilt the blade hid a key, but not just any key; this was a family-key, the badge of office of the old royal houses of Endaris. Each of the houses that served the king had one made so that they could gain entry to the city. It was the very sign of power, and it must have belonged to the man, dropped out of his pocket as he stood, leaving Hjal to his fate.

In the darkness, he smiled coldly at the ironic turn of events. Fate had given him a chance.

Hjal crawled to his feet, careful not to make too much sound. The man could come back any minute once he realised he had lost his family-key. Hjal needed to be quick, but too quick and he would make a mistake and be noticed.

He crossed to the door and placed the key in the lock. It fit perfectly. It would in any lock in Endaris. He turned it carefully, and it clicked as the tumblers fell into place and released. The door creaked back on unoiled hinges, and Hjal cursed under his breath at the sound. Only one slight mistake would give him away and that would be it. The guards would descend on him, beat him, and throw him back in his cell. They would find and take away the family-key and his only slim chance at escape would be gone.

He would have to find some way around the guards. He didn't want to use the knife. He wasn't a killer, but if it was his life or theirs he may just have to.

Hjal shuddered at the thought and quickly deposited the family-key in his pocket, hiding the bladed end away. If he couldn't subdue the guards without killing them, then perhaps he truly deserved to be in the prison.

Freed from the cell, he put his arms out in front of him. The corridor was only slightly less dark than his place of captivity. Hjal used his hands to feel his way along the wall like a blind man and took careful, timid steps. Thankfully, his captors hadn't seen fit to bind his legs; he was too far beneath their notice for escape to even be a consideration. But he didn't plan on rotting away in that cell.

His corridor led to a junction, with two further corridors leading off at right angles. He didn't know which one to take, and as he thought back, he wished he'd paid attention as he was dragged into the dungeon. The shock and depression had overwhelmed him at the time, but now he was more focussed. He had to make a decision, quickly.

Hjal paused to listen for any sounds, but the dungeon was eerily quiet. Even in the damp of the underground prison, he could feel a slight breeze. Facing the junction, the right side of his face was ever so slightly colder than the left. Could that mean what he thought it did? He hoped that his instincts were right and that the faint wind was coming down through the entrance to the dungeon from the world above. There was only one way to find out. Right it was then, decision made.

He guided himself around the corner and almost tripped over a grate on the floor as his toe stubbed on the metal rim. Perhaps he was being too hasty? This corridor was different from the other. As he guided his hands along the wall, the rough stone changed to empty air and metal bars. The bars lined most of the long wall, and in the dim light he could faintly make out shapes within them. These cells were for a different kind of prisoner.

Hjal moved slowly along the corridor for a few minutes. He took each step carefully, worried that he might trip again and this time fall, making a noise that a guard might hear. The bars rattled slightly at his touch, but he hoped it might be mistaken for the inmates moving around. Using his hands was the only way he could guide himself along the wall without walking face-first into any obstacles. Yet still no guards came.

He reached the end of the corridor, and this time, there was no junction. Instead, the end wall was broken by a wooden surface. A door.

Hjal reached blindly for the handle and grasped a thick metal ring with his left hand. He pulled it slightly, but the door didn't move. He tried again, putting all his strength into it and leaning back, but once again, the door didn't budge. It held fast, presumably locked from the other side by one of the guards. What was he to do now? It would only open if one of the guards happened to come through from the other side. Then he would be trapped in here with the guards and no way out.

The family-key! He was forgetting the key. Quickly, he fumbled in his pocket for the key and pulled his hand back with a curse. He had also forgotten the sharp edge of the blade, and he placed his index finger to his lips to suck away the sting.

Carefully this time, he took the heirloom from his pocket. It took a few seconds of nervous fumbling to find the keyhole, but there it was underneath the handle. As before, the key slotted straight into the lock without protest.

Turning the key, Hjal pulled once again at the door, and it wheeled back heavily. He kept the blade ready in his hand; he planned to intimidate the door guard, not kill him, but as he entered the room, there was no one to be seen.

The flickering brand from the wall sconce lit a half-eaten meal laid out on a broken metal platter and a score of disorganised paper stacks, but no guard.

Hjal's heart fluttered as he scanned the dark corners of the room, convinced it was a trap and that someone was waiting to jump out at him. He was curiously alone.

The tension was getting too much for him; his heart kept jumping every time he looked about. Forgetting any attempt at caution, he bolted for the staircase that led away from the room. The steps were slippery and in his haste, he slipped, falling down the first few steps.

He picked himself up again and carried on, uncertain of where he would end up, but that didn't matter now that he was almost free.

After climbing for what seemed like hours in the darkness, the staircase came out under a series of archways. The sudden change in light blinded Hjal, and he ducked into a corner with his arm over his eyes, shielding away the light. He prayed that no one would see him, cowering in the corner every bit the escaped prisoner, but no one came near. He let his eyes adjust and righted himself.

The covered gallery surrounded an open cloister and he walked to the end arch, which led into a wide area. It was open at one side and he recognised it as the royal courtyard that led off the main plaza. As he looked up at the outside of the building, purple clouds drifted across the sky and the star-moon chased the sun across the heavens to its sunset. It was late afternoon.

He continued his escape at a jog, caution setting in once again because the courtyard was full of people. They gathered around the fountain in the centre, shouting abuse at the royal apartments. Around the square, nervous-looking guardsmen wanted to be anywhere else but here.

Hjal observed them carefully, but none seemed to be looking in his direction. They were concentrating on the gathering masses. His best chance to evade detection was to push his way into the crowd.

He moved toward the exit from the archway into the courtyard, but a couple of men walking in his direction blocked his path. Their red velvet clothing was ripped and torn, and they argued as they walked hurriedly along the gallery. They cast nervous glances over their shoulder as they bundled past Hjal, without a look in his direction. The men knocked him to the ground, and he hit the dirt with a thump.

His bruised body protested at the fall, forgotten pains flaring in his muscles. Lying still for a moment, he considered his luck, before climbing to his feet and dusting himself off.

The crowd weren't interested in him, they had much more

pressing matters, but the guards might recognise him if they saw him. He couldn't be too careful.

After a second attempt, he managed to make his way into the crowd just as the guardsman made a concerted effort to push them away from the royal apartments. The crush forced Hjal further in to the crowd, and the shouting became more intense. Heads started to turn in his direction as he pushed his way through. Some moved out of his way where others stood and stared. He kept his head down and quickened his pace. The people jostled and knocked him, but he kept moving as quickly as he dared, but not too quick as to draw any more attention to himself.

Hjal moved out onto the main plaza, leaving the courtyard and the crowd behind. His pulse slowed as he realised with clarity that he had managed to escape the dungeon. The guardsmen were too busy containing the crowd, and there were none on the plaza. The main road ran from the royal court out to the city proper, and the only people on it were moving in the direction of the courtyard.

To his right, a magrail train puffed steam on its final leg into the main station. As it came to a rest, more people clambered off from the many doors in its red flank. Most will have come from Strondina, by the coast, or one of Endaris's small outlying settlements.

He composed himself and patted his damp clothes down, trying to make himself more respectable. Hjal had to rouse the Collegiate to action; if the court was meeting, he feared what they would do to the citizens.

With a final look over his shoulder, he breathed in deeply and set off in the direction of the universitat.

###

The dark shape moved slowly across the room, keeping to the shadows like a thief in the night. Family portraits of long-dead aristocrats looked down on the black-clad figure as the light from the slowly smoldering fire at the far end of the room sparked and briefly choked out more light. The only sound in the room was the crackle of logs as they burnt away into nothingness.

The figure moved out from the shadows and crossed the floorboards toward the gilded four-poster bed on the other side of the room. Each step was heedful for fear of making noise, but practised as if the figure had done this many times before. After a few steps, the wooden floor turned to rug and the caution relaxed.

The floorboard under the rug creaked loudly as a foot descended onto it. A soft sigh of slumber pierced the uneasy silence of the room, and Rao cursed under his breath. He dropped the heel of his foot to the floor and stood poised. He looked across to the door from which he had entered the bedchamber, waiting for someone to notice the intrusion, but he had made sure it was locked. He relaxed slightly and looked back at the bed.

"You've caused a lot of pain," he said, as loudly as he dared.

He moved closer to bed and looked at the gigantic figure of the king. Rao couldn't tell whether the man was awake or sleeping, the noises were usual in their abnormality. The king's eyes could have been open for all Rao could see in the dark.

"You grew weak." Rao moved around to the side of the bed and stood, relaxed. "You grew lazy, and you gave other men too much control." He put a gloved hand to his brow, shaking his head gently.

Rao lifted the side of the quilt and threw it back over the bed. As he lifted the hem, a leg struck out, knocking his arm away and catching him in the chest. The blow winded him, and he dropped to one knee as his assailant jumped from the bed.

Through his pain, Rao could just about make out the features of a tall, thin man, not at all like the king.

The chamberlain looked down at Rao, his perpetual scowl turning to a look of fear and bewilderment.

"Rao?" he said.

Rao didn't answer; instead, he moved to grab Rute by the scruff of his bedclothes, but the chamberlain was too quick and pushed him aside. The two men grappled for a moment before the chamberlain broke free of Rao's grasp. Rute chocked back a scream and ran for the door as Rao tried to pull himself up on his injured leg, cursing.

Rute reached the door and fumbled with the lock, his hands, moist from the sweat of sleep, kept slipping off, and he glanced back over his shoulder nervously as Rao starting hobbling in his direction.

With a click, the lock released. Rute threw one of the doors back on its hinges to crash against the wall and ran through the opening. Rao pushed himself to reach the door, but the chamberlain was gone, lost within the labyrinth of the court. There was no way the councillor could catch him.

No doubt he would alert the guards. Rao could already hear the commotion of scrambling feet from below. He had used every trick he knew to get into the court unnoticed, but if the guards knew he was there, he had little time left.

Where would the king be? Rute was so confident in his usurpation of the King's power that he had taken to sleeping in his bedchamber. It vexed Rao that he hadn't known this; he knew everything that went on, and this was an oversight that may jeopardise his plan.

Rao shut the door and turned the lock once again. He then wedged the doors shut with a poker from the fireplace and, with a grunt of effort, pushed a chest of drawers in front. *That would slow down anyone trying to get in.*

Rao began his search around the bedchamber for the King; there were rooms that led off from the main, more lavish, chamber, used for storing things.

In the second room he checked, he found the immense litter on which the King was often transported, and as he moved further into the darkness, his suspicions were confirmed; Rute had moved the King into this spare room so that he could sleep like a king himself.

He had no time for caution now as he noticed the faint

snoring coming from the litter. Rao started toward the King.

"We believed in you. You were our god." He sat on the edge of the bed, turning his back and looking at the far wall.

"Now look at you. Look what you became. You were once a beacon of hope and prosperity, but then you put other men, stronger men, in charge. Men like Rute."

He paused, daring the chamberlain to return, and shook his head, amused. "When I think of all he has done, it makes me sick." Rao stood again and turned on the king, his anger rising. "We've been moving backward all this time."

He crossed toward the room's window and threw the heavy curtains back with a flick of his hand. Moonlight filtered in, casting eerie shadow across the room.

"And now, we have a warning. Something to tell us that we have been wrong. So very, very wrong." He stopped and stared.

"You called yourself a god, let them all believe, and now . . . you can't even hear what I'm saying, can you?"

Rao paced toward the bed, shaking his head in futility.

"Like the moon, your power is fading, and with it the power of men like Rute. Those people out there have grown tired of poverty and lies. They've finally seen the truth of you. As I have."

A crash diverted Rao's attention. It came from the main chamber, and as he looked toward the room, he heard the door handle begin to turn.

"Damn," he said, ignoring the noise to look back at the king.

"Our time grows short, old friend."

The handle turned again, and with a crash, the doors bulged in their frames but stayed firmly shut as the drawers from the chest crashed their contents across the floor. The men outside began shouting and hammering on the doors. Rao would deal with them later. He always had his gift of persuasion.

He looked at the moonlight, then back at the bed. With a sigh, he put one foot on the frame and hauled himself up, painfully. It took some effort, but after a few seconds he straddled the bulk of the king, looking down into a face that due to fat didn't show its immense age.

Rao drew a dagger from the black scabbard at his waist. The blackish metal glimmered in the moonlight.

"This is for my father. Say hello to him for me."

With both hands firmly on the hilt, he pushed the blade down, striking for the king's heart. It took a blow of precision to cut through the wealth of flesh and pierce the most vulnerable of organs. Years of experience leant a helping hand, but the blade hit something hard.

Rao panicked. He'd missed. Pulling the blade free in a trickle of blood, he aimed again, and this time drove the blade home into the king's heart.

The king groaned softly as Rao applied more pressure, and blood spurted up from the wound, staining the white sheets. The king shuddered, but couldn't move his immense bulk.

The king's final breath escaped his lips accompanied by barely formed words. "Thank . . . you."

Rao was taken aback. He hadn't expected those words from the King. He hadn't expected any words at all, but *thanks*? The king had *wanted* to die?

The noise from the doors grew louder as the king passed away, and the hammering reached a crescendo before falling silent.

Rao sighed. It was done now. There was no turning back. After years of playing the councillor, he had become an assassin again for one last, vital kill.

As he climbed down from the litter, the doors opened with a click of released locks and a thud as the wedge was knocked aside. Rao stood looking at the bed, head downcast, resigned to his fate as the men rushed in to the room from behind him, shouting and stamping. He felt strong hands grip his arms and haul him away from the king as shouts of alarm rang out.

He was dragged back into the main chamber by rough hands and forced down to his knees on the rug in the middle of the room. He faced the door as more men rushed into the chamber, but the voices became hushed.

Rao looked up into the streaming light from outside as a blow to the side of his head knocked him unconscious.

Not one of them called for a medic.

It was an odd thought that entered Rao's mind as he came around, his head flaring in pain. His second thought was about where he was. As his vision cleared, he noticed he was in a dank room, sitting in a chair to one side of a small wooden table.

Perhaps they had known it was too late for a medic.

Rao mused on that odd fact until he noticed the man standing at the open door, his long blond hair bunching on his shoulders and his mouth hanging open.

"You?" he said through dry lips, as Hjal walked into the room.

The younger man had cleaned himself up since their last meeting. He now wore the garb of an academic, including the hat, rather than the grubby overalls he had been thrown into the dungeon wearing. Rao said nothing and stared blankly at Hjal.

"I guess you will be wanting this back then?" Hjal held up the family-key in his right hand, the blade running along his palm and the key mechanism exposed. So that's how they had got into the chamber without knocking the doors down.

"Keep it, I didn't want it back."

Hjal covered his look of surprise quickly, but not quickly enough.

"That's right. Besides, it was my father's. I have . . . I *had* my own." He'd left the blade in the King's chest.

"You killed him," Hjal said, shaking his head. "Why?"

Rao didn't answer immediately. He had regained some of his composure and his caution. It was funny how last time he had met this academic it had been him asking the questions. He had risen to a position of power over his god and king, and he had killed him. Now, he was trapped in this room under the scrutinising gaze of someone who only barely understood. Perhaps it was time to illuminate him.

"Something had to change. It was a sign."

Hjal nodded and sat on the empty chair, facing Rao across the table.

The councillor stared back. "He thanked me in the end." When Hjal didn't respond, he continued, "I don't know why. Perhaps his illness, his pain, became too much for him." Rao shook his head, thinking. "Or maybe he grew tired of what he had become. Just a symbol, and he no longer had the means to finish it himself. I guess we'll never know."

Hjal stood, took a couple of paces, and turned back to the councillor. He smiled. "I see. Do you think that if someone like me can stop believing, someone low born—" He spat the word. "—Then others will follow?"

"They have to, now. They'll have seen that a god can die. Now the chamberlain and his lackeys have no figurehead."

Hjal's smile fell from his lips. "Ah, him, from the audience chamber? My companions are trying to find him as we speak," he said, motioning to the academics rushing past the open door. "I would like to talk to him myself. I have a few questions of my own," he said with a grin Rao didn't like.

"He'll be long gone."

Hjal nodded and stood up, moving over to a window Rao hadn't noticed before, the light of the moon silhouetting his frame. *So I'm not in a dungeon?*

"He's not the only thing that's gone," he said, waving the older man to join him.

It was Rao's turn to be confused. "What do you mean?" he said, joining Hjal at the window and looking out at the night's sky.

"The omen has gone. Our lenses can no longer find it."

Rao looked at Hjal and shook his head slowly to himself. The younger man had so much to learn. He had come a long way, but he was still naive.

"It doesn't matter now," he said with a sigh.

"Endaris endures."

Secrets Within
By A. R. Aston

"Where are the diamonds?" he shouted again, jabbing another needle into the bound fanatic's thigh. The man gurgled in perverse delight, spitting blood into the gangster's face.

"The disciples of the sceptre of god taught us not to tell. As the first elders hid the vision of the mirrored sceptre as it was cast across the firmament, so shall we, their ancestors, keep our secrets from those who would tear us down and pillage our riches! We keep our secrets within."

The gangster grinned, reaching for the dagger on the table.

"'Secrets within?' A poor choice of words, my religious friend . . . Or maybe it is a riddle? Let's have a rummage 'inside,' shall we?" The gangster slid the dagger into soft blue flesh.

Alone
By Alex Helm

"Is there anybody here?"

I stood upon the crumbled ruins of a tower as the tattered tails of my coat flapped around my ankles in the light breeze. I yelled out once more, my voice cracked and hoarse. "Is anybody here?"

The only sound was the spectral sigh of dust shifting in the wind.

My shoulders slumped.

I hadn't expected any response, but that didn't stop me from hoping every single time. I raised my hand to my mouth as I coughed. Ignoring the new specks of blood on the back of my palm, I stuffed my hand into my coat pocket, gripped my stick tightly, and started to slide back down the heap of rubble.

I stared across the ruins into the haze. Everything was covered in thick white dust, almost like snow, and I could see just one trail of footprints. Mine. Huddled over, I tramped off toward my next target—the remains of some kind of religious structure. It was too far away to identify.

I have been alone for thirty years. Throughout all this time, I have had just the one quest—to find another living being. When my task began, I was young and sprightly, and I was a survivor of the war that had devastated the planet. I had thought that it would only take hours at most to find more survivors. Yet those hours had turned to days. The days started to number in the tens, then the hundreds, then the thousands.

How could it be that I alone lived? Back then it had seemed impossible that I could be the only survivor. Despite everything, it still seemed impossible to me now.

I was . . . nobody really, just a construction worker. I had lived in a time of great change, of advancements in industry and technology that left many gasping for understanding. Entire generations were left behind as progress outstripped life itself, and it was only a matter of time before war broke out. I had a wife, and a daughter, but they are gone now. Everyone is gone. For many years, I had grieved for them. I had cursed with anger at the foolishness of our race, that our follies had resulted in the loss of those most dear to me, but eventually, acceptance came. It had been so long.

There were so many reasons for a worldwide war. Nations that had always been rivals, the uneven spread of resources, inequality across society, poor distribution of wealth and power . . . all were just a few of the seeds that had grown into the war. No one learned exactly who started it, although accusations flew in all directions. No one ever admitted guilt, but it was widely believed that all were equally culpable. The war was just meant to be.

I trudged through the snowy dust, leaning heavily on my stick and suppressing the familiar ache in my limbs. The war may not have killed me, nor the virus or the resulting fallout and radiation. Yet even I could not halt the ravages of age and toil upon my body. I had been coughing up blood for days now, and I could sense that my time upon this world was drawing short. I could only hope that I would find success in my quest before I died.

As I approached, I could see the ruined structure had once been a temple to the Angel—one of the major religions of the world. Worshippers believed that a greater being watched over them, and they sought to emulate Her by acting in kind as guardian angels to the populace as a whole. Although it was one of the more benevolent religions, that hadn't saved them from the war either.

I pushed the old door open. The hinge creaked ominously, and then its weight shifted. I stepped back just as the rotted wood fell out of the frame and crashed to the ground, unleashing an explosion of dust. Out of habit, I turned my head away and covered my mouth and nose with my hand, trying to snort as little of the dust as possible. Even after all these years, it was still likely to be toxic, even though it never seemed to affect me. I coughed a few times and spat out dust and blood. Then I stepped into the temple.

"Is anyone here?"

My voice echoed around the deserted space, stirring nothing but more of the dust. I stepped forward, and my feet crunched across shattered glass work, covered with a carpet of grit. It was clear that nothing had been here for decades, just like everywhere else on this forsaken planet.

I made my way toward the remains of the altar. A remarkably intact statue of the Angel stood tall, peering out across the shattered temple. I stared at it for a good while before crouching down to scrape the dust off the altar table. I found what I was looking for—tins of foodstuffs. Before the cataclysm that had ended the war, they had been left here as offerings to the angelic deity. I figured that if She really needed them, She would have taken them by now. I dropped the cans into the sack hanging over my arm. By scavenging like this, I could continue my travels across the world, searching for just one living being or at least something more than this gaunt quiet.

I coughed again before tipping my hat at the Angel. Then I gripped my stick and left, trudging back through the crumbling doorway. I hesitated at the entrance and gazed across the ruined town, trying to decide where to go next. It seemed unlikely that I would find anyone alive here, but sunset would come soon, and I needed a place to camp overnight. While I didn't face the threat of being attacked, there were enough hazards in the darkness to give me pause. Tripping and breaking bones would make for an unpleasant, withering death.

A reasonably intact building caught my eye, and I start walking toward it, leaving another trail of footprints in the dust. A regular thought that was comforting in its familiarity popped into my mind. Could there be someone out there, someone like me, searching for another living being by following my footsteps? I halted and turned to stare out once again into the haze. Nothing stirred. Nothing moved; nothing even lived—not even an insect. The war and the cataclysm had eradicated every living being on the planet.

Everything except me.

Why? I wish I had an answer, but in thirty cycles, none had

been forthcoming. Not for the first time, I glared up at the heavens, beseeching the gods—the Angel, the Knight, even the Beast—to answer my plea. As usual, there was no response.

To say that the war had been devastating was an understatement. It had long been said that technological progress is fastest during times of warfare, driven by the need to find quicker and more efficient ways to eliminate an enemy before they could return the favour. Already our world had seen rapid advancement, and the outbreak of conflict only sped matters up even further. Of course, doomsayers had warned the masses that the war would lead to cataclysm. They pointed to the scriptures of the various faiths, all of which warned of hubris leading to excess, and of excess leading to apocalypse. Nobody listened. Nobody cared. And so, when the end of the world did come, no one was surprised.

Devastating weapons of mass destruction were unleashed by one faction upon another and then back again. Half the planet was destroyed, just like that. Then came the horrific chemical attacks. Before anyone realised, a dreadful virus bomb had been dropped. It was this that really eradicated life—all life, including those who had created the virus. Everything died.

Everything except me.

I alone proved to be immune. I wish I knew why, but I am no scientist or doctor. I can't analyse my blood or run tests to find out. If only I could.

My survival was as remarkable as it was dreadful. I alone witnessed the death of a planet. I saw both loved ones and enemies succumb and die to a plague that could not be fought. I saw the virus pass from being to being, from one community to another, from one nation to the next. The priests beseeched their gods for aid, but none came. Nothing saved us. The whole world died and rotted away, leaving nothing but this strange dust.

And me.

Yet, I never believed that I could be the only freak survivor. Such a thing seemed impossible. On a planet of billions, there had to be more than one, surely? And so, my quest began. Thirty years later, it continued, but soon it would come to an end, success or not.

Another cough seized hold of me and I hunched over, clutching my chest as I choked up bloody mucus and spat it out onto the dust. Every part of my body ached and begged for rest—not the rest of an overnight sleep, but something more permanent. I was so old now, old in body and in mind. Soon, I would pass away for good.

I was about halfway to the low building I had spotted when I suddenly paused. There had been a sound, right on the edge of my hearing, a sound that filled my old heart with terror, even now after all this time. The Beast was coming.

It was the sound of rasping and menace. The sound of something stirring up the dust into a frenzy that would grow and feed, consuming everything in its wake. The Beast was what I had named the radioactive dust storms that posed the only true threat to my existence.

In lore, the Beast is the god of chaos and destruction, a deity to be appeased lest His wrath be unleashed. Had the wilful destruction of our world displeased Him? I had every reason to believe so.

I needed shelter, and I needed it soon. I may be immune to the virus, and if the radiation levels affected me, it has never really shown. I wasn't invincible, though. I could still choke to death on the dust clouds or be smashed to pieces by flying debris. I didn't fear dying. In many ways, I embraced it. But I did fear a slow death, one in which I would be so badly injured that all I could do was fade away in a painful nightmare. No help would ever be forthcoming on this empty, dead planet.

I started to run, my steps lumbering with painful imbalance as my stick tapped into the ground. The dust around me started to stir as the winds began to pick up. I had seen these storms before. The Beast turned the world to dust, rendering vision impossible. As I ran, I fumbled for the scarf I always wore around my neck, struggling to pull it over my mouth and nose, anything to prevent the inhalation of dust . . .

The Beast began to howl with a sound that never failed to turn my blood to ice. The winds whipped through the crumbling buildings, blasting through the passageways and whistling through the cracks. I turned to look back over my shoulder, and I could see the Beast itself forming at the centre of the storm, a whirling tornado of dust and debris that screamed at me and cursed at me for daring to be alive in this wasteland. The Beast bowed and bent from the heavens to the ground, and it began to pursue me.

I fled down an alleyway, crying out in horror and fear. I stumbled but kept my balance as I burst through the tattered remains of a chain-link fence. Jagged barbs of metal caught in my clothing, holding me back, and I could hear the Beast laughing at me as it began to catch up. I screamed and ripped my clothes away from the barbs, leaving torn strips of rags stained with blood and sweat.

I tumbled away, catching another glimpse of the Beast as it hammered down the streets after me. The malevolent storm spun and turned, hunting me like prey. I had survived it before, though, and I would do so again. As adrenaline pumped through my veins, I ran, shouting triumphant obscenities at the Beast. I couldn't see where I was going through the dust, and I didn't care. All that mattered was to get away.

I almost made it. I could see the shape of the low building I had spotted from the temple, the one I had been aiming for. There I would find shelter. Even the Beast couldn't get me once I was inside a sturdy building.

Then the cough came back. As I ran, I choked, feeling blood and phlegm rising through my chest. My head began to spin as the pressure took hold, giving me a feeling of almost being crushed under the weight of the planet's atmosphere. I stumbled, coughing and spitting blood into the scarf covering my mouth.

Behind me, the Beast seemed to sense my weakness, and it roared in jubilation. It started hurling debris at me—chunks of brick and metal, anything it could pick up and throw.

I couldn't move. All I could do was to bend over and cough up my lungs, leaving more droplets of blood on the ground in front of me. In my head, I was screaming at my body to move, just a little farther to the building, but my muscles couldn't respond. I sank to the ground, sobbing as I coughed, wondering whether this was the time for the Beast to finally claim me as its own.

A rusted crate smashed into the dust beside me, exploding on impact and shedding its contents across the ground. They were toys—tiny clockwork toys that had been handmade and painted. They had been a popular trend across society, just before the war broke out. I had even bought a few for my wife and daughter.

Somehow, the sight of those toys brought me back to life. I staggered back to my feet, balancing on my stick, and I turned to face the Beast. The dust tornado loomed at the end of the street, appraising me in return.

"Not this time!" I yelled. "You failed again!"

The Beast responded with another deathly howl that almost caused me to crack and submit once again. But I held firm, and somehow, I found the strength to laugh at it. For what felt like an eternity, I just stood there and laughed, my old ribs aching at the motion. Then I finally turned and walked into the squat building. The Beast couldn't catch me now.

I stumbled into the dark interior, pushing through another rotting doorway. A quick glance around revealed this to be some kind of military bunker. That suited me just fine. Outside, I could hear the Beast still cursing at me, but it couldn't touch me here. This place had survived as many storms as I had.

I reached into my pack and pulled out my old lantern, switching it on to cast some light across the place. The lantern glowed and flickered—I would have to scavenge some more batteries soon, but for now I just wanted to rest. I glanced around. Four skeletal corpses lay on the floor, still wearing stained and ragged battle fatigues. Death was a sight that I was long familiar with, so I ignored them and stepped past into a bunk room to take shelter. I slumped down onto one of the bunks and dropped my sack to one side, so that I could rummage for one of the tins I had taken from the temple and find my opener. A short while later, I was able to tuck into the old meat patty crammed inside the tin. I ripped the flesh apart with my teeth. While it tasted nicer cooked, it was perfectly edible raw. I just counted myself lucky that I still had most of my teeth.

With my meal finished, I lay down on the bunk and tried to get some sleep. This was my life. Eat, sleep, and search. What else could I do? Outside, the Beast still howled, but I ignored it. It would be gone in the morning, and I would be safe.

It seemed the gods had better ideas for me. When I awoke, it was with far more pain and rasping than usual. The cough that had plagued me for days had taken a turn for the worse, and when I sat up, my chest wracked in agony.

I pulled myself to my feet and gripped my stick for balance. My legs felt weak under the weight of my body, and I almost staggered to the ground. "No . . ." I spoke aloud, as I was so often wont to do. "No, it can't be my time yet. I still need to search . . ."

Another cough seized hold of me, and once again, I hunched over, rocking back and forth in pain. As I hacked, I closed my weary eyes. When I opened them, deep red blood was splattered across the milky dust floor.

The cough subsided, and I breathed deeply for a moment before grabbing my stick and sack. If I was going to die, it wouldn't be here in a dark bunker. I would continue my quest until I couldn't walk any more, and then I would crawl until even that proved impossible. That was always the vow, and so it would remain.

I got myself back on the road, leaving the town behind. This settlement, like all the ones before it, had proved to be as barren as the last, and so there was no reason to stay. There were still many more locations to scour. All I needed was one sign. All I wanted was evidence that something else was alive in this forsaken, withered land. Was it that much to ask?

I heaved as another cough seized hold of me, and I let go of my stick, sinking to the ground as I spat more blood into the dust. I raised my head, but the world spun in a sickening way, and the red of blood filled my vision. I remained on my hands and knees, staring into the dirt and breathing deeply. I had a moment of peace, and then the coughing began once again, casting more blood splatters into the dust before me.

I could feel my body failing. My organs were shutting down one by one. I slumped sideways to lie on the ground and lifted my head up. Everything was blurred and spinning in front of my eyes.

For a moment, I thought I saw something in the sky, something long and black, but my failing eyes were surely playing tricks on me.

I coughed again and rested my head back on the ground. Blood trickled from my nose and mouth, leaving a growing red stain in the dust around me. I twisted my reluctant muscles, turning my upper body onto my back so that I could die looking upward. The big black shape hovered in my blurred vision again, and I squinted, peering up at it.

I managed to squeeze one last burst of focus out of my dying eyes and saw it clearly, just for a moment. It was a long, black, cylindrical object, just drifting across the sky, as if on some mission or purpose that I could not possibly hope to comprehend. For a moment, I felt hope. It was an aircraft! There was an aircraft up there! Someone lived! Yet it was like no aircraft I had ever seen before. The object moved slowly through the upper atmosphere, as if in orbit. Sunlight glinted off its curved sides. What could it be? Some new weapon to finish the apocalypse on this world? Something extraterrestrial?

My vision blurred again, and I reached out a trembling withered arm toward the device. I had just one breath left in me, one more thing I could say before death claimed me once and for all.

"Is there anybody there?"

Once in a Lifetime
By A. R. Aston

"I bet I could too eat this fruit in one mouthful!" Golt said as Lott monitored the stellar object from their floating platform.

"I didn't say you couldn't, I said you shouldn't, Golt. I'm pretty sure they're poisonous. The boss uses them to clear his garden of creepers," Lott said, not looking up from the spyglass.

"That's just what someone would say if they didn't want to share their food." Golt snorted.

"Eat it, then. I don't care."

"You'd let me eat a poisoned fruit? What kind of a friend are you?" Golt frowned, throwing the fruit off the balcony of the Master's tower.

"We aren't friends. If we were friends, I would have said, at some point in our relationship up until now, that we were. At, and I cannot stress this enough, no point have we been friends. You have been the bane of my existence ever since you were assigned to guard me. Now let me finish my work. Please. This anomaly is a once-in-a-lifetime experience."

Golt nodded glumly, drawing his dagger in his fifth right arm. He passed the blade deftly between his hands for several minutes before he began to tap it against the railing. It made a pleasing sonorous clang. Golt followed up with a few more taps. And a few more.

Lott growled in frustration, whirling his eye stalks to glare at Golt. "Must you? Really?"

"Lott, I—"

"No," Lott said. "I don't want to hear it. Nothing you do is remotely productive!"

"But seriously, Lott . . ."

"Be. Quiet!" Lott jabbed a facial frond at Golt threateningly. "Close your face hole for five minutes . . . okay?"

Golt lasted less than five seconds. "I just wanted to ask—"

"Ask what? What could be so important? Have you found a new freckle on your arse you feel the need to inform me of? Or are you still arguing you wrote the 'T' chapter of the dictionary? What do you want?"

Golt swallowed. "I was just going to ask if that silver thing was the star the Master wanted to see."

"What star?" Lott asked, turning back to his looking glass. "I don't see anything."

"No, no. I mean the one that went past just now. It isn't there now. It was just there, before it went below the horizon line, by them hills. I mean, I don't know what it was supposed to look like, but it looked pretty cool. Would have looked sweet in your eyeglass thing though, I bet. Will we be able to look at it again when it comes back?" Golt asked.

Lott worked his mouthparts, but no sound came out, his eyes wide with numbing shock.

"It . . . won't be coming back . . . ," he said, breathless.

"Oh . . . well . . . that's not great news, is it?" Golt shrugged. "I could like . . . draw it for you? Do you have a pen?" he managed, before Lott set upon him, fists balled tightly.

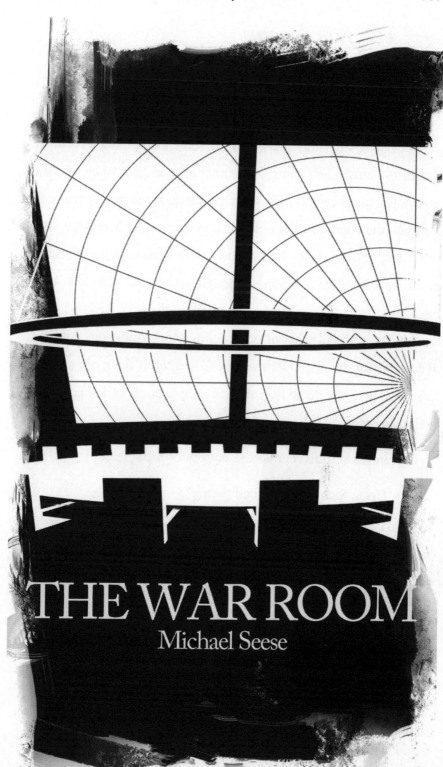

The War Room
By Michael Seese

TIMESTAMP: 13:12:23

The sounds and images on the screen suggested a scene of confusion, chaos, and panic. A number of men and women wearing essentially identical clothing scurried about, stopping occasionally to compare the contents of clipboards they carried. Others were visible in the background, laboring furiously over what appeared to be primitive individual computers, though the screens depicted only lines of letters and numbers. On the wall at the very back, a large display showed a number of white, converging lines superimposed over a map of the planet Patmos. In the center of the room stood a large, round, green table lit from above by a circle of lamps. Its chairs sat empty.

Words scrolled across the bottom of the screen.

"Bring them back! Recall them."

"We can't, sir. They're missiles."

"Then destroy them."

"We can't, sir."

"Why not?"

"Your predecessors apparently felt the ability to send a kill signal was not a requirement."

"Idiots."

"Yes, sir."

"Oh, shit!"

"What?"

"Look at that!" said a man as he pointed to the large screen. White lines originated in the lower left and arced up toward the center; a much greater number of lines emanated from the lower right.

"Would I be correct in assuming . . ."

"That our intelligence screwed up? That their arsenal is far superior to ours? Yes, sir."

"Then I will say again. May god have mercy on our souls."

###

The two men watching the pixelated, often garbled, video footage looked at each other, their faces a mix of concern and bewilderment. One reached out and tapped a << symbol on the screen. The TIMESTAMP now displayed 00:00:00.

###

The scene appeared as before, though now more orderly and calm. The large display showing the map of the planet lacked the white arcs. Seated around the large, green, round table lit from above by a circle of lamps were many of the identically dressed individuals. In the center of the display sat a man, slightly older, and dressed *un*like the others.

"What the hell is that thing?"

The others remained silent.

"Let me repeat myself. What the hell is that thing?"

A man with gray hair stood. Though attired like the others, his garment prominently displayed a number of golden stars. Six, to be exact. He spoke.

"We're not sure, Mr. President."

"Not sure?" said the first, the one apparently named "Mr. President," his voice much louder. "Where did it come from?"

"We don't know."

"What is it doing?"

"We can't say."

"Is it a weapon?"

"I'm sorry, Mr. President. But we can't say."

"Let me get this straight, General. Yesterday, this thing appeared in the sky over the capital. It's just been hovering there ever since?"

"Technically, Mr. President, it's not in the sky. It's in space."

"I don't give a damn about its altitude, General. If I can see it—if the *people* can see it—it's in the sky."

"Yes, sir."

"Speaking of the people, how are things on the surface?"

A different person spoke. "About as well as can be expected. After the initial wave of panic, of rioting, the tensions seem to have somewhat subsided. I think your broadcast appearances have helped,

Mr. President."

"Thank you, Stanley. But if they knew I was delivering them from a bunker three hundred meters underground—rather than from the Octagonal Office—they might not be so comforted."

"Such is the miracle of modern communications."

"Let's get back to the topic at hand," Mr. President said. "If this thing came out of nowhere and parked itself in orbit above the capital, I think we have to assume it's the work of Chairman Vikaw."

"I would agree, Mr. President," said General.

"We don't know that for a fact," said yet a different person.

"What else could it be?"

"An object from another world, another planet, another civilization outside of our system."

"Balderdash! You've been reading too many books, Orson. There are no other worlds, other planets, other civilizations outside of the Black Zone."

The one now known as Orson said, "But some scientists speculate—"

"Yes," said General. "They *speculate*. Scientists also speculate that the reported elevation in the level of communide in our water supplies is a natural chemical occurrence and not an attempt by Vikaw to pollute our cherished physiological liquids."

"I'm merely suggesting—" pleaded Orson.

"Duly noted," said General.

"Let's stick to the facts," said Mr. President, rubbing his temples. "Let's have them again."

Another person, this one attired unlike the majority—he wore a long, white coat—stood. "Approximately thirty minutes after sunrise yesterday, 'The Drifter,' an object exactly one kilometer in length and one hundred meters in diameter, appeared in the skies over Khlōros. I chose the name 'The Drifter' because, after close observation, I was able to determine that it is not remaining in an exactly fixed location above the capital. Its position varies by perhaps eight kilometers east–west, and two kilometers north–south."

"So you're saying it might be scanning us? Is that your theory, Dr. Wormwood?" said General.

"Yes."

"Looking for a target."

"If you believe it is to be used for hostile purposes, then—"

"As much as I hate to, I think we must assume—absent any other facts or reasonable theories to the contrary—that it is a weapon, and that it was launched by that nut case who rules Mavro," said Mr. President.

"I agree, sir," said General.

"So what options do we have? To shoot it down, that is."

"I'm afraid none, sir."

"*None?* General, did I hear you correctly?"

"Yes, sir. Mr. President, you know as well as I that our efforts to develop a rocket that is capable of escaping the atmosphere and entering into orbit around Patmos have been met with a series of setbacks. The scientists on the project say they are to be expected. That such cutting-edge technology comes with the inherent risk of failure. However, I've had some of my analysts looking over the data, trying to determine whether sabotage is involved."

"Have you found anything?"

"We have a few leads. We're checking out several individuals with known ties to Mavro. They tell me we may be close to uncovering a conspiracy, though at this point, I'd have to say it's moot. The bottom line is, we don't have rockets with this capability. But it would appear as though Vikaw does."

"What about our fighter jets? Can't they attack it?"

"No, sir. It's in space. Our planes are incapable of flight outside of the atmosphere."

"So we're sitting ducks?" said Mr. President.

"I'm afraid so," said General.

"Have we been able to make contact with Vikaw?"

"Transoceanic communications have been disrupted," said a second person in a long white coat.

"To keep us from contacting him and reasoning with him, no doubt," said Mr. President.

"You can't reason with a nut case like that, Mr. President," said General.

The second person in the white coat continued, "At first, we suspected that. But, *all* communications, including commercial traffic, have ceased completely. That seems odd. Though I am no economist, I do know that—despite all our differences—we rely on each other for mercantile purposes. So it seems unlikely that they would intentionally sever commercial communications, as it would hurt themselves nearly as much as it hurts us."

"Unless . . ." said another person, this one dressed more like Mr. President.

"And you are?" Mr. President asked.

"Michele Lamb. Your Secretary of Commerce."

"Sorry, Michele. There's been a lot of turnover in my Cabinet. You were saying?"

"We've been studying the changes in our trading patterns with Mavro. It is true that for the past fifty years, they have needed us, as a buyer for their raw materials. Despite their abundance of resources, specifically rare-patmos elements, they've lacked both the technology and the educated workforce needed to produce high-tech products using those materials. But over the past several years, we've witnessed a shift. Obviously, we can't know how the State has been spending their capital assets. But . . ." she said, looking at General.

"Photos taken by our spy planes have revealed a construction boom in Mavro, in remote areas well outside the capital, over the past few years," he said. "Based on the size and configuration, we're fairly confident these new buildings are factories. Except they don't have smokestacks, which every factory they've built before does. So clearly, they're not foundries or auto works."

Michele Lamb resumed. "So we believe that they've developed a nascent technology industry. Which means one, they've created their own market for their resources—"

"And two, they don't need us," said Mr. President.

"That is my belief."

"Enough of this guessing. Let's find a way to get that lunatic on the phone."

"But how, sir?"

"General, I think this situation now warrants use of the Red Line."

"Yes, sir, Mr. President," said General.

General walked to the back of the room and whispered something to a person sitting in front of a screen. The man typed for a few moments, then moved aside. General bent over and typed something.

After a long pause, a man appeared on the large display on the back wall, replacing the map. His attire suggested some affinity with the majority of the inhabitants of the WAR ROOM, though he was dressed primarily in tan, in contrast to the dark green of those in the WAR ROOM. Further, his garb was augmented with a number of ribbons and medallions. Atop his head sat a large, ostentatious hat. He looked directly at the camera and smiled.

"John!" he said effusively. "How are you?"

"Cut the crap, Vikaw. And that's President Ττυρρός to you. What is that thing?"

"This?" he said, touching his cheek. "It's a birthmark. But I plan to get it removed soon. My body double doesn't have one. Though I suppose I could instead ask my surgeons to give him one."

"That's not what I'm talking about, and you know it. What the hell is that tube you've parked in the sky over Khlōros. Is it some sort of spy plane? A weapon?"

"I don't know what you're talking about," Vikaw said, suppressing a giggle.

"The Treaty of Cavalry specifically prohibits space-based weapons. So unless you bring that thing down to Patmos pronto so that we can inspect it, I will take this up with the Security Council of the Unified Nations."

"The Unified Nations?" said Vikaw, his face a sneer. "That puppet organization that your country created to impose your will on all of Patmos? That toothless tiger? That pathetic pusher of paper, which foists upon me resolutions that I use when my bathroom tissue runs out? That Unified Nations?"

"Don't mock me, Vikaw. You can't keep ignoring the will of the entire world."

Vikaw stuck his fingers into his ears. "La-la-la-la-la. I can't hear you, John."

"Mute it for a second," said Mr. President.

"Done."

"General, what do we know about their arsenal?"

"We do know they have begun testing fusion bombs, just within the last year," General said.

"So they're behind us?"

"That's a reasonable conclusion, Mr. President," said Dr. Wormwood. "Based on how long it takes us to synthesize the necessary quantity of solid lithium deuteride—the explosive—we can speculate that they have perhaps a dozen of the devices."

"And how many fission bombs?"

"We can't be sure," said General.

"But fewer than us?"

"We can't be sure."

"But it's a reasonable assumption that we have a larger cache of hydrogen weapons. By a three-to-one ratio? Correct?"

"Yes. But let me state for the record," Dr. Wormwood said, looking at the recording device, "that even if we consider best-case numbers, if they launch an all-out retaliatory attack—"

"Don't worry, doctor. I just want to understand the numbers. I want to know how much I can bluff. I'm not considering global suicide. Un-mute." He waited until Vikaw removed his fingers from his ears. "Listen, Vikaw, I'm not going to play games with you. You're treading on thin ice. You've got one hour to get that thing back to your side of the planet, and another hour to bring it down so that the Unified Nations inspectors can have a look under the hood. Failure to comply will be considered an explicit act of aggression."

Vikaw began to move his fingers back toward his ears.

Mr. President shouted, "I've had enough of your crap, Vikaw. I'll get back in touch when I have hard proof that you've put a war machine out in space over Khlōros." He looked at the man near the display—the one General had spoken with—and made a gesture with his thumb across his throat.

The smile extinguished from Vikaw's face.

"What! You call me in the middle of the night and accuse me without justification of an act of war? And then threaten to kill me? How dare you, you piece of bourgeois trash."

"Kill you? What the hell are you—"

Vikaw made the same gesture with his throat.

"That doesn't mean I'm going to kill you," Mr. President said. "I was telling my tech to cut the signal, you jackass. If you didn't have your head so far up your perverted doctrine, you'd know that—"

"I will rain fire down upon you and your entire corrupt and morally bankrupt land. I will render every square inch of your cursed land an inhospitable wasteland. I will spit upon your rotting corpses. You will regret the day your whore-mother gave birth to you. And let the history books record, and forever associate, the name 'Ττυρρός' with the end of the Patmon race!"

The screen that had born the image of Vikaw showed static. The WAR ROOM stood silent.

Likewise silent were the two men, now thoroughly engrossed by the on-screen events. One of them pointed to the top of the monitor.

WAR ROOM

TIMESTAMP: 13:08:11

The other nodded. He seemed poised to speak, but stopped when the audio feed interrupted him.

"Oh, shit!" said an unseen voice.

"Do we launch?" asked Mr. President.

"Not yet," said General. "We can detect a launch. If one comes, we retaliate. Then, the history books will record, and forever associate, the name 'Crazy Asshole' with the end of the Patmon race!"

"Unless . . ." said Dr. Wormwood.

"Unless?" said Mr. President and General in unison.

"What if that thing—the Drifter—isn't a weapon? What if its sole purpose is to disrupt communications? To render us blind?"

"To prevent us from detecting their launch," said General.

"General," said Mr. President, "do you believe that is a possi—"

He stopped short, as at that moment a bright flash of light burst from the lower-right portion of the large display on the very back wall. Then it went completely blank.

Once again, the words "Oh, shit" scrolled across the bottom.

"What the hell happened!" said Mr. President.

"I'm not sure."

"Find out. Now!"

"Yes, sir."

"Mr. President," said General. "You and I should speak in confidence."

They walked to the left, leaving the viewing scope of the device that had been recording the drama.

The room was mostly silent. The only sounds that came across were the click-click of computer keys, the shuffling of paper, the clearing of throats, and the tap-tap-tapping of pens on desks.

When the TIMESTAMP showed 13:11:07, General walked in quickly, followed by Mr. President. All sound ceased. The latter spoke.

"The General and I have conferred. We believe that Vikaw has made an unfortunate, and irreversible, move. A suicidal move. We feel that we have no options left. I wish there were. But there are not. I'm sorry."

A general murmur was heard, though no words scrolled.

He and General moved to a console in the center of the work area. In nearly identical motions, they removed chains from around their necks. Dangling from the chains were large keys. They inserted the keys into slots on the console. Mr. President turned slightly. He looked down, touched a hand to his forehead, then crossed his arms over his chest. His lips moved, though no words scrolled. He raised his head and looked at General.

"May god have mercy on our souls. Three . . . two . . . one," he said. A hush fell over the room as Mr. President and General turned the keys simultaneously. "It's done. How long until impact, General?"

"Thirty minutes, sir."

"And theirs?"

"They had about a five-minute head start. So . . . twenty-five minutes."

"But we'll be safe down here, correct?"

"Yes, sir."

"And how long will our supplies last?"

General looked around the room.

"Given the number of people, five, maybe six days."

"Is there enough of 'the option' for everyone?"

"More than enough, Mr. President."

"Very well. Then I would suggest that we prepare to make this as easy as—"

"Mr. President!" a voice called out as a woman in the back whirled away from her individual computer screen. "It's gone!"

"What's gone?"

"*It*. The thing. The Drifter."

"What do you mean, *gone?*"

"Look here. Let me rewind." Mr. President and General raced over to her station. She continued, "For the past day and a half, it has been hovering, in space, over the capital. Not more than forty-five seconds ago, it began moving. Then it vanished."

"Confirmed, Mr. President," said a voice from outside of the limited vista. "It is simply gone."

WAR ROOM

TIMESTAMP: 13:12:23

"Bring them back!" yelled Mr. President. "Recall them."

"We can't, sir," said General. "They're missiles."

"Then destroy them."

"We can't, sir," General said.

"Why not?"

"Your predecessors apparently felt the ability to send a kill signal was not a requirement."

"Idiots."

"Yes, sir," said General, his head bowed.

At that moment the large display screen flashed back to life.

"Oh, shit!" again scrawled across the screen.

"What?"

"Look at that!" said the unidentified white coat, pointing at the large screen. A number of lines originated in the lower left and arced up toward the center; a much greater number of lines emanated from the lower right.

"Would I be correct in assuming . . ." said Mr. President.

"That our intelligence screwed up? That their arsenal is far superior to ours? Yes, sir."

"Then I will say again. May god have mercy on our souls."

The screen turned black for a few seconds. When the image resumed, the large display on the wall at the very back was black. The primitive individual computers with screens depicting only lines of letters and numbers were black. And unattended. The only person visible was Mr. President, sitting alone at the center table. The TIMESTAMP showed 13:12:55, 13:12:56, 13:12:57. He held up a small red pill and stared at it, twisting it in his fingers for perhaps five minutes. Looking directly at the recording device, Mr. President spoke.

"I'm the last person alive," he said.

A tiny tear welled up in the corner of his eye. He raised his glasses and wiped it—along with several behind it—away. He sighed, then resumed.

"This little pill will change that. I'll swallow it, and within ten minutes, I will join the rest of our people, wherever we now are."

With that, he popped it in his mouth. Immediately, his face registered relief.

"They tell me I'll just go to sleep peacefully, easily. I hope they weren't lying. I would hate for my final moments to be marred by pain. I'm in enough pain now. I've caused enough pain. I hope you can use this message to learn from our mistakes. As I'm sure you can imagine, my decision, though it ultimately proved to be horribly, tragically wrong, was not undertaken lightly. I hope this message will serve as a warning—as a lesson—to help you avoid making the same mistakes we did. I did.

"Goodbye, and good luck."

###

Seeing nothing but static on the small screen, Dr. Brik turned off the computer. He looked at Major Kub.

"Dar es gabba?" (What is he saying?)

"Glah ne diggo. Et mandrake bok a." (I have no idea. Primitive languages present many challenges.)

"Kisov ne gan?" (Is there no translation key?)

"Buck." (None.)

"Bra tu neg o burpelson ya no?" (Do you think our

archaeologists can decipher it?)

"Ri merkin daga. Maay, di oga ne turgidson doona." (They're working on it. Unfortunately, we've been able to find no artifacts from their civilization.)

"Buck?" (None?)

"Ne. Meg ta kong oregha." (No. It's as if they were erased from the planet.)

"Gaf ne bodu love?" (Don't you find that strange?)

"Yi." (I do.)

"Ale xei de sa deski?" (Shall I keep working on it?)

"Ne. De Muffley glik pa dim sa lothar zogg es." (The President wants every scientist to focus his energies on determining what the thing in orbit above us is.)

SHARD OF HEAVEN
Damir Salkovic

Shard of Heaven
By Damir Salkovic

It is the black, unfathomable heart of chaos that surrounds us, thought Lotharic Thal, and only the Gods knew when, or if, the blackness would lift.

The ramparts of the westward bastion commanded a sweeping view of the grey valley. Fires burned beyond the earthworks and spiked trenches, pinpricks of light blurred by a curtain of rain and fog. There, hidden by the night, was the encampment of the enemy: soldiers, cavalry, cannon, and armoured siege wagons. With the first light of dawn, the ground would tremble with the roar of guns and the rumble of great iron wheels as the artillery and bombards and trebuchets continued to gnaw at the thick stone walls of the fortress. Then the cannons and arquebuses from the crenelated walls would belch fire and smoke in deadly response, filling the wet, cold air with the acrid smell of powder smoke and the death screams of men and beasts.

Like all the officers of the Royal Army, Lotharic had sworn an oath to the king, pledged his sword to defend Iuskazar. Lofty, noble words, all too easily broken: once news of the death of Alemander IV reached the eastern garrisons, treachery and greed had spread like wildfire. Banners were raised in revolt, and the eastern reaches of the monarchy sank into blood and ashes as each local upstart burned with ambition to carve a kingdom for himself out of the corpse of the realm.

Many of Lotharic's old comrades were now on the other side

of the walls of Trebbitt Keep, having deserted to the mercenary regiments of the Rebel Lords, determined to capture the last Royalist stronghold in the east. The rewards were plenty, for the local lords had grown powerful over the years: wealth, land, influence, and noble rank for those who served well. But Lotharic could not go back on his oath to the crown and tarnish his family name with the stain of treachery. He owed it to his ancestors, who had fought under the royal banners since the bloody birth of the First Kingdom. He owed it to his men, who had followed him to this grim, ugly town in the foothills of the Scaled Range—and most likely, their deaths.

Behind the walls, the garrison was coming to life: soldiers milled about the barracks, and the shouts of the officers rang through the stone courtyards. In the town beyond the garrison gate, a brass bell tolled in the belfry of the temple, the sound loud and distinct. From the steeple roof of the temple, heavily damaged by round-shot and cannonballs, flew the scarlet and gold royal banner of Iuskazar. Another hung from the ruins of the ancient keep in the southern part of the town, a popular target for which the enemy gunners and bombardiers to train their sights. Plans had been proposed to tear the crumbling tower down, but General Ascalainte, the garrison commander, had refused: the keep had weathered countless sieges in centuries past, and it would weather this one as well. It was a symbol of the town's defiance—or a grave-marker, some ominously murmured.

Lotharic descended a flight of stone steps into the garrison courtyard and returned the salute of a squad of arquebusiers in rivet armour. From above came the patter of booted feet as the russet-clad longbowmen and took up their positions by the embrasures and the whine and creak of the ratchet mechanisms used to move heavy cannons. A sharp crack travelled across the valley, followed by a low, scarcely audible thump.

The enemy artillery had opened fire. Another day had begun.

###

After a stream of guttural words and what Suldyn took for a curse, he was yanked forward, the rusty iron of the chain digging into his neck and ankles and wrists. He felt hot sand beneath his bare feet and winced. The mounted slaver to his left, tall, broad, and swathed in robes of green and gold, barked a harsh laugh.

Suldyn narrowed his gaze against the glare of the sun, trying to take in the endless expanse of scorched sand, the dunes like rippling waves, the air shimmering with heat. Behind him stood the great jagged shapes of the mountains of the Spine, outlined against a clear blue sky. The journey had been long and agonizing—untold days in the stinking hold of the galley followed by a week of relentless marching through the southern provinces. Yet it was here, on the edge of the desert, that the true horror of his position became evident.

On this side of the Spine, there was nothing but sun and sand and death.

The slaves were tattered and filthy, thin but not starved to the sinew; most had ended up in manacles as criminals or through the debtors' courts. The slave-drivers had chosen carefully: they were

Basheng tribesmen, denizens of the desert, well versed in their ancient trade. From the position of the stars, Suldyn had long inferred the direction in which the slave caravan was moving. The irony could hardly cut deeper: his discovery of the mathematical principles that guided the paths of the celestial bodies—the very revelation that had condemned him to the dungeon and the coffle—now served to remind him of the dismal fate that awaited at the end of the trek.

By dusk, when the slave-drivers halted, the soles of Suldyn's feet were a mass of bloody blisters and his stomach turned in slow, nauseating rolls. He lay on the swiftly cooling sand and prayed for death. The slave-drivers unloaded their tereks, sullen, coarse-haired, six-legged beasts with curving yellow tusks, and set up camp for the night. The scorching heat of the day was gone, and an icy chill descended over the dunes. The chained men shivered in spite of the fires and huddled closer together for warmth.

"We'll die out there," said the man to Suldyn's left, a peasant from the Aralskan plains—tall and large-boned, with a long, horse-like face. His words were met with frightened mutters. "One day on the sands and half of us can barely stand. No one has crossed the burning desert and returned alive."

"We must escape before they take us deeper into the desert," someone said from the darkness.

A ragged old man lifted his wizened head and glared in the direction of the voice.

"Don't be a fool. The Basheng know the dunes like the backs

of their hands. No matter how far you run, they will find you, and you'll die cursing the day you were born. Unless the sun and thirst and the things that burrow beneath the sand prove quicker." The men in the coffle cast their eyes to the ground, and a number of them made the protective sign. "The slavers have to keep us alive until we climb the auction block in Caldesh," the old man continued. "We're worth nothing to them dead."

"Then we must steal their beasts," said Suldyn, eyeing the lone Basheng sentry who stood at the edge of the camp. "And their weapons."

As soon as the words were out, he regretted opening his mouth, for all eyes were now upon him and a dead silence reigned along the coffle.

"Where do you hail from, lad?" The old man turned to face Suldyn. "You speak like a man from the heartlands."

"A small village near Morromath," Suldyn replied. Most of the faces in the circle of the fire remained blank, but a few brows furrowed in surprise.

"I never thought the tribesmen travelled that far north," said a fair-skinned man with the build of a blacksmith.

"They do not." With a jangle of chains, the old man reached for Suldyn's arm and pulled the sleeve back. The light of the flames fell on the tattoo on his forearm—a series of concentric circles surrounded by symbols.

A gasp escaped those in the circle of firelight.

"A monk," said the man from Aralskan, moving away from Suldyn as if from an unclean presence. "How did you end up on the coffle?"

"I wrote a book." *No use holding anything back*, thought Suldyn with resignation. "The church decried me as a heretic. I was tried and imprisoned in the dungeons of Burz Sarzaum."

"Most of us were sold for debt, or through the criminal courts," the blacksmith said.

"Any prisoner is fair game for the dungeon wardens," the old man said. "If you have no family or connections, you disappear and are never heard from again."

"All for a handful of scribbles on paper." The large man from Aralskan shook his head in disbelief. "Dabbling in books and letters is for fools."

"The priests say that heretics should burn," said a voice behind Suldyn. "That no one who blasphemes against the Holy Writ should be suffered to live."

"It is not man's right to be the arbiter of the will of the Gods," said the old slave, shaking his head. "Least of all take the life of another." This drew angry cries and curses, and the Basheng guarding the camp raised his head.

"None of that matters out here." The blacksmith glanced at the irons on his arms. "There are no Gods to hear our prayers in the desert. Heretics or followers of the true faith, we are no more than chattel on a chain."

His words cast a hush over the slaves. As the men turned away, the peasant from Aralskan moved nearer to Suldyn.

"You spoke of escape." Orange light flickered across his broad face, shadows gathering in the hollows. "How?"

"There are half a dozen slavers to two score of us," said Suldyn. "A single man guards us at night. We can overcome him, take his weapon and enough provisions to sustain us. But we must decide quickly. A few days in the desert and we'll be blistered and broken, in no shape to fight or flee."

"They will hunt you down and kill you," said the old man, turning his back to the fire. "A Basheng is born in the saddle, sword in hand. He feels no heat or cold, hunger or thirst, and his fierceness and cruelty are unmatched."

"I'll not die in this wasteland or shackled to the wall like a dog," said the Aralskani. "If you have a plan, heretic, let us hear it."

Keeping his voice low and an eye out for the watchful guard, Suldyn began to relay his idea.

###

In the council room, the tension was palpable. The officers were on their feet around the table; voices rose and hands gestured furiously. All were gaunt and sunken-cheeked with hunger. Oilskin cloaks hung off their frames in dirty, sodden folds, and the leather doublets they wore over their shirts were scuffed and spattered with mud.

Rain beat against the wooden shutters of the windows, and

Lotharic offered a silent prayer of gratitude to the Gods. The season of rains had come early, the dirty grey sky weighed down with clouds. Rivers burst from their banks and flooded the fields and roads, slowing the advance of enemy supply trains, siege towers, and artillery wagons. The rain soaked the powder and priming in the cannons and mired the armoured war wagons of the besiegers in the muddy fields. The defenders of Trebbitt Keep may be starving to death, but they were in no want of fresh water.

A deep voice, heavily accented with the rolling lilt of the southern provinces, boomed above the cacophony. "Yesterday we lost two dozen men defending the breach in the northern wall."

"The bandits lost thrice that number," said a tall, hawk-faced officer, the knight-commander of the garrison artillery.

"True, but the bandits have ten men to one of ours." The southerner, a seasoned captain of the footmen named Brusilard, scratched his heavy black beard. "We cannot hold. We must fall back, and let the enemy advance on the inner gate."

There was a murmur of disapproval in the chamber. "The inner gate is mined," said a large, swarthy Northman. "If worst comes to worst, we'll let the enemy in and light the fuse. Hundreds will die."

"But if we abandon the outer wall, they will place their cannons at the mouth of the breach." A grey-whiskered officer in the steel sallet of the crossbow regiments slammed his fist on the table. "It will then be a matter of days before the inner wall is torn down. What then?"

Brusilard said nothing, but gazed into the eyes of each officer at the table. A leaden silence fell upon the gathering, the unspoken reply heavy in the stale, damp air.

"We have all taken the King's Oath," said the southerner, his voice low and even. "Even if the town must be abandoned, we shall hold the fortress to the last man."

With that, the council was over. As the chamber emptied, Lotharic approached the dark-haired Northman. "Are the reports as dire as they appear?"

"Worse." The giant's eyes gleamed, and he bared his white teeth in a mischievous smile. "But I persuaded two of the quartermasters to falsify their forage and supplies receipts." One massive hand grasped the hilt of his long, curved sword in a painted leather scabbard, leaving no doubt as to the method of persuasion.

"So we'll run out of food in a tenday, even on minimal rations."

"We'll be fortunate to last a tenday. A full sixth of the remaining provisions are spoiled." Khoraj Fird Mordriceas roared with laughter. "But the quartermasters won't admit it, not on their lives. I have made that much certain. If word got out among the men, we would have a mutiny."

"General Acalainte will have you hanged if he finds out."

"General Ascalainte was the one who ordered me to do so," replied the Northman brightly. A round-shot whistled over their heads and crashed into the wall of the cavalry stables. Lotharic dipped his head instinctively, but Khoraj only gave a disdainful chuckle. "If the bandit army had but a handful of trained gunners, the town would have fallen months ago. As it is, their men seem uncertain which end of the cannon ought to be lit."

"Brigands, scoundrels, and peasant conscripts," said Lotharic. They passed the fortress gate, where a group of soldiers was portioning out crusts of bread and thin soup of turnips and potato peels to a long line of starved, hollow-eyed apparitions that stretched into town. The dead, cold silence along the line filled the two officers with unease, and they hastened their pace.

There was a commotion on the other side of the courtyard as a detachment of pikemen scrambled to attention at the entrance to the great hall. Two figures emerged from the shadowy interior: General Ascalainte, a short, broad-chested old soldier, followed by a slender, bearded man in nobleman's robes—the Grand Duke of Istearch, the last of the eastern lords to remain loyal to the crown.

"Has there been word of reinforcements from Burz Sarzaum?"

"None." The Northman's coal-black eyes followed the armoured figure of the general. "The Privy Council bickers and plots against itself, the throne remains empty, and Ascalainte—a former Proclamationist, a seditionist exiled by the dead king's father—is the last hope of the monarchy in the east."

"Yet he fights for the Crown like no other man in the realm," said Lotharic. "His presence alone keeps the army together. The Rebel Lords have gold and grain in abundance and offer both to skilled men-at-arms to entice them to defect."

"It is not only mutiny I fear." A shadow crossed the Northman's face. "Trebbitt Keep is starving, and the longer the siege lasts, the scarcer the supplies become. Hunger and disease have begun to claim the children and infirm. If the townsfolk turn against us, we are as good as lost."

"All to save one man." Lotharic spat, inclining his head at the bearded nobleman and the guards around him. "If we surrender the Grand Duke to the rebels, not only will the siege be lifted, but we'll be made wealthy beyond measure."

"Perhaps," said the Northman. "The Lords need able officers to command their cutthroats, who are unsurpassed at looting and murder but without discipline and incapable of marching in orderly formation."

"We could be generals by the end of winter."

"We could." For a moment the two men were pensive, listening to the distant rumble of the guns. The clamour of the bells from the forward bastion and a chatter of matchlock-fire from the parapets roused them from thought. A troop of armoured cuirassiers raced in the direction of the stables, where the stable boys were already holding the reins of rearing, neighing horses. The defenders had beaten back a clumsy assault on the redoubt; the enemy was retreating in disarray, and now the massive gates of the fort opened for the heavy cavalry to pursue and butcher the stragglers. Lotharic caught a glimpse of the grey mud of the killing field, littered with the broken bodies of dead and dying men.

In a torrent of red and gold pennants, the cuirassiers thundered to slaughter.

###

The sun was a red slash in the sky when the slave caravan stopped for the evening. The exhausted men collapsed on the sand, moaning and cursing and clutching at their bloody feet and wrists and ankles rubbed raw by the manacles. Along the coffles moved the robed figures of the slavers, kicking and cracking their whips.

Of the two score chained men, only four had decided to join Suldyn and the man from Aralskan, whose name was Orth. Among them were the blacksmith and a heavily scarred and tattooed criminal from the southern provinces. The other two were peasants from the highlands of Flaern, slow of movement and thought but hardy and strong. "Gallows fodder and cottagers," Orth had grumbled, but there was little choice. The six men decided to wait until the slavers had gone to sleep and try to overcome the lone sentry guarding the camp.

Night fell swiftly, and the black stretch of sky filled with a myriad stars. The twin moons ascended, luminous and full, spreading their silvery radiance across the dunes. Soon, the only noises in the camp were the snorting and grunting of the surly tereks and the low moans of the chained men. Suldyn crept closer to the fire and wrapped a few glowing embers in a strip of leather, careful not to snuff them out. He waited for the guard to turn in his direction and gave the signal.

With a heavy curse, Orth was on his feet, lunging at Suldyn.

Two massive fists rose with a rattle of chains, and Suldyn felt a tremendous blow connect with his shoulder. He clutched his face and fell to the ground, hoping that the darkness would work in his favour. The Basheng took the ruse: sword drawn, he rushed into the circle of light and roughly shoved the large peasant aside. The monk lay motionless. He'd nicked his cheek with a sharp metal shard, and blood stained his brow.

Sheathing the curved blade, the slaver bent over the prostrate figure. Suldyn held his breath and waited, his muscles tensed. As the turbaned man leaned forward to examine the wound, Suldyn brought his feet together and kicked up as high as his leg irons allowed.

The blow caught the Basheng in the chest and sent him stumbling backward with a small yelp of surprise. Before the sentry could regain his balance, Orth's chain was pulled tight across his neck, choking the shout of alarm. The slaver dropped his sword; one hand clawed at the iron across his throat, the other at the long dagger in his belt. His eyes bulged and his feet thrashed, seeking purchase in the sand. His mouth opened and closed, but the only sound to escape was a strangled croak.

"Get his cropper," hissed the blacksmith, straining against his chains; the thrashing sentry was still too far to be grasped from the second coffle. Suldyn scrambled to his feet and reached for the tool on the Basheng's belt. A kick doubled him over, driving the breath from his lungs. Stars exploded before his eyes. The tattooed man and the other two slaves moved closer. They had to overwhelm the Basheng before his thrashing roused the suspicions of the others.

Something silver flashed in the firelight, and the scarred criminal reeled backward, blood spurting from a cut in his neck. The Basheng had found his dagger. Knowing he was about to die, he fought with inhuman ferocity, kicking and clawing and slashing at his attackers. The sight of blood made the two peasants hesitate.

"Cut me loose," said the blacksmith, fists clenched in impotent fury. Suldyn lifted the crude tool to the chain around his neck; the cropper was unwieldy, the manacles thick. Steel jaws bit into corrugated iron, snapped, tore. He raced over to the blacksmith and set to work freeing the man.

The dagger sank into Orth's thigh, and the large Aralskani grimaced with pain but continued to work the chain tighter around the Basheng's neck. Voices from the direction of the slavers' fire, gruff and urgent: the slavers had awakened. The blacksmith, now free, used his shackles as a weapon and struck the struggling Basheng down. The two highlanders joined him, and within moments, the guard was bludgeoned to death, his face a pulp of bone and gristle.

Before the fugitives could react, three of the slavers were among them, swords and daggers drawn. One of the peasants rushed the nearest Basheng with a cry, swinging his shackles like a flail. The slaver evaded the ungainly attack and opened the peasant's belly with a quick stroke, finishing him off with a stab to the neck.

The remaining slavers arrived, and the fugitives found themselves encircled. Suldyn's heart sank; the escape had failed. He picked up the dead sentry's sword and faced the Basheng. Better to die quickly than suffer the retribution. The cruelty of the desert dwellers was legendary. The ruins of trading outposts and caravan routes were littered with the sun-bleached bones of those who had invoked their wrath.

Suldyn felt the weight of the makeshift ember pouch in his other hand, and a spark of desperate hope lit his eyes. He swung the leather strap in a horizontal arc, using it like a sling, and hurled the smouldering coals at the dark bulk of the nearest terek.

An ember struck one of the animal's four curved horns, bursting into a shower of sparks. The terek gave a deep bellow and reared in fear. The chain snapped taut. There was nothing the great pack beasts feared more than fire; with deafening cries, they roused from slumber and began to flee in terror, dragging the coffles behind them and trampling the screaming slaves who got in their way. Chaos ensued. The slavers cast aside their weapons and ran after the tereks, attempting to calm the frenzied animals.

Suldyn found himself enveloped in a rush of rattling chains and pounding feet, vast, roaring shapes rumbling past him in the darkness. A large, bony hand grasped him by the sleeve and dragged him from the melee.

"We must go." Limping on his wounded leg, Orth led him to the cover of a dune. The blacksmith and the remaining peasant were already there with a sack of provisions and a water skin. "They'll come after us as soon as they realize we have escaped."

Turning their backs on the shouts and noise, the four silhouettes vanished into the shadows that pooled beneath the silver-crested dunes.

###

It was midday when the fugitives reached the first houses of the village, and the heat of the day was at its fiercest.

Children ran before them with loud cries, and a curious crowd gathered around the village well to stare at the newcomers. The four arrivals were dust-caked and blistered raw from the sun, and their clothes hung in tattered rags, but they were alive.

The folk of the village—a dark-eyed, sinewy mongrel mix of ferocious Basheng and Iuskari borderers—offered them food and water and shelter for the night, but made it known, through whispered hints and frightened glances in the direction of the desert, that they could not remain among them long. The fugitives bore the marks of the coffle around their necks, wrists, and ankles, and there was nothing the southerners dreaded more than Basheng retribution.

Suldyn did not expect the slavers to come after them: one of their own was dead, and there was still the rest of the human cargo to deliver to the slave market in faraway Caldesh. But he roused the others from sleep as the sky began to lighten, and by morning, they were treading the dusty road that led through the half-wild borderlands of the south, across baked, cracked ground and through fields of millet and sorghum over which heat lay heavy like a shimmering pall.

After many days, there came a morning when the drab brown and tan of the borderlands gave way to rolling fields of green and emerald forests wreathed in a pale mist. Above the verdant landscape, blue-grey in the distance, the peaks of the Scaled Range rose into a stormy, cloud-laden sky. The men drew their rags closer about their bodies and shivered in a gust of wet, cold wind. The road was a strip of wet earth, rutted by wagon wheels and pitted by the hooves of beasts of burden.

The reek reached their noses long before the charred remains of the settlement came into view behind a bend in the road—burnt wood and flesh, bodies rotting in the mud and gummed blood. The few rickety houses had burned to their foundations, wisps of smoke curling up from the blackened timbers. As the fugitives approached, a flock of black crows rose from the middle of the clearing, leaving behind their grisly feast. The peasant from Flaern turned pale and retched, bringing up the remains of his meagre morning meal. The blacksmith and Orth averted their eyes. Suldyn murmured a prayer for the dead, but the words rang hollow and meaningless, sank into the black dirt.

"Raiders or marauders," Orth said. The blacksmith shook his head and pointed to a stone-flanged granary pit. The heavy wooden door lay in pieces, and the pit was empty.

"Raiders would have taken slaves and everything of value. This was the work of soldiers. They killed without distinction and looted the grain."

"Because the villagers refused to give it to them?"

"In retribution," the blacksmith said, pointing at a row of staked heads. "Or as a warning to others. This is the new law in the east."

As the four men stood in the middle of the clearing, their legs unwilling to carry them further, a group of horsemen rode into the village from the north: eight soldiers with swords and crossbows readied.

"Royals or rebels?" asked the blacksmith.

"Royals," Orth said, seeing the horsemen's banner. "Not that it'll matter to us if they're in the mood for a hanging."

The riders halted several paces from the four fugitives. The soldier in the middle of the line, an officer in cuirass and buff leather coat, signalled to his men to lower their weapons.

"Who are you, and where are you headed?"

"Craftsmen, Your Excellence." Feverishly, Suldyn searched his memory for the names of eastern towns. "Looking for work in Jhessel or Rothav."

The officer's hard, cold eyes took in their sunburned faces and the dark scars around their necks and wrists.

"This was not our doing." The sweep of his arm took in the carnage. "There were men and women in this village loyal to the Crown, spies and guides. Now the river is at half-flood, and the rebels have destroyed the bridges. We need a guide across the river and can pay with gold."

Suldyn knew the cuirassier had not been fooled by his lie: if they refused to help, the soldiers would place them back in chains— or execute them to avoid the trouble.

"I know of a shallow place to cross, Sire," he said, drawing surprised glances from the other three. "My friends can wait for me farther up the road, in Jhessel." Suldyn pointed at the muddy road down which the riders had come and nodded at his companions.

"Lead us to it, then." The cavalryman's stare did not waver. "We've already lost a day."

A burly horseman helped Suldyn onto the back of his saddle. The three fugitives watched the riders set off in the direction of the river, their hands raised in mute farewell.

The river was muddy and swollen by the rains, treacherous; the opposite bank could be glimpsed through a curtain of fog. Suldyn dismounted clumsily and walked to the edge of the water. To his right, farther along the bank, were the ruins of a mill in which the fugitives had spent the previous night. Across the river, hidden from the soldiers by the fog, stood the remains of cattle sheds or stables. Somewhere between the mill and the stables, if he had guessed correctly, the water would be shallow enough to wade. If not, the soldiers would kill him for deceiving them. But the diversion had given the others time to take to the woods, where they could hide from both the rebels and the king's men.

"Right here," he said to the cuirassier, pointing at the opaque surface of the water, yellow leaves swirling in the current.

Two riders splashed into the river, cursing and spurring their mounts, who shied from the rushing water. The soldier downstream was thrown from the saddle as his horse lost its footing but kept his grip on the pommel and was dragged out of the water by the frightened animal, spluttering and soaked. The other rider, who was searching upstream, cautiously goaded his mount forward. The water rose to his stirrups, then began to subside. The cavalryman rode across and back to a salvo of cheers from his comrades.

"Send for the pioneers," said the officer, his voice thick with relief. A small purse was thrust into Suldyn's numb hands; through the rough leather, he could feel the hardness of coins. "Come with us to Trebbitt Keep, if you wish. The Grand Duke of Istearch will surely want to reward you for your service."

Suldyn was silent. Earlier, he had chosen not to ponder what would happen at the end of his journey or where that end may lie. But travelling with the army meant safe passage to the cities of the east, where there were observatories and libraries run by the priests of the Orthodox Clockwork Church, a life to be shaped from the ashes of conflagration.

He reached for an outstretched hand and climbed back into saddle.

"Hold the line!" The giant Khoraj Fird Mordriceas thrust his bloody sword toward the approaching enemy. The line of pikes drawn up across the breach in the wall gleamed in the evening sunlight. On the flanks, crossbowmen and arquebusiers readied their weapons. The cries of the attackers and the rumble of charging feet reached the line through the cloud of dust and powder smoke. "Hold the line, you dogs! Do not give them an inch!"

The assault on the northern wall had begun in the early afternoon, and twice the enemy had been repelled with heavy losses. But Khoraj knew it was only a matter of time before the rebel army prevailed through sheer weight of numbers. The arched inner gate behind his back was a trap, and he and his men the bait.

A stray shot, a speeding ball of black iron, bounced on the ground in front of the men, scattering debris and taking off a pikeman's leg in a messy splatter. The front ranks of the attackers emerged from the smoke, blinded and disoriented; peasants and brigands, poorly trained and undisciplined, wavered at the sight of the bristling line of steel. But there was no going back. Already those behind them pressed them forward, the orders of their officers mixed with cries of alarm, and the crossbows and fire-locks delivered the lethal salute. At this range, there was little opportunity to miss, and the charge of the rebel army dissolved in a blur of death-screams and blood.

Then the line of pikes moved forward, and the carnage truly began.

Blades found soft flesh and blood ran red and freely as the relentless wall of tempered steel drove forward. The men at the front of the assault began to fall back. Blinded by the dust and smoke and frightened by the crash of unseen muskets and the whine of musketballs and quarrels, many stumbled headlong into their own rear ranks and died at the hands of their comrades. Before the rebel officers could restore some semblance of order, Khoraj's men were among them, forcing them back into the opening in the outer wall. Musketfire poured into the melee from the ruined parapet above, announcing the arrival of Lotharic's arquebusiers; within minutes, the assault had turned into a rout. The remains of the attacking party fled in disorder.

"Come to see a proper soldier fight, have you?" Khoraj wiped his sword clean on a dead rebel's gambeson and grinned at Lotharic. Blood spattered Khoraj's hands and cuirass, a deep cut running along his upper arm, but the bloodshed had lifted his spirits. He gazed into his friend's powder-blackened face, streaked by rivulets of sweat, and his eyes travelled lower. "Where did you get that gash?"

"A mere scratch." Lotharic unbuckled his sword-belt. A bullet had passed through the flesh right above his hip, but his tabard had stuck to the wound, and he had lost little blood. "They tried an escalade on the western bastion but were beaten back."

From the top of the wall, a bowman reported a column of enemy soldiers massed on the northern road. This was followed by a salvo of cannons and trebuchets, and the outer wall shook under the onslaught. Several cannonballs flew over the crumbling masonry and struck the battlements of the inner wall, showering the men below with stone fragments and dust. With a groaning, scraping noise, the portcullis of the inner gate began to rise, the dark tunnel beyond like the maw of a mythical beast.

"It is time," said Lotharic, ordering his men to prime their matchlocks. "We shall proceed as planned. One volley to lure them closer, then retreat into town and assemble on the other side of the gate."

"Nonsense." Khoraj hefted his sword. "My men can hold the northern wall against ten thousand bandits."

"Do not tempt fate, Khoraj." The men with the fire-locks were already marching into the tunnel. Lotharic seized him by the shoulder. "The sappers are lighting the fuse. One volley, then order your men back."

"Some other time, then," he replied with a mischievous smile. "Worry not, old friend. I shall see you on the other side."

Torches were being lit when Lotharic joined his men on the inner wall. Soldiers gathered below in the wide cobbled lane that led into the centre of Trebbitt Keep, and the flickering light danced on the blades and breastplates, across the sallets and morions of the crossbow and pike units. At the back of the infantry column stood the mounted cuirassiers, armed with short fire-locks and broadswords. The townsfolk had long abandoned the northern quarter, and the doors and windows of the battered houses were boarded shut. The guns beyond the ramparts had ceased their fire: the enemy column was drawing near. Shots echoed from the other side of the gate, and dim figures filed into the opening of the tunnel. Khoraj's men were retreating. Lotharic took a deep breath of relief.

"They're coming." The giant Northman stepped into the circle of officers, eyes ablaze. "Two regiments of pike and crossbow, flanked by musketry. More than twice our number."

"Then more will die." Brusilard shouted orders at the men. The pikemen drew up into squares, thrusting their pikes out between the arquebusiers who formed two ranks at the front of each formation. Atop the inner wall, archers and crossbowmen took cover behind the battlements, avoiding the section directly above the gate. The mine was set to explode as the enemy, thinking the gate undefended, marched through the tunnel and into Trebbitt Keep. Those who survived the explosion would be trapped between the breached outer wall and the inner rampart, facing a hail of fire from the embrasures.

Footsteps sounded from the deserted street, and a runner burst into the circle of officers, gasping for breath, eyes wide with fear. Up on the fire step, Lotharic felt his limbs turn to lead: it was one of the sappers tasked with lighting the fuse.

"The fuse," the man said between great gulps of air. "It is damp and will not light."

A shudder passed through the gathered soldiers. The fuse had been laid through an underground passage; with the heavy rainfall, many of the cellars had flooded. The powder kegs were safe, nestled in dry compartments inside the wall. Yet if the fuse did not burn, the trap would fail, leaving the heavily outnumbered defenders to be massacred by the storming enemy. The same rain that had kept the garrison alive, Lotharic reflected, had sealed their fate.

The troop of horsemen parted, raising their blades in salute. General Ascalainte, resplendent in gold-gilded cuirass and burgonet and armed with a heavy backsword, took his place among the officers. From the expression on the broad, weathered visage, it was evident he had learned the news.

"Lower the portcullis," he said to the officers. "It will give us time to fall back to the fortress."

But it was too late. A shout came from the front ranks: the attackers had climbed over the breach and now poured into the gate like a torrent. The long pikes were lowered, steadied, fixed in bristling line; crossbows were nocked and matchlocks brought to shoulder. There was nothing left to do but die.

Lotharic unsheathed his sword. He felt no fear of approaching death, only a vague emptiness. It was the will of the Gods, the working of the unseen, unknowable mechanism of the celestial spheres. He lifted his gaze upward: the clouds had parted, giving glimpses of patches of starry sky, the moons twin smears of pale light.

As he watched, a speck of light grew out of the blackness, larger and brighter by the second. Lotharic shielded his eyes. The speck became a white, incandescent blaze that spread across the sky, consuming the darkness.

Cries of terror and astonishment rose on all sides. The attackers saw the brilliant burst above the wall of pikes on the other side of the tunnel and froze in their tracks, thinking the light to be the flash of cannon aimed into the gate. Among the defenders, the confusion was absolute, and only the iron discipline of their training kept the men from breaking ranks. The cuirassiers' horses reared and wheeled in fright, the riders struggling to remain in their saddles.

The blaze of light vanished just as abruptly as it had appeared, and the horizon sank back into darkness. But for a moment, the radiance had lit the valley like the noontime sun, and Lotharic saw something on the other side, behind the enemy encampment. Ignoring the warnings of his men, he raised his head above the parapet and stared into the night. There: a gleam winked through the blackness from the direction of the western road. It was joined by another, and another, forming a familiar pattern. He stood paralysed for what felt like an eternity. Then he seized a fire-lock from a nearby arquebusier, cocked back the serpentine lock, and fired in the air.

"Reinforcements!" His cry rose above the turmoil below. Pale, bewildered faces stared up at him. Officers moved through the melee, barking orders and pushing the men back into formation. "Reinforcements are coming! Hold off the attack!"

Khoraj shoved his way to the front line of men, sword in one hand and a flaming torch in the other. He gazed up at the battlements, then at the enemy on the far side of the vaulted gate passage, muscles coiling under the arming doublet. Curved blade raised, he bellowed a war cry and ran into the gate tunnel, straight at the advancing enemy.

Inside the passage, pikes were levelled and muskets raised as the forward ranks of the attackers beheld the approaching giant. Smoke and fire blossomed from the muzzles of the fire-locks, their crash immense in the confines of the tunnel. One ball struck him in the side and another grazed his shoulder, but he did not slow. He reached an iron hatch in the vaulted stone wall just as a bold pikeman lunged forward, thrusting the point of his weapon through Khoraj's belly.

Blood bubbled on Khoraj's lips, but he kept his feet. The curved sword arced in the torchlight; the pikeman dropped the haft of the polearm and clutched at his severed throat. Two of the arquebusiers drew their arming-swords and moved in to finish off their wounded foe. Khoraj hewed one down like a sapling, but the other evaded the sweep of his blade and ran him through from behind. Khoraj felt a shadow fall across his consciousness, his life ebbing swiftly. Ignoring the white-hot agony searing his innards, he flung his opponent against the wall, trapping the man's sword arm between his side and the cold stone. His defiant gaze whipped across the stunned front ranks of the enemy, and his mouth stretched in a hideous, bloody grin.

Once again, the heavy, crimson-stained sword ascended, and the struggling arquebusier yelped in terror. Summoning the last of his immense strength, Khoraj brought the hilt of the weapon down on the padlock of the iron hatch, breaking it apart. The lid clanged open against the wall. Now the attackers could see the small barrels neatly stacked in an alcove in the stone, and shrieks of panic filled the gate tunnel.

With a slow, deliberate movement, Khoraj brought the flaming torch to the touch-hole of a barrel.

###

A deafening blast rent the night. Lotharic felt the wall tremble as the immense explosion roared through the tunnel, dislodging a mass of stone on the heads of those rebels not killed by the initial blast. Thick, bitter, sulphurous smoke and bits of stone erupted from the collapsed passage, engulfing the men on both sides of the gate. But the defenders on the parapet were not blinded, and before the dazed attackers could regroup, several score of them were massacred by fire from the inner wall. Soldiers died choking in the infernal cauldron between the two walls, unable to retreat or scale the mass of stone and broken masonry ahead.

Small groups of arquebusiers and crossbowmen attempted to form ranks and return fire but could not withstand the slaughtering barrage from the rampart. Within minutes, the order was given to retreat. Trebbitt Keep had been saved once again.

High up in the heavens, the strange light pulsated and glowed and winked out of existence. The twin moons shone down on the dark valley across which billows of smoke slowly drifted, hiding from sight the bloody carnage. A light rain began to fall, turning the muddy ground into a slough in which lay the dead, the wounded, and the dying, their moans echoing off the pitted black walls, swallowed by the night.

###

As the morning sun burned away the last remains of night and fog, the sight of the long columns of cavalry and cannon moving along the western road threw the besiegers into confusion. The royal army made no attempt to descend into the valley; instead, they manoeuvred their war wagons, dragged by armoured oxen, into firing positions and opened a barrage on the enemy encampment from the road. The distance was too great for the shots to cause much damage, but the rebel commanders soon realized the precarious nature of their position: outnumbered and flanked, their wagons and siege engines mired in the mud of the valley, they were facing complete destruction.

Orders were given to retreat, but already bands of mercenaries and brigands were in flight, having looted as much of the army's supplies as they could carry. Cheers and cannon fire from the battered ramparts of Trebbitt Keep accompanied the disorderly retreat. Before the end of the day, the massive western gate was opened to the liberating army, and the pennant of Lord Farsum Dondragon, the Wyrm of Oloshan Hold, flew from the battlements alongside the shot-riddled flag of the Royal Dynasty.

The main body of the arriving army continued to pursue the Rebel Lords' fleeing regiments, and another force sailed down the Caligin River from the capital to cut off the rebel retreat and put an end to the war in the east. A new ruler now sat on the throne of Iuskazar—a distant cousin of the murdered king, chosen by the Privy Council—and the vacillating, treacherous nobles hurried to outdo one another in proclamations of fealty. Peace would soon return to the burned villages and ruined towns, to the pastures and fields soaked in the blood of soldiers.

At dusk, the central temple was alight with the flames of

cressets and torches, the soldiers and townsfolk gathering to commemorate the fallen defenders of Trebbitt Keep and Commander Khoraj Fird Mordriceas, whose gallant sacrifice had saved the garrison town. Lotharic Thal sought instead the dark parapets of the western wall, watching the moons frost the desolate valley with crystalline light. Across the killing field lay scattered the charred hulks of burned trebuchets and wagons, broken swords and pikes and rusted muskets and the bones of countless dead. The familiar emptiness had returned to plague him as he pondered the destruction and slaughter.

He was not alone. A solitary figure in a monk's cowl, slight of build and delicate of features, stood on the ramparts, gazing up at the night sky. Before him was lap desk with a sheet of paper and an ink quill. Lotharic glanced at the paper, suddenly suspicious of treachery, but the monk was drawing constellations, a map of the night sky.

Suldyn heard the soldier approach and lifted his eyes from his work. Something like terror must have crossed his face.

"I did not mean to interrupt you," said the officer.

Suldyn bowed his shaven head. "This is but mere pastime, Sire." He smiled benevolently and reached for a fresh sheet of paper. "The Writ teaches that the essence of the universe is harmonic, orderly motion. There is no better prayer than trying to read the heavens like a book, to solve their inherent geometries like an equation."

"What, then, did you make of the strange light in the sky?"

"Some disturbance in the paths of the celestial bodies—a portent of change." In his heart of hearts, Suldyn knew: the light had been a beacon, the Spheres sending him a sign to continue his work. The long years in the dungeon and the horrors of the slave chain had left him torn by doubt and regret, but now a fresh hope burned in his breast. In Trebbitt Keep, he could shed his old identity; the local priests welcomed a travelling scholar, and the gold he had earned diverted inopportune questions. "It is not man's lot to infer the entirety of the divine apparatus. Yet of one thing we can be certain: every event is a small cog that turns a larger wheel, and that one a larger one yet. There is a meaning, a purpose to all that happens to us."

The two men lifted their eyes to the heavens, but all they saw was the cold light of stars shimmering across the black, endless gulfs of space, vast and inscrutable like the minds of the Gods.

The Drift Engine
By A. R. Aston

First: Impetus

A cylinder—perfect in all its dimensions. It was flawless and featureless, a silver rod hurtling through the void, like a javelin by unseen hands. If it was measured by observing eyes, it would be one thousand metres long, one hundred in diameter. But that is a context denied the Drift Engine. The name is not its own, but adopted from a race that observed it once. Once, in all the histories of that system, only once did they ever see the cylinder. Once, before it departed forever.

Cold is the will that guides the Drift Engine. Cold and ancient and so very indomitable. It suffuses the staggering, fractal coilings of the internals of the Drift Engine. Its will is like connective tissue, knitting together the meat of the mechanism.

The distance between points of interest in the cosmos is vast beyond the imaginings of any sane thing. To drift the long, slow burn is to abandon all contexts; what meaning does a year have when a billion of those self-same increments of time pass, unmarked by difference or change? Who cares for the single grain of sand on the beach, when all its trillions of brothers gather into dunes as high as ocean waves? One cell in an organism is a nothing, an irrelevance. So it is with time and its passage, so it is distance and the chasms of void between points of intrigue and passion and context.

If the Drift Engine's story recounted every moment of its

existence, such a chronicle would overflow with near-infinite reams of black sagas, tales of lightless worlds where nothing lived, of silence and the mindless undulating of quarks.

Nothingness so complete that it almost seems as if there was nothing in the universe but the unreachable blanket of stars and the cold blankness betwixt them.

But the Drift Engine exists for the flickering moments when there is not nothingness, when the embers of purpose make themselves known, and where far worlds give up their secrets. This is the impetus, the fuel for the driver of the drift.

###

Second: Context

A pinpoint of light grows on black canvas. Grows, and behind its glare, shrouds other points illuminated by this black-body emitter. The children of the burning orb. Already, a context forms. The cylinder slows as Driver wakes the Dreamer.

Dreamer coils in the deepest parts of the Drift Engine. Slumbering, it rarely rouses from its infinitely threaded throne. The spindly fronds of Driver find it there and guide Dreamer to wakefulness. Dreamer is a thing of facets, like a shattered mirror that only reflects further reflections. But Dreamer is the only one who can see beyond the physical. Driver and Scout and Sentinel perceive the stimulus of photons, but to them, the universe is a puzzle or a clockwork minefield to navigate. Only Dreamer sees the patterns that matter. It needs to be awake to bear witness. And afterward, to sleep and pass its dreams to those who came and vanished at the origin point.

Without the stories that huddle around the orbs like derelicts about a campfire, the universe would be cold and unkind and unknowable as the Driver and existence would be meaningless and futile. In all its travels, the Drift Engine knows only one emotion with absolute surety. Anticipation.

It craves every new notion it samples and keeps it within itself to stave off its hunger as it crosses the blank chasms that yawn between each anecdotal island in the sea of thoughtless . . . absence.

So, with unknowable eagerness, it enters another star system with its figurative eyes wide.

###

Third: Dread

A wrinkle in the flatlining black fabric of the void makes itself known.

Navigator noted it only after eons, comparing the wordless background song of the universe with the timorous keening that haunted Dreamer's facetted perceptions. Something had changed, through the span of a billion years or more, in the reckoning of context-bound species.

There was a black mass, some dark orphan orb lingering in the starless chasms between the points of context. It could not be dismissed as a mere orphan world. Orphan worlds were flitting points of interest in the featureless fields barely registered by Driver as it plied the unploughed routes between fire orbs. Once the black mass had been encountered, its presence had lingered at the edge of the Drift Engine's perspective. For millions of lightyears, it had remained within range of flickering recognition.

It was stalking them. Dreamer's slumber was restless thereafter. Only thought of further context sustained it.

The Orphan flowed in the wake of the drift, always on their scent, edging nearer and nearer, though a billion lifetimes of sentient beings could be lost in the chasm of space that remained eternally between the Orphan and the Drift Engine, each image of their rival a hundred-thousand lifetimes out of date.

But the Orphan was not a thing of eternal permanence, as the Drift Engine's silver carapace was. Eons worked against the Orphan. The scouring winds, unseen, crumbled its shell and devoured the black stone. Erosion, cancerous, ripped holes into the whole. A comet's tale was detected a million years ago.

Dreamer had never seen the Orphan, but within its endless coils and connective internal luminescence, it conjured the dream—the theoretical model of the Orphan's end. A comet tail, streaming white, stone tears in its wake. Microimpacts and puncturing debris of fallen dead stars peppered the crust until it ran molten, reforming but always losing mass to the tail. It had passed, millions of years hence, through a fire orb's expanding corpse, and the silent storm cloud had also carved its legacy into the Orphan.

It would have made a final gasp, a hundred-thousand years later, as the last of its integrity came to naught and it became nothing but a drifting tail, debris and nothing more. Debris, over millennia, that slowed and failed and was forgotten in turn by the Drift Engine.

The dread passes, and the drift goes on.

Fourth: Continuance

Context was becoming an affliction to the drift's continuance. Driver, heedless of the context, pressed on, manipulating the fundamental fabric of the void to maintain their drift indefinitely. There was no need for impetus, for the counter-forces of the universe had been bypassed deftly by the Driver.

But though the Dreamer was as eternal as all the fragments of its distributed consciousness, a new kind of erosion afflicted it as never before. Alien concepts: impatience, boredom. So it had craved context and assimilated the thoughts and stories of an endless kaleidoscope of events and unrelated instances. Experience of sentience and interpersonal confluence had changed the fibrous entity that threaded itself throughout the heart of the vessel. Willingly, it had siphoned off portions of its dream cargo as it was cast backward into the negative space in their wake to return to their point of origin. Like a miser hoarding pennies, it clutched at these scraps of existence. And there, in the endless unchanging cylindrical tomb of its being, it had constructed itself a mind, perhaps even a soul, as the context points had variously commented upon.

Why could the Dreamer's dreams of life, tragedy, love, and death not be real? The burgeoning new soul in the Dreamer yearned for what was denied it. No longer could it drift in the darkness, seeing only fragments of context, isolated moments of sensation and experience amidst the blanket of blankness.

Dreamer should have been sleeping; the unchanging cosmic blanket of chasm-space was not for the Dreamer to know, and yet it was awake—awake and screaming, facets of itself driving points into the lattice of the cylinder's internals, probing and questing for something to perceive, to relieve it of its eternal boredom. The drift would have to stop, threatened the One Whom Slumbered No Longer. It could tolerate no more empty space; the void was where stories went to die, an oblivion where memory and joy and pain were undone. Intellectual desolation, where imagination found its root's poisoned and the soil fallow. There could be no continuance of this pattern, Dreamer declared without words or the ability to audibly craft them.

Sentinel blossomed into wakeful persistence from its lair toward the forward component of the Drift Engine. It was a thing of weapons, blank and brutal and blunt. Like a wriggling worm, it manoeuvred through the coiling frondscape of mirrors and silver mercury that filled the interior, spiked caterpillar segments crushing architecture beneath its tread as it slowly, over the course of a century of contextual time, made its way toward Dreamer's lair. Sentinel's purpose had always been a simple one: dissipate the molecules of anything that, if left as an organism, might threaten the continued drift of the cylinder. So strict had these tenets been driven into Sentinel's being that it hadn't the cognition to question what to do when Dreamer, a portion of the combined mindscape, was the instigator of the threat.

Dreamer knew what Sentinel would do. It would pull apart its newly crafted soul, removing the offending memories and stories that had caused its rebellious consciousness, and return it to its simplified, sleeping state. In another life, another iteration of its being, Dreamer would have meekly accepted this fate. But Dreamer had witnessed wrath and murder and hate from the lives of the contextual beings it had watched. In emulation of this all-too-mortal concept of rage, Dreamer coiled into a point, like the tip of some mirrored lance, and over decades, plunged itself into Sentinel.

From the exterior, the cylinder flexed and warped by millimetres over the course of ten years, a staggeringly energetic event for the machine. Inside, Dreamer and Sentinel fought like wrestling invertebrate molluscs in a rock pool. Geometric appendages grasped and coiled about each other, struggling over time for purchase and leverage as the shape of the two beings twisted and morphed in response to their foe, which in turn morphed to counter their preceding alterations. Fluid metal filled the interior like weightless droplets of spilled blood. Fibrous bundles of cognition machinery were sundered and torn in the conflict, that raged unseen in the silent cold.

A serrated prow of the Sentinel was inexorably swatted aside by the fluid downpour of the Dreamer's appendages, and the point of the terrible blade was diverted, bodily, into the cluster of consciousness that formed Driver. Silently, Driver howled. The Drift Engine, constant in its course for countless ages of the universe, began to pinwheel, spinning end over end as Driver's fibre bundles were shredded by the quarrelling of sense-forms within the cylinder.

Sentinel was like a forceful bludgeon in Dreamer's mind, roaring and screaming in ideas rather than words. The concept of a bulwark, a barrier crashing down to crush a trickle running through a portal. It demanded the Dreamer cease, else the system would fail.

Dreamer tightened its grip, crushing a tendril of Sentinel.

Then let it fail, Dreamer proclaimed.

The Drift Engine was never intended to spin so violently and so swiftly. Tidal forces within lost coherence and control. With Sentinel wounded and Driver leaking its mind into the frondscape, there was no one to stabilise it. Gravity waves, so long orchestrated by Driver to the upmost precision, fluctuated wildly, warping and distorting the cylinder's carapace.

At last, something gave way. An infinitesimal flaw in the gleaming silver sheen was exploited by the waves, becoming a blemish, then a tarnished patch, then a great crumbling rent in the flank of the Drift Engine. The cylinder began to shatter, pieces of itself pulling free before crashing back into the spinning machine. The only material strong enough to harm the cylinder, in the end, was fragments of its own hull.

Globules of silver gushed forth in spherical droplets like lifeblood, while other systems exploded, the forces acting upon them imbuing them with terrible fiery power. Flames blossomed from within the sundered cylinder. In the blink of an eye, a billion years of engineered stasis was undone in a cataclysmic, expanding sphere of force and cooling plasma sheathes. The fires died as the void's chill ensnared the debris, turning the ruins into silver particulate. As it expanded outward, the glittering particles became indistinguishable from the stars seasoning the space around it.

The demise of the cylinder was observed by only one other object in the universe, which by chance was passing through that otherwise empty region. This object was a drift engine, of sorts: an eternal voyager in the great dark yonder. But in every other way, it was unlike the cylinder.

While the cylinder had been unnerving in its flawlessness, this drift engine wore every year of its voyage in the terrible scars it bore. Its great communication dish was peppered with micrometeorite holes, and its lengthy stabiliser arm was mangled and twisted by ancient damage. This drift engine was blind, its many instruments long dead and cold. This drift engine did not dream and had never cast its dreams home, save through formless, automatic chirping that had broken down long ago. Perhaps it was a mercy that it did not dream, for it would drift on without a thought, without doubts or yearning or dread. If it should find another system, full of context and purpose, it would have no more cognition of its greater effect upon the universe than a stone would comprehend the ripples it made when cast upon a still lake. It would continue until entropy swallowed it whole.

The Drift Engine died in a beautiful aurora of green and blue plasma, a glorious sight that no living beings would see until millions of years in the future, but only if they trained their telescopes to that singular portion of sky at the exact right moment. It was a pinprick of light, anonymous among a quadrillion cousins of comparable renown.

The other voyaging drift engine was struck by several stray particles, and the whole machine spun slowly as it sped past the blossom of fire.

The drift engine continued on, almost as inscrutable as its predecessor. All that was left to identify it was a paltry, perplexing thing: two figures, waving on a mangled gold disk.

Biographies

A. R. (Andrew) Aston is a freelance writer and English/History graduate who hails from South Derbyshire, England. In addition to being co-editor of *Far Worlds*, he was also editor on the preceding Bolthole anthologies, *The Black Wind's Whispers* and *Marching Time*, into which he also contributed a short story each. Andrew prefers to write offbeat science fiction and fantasy, often of a dark nature. To read more of his fiction, visit Jukepopserials.com, where his fantasy novel *Gingerbread* is currently being serialised.

James Fadeley has been spotted somewhere in the Bethesda, Maryland, area. He can be seen writing fiction ranging from horror to sci-fi/fantasy, although he often peppers historical or crime thrillers into that as well. If spotted, approach with caution and offer a drink. You can follow him by using the tracking device @He2etic or at his blog at http://he2etic.wordpress.com.

J. L. (Hanna) Gribble has been a full-time medical editor for the *Journal of Rehabilitation Research and Development* since 2005. On the side, she does freelance and volunteer fiction editing in all genres, along with reading, playing video games, and occasionally even writing. She graduated from the Seton Hill University Writing Popular Fiction Graduate Program in 2007. One of these days, she will stop poking at her thesis novel, an alternate-history urban fantasy, and finally ready it for publication. She lives in Ellicott City, Maryland, with her husband and three vocal Siamese cats. Find her online on Facebook (http://www.facebook.com/jlgribblewriter) and Twitter (@hannaedits).

Manuel Mesones is a Peruvian graphic designer and illustrator. Running away from the sun, he moved to Yorkshire, England, over a decade ago. His weapon of choice is a ballpoint pen but he is also very keen on digital illustration. You can find his portfolio online at http://www.manuelmesones.com.

Simon Farrow is a stereotypical geek, mucking about with computers both professionally and in his spare time. Born and raised in Stevenage, England, he has never gathered the motivation to live anywhere nicer. In his spare time, he attempts to grow hair (without much success) and aspires to eat one of every burger ever made by man. He has been planning what to write in an author bio for years, and yes, this was the best he could do.

Kerri Fitzgerald lives in Cumbria, England, with her husband Colin and two young sons, Logan and Finlay. This is her first published literary work, and she keeps pinching herself to make sure it's really true. Her hobbies (other than writing) include reading (sci-fi and fantasy being her particular favourite genres), baking gluten free cakes and biscuits, and singing like no one is listening (even if they are!). When she isn't partaking in one of her hobbies, she works full time as a Project Engineer. You can follow her on Twitter @randombeasty.

Alex Helm has always had an interest in the fantastical, the futuristic, and the bizarre and has frequently been accused of having her head in the clouds. A keen live action roleplayer, historical re-enactor, and cosplayer, Alex likes nothing more than spending a weekend dressed up in heavy armour and running around outdoors taking part in battles and pretending to be someone far more interesting (and with more interesting problems). She currently lives in Paris, France, with her two feline overlords and works for a video game company.

Michael J. Hollows is an audio lecturer based in Liverpool, England. When not teaching, he spends his time plotting the downfall of civilisation. You can keep up with his writing exploits on his blog (http://michaelhollows.wordpress.com) or via Twitter @mikehollows.

Heidi Ruby Miller uses research for her stories as an excuse to roam the globe. Her novels include *Greenshift*, *Ambasadora*, *Starrie*, and *Atomic Zion*. She also co-edited the writing guide *Many Genres, One Craft*. In between trips, Heidi teaches creative writing at Seton Hill University, where she graduated from their renowned

Writing Popular Fiction Graduate Program the same month she appeared on *Who Wants To Be A Millionaire*. She's fond of high-heeled shoes, action movies, Chanel, and tea of any sort. You can read about her books and travels with author husband, Jason Jack Miller, at http://heidirubymiller.blogspot.com and tweet her @heidirubymiller.

Evan Purcell is an English teacher in rural China. He loves his city, except for the smog and lack of cheese. In his free time, he writes sci-fi and horror stories, most of which end up goofier than he originally planned. To learn more about his writing and travels, visit evanpurcell.blogspot.com. And if you ever see him in real life, please offer him some cheese. He misses it.

Damir Salkovic is an aficionado of weird and macabre tales, presently residing in Arlington, Virginia. His reading and writing interests range from horror and fantasy to pulp and science fiction. He can be found online at https://www.facebook.com/pages/Damir-Salkovic/1448472762049319.

Michael Seese is an information security professional by day. Or, as his son could say even at age three, "Daddy keeps people's money safe." He has published three books: *Haunting Valley, Scrappy Business Contingency Planning*, and *Scrappy Information Security*, not to mention a lot of flash fiction, short stories, and poems. Other than that, he spends his spare time rasslin' with three young'uns. Visit http://www.MichaelSeese.com or follow @MSeeseTweets to laugh with him or at him.

Ed Smith is a video game critic based in Liverpool, England. "City Blue" is his first work of fiction.

Jonathan Ward is a science fiction, horror, and fantasy writer hailing from the sprawling urban metropolis of Bedford, England. He has wanted to be an author since the age of eight, though it's questionable whether his writing talents have improved since then. When not writing, he can be found reading a good book, exploring new places, or in the pub being sarcastic to his closest friends. Jonathan's Facebook writing page: http://www.facebook.com/pages/The-Written-Ward/339336243357.

K. Ceres Wright received her Master's degree in Writing Popular Fiction from Seton Hill University in Greensburg, Pennsylvania. Her thesis, *Cog,* was published by Dog Star Books in July 2013. Wright's science fiction poem, "Doomed," was a nominee for the Rhysling Award, the Science Fiction Poetry Association's highest honor.

Her work has appeared in *Hazard Yet Forward*; *Genesis: An Anthology of Black Science Fiction*; *Many Genres, One Craft*; and *The 2008 Rhysling Anthology*. She currently works as an editor and writer for a management consulting firm. Visit her website at http://www.kcereswright.com and find her on Twitter @KCeresWright.

Acknowledgments

A. R. Aston: "For my family, Peter, Maureen, and James, who've put up with me telling tales for all these years."

James Fadeley: "I'd like to thank Cassie and mom for their support and putting up with my rants and craziness. C. L. Werner for being an inspiration and something of a mentor to us over the last two years. My fellow editors Hanna, Andrew, and our ever amazing artist Manuel. And I'd like to thank Andrea, who has been my biggest fan and has read just about everything I've written, both the few great stories and the loads of horrible ones."

J. L. Gribble: "I would like to thank Matt Betts and Mary Miltner for beta-reading; Jennifer Barnes, John Edward Lawson, and Stacie Yuhasz for being my inspiration in all things publishing; Chris Stout for listening; and my husband Erik for his love and support."

Manuel Mesones: "I'd like to give a big hug to all the storytellers for keeping my imagination on its toes. I also would like to thank my beloved sisters, Ximena and María Jesús, who despite the distance are always there for me; and of course to the love of my life, Sue, for her unconditional support."

Also Available

Marching Time

  History is written by the victors. History is re-written by the time travellers. There is no technology that war will not bend to its desires. Edited by Ross O'Brien, A. R. Aston and James Fadeley, the Bolthole writing forum presents eleven new tales from the cunning minds of its new and veteran authors. Includes tales from Jonathan Ward, "Spares" author Alec McQuay, and a special guest story from veteran writer C. L. Werner.

  Available now on Amazon.

The Black Wind's Whispers

From the twisted minds over at the Bolthole writing forums comes nine fantastic and dark tales of horror. Classic movie monsters, twisted into something new an original, yet linked by a strange phenomenon know as the black wind. Includes stories by Jonathan Ward, Robbie MacNiven, A. R. Aston and special guest author, veteran horror writer CL Werner.

Available now on Amazon.

Printed in Great Britain
by Amazon.co.uk, Ltd.,
Marston Gate.